DIAMOND RING
FOR THE ICE QUEEN

BY
LUCY CLARK

MILLS
BOON

To the staff of the Whangarei Hospital. Thank you
For making my mother smile on her voyage of discovery. Ps 19:1

First published in Great Britain 2012
by Mills & Boon, an imprint of Harlequin (UK) Limited.
Harlequin (UK) Limited, Eton House, 18-24 Paradise Road, Richmond, Surrey TW9 1SR

© Anne Clark & Peter Clark 2012

ISBN: 978 0 263 89171 3

Harlequin (UK) policy is to use papers that are natural, renewable and recyclable products and made from wood grown in sustainable forests. The logging and manufacturing process conform to the legal environmental regulations of the country of origin.

Printed and bound in Spain
by Blackprint CPI, Barcelona

'You must be the Ice Fairy.'

As he spoke, one of the nurses standing behind Darla suddenly started to choke. The man held out his hand, seemingly not at all scared of her. Darla slid her hand into his outstretched one, ensuring the shake was firm and direct. She went to withdraw her hand, ignoring the momentary warmth his touch had evoked, but he stepped forward and warmly cupped her hand in both of his.

'A little icy—but then the air-conditioning can get rather cold in here. Especially if you've been sitting in your office poring over case-notes,' he stated, his gaze flicking to the pile of notes she'd left on the desk. 'And I thought fairies were supposed to be sweet and happy and loving.' He smiled at her, dazzling Darla with his straight white teeth—a perfect smile.

Her mouth went dry as she tried to control the unwanted sensations this stranger was evoking. As she wasn't all that experienced when it came to any sort of relationship, it took her a few moments to realise the man was actually trying to *flirt* with her, and from the way she appeared to be affected by his nearness, his subtle spicy scent and the warmth of his hands over hers, she realised he was succeeding...

Dear Reader

Canberra is the capital of Australia and where we spent quite a few of our teenage years, running amok and generally having a good time before settling down to the seriousness of life. It's a lovely city with great sights, great food and great people.

Canberra is also the closest capital city to the fictitious town of Oodnaminaby, the setting for our two previous books in the *Goldmark Family* series: THE BOSS SHE CAN'T RESIST and TAMING THE LONE DOC'S HEART.

When creating this story, we both knew Benedict Goldmark needed a woman who would challenge him. Beautiful Darla Fairlie was the answer. We did feel a little sorry for Darla as we really put her through the wringer, creating a past for her we wouldn't wish on anyone, but in doing so we were able to shed some light on a serious issue. Thank goodness Benedict came into Darla's life to help her let go of the memories that haunt her, to shine light into her world, and to help her step from *existing* to *living her life*.

Act Now is a fictitious organisation, but there are many organisations out there every night, helping and encouraging people to change their lives. They are the *real* unsung heroes.

We hope you enjoy Darla and Benedict's journey.

Warmest regards

Lucy Clark

CHAPTER ONE

DARLA FAIRLIE was met with a round of girlish laughter as she walked into the accident and emergency department of Canberra General Hospital. The laughter was blended with a rich, deep, modulated voice. Darla scowled as she adjusted the armful of case-notes she carried and headed to the nurses' station determined to set things to rights. This was a busy hospital department, not a nightclub where they could all stand around laughing and joking.

Trying not to grind her teeth in frustration, Darla dumped the case-notes on the desk, the noise they made resounding beautifully and causing a few of the staff to jump. They spun around to see what was going on and when they all saw her—*their boss*—the mirth slid from their faces as they quickly busied themselves with work. They tided the desk, picked up the phone to make calls or headed to examination cubicles to check on patients. Busy little workers, keeping their ice fairy happy.

Satisfaction flowed calmly through her as she watched A and E return to its proper rhythm. The ice fairy was in her castle and she wasn't the type of matriarch to tolerate insubordination. She knew her staff called her that and she welcomed it, the name keeping a nice professional distance between herself and the rest of the A and E crew. As far as she was concerned, it was the only way to run an efficient and productive department. If they were scared of her, so be it.

The only person who didn't seem to be doing anything, didn't seem to be scurrying away, pretending to be at all busy, was a tall, dark and—she reluctantly admitted—handsome man who continued to lean against the desk, arms crossed over his chest, watching her with open interest.

Darla fixed him with a firm glare but he still didn't move. The realisation that she couldn't reduce him to a shrivelled mess with one of her withering stares was a little disconcerting. She had no idea who he was but the stethoscope around his neck gave the clear indication he was a doctor of some sort.

She straightened her shoulders and folded her arms firmly across her chest. 'If you've quite finished flirting with my female staff, I'd thank you kindly to head back to your own department.' She delivered her speech with ice to her words, hoping it would do the trick of removing the man, whose deep blue eyes seemed to be watching her with a hint of mockery.

'You must be the ice fairy.' As he spoke, one of the nurses standing behind Darla suddenly started to choke. The man held out his hand, seemingly not at all scared of her. Darla tried to quell her annoyance at his lack of fear. Logic dictated that if he was this relaxed around her, he must be someone of consequence. Someone from hospital administration? Had he been sent to evaluate her?

She'd been acting director of the accident and emergency department for twelve months now and although she had officially applied for the job in the hope of making it permanent, the hospital board had yet to make a decision. She knew they were waiting for the return of Dr Benedict Goldmark, who had been on sabbatical for the past twelve months. If Dr Goldmark wanted his job back, then she'd be forced to find a new job, to make way. If he didn't, the hospital would be insane to pass up an A and E specialist of her calibre running their A and E department.

Now she was faced with a man who didn't seem to care he was disrupting her staff and the best way to get rid of him quickly so she could concentrate on her job was to be polite. Darla slid her hand into his out-stretched one, ensuring the shake was firm and direct. She went to withdraw her hand, ignoring the momen-tary warmth his touch had evoked, when he stepped forward and warmly cupped her hand in both of his.

'A little icy but, then, the air-conditioning can get rather cold in here, especially if you've been sitting in your office, poring over case-notes,' he stated, his gaze flicking to the pile of notes she'd left on the desk. 'And I thought fairies were supposed to be sweet and happy and loving.' He smiled politely, dazzling Darla with his straight white teeth—a perfect smile.

Her mouth went dry as she tried to control the un-wanted sensations this stranger was evoking. Usually when a man showed the slightest bit of interest in her, Darla's defence was to shut him down, stat. However, if this man was here to review her, she needed to play her cards very carefully. So she ignored his subtle spicy scent and the warmth of his hands over hers and lifted her chin a little higher, narrowing her gaze but fixing her smile in place.

'So why do you suppose, Dr Darla Fairlie, the staff here thinks you have a heart of ice and glare of steel?' he continued, and with a shock she realised he was teasing her. Teasing her! Darla started to see red. How dared he come into *her* department and tease her in front of *her* staff? She may only be *acting* director but it was *her* department until she was told otherwise. Darla tightened her grip on the man's hand and held his gaze, ensuring her tone was controlled.

'You appear to have me at a disadvantage, Dr...?'

His smile increased and a deep chuckle filled the air around them. 'Oh, if I told you, it would spoil all my fun and I *am* having such a good time.'

Darla could hear the muffled twittering from behind her and realised this discourse was being eagerly observed by the staff presently on duty. They coughed and cleared their throats, disguising the fact that they were enjoying seeing their present leader, their boss, their ice fairy, being brought down a peg or two. Well, she wouldn't have it.

With her temper rising to an all-time high for the first time in well over a decade, Darla jerked her hand from his hold, relieved the contact had ended. Her main focus now was to regain power over the situation and as such it was best to deal with this larrikin in private. 'Why don't we continue this in my office?' Without another word, she turned and stalked away, ignoring the smattering of quiet female giggles. No doubt *he* had pulled some sort of face behind her back, bringing forth everyone else's mirth.

Darla ignored the pain that pierced her chest. She'd been laughed at many times, too numerous to mention, and she loathed being taken for a fool. Growing up, she'd often struggled to fit in at school, eventually deciding it wasn't worth the effort to form friendships with such shallow people. She'd learned at too young an age that everyone always had an agenda. Everyone always wanted something. Keeping to herself had been her only form of protection and over the years she'd managed to perfect it. Now, when she felt incredibly uncomfortable, she was able to detach her emotions from the situation and look logically at the facts. Distance. Focus. Self-control. Those were her staples.

Without checking to see if *he* was following, she continued towards her office, her back straight, her eyes focused on where she was going, her thoughts sorting themselves into a neat order. She swiped her pass-card through the slot in order to open her office door. It was only then she glanced over her shoulder and saw that he *had* indeed followed her but was definitely taking his time, dawdling along, waving a hello to a few people who passed him. Deciding he was taking too long, she let her office door close, determined he could jolly well knock and wait for her to admit him, rather than her waiting for him.

Settling herself behind her desk, she straightened her blotter even though it was already in perfect alignment and shifted her in-tray back half a centimetre. She tapped her foot beneath her desk. Where was he? Had he thought her closed door meant she'd changed her mind about talking to him?

Darla tried not to let her impatience win. Distance. Focus. Self-control. She closed her eyes for a moment, drew in a deep, calming breath and centred her thoughts. Upon hearing the sound of his deep voice outside her door, her eyes snapped open and she decided it was her turn to keep him waiting, picking up the phone to ring CCU and check on a patient who had come into A and E last night with cardiac arrhythmias. She watched her door as her call was connected to the ward. She waited for his knock on the wooden panel separating them. It didn't come.

'This is Dr Fairlie.' She spoke into the receiver once the call was answered. 'I wanted to check on Mrs—'

The next instant, Darla's office door opened and in he walked. Pass-card in hand. Eyes alive with repressed mirth. Whistling softly. She couldn't help it. She gaped, losing her train of thought as he clipped the pass-card to the pocket of his chambray shirt.

He stopped whistling the instant he realised she was on the phone. 'Sorry,' he whispered, and closed the door behind him, before looking around the room and smiling at the generic paintings on the wall and the single potted plant in the corner. The décor hadn't changed.

'Hello? Dr Fairlie?'

The ward sister's voice snapped Darla out of her confused stupor. 'Er…Mrs Carey. How is she?'

'Progressing nicely. I can email you her most recent report, if you'd like?' Sister offered.

'Thank you.' With that, Darla disconnected the call and stood, both hands flat on her perfectly clean blotter. '*Who* are you? *Why* do you have a pass-card to my office and how *dare* you speak to me like that in front of my staff? I do not tolerate insubordination in my department.'

'*Your* department?' He shook his head and turned to face her. 'Is that right?'

Darla stood there for a split second, looking at him as though he'd grown an extra head. Slowly, she began to process his words and as she did, all the fire seemed to drain out of her as she realised *exactly* who he was. After all, who else would have a pass-card to this office but the man whose job she'd been babysitting for the past twelve months?

Straightening her shoulders and meeting his gaze, she spoke clearly. 'Dr Goldmark, I presume.'

He spread his arms wide and turned slowly in a circle. The open gesture gave Darla the opportunity to really look at him and when he was facing her again she wished he hadn't. Her gaze had quickly taken in the breadth of his shoulders, the length of his legs, the firmness of his torso and the humour in his eyes. 'In the flesh and…' he performed a little bow '…at your service.'

He was handsome and he knew it. The realisation was enough to help clear her thoughts from the vision before her. She slowly eased herself down into her chair—which she realised was really *his* chair—and clasped her hands calmly in front of her.

'You weren't expected until tomorrow,' she stated.

'Well…' He settled himself in one of the two chairs located on the other side of her desk. 'I was in hospital Admin, completing the mounds of paperwork so I was all ready to begin my shift tomorrow, when I decided just to stop by and say g'day to some of the staff.'

He'd been to the hospital administration department? Did that mean he'd made a decision? Was he going to resume his previous post as director or not? She hated feeling so conflicted in her thoughts and emotions but until she knew for sure, she needed to play it carefully.

'Saying g'day? From where I stood it looked more like you were disrupting the working environment.' She attempted to keep the censure from her tone but she wasn't sure she succeeded.

'Ah, that's because you didn't hear the great story I was telling. You see,' he continued when she didn't say anything more, 'when I was in Tarparnii, I was in the middle of nowhere, stitching up a man who'd been involved in an…altercation, when this monkey came along and—'

'I'm not particularly interested.' Darla's brisk tone cut through his words. 'Dr Goldmark, your—'

'Please, call me Benedict or Ben. Your choice. I answer to both. I also answer to "hey, you" and *"ea-wekapla"*, which is actually Tarparnese for "hey, you" and—'

'*Dr Goldmark!*' Her tone was filled with complete exasperation.

'Yes?' he answered innocently, realising he was starting to push her to the edge of sanity. He was intrigued by the woman who had taken over his job while he'd been on sabbatical and he was enjoying ruffling her feathers a bit, especially as it appeared most of the A and E staff were more than a little wary of her. In his opinion, that was the wrong way to be with staff. Being relaxed, having them on side, usually produced a more pleasant and productive working environment. However, when he'd been in Admin earlier that morning, he'd read the statistics for A and E during the past year and realised that under Darla's guidance things had been flowing smoothly. That news alone had helped solidify his decision not to resume the post of Director. Having been on a year-long sabbatical whilst working in Tarparnii with Pacific Medical Aid, where there had been very little red tape, had helped confirm that he could do without the excessive admin. He'd worked in Darla's job for almost two years before his life had changed but now was not the time to dwell on the past. Darla was talking and he'd do well to pay attention to the woman who was probably going to be his new boss.

'I am still acting director of this department until otherwise notified and as your shift doesn't officially start until tomorrow morning at seven o'clock, I would ask you to kindly leave the hospital immediately. I would also like to remind you that this is an accident and emergency department and as such staff are required to be one hundred per cent focused at all times.' Darla held his gaze firmly as she spoke. 'Something they don't seem able to do when you're around, joking and laughing with them.'

Benedict hung his head a little. 'You're right and I apologise. Consider me suitably chastised for my behaviour. Having worked in a loose and relaxed environment for the past year, I may have temporarily forgotten the protocols governing hospital departments. Rest assured, I will not forget them again.'

Darla breathed in a calming breath, pleased he was finally taking her seriously.

'However,' he continued, lifting his head, his blue eyes twinkling with delight, 'I'm sure you'll agree that during quiet times in A and E it's good for the staff to simply stop for five minutes, have a bit of a laugh together—which promotes unity and team bonding— ensuring they're not as fatigued, given laughter not only releases all those happy endorphins but loosens the body, and then return their focus to their work.'

'Ugh!' Darla stood and threw her hands in the air, shaking her head in total frustration. 'There's no getting through to you, is there?' she stated rhetorically. She planted her hands firmly on her hips and glared at him. 'This is still *my* department. You can't just waltz in here after twelve months of being away and think it's acceptable to upset the apple cart.'

'I wasn't trying to—'

'Quiet!'

There was a thread to the word that made Benedict

think he may have just pushed her a little too far. His older brother Edward had often said it was one of his worst traits, to needle and cajole until he went too far and often pushed the other person right over the edge. Of course, when he'd been growing up, usually the other person had been his younger brother, Hamilton, but Benedict actually couldn't remember needling anyone like this for years. He was a trained A and E professional who was good at his job. The way he was behaving with the stunning Darla Fairlie was even starting to puzzle him, but for some reason he didn't seem able to stop.

He'd spoken to a few of his Canberra General colleagues during the past year and whilst they all respected Darla in a professional capacity, none of them actually knew much about her. She ran her department like clockwork and kept her emotional distance from all staff. Why was that?

'But she's a good-looking woman,' Matt, one of his colleagues, had stated. 'A real beauty with her blonde hair and brown eyes.'

'You're a married man,' Benedict had pointed out.

'Very happily married, too, but that doesn't mean I can't appreciate a woman's beauty,' Matt had continued. 'She's a brilliant doctor, runs a tight department, is talented with administration and arbitrates disputes with an intense fairness. She keeps to herself, though. She's been here almost a year and none of us really know her.'

'So the staff respect her but don't like her?'

'Basically, yeah.'

It was why he'd decided to visit A and E after his meetings. He'd wanted to see the ice fairy in action, to get a fix on how she really behaved, and he had to admit, she'd given him a run for his money. What he hadn't been prepared for was her classic beauty. Her slim figure was clothed in a power-suit and he couldn't help but be pleased that she'd chosen a skirt over trousers as it revealed her smooth legs, the sensible court shoes still managing to highlight the natural curve of her calves and ankles.

Her blonde hair was pulled back into a tight bun, which on someone else would have made them look washed out and austere but not Darla. With her head held high, revealing her long, perfect neck, her lips pursed, her chocolate-brown eyes glittering with anger, the hairstyle complemented her overall look and she definitely portrayed the vision of a woman in power who knew exactly who she was—but did she? Perhaps her efforts to appear cool, calm and collected helped give her the confidence to run such a stressful department as A and E.

'Dr Goldmark,' she began, her tone clipped, brisk and direct. Benedict brought his thoughts back to the present and focused on what she was saying rather than intently watching the way her pink lips, which were covered in the mildest sheen of gloss, formed the words.

'That is quite enough. You may have been on sabbatical for the past twelve months and you may be coming back here to resume your duties as director, but until I am officially notified otherwise, this is still *my* department. You have no licence to swan in here and run roughshod over the governing rules and regulations such an intense department demands, and I would thank you to curb whatever natural impulses you seem to possess in regard to being an annoying presence whilst you are within hospital grounds.'

Darla kept her tone firm and clear as she continued to look directly into his hypnotic blue eyes. She hadn't missed the brief appraisal he'd given her and she'd flatly ignored the way her body had momentarily warmed at such an action. 'Understood?'

'Yes. But—'

'No.' She held up both her hands, palms out as though to stop him. 'No buts, Dr Goldmark.'

'But I was only going to—'

'I don't want to hear it.'

Benedict stopped and watched her closely for a moment before slowly nodding. He rose to his feet, thoughtfully stroking his chin with thumb and forefinger. 'You've made some valid points, Dr Fairlie. I'm presuming there's a list of all new departmental protocols somewhere?'

Darla frowned, unsure of his easy acquiescence. Was this another trick of some sort? Could she trust him? Did he want to look them over so he knew exactly which ones to revoke when he resumed his directorship duties? A fleeting sense of panic filled her. Had she been too overbearing with the man who could end up being *her* boss? 'Er…yes. There are.'

'Great.' Benedict rubbed his hands together. 'Then I look forward to discussing them with you at dinner tonight.' With a nod, he turned and took a few steps towards her door.

'Dinner?'

He turned back to face her, a wide smile on his handsome face. 'Yes, a working dinner, Dr Fairlie.' He spread his hands wide. 'We've both got to eat. Let's say seven o'clock? Across the road? *Delicioso?*'

With that, he opened the door and walked out without giving her the opportunity to turn him down, to tell him she didn't believe in 'working dinners' and that he'd be eating dinner by himself tonight. That was that.

CHAPTER TWO

IT WASN'T three minutes since Benedict Goldmark had walked out of her office when a 'code blue' was called.

Darla rushed from her office, heading towards the emergency bays, when she caught up with Matrice, the triage sister.

'Two ambulances. More on the way.' Matrice gave Darla a full update as they readied trauma rooms one and two.

'Call in extra staff and notify the orthopaedic department.' Darla pulled a protective gown over her clothes as the ambulance sirens drew ever closer.

'Report?' a deep familiar voice asked from behind her, and she turned to see Benedict Goldmark heading to the sink to wash his hands. She glared at him, almost desperate to dismiss him, to inform him they didn't need his help, that they could all cope quite well without him, but she also knew it would take a good twenty minutes or longer for extra staff to arrive. The patients were what mattered most and because of that, Benedict was a valuable asset. Professionally, she needed him. Personally, she wished he'd leave. Her world was nice, neat and ordered, or at least it had been until she'd encountered *him*.

'MVA between a tourist bus and a school bus. Both

drivers are badly injured, the school bus driver was thrown from the vehicle. There are two parents and a group of children still trapped in the bus but reports at this stage indicate they're not critically hurt.'

'No doubt they're in shock.' Benedict nodded. 'They'll come later. What else?'

'Whiplash injuries, lacerations. Thankfully the tourist bus was equipped with seat belts but the school bus wasn't.'

Benedict shook his head. 'Disgusting in this day and age.' The ambulance sirens had stopped and Benedict finished pulling on a protective gown and a pair of gloves.

'There are three children, aged…' Darla stopped and quickly scanned the piece of paper triage sister had handed her '…ten, eleven and ten, who have suspected multiple fractures. They're still at the crash site. Arriving now are the two bus drivers. From reports, the tourist bus driver is nowhere near as bad as the man thrown from the school bus. Benedict…' She glanced at him. 'You and I will take that patient. That way, we'll be finished sooner and readily available for the next lot of casualties.' She'd also be able to assess his skills, to see if he really was as good as she'd heard.

When she'd first arrived as acting director, so many staff had mentioned Benedict's skill, his attention to detail, his ability to adapt to whatever situation was presented. Darla was eager to see that in action because if she was forced to relinquish her hold on this department, she wanted to make sure the A and E was in good hands.

She turned to speak to Matrice, who was on her way to meet the ambulances. 'I want you and Dr Carmonti in TR2 as lead,' she said.

'Yes, Doctor,' Matrice replied, and within another few minutes, Benedict's first patient at Canberra General Hospital was wheeled into trauma room one. He couldn't help but wonder whether Darla had wanted to work with him so she could suss his technique, to see if he was worthy of returning to the fold. When she permitted him to take the lead, he knew he'd guessed right.

'Cross-type and match.'

'Get an IV line in.'

'What's his name?'

'Pupils equal and reacting to light.'

'Carlos? Carlos? Can you hear me?'

'BP is dropping.'

'Get that plasma going, stat.'

'Patient has voided.'

'Carlos? I'm Ben. You're safe now. We're going to take care of you.'

'He's moving. Fighting.'

'Hold him.'

'Carlos? I'm Ben. I'm a doctor. You're in hospital. Just relax. We're looking after you.'

'I'm Darla. Stay nice and still, Carlos.' Her sweet feminine voice seemed to calm the patient and Benedict was grateful for that. 'We're getting you something for the pain.'

'That's it. Nice and steady.' Ben glanced around the room at the staff, pleased to see no one had been hurt during Carlos's struggle. As the nurse finished cutting off what remained of Carlos's clothes, Benedict continued to treat his patient. Finally, things started to settle down.

'He's as stable as we can get him. Suspected fractures to the right ulna and radius; fractured left tibia and fibula; possible pelvic fracture.'

Carlos had a non-rebreather oxygen mask over his mouth and nose, his blood pressure was still low but stable. Benedict wrote up the radiology request forms, having momentarily forgotten that as he was now back in a hospital, the red tape and regulations had to be followed.

'Well done, Dr Goldmark,' Darla said without the slightest hint of praise in her voice as Carlos was wheeled off to the radiology department. Benedict raised an eyebrow as he pulled off his gloves and gown.

'Thanks for the approval, Dr Fairlie,' he returned, and Darla was almost sure he was teasing her. She hadn't been teased in a nice, friendly way much throughout her life. Most of the teasing she'd endured had been filled with ridicule and spite. She nodded once, unsure how to respond.

'And now that I've earned your positive opinion of my professional skills, I hope you'll agree to grace me with your presence at dinner tonight.'

When she looked away, trying desperately not to roll her eyes, Benedict wanted even more to obtain a firm positive that she'd come. He wanted to tell her himself that he'd already officially resigned as director and was more than happy to take the post of deputy director. First, though, he had to get her to agree to the dinner date.

'Seriously, Darla, think about it. Going over those new protocols with me is probably the only way you can be assured I know what the new rules are.'

'You're not a five-year-old, Dr Goldmark, and I don't see why I need to hold your hand and explain the meaning of life.'

Benedict couldn't help but smile. The ice fairy was definitely cute when her eyes flashed with defiance. He took a small step towards her. Although there were other staff in the room, they were busy tidying and cleaning, getting TR1 ready for the next patient. Benedict spoke softly, ensuring they weren't overheard. 'I've already heard the meaning-of-life talk, Darla. Why don't you skip straight to the good stuff—the birds and the bees?'

Darla gave an audible sigh. 'Don't you *ever* stop?'

'Only when I get my way. I know you plan to leave me sitting in that restaurant all alone, imagining me a fool. That's not going to happen.'

'You're wrong. I can always imagine you a fool.'

Benedict's rich laughter rang out at her dry words and Darla was astonished to find a warm and fuzzy sensation flooding through her at the sound. She'd made him laugh! As far as she was aware, she'd never made anyone laugh before. It was a nice feeling but she quashed it as quickly as it had come.

'I can't tonight,' she finally said, and momentarily closed her eyes.

'Really? Darn. I'm busy for the next two nights and by then…my bad habits may not be so easily altered.' Benedict knew it was a long shot but he now felt an urgency to get her to agree to have dinner with him. There was no doubt Darla was not only an exceptional doctor but a good administrator yet none of the A and E staff had a clue who she was, other than their brisk, efficient boss.

Who *was* Darla Fairlie? Why did she appear to be wound so tight? What had caused her to be this way? In his past relationship with Carolina, he'd been lax in asking too many questions, content to accept people as they appeared. Not that he was looking for any sort of personal relationship with Darla Fairlie, or anyone else for that matter.

Settling back into his Australian life after spending a year working in Tarparnii was important but he'd been made to look a fool in the past and he'd vowed never to allow that to happen again. He'd be required to work closely with Darla and the urge to know more about her was definitely spurring him on.

Her eyes snapped open and she looked at him. 'Fine. Seven o'clock. Don't be late.' She pointed to Carlos's case-notes. 'And get them written up. Stat.'

'Yes, Dr Fairlie.' He gave her a mock salute, which accompanied his wide grin, as she stalked from the room. He clicked his pen and opened the notes. 'Success!'

Benedict couldn't help keeping an eye on the door, watching for Darla's arrival. Would she really come? Was she a woman who kept her word? He guessed time would tell but in the meantime he'd continue to be cautious.

The emergencies that afternoon had meant his day hadn't turned out as planned but that was the life of a doctor. Over the years he'd learned to juggle the busy times with the quiet times, eating and sleeping when he had the opportunity, but during the past twelve months in Tarparnii he'd also learned how to appreciate down time far more. In the jungle he and the rest of the Pacific Medical Aid team worked as hard as any of the staff at a busy hospital but the quiet hours were spent swimming in the waterhole or joining in with the locals and village life. He'd learned how to bake flatbreads by hand, how to string flowers into garlands and how to climb a coconut palm tree without shoes. Life there had seemed to make sense and now that he'd returned to Australia he wondered how long it might take for him to feel that same sense of calm satisfaction.

Surely having dinner with a beautiful woman was a start, and whilst he acknowledged that Darla's looks weren't the real reason why he'd pressured her to have dinner with him, he wasn't about to kid himself into thinking they also had nothing to do with his decision. She was stunning, with her slim build, her blonde hair and rich brown eyes that seemed to be hiding all sorts of secrets. It was the secrets that had propelled him forward, his gut instincts telling him there was far more to her than met the eye. As they were going to be working closely together from now on, he wanted to know what those secrets were. He had learned the hard way that caution was necessary and, by golly, he was going to get to the bottom of whatever Darla was trying so desperately to conceal. So instead of heading back to the house he shared with his two brothers, Bartholomew and Hamilton, he'd come to the restaurant early, determined to watch every move she made so he could analyse it.

With the restaurant being situated across the road from the hospital, it was heavily populated with staff either just finishing or just beginning their day. Bacon and eggs were served alongside pizza and pasta. George, the proprietor, was in his element, greeting people and laughing his robust laugh. Everyone at the hospital knew George and George knew everyone at the hospital. Even tonight, when Benedict had walked through the door, George had greeted him like a long-lost friend, pleased to see him back home once more.

Benedict turned his head to glance at a table of nurses who were laughing and having a good time, obviously letting off steam after a hectic shift, but when he focused on the front door again, he noticed the woman he'd been waiting for was already heading in his direction. He sat up a little straighter in his seat, watching as George made a beeline to intercept her. He'd told the proprietor of their 'working dinner' and as George spoke warmly to Darla, he indicated the table across the room where Benedict was waiting.

Darla didn't even bother to glance in his direction, instead giving George her undivided attention. He watched as Darla spoke brightly to George and when she smiled Benedict's jaw almost dropped and he was positive his heart skipped a beat. What a vision of loveliness. The smile touched her mouth, curving her lips up at the edges, her eyes alive with sincere pleasure. With George, it was clear, she wasn't the strict and demanding ice fairy everyone knew at the hospital and Benedict realised he was catching a rare glimpse of the *real* Darla. He had to admit…she was breathtaking.

She was still wearing the same suit, with her hair still pulled back into its sensible style. In her elegant hands she carried a manila folder, her handbag on her shoulder. With George she was easy, relaxed, friendly, and Benedict wondered how he might get Darla to look at him in such a non-threatening way. It would be the best way to see what really lay beneath the surface.

He continued to watch her progress through the busy restaurant, her movements smooth and controlled, her spine straight, her shoulders back. She walked with purpose yet also seemed to glide with perfect grace.

'Here you are, Ms Darla.' George indicated the table where Benedict was sitting. Benedict quickly rose to his feet and moved swiftly around the table to hold Darla's chair for her, beating George.

'Ready?' George asked quietly, giving Benedict a little wink.

'Yes, thanks,' Benedict replied as he sat back down. George excused himself and the instant he was gone Darla put the manila folder on the table between them, determined to establish an air of professionalism.

'I took the liberty of printing out all the A and E departmental protocols for us to go through, just to completely refresh your memory.' She glanced pointedly at her watch. 'I only have one hour so if we could get started, I'd appreciate it.'

'Are you sure you wouldn't like a drink first? Some wine perhaps? Or a beer?'

'I don't drink alcohol.'

'Really?' It was something personal about her and he filed the information away.

Darla half expected him to question her, to find out *why* she chose not to drink, but he didn't. Instead he simply nodded, accepting her statement, and offered her another choice.

'Soft drink, then? Mineral water?' As he spoke, a young teenage waiter came over to their table, and while she'd been about to tell Benedict she didn't want a drink, that she'd rather get their work out of the way so she could leave, she found herself ordering a glass of iced water.

'Make that two,' Benedict added, smiling at the waiter and offering his hand. The two men shook hands warmly. 'How are things going, Eamon? I heard you were working here.'

'Yeah. Good,' the teenager replied. 'George has been very patient. Teaching me stuff, you know?'

Benedict nodded. 'Well done. Keep up the good work, mate.'

When the young man had left, Darla slowly opened the manila folder. 'You know the waiter?'

Benedict shrugged. 'Sure. It's the first time I've seen him in over a year.' He nodded. 'Good to see him turning his life around.'

Darla was intrigued by his statement, knowing a lot of doctors wouldn't give the waiting staff the time of day, apart from expecting them to do their job in as unobtrusive a manner as possible.

'So protocols,' Benedict continued, pointing to the stack of papers before them. 'What changes have you made to the department in my absence?'

Darla picked up the first piece of paper and handed it to him. 'Wait a moment. You said *the* department. Not *my* department.'

'I don't own the department, Darla. I merely work there.'

'But most heads refer to departments as…' She paused. 'I refer to it as *my* department.'

Benedict smiled. 'I know, and so you should.'

'Wait. What?' Clearly puzzled, she shifted in her chair and leaned forward a little. 'What do you mean?'

'Ben? Ben, is that you?' A woman's voice cut through her words and Benedict's attention was quickly drawn from her. Darla tried to quell her impatience at the interruption. Was Benedict trying to tell her that he didn't want his job back? That instead of being *acting* head of department, the job could be hers? Permanently?

'Jordie!' Benedict quickly stood and held his arms out wide.

'It *is* you!' With delight, his good friend Jordanne Page embraced him warmly. Darla tried not to frown at the way the other woman appeared to be hugging Benedict close. 'When did you get back?'

'Two days ago. Just enough time to get over jet lag before starting at work.' With his arm still around Jordanne's waist, he turned her to face Darla. 'Jordie, do you know Dr Darla Fairlie? She's the A and E director.'

Darla squared her shoulders. There. He'd done it again. Referred to the department as though it *was* hers. Was it? Had he decided he'd had enough of administration work and was instead more content to simply be a part of the department team rather than running it?

'No. We haven't met.' Jordanne disengaged herself and held her hand out to Darla, who accepted it in a daze of confusion.

'Jordanne's an orthopaedic surgeon who, alongside her husband, worked with me in Tarparnii for the first few months I was there.'

'Those were good times,' Jordanne sighed longingly. 'Such a beautiful place.'

'Jordanne and Alex are both orthopaedic consultants at the hospital,' Benedict continued.

'You've probably seen our names on operation lists and met our registrars but life gets so busy sometimes there just isn't time to meet everyone.' Jordanne laughed and released Darla's hand, then pointed to her table. 'I'd better get back to it. Just going over some things with my registrars and new interns. It was great to see you again, Benedict. Give me a call and we'll fix a time to get our families together for a meal.'

'Sounds great.' Benedict sat back down as Jordanne left and picked up the protocol Darla had handed him earlier.

He had a family? As far as Darla was aware, Benedict was single and very much unattached. 'You certainly seem popular.'

Benedict shrugged. 'When you've been away for

twelve months, there's bound to be people to catch up with.' He glanced at the first protocol. 'Still, no rush. Let's take a look at these changes.' He started reading, giving the document his undivided attention. It was what Darla had wanted, for him to be serious, to study the changes she'd made to the department, to approve of them, but now all she wanted was for him to answer the questions that were hammering around in her mind, causing her apprehension and underlying excitement to increase.

'Uh… Benedict, you were saying something before Jordanne came over,' she prompted, unsure exactly how to broach the subject. 'You've…implied… That is to say, you've sort of alluded to the fact that you no longer want—'

'Here's your water,' Eamon announced, and placed the two glasses on the table. 'Phew! Didn't spill a drop.'

Benedict looked up from the page he was reading and smiled brightly at the waiter.

'Good lad,' Benedict praised, and then pointed. 'And here comes George.'

Darla glanced over her shoulder to see George heading in their direction carrying two hot plates piled high with steaming, delicious-looking food.

'Excellent.' He placed the page back on top of the pile in the folder and closed it, shifting the file to the side of the table out of the way. 'I'm famished.'

Darla looked from George to Benedict, completely confused and unable to make sense of what was happening. She'd come here to discuss the protocols with Benedict. Then he'd thrown out such disarming remarks that she wasn't sure what he'd meant, and now George was bringing them food?

'Here you go, fairy princess,' George said sweetly.

'*Fettuccine alla panna* for you and for Dr Ben we have *spirelli caprisio*.'

'But…I didn't order anything!'

'I figured you'd be hungry. That was one gruelling session in A and E and you've no doubt been catching up on admin work before that,' Benedict replied. 'So I took the liberty of ordering for you and, well, George knows what you like so I left the selection up to him.' He breathed in the aroma. 'And you didn't disappoint, George. Thank you.'

George bowed his head, then left them alone. Darla sat there, too stunned at the unfolding events to move. Benedict picked up his glass of iced water to toast. 'Here's to fine dining in a rush,' he announced, and then instead of clinking glasses with her he gave her a wink and a smile.

The teasing action caused a rush of warmth to flood through her body and for a second she wasn't sure if it was because she was actually enjoying his confusing company or whether she was boiling mad at him. The latter. Of course it had to be the latter.

He was probably winding her up, throwing out ambiguous comments about the department to simply play a joke on her. Well, little did Benedict Goldmark know it but she was an expert at recovering from teasing, ill-timed jokes. It had happened all through her school years as well as throughout her home life. Being put down, being brushed aside, being thought *persona non grata* was something she'd lived with for so long, she knew how to deal with it.

Straightening her shoulders, she desperately tried to ignore the delicious aroma emanating from the food. It was true she still had a full night of work ahead of her and would probably find no other time to eat but she

could resist. She had questions. The man sitting opposite her had the answers. She wasn't exactly sure why
he'd asked her to meet him here but she intended to turn
the situation to her advantage.

'Benedict.'

'Yes?' He started to eat, his eyes momentarily closing
in delight at that first mouthful. He chewed then swallowed. 'Mmm. I'd forgotten how good the food tastes
here.'

'Benedict.' This time she couldn't control the impatience in her tone.

'Yes?' He held her gaze this time, raising his eyebrow in surprise. Darla's determination faltered for a
moment before she continued.

'Do you plan to resume your position as head of A
and E?'

'No.' He scooped up another forkful and held it near
his lips. 'I did try to mention it earlier today but, well,
things don't always work out as planned.' He glanced
down at her food. 'Aren't you going to eat?' he asked
before continuing with his meal.

'What do you mean, "No"?'

Benedict chewed his mouthful thoughtfully before
swallowing and saying, 'I'll tell you if you'll agree not
to waste the delicious food in front of you. I know you're
hungry.'

'How could you know that? You know nothing about
me, Dr Goldmark.'

'I worked in your job for almost two years, Darla.
I know how hectic it can be. Please eat. If not for me,
for George?' Benedict indicated to where George was
standing on the other side of the room, watching her
with a concerned frown. 'He worries about you.'

'He shouldn't. I can take care of myself.' It was her

policy not to rely on anyone else, not to expect favours from other people and to make do with what she had. It was the only way she could ensure she didn't get hurt.

'No one's saying you can't. Besides, it's nice to have someone worrying about you.'

'Just as long as their motives are visible,' she murmured, before reluctantly picking up the fork and starting to eat. At the first mouthful her entire body seemed to sigh with relief, the food absolutely delicious, as always.

'Ahh… Good.' He smiled across the table at her. 'I thought for a moment you might pick that up and throw it at me.'

'And waste food?'

Her reply made him smile. 'My mother used to say that good food was made to be enjoyed and she was right.'

Darla noted the use of the past tense and it intrigued her. On one hand, she didn't really want to know anything personal about Benedict, preferring to keep their relationship strictly professional, but, on the other hand, perhaps getting to know him a little better would help her to control him within the work environment. Logic won out.

'Your mother—she passed away?'

'Yes. When I was thirteen.'

'That must have been difficult.'

'Losing a parent is never easy and I lost both in one horrific accident.' He put down his fork and reached for his water glass, taking his time. 'Thankfully, I have three older brothers. Edward was twenty-four when it happened so he gave up everything, all his own dreams, to take over the family medical practice and to raise me and my younger brother, Hamilton.'

'Your parents were doctors?'

'Yes. They were killed in an avalanche whilst out on a medical emergency call.' There was no smile on Benedict's face now and Darla could hear the love for his parents radiating throughout his words. He was lucky. At least he'd *felt* parental love.

She clenched her jaw and rejected the dull ache of envy she had long conditioned herself to ignore. 'So, the job?'

Benedict watched her, noticing a fleeting look of pain in her eyes before it was pushed aside. He'd been right. There was a lot more to Darla Fairlie than first met the eye and he was even more intrigued than before.

'I informed the CEO this morning that I have no wish to continue as director. That, whilst I enjoy the work, I'd rather not be snowed in under a mound of paperwork. They've offered me the job of deputy director and I've accepted. As you'd be aware, they need to formally advertise the director position and someone will no doubt contact you tomorrow to inform you of the required protocols to follow in this instance.'

'And you're not pulling my leg? Teasing me? Having a laugh?'

Benedict was surprised at her question. 'Why would I do that?'

Darla dismissed the thought and shook her head, relaxing a little. He didn't want the job. She'd already sent her updated résumé to the CEO. She could breathe a little easier, confident of getting the job, a job she really liked.

They sat in silence for a minute, both of them eating, Benedict glancing at her, trying to read her emotions, but she appeared very adept at concealing them. Darla swallowed her mouthful and looked intently across the table at him.

'Why did you really ask me to join you, Benedict?' she asked, her voice soft and a little uncertain, as though she could sense he had an ulterior motive. 'I'm fairly sure it wasn't to discuss the protocols.'

'No. You're right. I've already read the updated ones. You've done a good job.'

'Then why?'

'Why?' Benedict put down his fork. 'Because you intrigue me, Darla, and when I'm intrigued, I can't help but discover why.'

Discover? That was the last thing she wanted. To have someone as handsome and as enigmatic as Benedict Goldmark poking around in her neatly controlled life. The fact that he was intrigued by her was reason enough to stand up right now and walk out, reason enough to maintain a clear professional distance from him, reason enough to ignore the way he'd started to get under her skin. Already he'd managed to rile her, to tease her, to make her *feel*. She didn't like to feel. Feelings clouded issues. Feelings let you down. Feelings got you hurt.

CHAPTER THREE

'YOU'RE very quiet tonight,' Hamilton remarked almost a week after Benedict had returned to Canberra. The two of them were sitting in a small first-aid van, stocked with medical supplies, waiting for patients. Benedict looked over at his younger brother and frowned a little.

Hamilton shrugged in defence of his statement. 'What? This is the first real chance we've had to catch up since you returned and usually when you get back from Tarparnii you're always Mr Chatty, telling me all about your wacky escapades there.' Hamilton sighed with longing. 'I can't wait to go back. How was Nilly?'

'Nilly was great. In good health. Always shiny,' Benedict replied, smiling at the memory of their good friend who was matriarch of the village they usually used as their base for medical clinics when they were in the small Pacific Island of Tarparnii. Belonging, being grounded, surrounding himself with people he loved, was Benedict's idea of happiness. He had a great family and knew he was a fortunate man. He didn't ever want to forget it, especially considering what had happened with Carolina.

He closed his eyes as she swam into focus. Dark hair, dark eyes and buried deep down beneath…a dark heart. Of course he hadn't known about that in the beginning.

No. Carolina had taken great pains to hide her true motives. She was a misguided woman who had made a fool out of him.

He pushed the memory away and opened his eyes, forcing himself to focus his thoughts. He checked his watch. It was still early yet. Only eleven o'clock in the evening. It usually wasn't until after two in the morning when people started arriving at the van, looking for help. Benedict had planned on getting some sleep before his volunteer shift began but an emergency case had come in to A and E just as he'd been about to leave. As Matt had called in sick, Benedict had decided to stick around the hospital and help out. He'd also hoped Darla would finish up her meetings early so they could chat.

The woman was beautiful, intelligent and also highly intriguing. He could tell she was hiding something but he had no idea what. As far as work went, she was excellent both in administration and in dealing with the patients. He'd been very impressed and had also mentioned these facts to the CEO. It didn't matter that Benedict had been unable to stop himself from thinking about her during the quiet hours. The woman was intriguing. There were no two ways about it and the more he watched and listened to her, the more he wanted to uncover whatever it was she was trying to protect.

His colleague Matt had been right when he'd said Darla didn't mix with the other A and E staff. She was clear, concise and fair but Benedict hadn't seen her sitting in *Delicioso* with her registrars and interns, having an informal chat, as had his friend Jordanne. But, then, he shouldn't compare apples and oranges. Jordanne was a people person, so was his sister-in-law Honey, and, Benedict had to admit, so was he. He liked being around people, helping them both in a medical and mental ca-

pacity. It was why he'd taken the sabbatical, to go to
Tarparnii and help people, especially when he hadn't felt
too comfortable with the way his own life had turned
out—thanks to Carolina.

'When you help other people,' he remembered his
mother saying, 'you stop thinking about only yourself.'
On that occasion, when she'd first said those words to
him, Benedict had been about eight years old and his
mother had been rushing about the house, checking her
medical bag so she could go and deliver a baby. It had
been his bedtime and he'd wanted her to stay and read
him a story, to cuddle him and stroke his hair and kiss
his forehead as she whispered lovingly, 'Goodnight,
my Benny-boy.' As his father had also been out on an
emergency call, it had fallen to one of his older brothers to make sure he and Hamilton got to bed on time.

As an adult, he understood what she'd meant and
when he'd realised the truth of Carolina's duplicity,
Benedict had taken his mother's advice and, instead of
wallowing in his own misery, had taken a sabbatical to
go and help others. It was why he was more than willing to continue volunteering with ACT NOW.

For years his older brother Bartholomew had been
involved with ACT NOW, a Canberra-based agency
that provided Nocturnal Outreach Welfare to those who
needed it. Every night, there was a first-aid van and a
van with hot food, coffee and even an array of clothing.
There were vans situated in the north, the centre and
the south of the Australian Capital Territory. The vans
always rolled out together, usually carrying a total of
six or seven volunteers each evening. Lawyers, medics,
police officers, chaplains, as well as other volunteers
with a heart to help were usually rostered on at least
once a week, sometimes more.

Bart was presently at the food van, mixing and talking with some of the young adults who preferred hanging out with them until it was safe to head home.

'Once my old man's drunk himself stupid,' he could hear one boy saying, 'then I can sneak in and sleep in my bed, but if I go home too early, I'm nothing more than his punching bag.'

Benedict shook his head as the matter-of-fact words floated on the cool breeze. Hamilton, who was far more hot-headed than the rest of his brothers, growled with disgust.

'Those poor kids. Makes you realise how easy we had it, even after Mum and Dad died.'

Benedict nodded in agreement. 'You're helping, Ham,' Benedict pointed out. 'You're making a difference. Focus on that.'

'Yeah.'

The two of them sat in the van. Waiting. It had often been just the two of them doing things together when they'd been growing up. Out of the five Goldmark boys, they were the youngest and had often gone off on explorations together. After the deaths of their parents, they'd been raised by their older brothers, and family friends BJ and his daughter, Lorelai.

The five boys had stayed in their family home, continuing to live their lives, going to school and somehow managing to deal with their grief. His parents, Hannah and Cameron Goldmark, had been so happy together, filling their home with five rowdy boys and a lot of love and laughter. It was the ideal picture and one he realised he still wanted for himself, even after what had happened with Carolina. The question was, would he ever be able to really trust a woman again? For some strange reason, an image of Darla Fairlie entered his mind and he quickly sat up straighter in his chair.

He'd do well not to think about a woman he knew very little about. Wasn't that the way things had gone wrong with Carolina? Had he learned nothing from the pains of his past? Even though he'd been watching Darla throughout the week, watching the way she barely interacted with the staff but still managed to achieve good working results, keeping her departmental statistics up to their usual standard, Benedict had also noted she seemed to knowingly hold herself aloof.

He'd made the effort quite a few times to talk to her about non-hospital things, to ask her where she lived, whether she had any hobbies, any family, but to no avail. All he'd learned about her was that she didn't like to answer personal questions. She was closed off, cagey and cautious. She was hiding something and it was that which brought his distrust.

Most people liked talking about themselves, sharing anecdotes, telling jokes, laughing together. Those were natural human instincts yet Darla did none of those things and it was enough to keep him suspicious. It also made him more interested to discover exactly what she was trying to hide.

Carolina, on the other hand, had been bright, bubbly and bouncy, putting on a show to ensure she achieved her manipulated goals in the end—namely, securing herself a successful husband. As he'd been offered the position of director whilst still quite young, due to his experience working with ACT NOW and heading to Tarparnii as a medical student, Benedict's knowledge of emergency medicine had impressed the hospital board. Carolina had been impressed as well and he'd realised it hadn't been until he'd accepted the directorship that she'd really started paying him any serious attention.

Her deception had run deep and when all had finally been revealed, Benedict had come to see her for what she was—a conniving, manipulative liar who had confessed to never really loving him in the first place.

Why couldn't people simply be who they were? His parents had raised him to be true to himself, to be honest and to help others. Why couldn't he find a woman who was like that? One who didn't appear to have an agenda or an ulterior motive. He had always been so accepting, so willing to give people the benefit of the doubt, but that had been before his trust had been shattered. Now he had to tread carefully to avoid getting hurt. He didn't like it but he didn't see any way around it.

'Ham, do you think about Mum and Dad a lot any more?'

'Yes. Almost every day,' Hamilton replied. 'Although I was only nine when they died and my memories might not be as clear as those of the rest you, I had some great times with them both. Most of the time, though, I just wish they were here to talk to, not necessarily for guidance but just to talk, you know?'

'Yeah, mate. I know.'

Bart banged on the side of the first-aid van. 'You're up,' he called, and Benedict stood, having to bend his head down a little as he opened the door, which had been closed against the cool April evening.

'Hi,' Benedict said, smiling warmly at the woman who was being escorted by Yvonne, one of the other female volunteers. 'I'm Benedict. This is Hamilton. Come in. It's warm in here.' He held the door for the two women to come in. It was policy for a woman to always be present if the patient who came for help was female.

'This is Paloma,' Yvonne said and it wasn't until the two women were inside that Paloma opened the almost threadbare long winter coat she wore to reveal a six-month-old baby asleep in a papoose around her chest. 'And this is baby Frankie.'

'He's gorgeous,' Benedict said, then waited for Paloma to speak, to let them know why she'd come to the Nocturnal Outreach Welfare van. Benedict wasn't bothered by the silence. It was quite a common occurrence. People wanted help, were often desperate for it, but felt that if they gave in, if they revealed too much about themselves, that they'd be metaphorically pushed into a little box and shipped off to social services.

With two more people in the first-aid van, it was starting to become a little overcrowded so Hamilton quickly offered to get some soup. Paloma declined but Yvonne accepted, the experienced woman sharing a knowing look with Benedict and Hamilton. It was clear Paloma was cold, tired and hungry but felt highly self-conscious accepting the help NOW offered.

'Paloma's been sent by *the angel*,' Yvonne remarked seriously once Hamilton had left the van.

'The angel?' Benedict couldn't help the bewildered look on his face.

'She comes to the park, to the estates where she knows we live,' Paloma said quickly, as though she couldn't bear for Benedict to be ignorant of her. 'I don't know how she finds us but she does. She is an angel with her shiny hair and big brown eyes. She talks to us, tells us to get help, to get off the drugs, to think of our babies. She has fire in her voice like she knows what it's like, that sometimes there isn't a way out so you keep going on down and down.' Paloma stroked her sleeping son's downy head, her voice cracking as she spoke, emotion pouring from her words.

'She keep saying, "Think of the kids", "Think of the baby", "Think of Frankie". She say to me tonight, "Go to the van". I say to her, they will take my baby. They will take my Frankie.'

Paloma looked at him with pleading eyes. Benedict felt his sympathy for this brave woman increase.

'She says you don't do that. She says you can get me off the drugs and she says that you can keep my baby with me.' Paloma's eyes filled with tears and one ran down her cheek. 'Angels do not lie.' She kissed Frankie's head. 'I want to get clean. I want Frankie to be clean, too. I want to be a good mother.' Her eyes were pleading. 'Angels do not lie,' she repeated, her voice barely a whisper.

'No. They don't.' Benedict had no idea what all this angel talk meant but right now he didn't really care. Paloma had gathered her courage and come to them. She was trusting them and the next few minutes were crucial if they were going to be successful in helping her. 'Your…angel was right. At ACT NOW we have programmes that help mothers go through detox and stay clean, all the while keeping their children with them. We believe it's important the children be a part of the recovery so they can see that things are really going to change, that their mother is making the effort *for them*, for their future as well as her own. In Frankie's case, though, he'll need to go through detox too and for that he'll need to be closely monitored.'

'But you won't take him?' Her hands were wrapped firmly around the sleeping baby.

'No. He still needs you, Paloma. You're his mother.

He needs you to care for him. I presume you're still breast-feeding?'

Paloma nodded, the desperation in her eyes almost causing Benedict's heart to break. He smiled warmly and took her hand in his, giving it a reassuring squeeze. 'You're very brave. Coming here tonight would have been so difficult for you but you've done it. Your angel would be proud.'

He released her hand and reached in his pocket for his phone. 'First of all, let's get you sorted out with accommodation for tonight. There's a place specifically set aside for breast-feeding mothers but we won't be able to get you in there until tomorrow.' Benedict punched a number into his phone and smiled warmly at Paloma. 'We'll get you and Frankie sorted out,' he promised.

An hour later, Yvonne had taken Paloma and Frankie to the temporary night accommodation run by one of the local church groups as a women's shelter. Benedict had also been able to secure a permanent place for Paloma and Frankie over the next six months in one of the staffed houses where ACT NOW helped women in exactly this predicament.

He'd given both Paloma and Frankie a check-up and had just finished when Hamilton returned with warm soup and bread rolls for all of them. Benedict was pleased when Paloma accepted the food, eating as though she hadn't had anything for days. It was a sad predicament she was in but he wasn't here to judge, he was here to help.

'What I *don't* understand,' he said to Bart a while later, 'is the vision of the angel. Paloma was one hundred per cent certain she'd been visited by an angel and told to come here. Not that I'm quibbling,' he said, raising his hands to show he meant no disrespect. 'It's just…odd.'

'No, it's not. The "angel" isn't a vision, Ben, she's a real person,' Bart replied.

'Really? Does she work with ACT NOW?'

Bart shook his head. 'Nope. We've never met her, don't have a clue who she is but over the past twelve months we've had a dramatic increase in the number of single mothers coming to us for help. They all arrive here with the same story. A woman with blonde hair and brown eyes visits them. They say she seems to just *know* where they are, gives them an option to get out of their present despair, urging them to come to us for further assistance.' Bart sipped his warm cup of coffee. 'She somehow connects with these women, gets them to trust her and then sends them our way. It's as though she's that first step, that foot in the door. Not all the women who come here are addicts. Some are in abusive relationships and she offers them a safe way out. Others are homeless, often sheltering with their children in doorways because the temporary accommodation is overcrowded.'

Benedict listened intently to what his brother was saying. 'The past twelve months,' he muttered.

'Yep. Don't have a clue who she is or where she came from but with the results she's getting I don't care. As far as I'm concerned, she *is* an angel and she can continue on saving one woman after another, knowing she not only has our respect but our backing and support if ever she should need it.'

'I guess.' Benedict frowned, something niggling at the back of his mind, something obvious, but whatever it was it was slightly out of focus. He shook his head to clear his thoughts and looked over to where Hamilton was having twenty winks.

'Aw, poor little medical student,' he said softly, his tone laced with teasing. 'Wait until he's pulling all-night shifts in A and E. *Then* he'll know what exhaustion is.'

Bart chuckled but his laughter soon died at a loud commotion coming from outside, not too far away. Angry male voices, getting louder and louder. Hamilton sat up with a start and after a brief shared look, one that between brothers required no words, Benedict and Bart grabbed their coats and a medical kit and rushed out the door, leaving Hamilton to hold the fort.

The rest of the night ended up as busy as his afternoon at the hospital. The noise they'd heard had been a brawl between two rival gangs. Bart had called the police the instant they'd seen a number of men fighting. Benedict had called an ambulance as he was sure he'd seen the flash of metal, probably knives, as the violence had escalated.

After sending two gang members to A and E and several being taken away by the police, the dawn was well and truly upon them by the time Benedict was able to catch his breath.

'You did well for a man who's been used to lazing back in Tarparnii, sipping fresh coconut milk and applying the odd sticking plaster here and there to patients who've scraped their knees,' Bart joked, clapping Benedict on the back. He laughed at his brother's words, both of them knowing that providing medical aid in Tarparnii was nothing like that.

'Thanks.' Benedict yawned. 'I'm going to get some sleep. Ham, can I take your car?'

'Sure.' Hamilton tossed his brother the car keys. 'I'll

finish up with Bart. The car's parked two blocks down.'
Hamilton continued to give Benedict clear directions.
'And don't scratch the duco,' he continued. 'I still have
a few years to go before paying it off.'

Benedict laughed. 'A few more than a few, Ham.'

Hamilton shrugged but called after his brother, 'And
perhaps think about getting a car of your own, eh?'

Benedict nodded as he smothered another yawn, waving to his brothers as he headed off to find Hamilton's
car.

Two blocks down, he rounded the corner into the
street where Hamilton's shiny sports car waited and was
astonished to see a woman, slim build, wearing jeans,
boots and a long, thick jacket, on the other side of the
street, heading towards him. She'd pulled the hood of
her jacket over her head, obscuring her face. She took
keys from her pocket, pressed the button and the lights
of the car parked in front of Hamilton's flashed briefly.
Benedict watched her as she walked, checking the street
to make sure she wasn't being followed. The woman
appeared to be alone and he was instantly concerned
for her safety. She shouldn't be out here, on the streets,
alone, at this time. She could get hurt.

The woman's gaze was focused on the ground, con-
centrating as she walked. It wasn't until she went to
cross the road that she looked up to check for cars. It
was then she saw him. Her step faltered, just for a fraction of a second, in the middle of the road before she
actually stopped and stared at him. Did she think he
was some sort of lunatic? That she wouldn't be safe in
his presence?

'It's OK. I won't hurt you,' he said, and held up
Hamilton's car keys, jangling them in his hand before

pressing the button to unlock the sports car. 'I'm parked just here.'

'Of course I know you're not going to hurt me,' she retorted, and it was only then Benedict recognised her voice.

'Darla!'

She was the last person he'd expected to see walking the streets this early in the morning and, in fact, she'd been equally surprised to see him.

'What are you doing here, Dr Goldmark?'

'Er…' Benedict was too flummoxed to reply, still trying to process that the woman he'd thought about during the past week, more than he'd cared to admit, was now standing in front of him. 'Er…I could ask you the same question.'

'So ask.' It was only then she realised she was still standing in the middle of the road and, after checking for traffic, continued on towards her car.

'OK, then.' Benedict cleared his throat and took a few steps towards her. 'What are you doing here, in the middle of a deserted street at this ridiculous hour of the morning, Dr Fairlie?' And did it have something to do with the secret he could sense she was hiding?

She shrugged a shoulder, the action barely perceptible beneath her big jacket. 'Running some errands,' she remarked, and opened the driver's door.

'At five-thirty in the morning?' His tone was disbelieving.

'There are plenty of people who are up at this hour of the day.'

'Name three—and not emergency crews, that's too easy,' he said quickly.

'All right. Bakers, garbage men and radio show hosts. Satisfied?' Still standing, she slipped the key into the ignition then turned to face him, pulling the car door close around her body as though using it as a protective shield against the man who had annoyingly entered her thoughts far too many times since their impromptu dinner last week.

A small smile touched his lips. He couldn't help it. He liked her style. She wasn't going to let anyone intimidate her and he appreciated that. 'I guess I'll have to be.' The silence started to envelop them, the chirping of birds in the trees plus the sound of cars in the distance the only noises as they stood there, looking at each other. Where he'd felt utterly exhausted when he'd left his brothers only minutes ago, he now felt completely refreshed and restored. He couldn't deny that simply a few minutes in Darla's company had changed his mood. She was an enigma and one that seemed to be drawing him closer and pushing him away at the same time. It was an odd sensation.

'As we're both up and about, would you care to join me for breakfast?'

'How do you know I haven't had breakfast already?'

'Have you?'

Darla gritted her teeth, annoyed she couldn't lie to him and equally annoyed that he still didn't seem to read the 'keep away' sign she was desperately trying to project. She shook her head and the hood of her jacket fell backwards. 'You're obsessed with eating.'

Benedict looked at Darla, trying not to gasp at the lovely blonde locks flowing loosely about her face and shoulders. The early-morning sunlight glinted off her blonde hair and her tired brown eyes were looking at him as though she wished he would leave her alone. But he couldn't help but admire how incredibly stunning she was. 'It's something I tend to do a few times a day in order to fuel my body, but the fact that you're getting ready to drive away from me leads me to believe you're rejecting my generous offer of food, even after I've already proved myself to be a perfect dining companion.'

She tried not to smile at his words. What was it with this man that he wouldn't take no for an answer? He was her colleague and for all intents and purposes she was his boss. She didn't mix her professional and private life. In fact, she didn't mix her life at all. She had her work at the hospital and then her work here on the streets. Both were vitally important and the last thing she needed was to lose focus. The last time she'd lost her focus, she'd ended up with a broken heart and no job. She wasn't about to sacrifice her hard work just for a man. Never again.

'Maybe another time,' she mumbled as she tried to stifle a yawn. Darla climbed into the driver's seat, trying to ignore the fresh, earthy scent he wore, which seemed to be drugging her senses, wanting to know more about him, to discover why this man appeared intent on wanting to spend time with her. Although the morning was nice and crisp, there was a warmth emanating from him that was drawing her in.

Benedict stepped forward and grasped her car door before she could close it, stepping into the gap she'd just vacated. He crouched down so he was at her eye level.

'A rain-check? I'll hold you to that.'

'You do that.' She tried to convey nonchalance, his closeness starting to unsettle her.

'Seriously, Darla. It's not safe for a woman to be alone on the streets at this time of the morning.' His voice was soft, smooth and serious.

'I can look after myself.'

'Perhaps against one man. Maybe two, but tonight, only a few blocks north-west of here, there was the beginnings of a gang war. It wasn't pretty and it certainly wasn't safe. Thankfully, the casualties weren't too bad but a few were sent back to the hospital for surgery.'

Her eyes widened at this news, although she wasn't startled by it. She'd seen many a gang war in her time and she'd broken up plenty of fights. She also knew when to walk away and hide. She'd become very good at protecting herself.

'So you just happened to be passing by when this gang war happened and stopped to lend a hand? Partying hard with friends?' she queried, rubbing her hands together to indicate she was getting cold and he was blocking the means of her closing the car door.

Benedict frowned, unsure where her question had come from. 'I was with my brothers.'

'Well, after your early-morning gang war patch-up session, you're probably exhausted. I'll be expecting you one hundred and ten per cent alert and ready for work at one-thirty this afternoon, Dr Goldmark. No excuses.'

She was dismissing him—again. He found it quite endearing. 'You're right.' As he straightened up, something shiny hanging from her rear-vision mirror caught his eye. A small crystal angel twirled in the early-morning sunlight spreading out all around them. It was pretty. Then he noticed a small angel badge pinned to the collar of her russet-red shirt, just visible beneath her jacket.

His eyes widened as his sluggish brain started to put two and two together and come up with four. The angel. Blonde hair. Brown eyes. Out at this ridiculous hour. Cagey about what she'd been doing. Saying she could look after herself.

'Oh, my gosh.' He stared at her for a moment, the penny finally dropping.

'What? What is it?'

'It's you.' He stared at her in stunned disbelief. 'You're *the angel*!'

CHAPTER FOUR

'WHAT?' Darla simply stared at him in stunned disbelief. How could he have known? It wasn't a name she'd given herself but after a few people had started calling her that, it had somehow seemed to catch on and she hadn't been able to quash it. Truthfully, part of her hadn't wanted to and when she'd seen the crystal angel in the shop, she'd indulged herself and bought it, as well as the lapel badge.

It felt nice to be needed, to know she really was doing some good. She knew how these women felt, she knew what they were going through, she knew what their children were going through, and it was her gift to be able to help them in such a small way as to urge them to seek help.

Her thoughts continued to tick over quickly as she gaped at Benedict Goldmark. How had he clicked so quickly and…? Wait a second. How did he know of *the angel* in the first place? She pondered this for only a moment before realising that if he knew of the mysterious and elusive *angel* then… 'You're working with ACT NOW?'

'Yes.'

'You've done this…sort of work before?'

'Before I went to Tarparnii, yes, although my brothers, who also volunteer, have been telling me about the increase in women seeking help during the past twelve months. Those would be the same twelve months since you, dear Darla, arrived in Canberra. Even tonight a young woman, Paloma, came in with her tiny baby desperate for help.'

At this news he saw relief wash over Darla's face and if he'd had any doubts that she was indeed *the angel*, he didn't now. It also clarified that *this* was probably Darla's big secret. She would head out onto the streets at night, seeking out women who needed help, and she'd help them. Her secret was that she was working hard to make a difference in other people's lives, other people who were worse off than either of them.

Benedict's heart seemed to fill with pride on her behalf but still it didn't explain why she held herself so aloof at the hospital. Did she think people wouldn't understand her cause? Or perhaps they'd see her as some sort of modern-day saint? And why wasn't she working alongside ACT NOW as one of their volunteers? At any rate, Benedict was happy to note her motives were real, genuine and selfless. He'd seen first-hand what Darla's influence could produce and actions definitely spoke louder than words.

'Paloma and Frankie are safe,' he continued. 'One of our workers, Yvonne, has booked her into a temporary women's shelter for the night but later today she'll be taken to a small house and welcomed into a community of women who are not only in the same boat but also determined to fight for a better future for their families. And it's all thanks to you—angel Darla.'

He smiled at her, half puzzled, half impressed, and after a moment couldn't stop the question from tumbling off his tongue. 'Why don't you work with ACT NOW? Why do you do your angel work alone?'

'That's not what this is about.'

'Then what is it about?'

Darla rubbed her arms again, feeling more self-conscious rather than cold. There was no way she could tell Benedict why she did what she did, why she felt such a driving need to go around saving other women. There was no need to tell him it was her choice of penance for not being able to save her own mother.

She straightened her shoulders and lifted her chin with defiance. 'I really need to go. And so do you.' Darla met his gaze, trying to stare him down, to get him to move by sheer willpower.

He stayed where he was for a long moment before acquiescing. 'OK. You have a point. We both need sleep.' No sooner were the words out of his mouth than her stomach growled. She closed her eyes, unable to believe the betrayal of her own body. When she glanced up at Benedict, he'd raised his eyebrows. 'Are you sure I can't buy you breakfast? I know a nice little place, not far from here. Lovely food. Great big chocolate muffins. Hot coffee. Yum, yum.' He rubbed his stomach with his hand and she couldn't help the laughter that bubbled up.

'You are both persistent and quite silly, Dr Goldmark.' She shook her head in bemusement, unable to remember the last time a man had made her feel this way. It only served to reiterate what she'd been telling herself all week long—that Benedict Goldmark was a dangerous man to be around. He was nothing but another colleague. Period. 'I'm tired and I need sleep before starting work in a few hours' time.' She smothered a yawn. 'I don't have time to eat, please go away and leave me in peace.' Although she was chastising him, her tone didn't hold any hint of her earlier annoyance. All Benedict heard when she spoke was sheer exhaustion. 'I don't have the energy to argue with you.'

Benedict smiled. 'I'll remember that for future reference.' He held up his hand and ticked the points off. 'Doesn't drink alcohol. Guides women seeking help. Has a secret identity and when hungry doesn't have the energy to argue.' He smiled. 'See? I *am* getting to know you.'

Darla swallowed, a little scared to discover he was taking mental notes.

'Right you are, then, Dr Fairlie,' he said after a momentary pause. 'Away with you to your bed, and sleep.' With that he stepped back from the car and closed her door. 'And remember to drive safe,' he remarked, then whistled as he walked towards his brother's sports car, twirling the keys on his finger. He looked over his shoulder as Darla drove away, giving her a brief wave. He was sure if he'd pressed her just a little harder, she would have accepted his breakfast invitation. Still, the fact she hadn't, combined with the fact that he'd enjoyed having dinner with her, only made him look forward to the next time he could somehow get Darla to join him for a meal.

As he climbed into Hamilton's low-slung sports car, he pondered what the real reasons were for Darla not wanting to join ACT NOW. The organisation did a lot of good but they also had a lot of resources at their disposal. Darla was out and about on the streets by herself, in dangerous neighbourhoods all alone. It wasn't safe. Even ACT NOW operated under the policy that one person was never to go out into the streets by themselves. It was imperative they were either in pairs or in a group of three or more.

Even the ACT NOW vans travelled in pairs, the food and clothing van paired with a first-aid van. Safety in numbers. To think that Darla was out on these streets alone, by herself night after night, sent shivers of concern down his spine. He recalled Bart and Yvonne telling him of the good work the angel had done over the past twelve months, of the number of women and children she'd managed to help, and he couldn't figure out why Darla couldn't do all that good work with another person watching out for her.

He clenched his jaw and gripped the steering-wheel tighter as he drove through the quiet city streets, making a mental note to ask Darla those questions. For now, he'd do well to head home and get some sleep. His own stomach grumbled and he realised just how hungry he was. Perhaps he could stop at his favourite bakery on the way. Although the shop wouldn't be open yet, he was sure he could persuade his friend Tom to open up and give him something fresh from the ovens. His mouth watered as he thought about it.

'You don't know what you're missing, Darla,' he murmured to himself as he parked the car and made his way to the bakery, the scents of freshly cooked breads and cakes filling the air. The greengrocer next door was setting out his fresh fruit and vegetables for the day. It was while he was talking to Tom, sitting on a stool in the corner of the bakery, that Benedict was struck with a very good idea.

'If Dr Fairlie won't come out to breakfast…' He didn't finish the sentence but a wide grin spread across his face.

* * *

Darla wasn't sure how she managed to sleep after the night she'd had but for some reason the three hours she managed to squeeze in seemed to have rejuvenated her as never before. She hadn't planned on being out all night, it was just the way it had happened. Some nights she was able to talk to more women, to get through to them, and other times she felt as though she hadn't made any difference whatsoever. Those were the nights when she would come home early, the nights when she would sit and think things through, to figure out whether she needed to do something new or different. She'd think back to her own past, about what she'd been looking for back then, but that sort of digging usually left her with a terrible headache. It was her past that now drove her present life, which fuelled her burning desire to really help, but at the same time the last thing she wanted to think about was that horrific, upsetting and downright depressing time of her life.

Tonight, however, had been one of the good ones, and to hear Benedict saying that Paloma had followed through, that she'd sought out ACT NOW and had entered into their programmes, had been like music to Darla's ears. Even now, it made her smile to think she'd finally been able to get through to Paloma after months of talking to her. Paloma had done what was right and Benedict had been the doctor to accept her, to treat her and Frankie, ensuring they were placed into the correct housing situation.

Benedict. Why was it he had been her first thought when she'd woken this morning? As Darla walked towards the accident and emergency department, she rationalised he'd been the last person to annoy her before she'd gone to sleep so subconsciously it was natural he should be her first thought when she awoke. Yes. That had to be it.

Nothing at all to do with the way his smiles and his rich, deep chuckles could cause butterflies to churn within the pit of her stomach. Or the way she'd been so incredibly close to accepting his offer of breakfast because if she had, she wouldn't be putting up with a growling stomach now. She'd only had time to sleep and shower before heading to the hospital, incredibly grateful her first meeting hadn't been scheduled until nine-thirty.

'Coffee,' she murmured, and stopped at the vending machine near her office, quickly inserting money and pressing buttons, but to no avail. She tried again but it didn't work, just ate her money. Her stomach growled and its impatience started to match her own mood.

Trying not to stomp like a five-year-old having a tantrum, she continued towards her office, her annoyance increasing when she discovered her secretary wasn't at the desk. What was the point in having one if she was never around?

Darla walked on and stopped short in the doorway of her office as she watched her secretary placing an enormous basket on the desk.

'What's all this?' Darla asked, and Syd turned around to face her.

'Dr Fairlie. You're just in time. This was just delivered for you and, my goodness, does it all smell perfect, or what?'

'Or what,' Darla replied drolly as she took a few more steps into her office. 'This' turned out to be a large wicker basket of delicious muffins—she could see at least four different varieties—with some fruit on the side, and, lo and behold… Was that a Thermos of coffee?

Darla could almost feel Syd looking at her, watching her every move. 'Uh…do you have the file for the departmental heads meeting? I'd like to review it before I leave.'

'Of course. I'll get it for you now.' Still beaming brightly, Syd headed for the door. 'There's a card,' she pointed out, a cheeky twinkle in her eyes, before closing the door behind her. Darla put down her bag and took off her coat and scarf before reaching for the card. There was no envelope to disguise who it was from and when she saw Benedict's bold, but surprisingly legible writing, she knew there'd be no keeping it from the rest of the A and E staff. By now Syd, a great disseminator of useless information, would have told anyone who would listen.

Darla clenched her jaw as she read what Benedict had written. 'I can still hear your stomach grumbling from here! Benedict.'

As though on cue, and probably due to the delicious scents emanating from the goodie basket, Darla's stomach grumbled. Why did he have to be so…considerate? She found it immensely annoying yet at the same time she was touched by his thoughtfulness. She'd been raised not to expect anything from anyone and she knew that on the few, very rare occasions she'd let her guard down, she'd ended up hurt.

And now here was Benedict Goldmark, being sweet and kind and thoughtful, and it was the last thing she wanted. He'd been back at the hospital for only a week and he was already creating havoc. Darla shook her head and walked slowly around to the other side of her desk, eyeing the basket carefully as though something bad might jump out at her any moment. Was this a practical joke of some kind? Were the muffins laced with laxatives?

Her stomach growled again and as she sat down in her chair she pulled the basket closer, breathing in deeply. No. Although she wouldn't put schoolboy pranks past the likes of Benedict Goldmark, she honestly didn't think he'd be so cruel as to lace the muffins.

Where had he found them? How had he organised all this? She breathed in deeply again and this time felt her self-control snap. She was not only hungry, she was now starving. She had to keep reminding herself not to be drawn in by this smooth, handsome man she knew next to nothing about.

'Except for the way he wants to feed me all the time,' she murmured as she removed the Thermos from the basket. She unscrewed the lid and closed her eyes, almost sighing with relief as the scent of percolated coffee floated around her. Another minute later and she was sipping a cup of the piping-hot liquid and elegantly devouring a muffin. Then her phone rang. She quickly swallowed her mouthful before picking up the phone.

'Dr Fairlie.'

'Top of the morning to you—again.' Benedict's rich tones floated down the line. 'How did you sleep?'

'Fine.' She knew she shouldn't be curt with him but she couldn't help it. Every time he spoke to her or was near her or did something nice for her, she found herself completely off balance. For a woman who prided herself on always being in control, this wasn't a sensation she was enjoying. In her experience, men were only nice to you when they wanted something. So what *did* Benedict want?

'Did the basket arrive?'

'Yes.' A pause. Darla closed her eyes. 'Thank you, Benedict. You shouldn't have but…thank you.'

'Believe me, Darla, it was my pleasure. Anyway, I won't keep you. I'm presuming your schedule hasn't changed much from when I was doing the job and that would mean that Wednesday morning is the departmental heads meeting.'

'*Correct.*'

'Yep, I remember the drill, which is why I wanted to catch you before you left. I thought I'd check to see if things had gone according to plan.'

'And what plan is that?'

'The plan to make sure you eat more regularly. You see, Dr Fairlie, I think it's only right, as deputy director, to warn you I've appointed myself as your caretaker. I know how incredibly stressful your job is. I also know you don't seem to take a lot of time out for yourself, preferring to spend your evenings helping others. Anyway, after you drove away earlier this morning, after you flatly refused to indulge my whims and join me for breakfast…' His tone was become quite theatrical and Darla already felt her lips starting to twitch, just a little. 'And after breaking my heart and discarding me like…' He stopped. 'Oh, hold on,' he said in his normal voice. 'That was the one thing you *didn't* do.'

'Yet,' she added, and was rewarded with a deep chuckle for her efforts.

'Anyway,' he continued, his jovial tone coming down the line, making her feel all sweet and lovely and feminine, 'I was concerned you wouldn't get time to eat. That's all. Nothing sinister behind the gesture. Just *wanted to make sure you had the opportunity to put some food in your belly so it didn't growl all the way through your meetings.* Enjoy and I'll see you later.'

In another moment he'd disconnected the call, leaving Darla still completely perplexed as to what he was playing at. All men had agendas. All men manipulated women for their own selfish gains. Benedict Goldmark wasn't any different from any other male on the face of the earth…and she'd do well to remember that because right now, just for one split second, she desperately wanted to believe he was different.

'Benedict? Trauma Room Two,' the triage sister said when Benedict came back into the nurses' station, putting the case-notes he carried on the desk.

'Right you are, Matrice.' He pointed to the notes. 'I've finished writing those up. They can go to the ward with the patient.' With that he headed to TR2 to see what new emergency awaited his attention and was astonished to find Darla pulling on a pair of gloves and disposable gown. 'What are you still doing here?' he asked, his brow furrowing into a frown. 'It's almost six o'clock, Darla. You should have left at least half an hour ago.' He crossed to the sink to wash his hands and felt her cold stare digging into his back.

'You're not in charge any more, Dr Goldmark,' she remarked briskly. 'Kindly remember that.' She turned away and spoke to the attending nurses.

'Status?'

'Lydia Galgonthon. Twenty-one-year-old female. Ambulance called for by university. Patient was reportedly sitting and staring into space after her lecture ended, then collapsed. She briefly regained consciousness but was disoriented. According to paramedics, one of Lydia's fellow students mentioned she'd been involved in a car accident four months ago.'

'Do we have her hospital case-notes here yet?' Benedict asked as he came to stand beside Darla.

'They're on their way.'

'Obs.' Darla checked Lydia's pupils. 'Pupils equal and reacting to light.'

'Good.' Benedict looked at the treating nurse. 'Order an ECG, EEG and let's get an IV into her. Complete blood work-up to start with.'

As Heather, one of the nurses, started to wind the BP cuff around the patient's arm, Lydia started to shake and twitch, the muscle contractions increasing in severity with each passing second.

'She's fitting,' Darla stated. 'Benedict, check her airway.'

The nurses helped protect Lydia's arms and legs so she didn't hurt herself. Heather quickly loosened Lydia's clothing.

'Airway is currently clear,' he reported.

'Get ready to intubate if necessary.'

'Patient's voided,' Heather announced.

'Noted.'

'Two hundred mils of phenytoin, stat,' Benedict ordered. Once the injection was drawn up and administered, Lydia began to calm down, although her body was still alternating between rigidity and relaxation.

'Tonic-clonic seizure. First muscle contractions, followed by jerking,' Benedict remarked as Darla rechecked Lydia's airway and pupils.

'Airway is clear, pupils still equal and reacting to light. Lydia?' she called. 'Lydia, can you hear me?'

The patient started coughing.

'Take it easy,' Benedict soothed. 'You're in Canberra General Hospital, Lydia. You passed out at one of your lectures. Do you remember?'

Lydia opened her eyes, her gaze indicating complete confusion.

'It's all right, Lydia. I'm Benedict. This is Darla and together with our team of extraordinary nurses we're going to take care of you. You're all right now.' His tone was deep, placating and soothing. As he was speaking, Lydia tried to sit up but Darla eased her backwards.

'Rest now. Everything's fine. Just rest.' As Darla looked down at the young woman, Benedict watched his boss closely, at the way she seemed able to look right into the heart of their patient and out came such caring and genuine compassion. He had no idea how any of the staff could say her heart was only filled with ice.

'Dizzy?' Darla asked.

'Yes.' It was a whisper.

'Close your eyes for a moment. We're just waiting for your case-notes to come up from Medical Records. There are a few things we need to check.' They could ask Lydia their questions, such as whether she was allergic to anything or whether she'd sustained mild head trauma in her previous car accident, but as she was rather dazed at the moment, the information they received might not be accurate. No, it was better to wait for the notes. It was better to err on the side of caution, and as Lydia was now relatively stable, there was no need to rush.

'This is an oxygen mask, Lydia,' Benedict said as he gently placed the mask over Lydia's mouth and nose. 'Your oxygen level is a bit low.'

Darla put her fingers into Lydia's hands. 'Can you squeeze for me?' She did. 'Good.'

'Have you ever passed out before?' Benedict asked. 'No.'

'Have you ever had a seizure before?'

'No.' Lydia opened her eyes, her previously worried gaze now frantic. 'Not that I know of. How would I know?'

'Shh. It's all right. We're just checking.'

'Glasgow coma scale is thirteen,' Darla told Heather quietly, and the nurse noted the information. 'Lydia, is there someone we can call to let them know you're here?'

'My…my mum.'

'Your mum? Sure. Do you know her number?'

Lydia sighed, obviously exhausted from the seizure. 'My backpack.'

'In your backpack?' At Lydia's nod, Darla rested her hand on the woman's shoulder. 'We'll take care of it. You rest for now.'

Darla headed out to the nurses' station and Benedict followed, leaving Lydia in Heather's capable hands. Darla checked the local phone directory and found the number for the university. She picked up the phone but Benedict took it out of her hands.

'What are you doing? I need to get the contact details for Lydia's mother.' There was concern in her voice as well as annoyance.

'Breathe now, Dr Fairlie. Think. Surely one of Lydia's friends would have come with her to the hospital.' He angled his head to the side and listened. Darla frowned at him and snatched the receiver back, her impatience beginning to grow.

'Her mother needs to know.'

'Hark!' Benedict cupped his hand around his ear. 'What's that I hear out in the waiting room? Could it be the sound of concerned "Oh, my gosh"-ing by a gaggle of twenty-year-old females? I do believe it is.' He winked at her and headed towards the waiting room.

Darla listened, then put the phone down, reluctantly following him.

He pushed open the door to the waiting room and there, in the corner, were four girls and one boy, backpacks surrounding them as they sat either talking or texting on their cellphones.

'*Et voilà, chérie.*' He smiled at Darla.

'I'm not your *chérie*,' she said between gritted teeth as she walked towards the students. 'Are you Lydia's friends?' she checked, one very small part of her wishing to prove Benedict wrong.

The texting and talking stopped as the collective turned to stare at her. 'Yes. Oh, my gosh, *yes*.'

'Is she all right?'

'What happened?'

'We were all so worried.'

'It was so freaky.'

Words tumbled out of their mouths and even when Darla tried to speak, none of them seemed to register what she was saying, they were all too caught up in their concern for their friend.

'Excuse me,' Benedict said calmly as he walked towards them. The deep resonance of his tone seemed to vibrate around them, causing their chatter to cease. 'Has anyone called Lydia's mother?'

'I have,' one girl said. 'She's on her way right now.'

'Should be here soon,' another volunteered.

'Can we see Lyds?'

'Not just yet but soon,' Darla answered. 'Did any of you bring Lydia's backpack to the hospital?'

'Yep, of course,' one girl said.

'Here it is,' another replied, handing the bag to Darla.

'Thanks.'

'Her phone's in the front section. Her mum's name is Irene.'

'Great. Thanks for that.' Darla turned and headed off.

'When can we see her?' one of the girls asked.

'We're all so worried. We need to see her or we won't sleep tonight.'

'I was so scared,' another repeated.

'I'm still shaking. Look at my hands. See? Does that mean I'm in shock?'

Their words filtered into background noise and Darla decided she'd leave Benedict to continue fielding their array of questions. After all, he'd proved himself to be such a dynamic people person, who was she to deny him the opportunity to use his natural talents?

CHAPTER FIVE

'NOT fair,' he murmured, coming to stand behind Darla as she read Lydia's EEG report. His voice was low and quiet but she could hear the hint of jesting in his tone. 'Leaving me to fend for myself. What sort of boss are you?'

'I'm the ice fairy, remember?' She turned her head to glance at him over her shoulder then immediately wished she hadn't. Not only could she feel the warmth emanating from his body, surrounding her with a delicious sense of protection such as she'd never felt before, but until she'd turned her head, she hadn't realised just how *close* he was.

Their gazes met and held, awareness surrounding them causing the atmosphere to thicken. It was similar to the moment she'd experienced earlier that morning when he'd knelt down beside her car, just before he'd realised she was the angel, although this one was far more intense. Benedict's blue eyes dipped momentarily to take in the plump contours of her mouth, before looking into her eyes once more. He swallowed, his Adam's apple sliding up and down his smooth neck, and she couldn't help but follow the action, her gaze resting on the undone top button of his shirt, his loose tie giving him a rakish look.

'What were you saying?' His whispered words were enough to snap Darla free from the intense atmosphere surrounding them. She looked down at the printout in her hands, the rest of TR2 coming back into focus. Heather was attending to Lydia, who was now dozing peacefully.

Darla cleared her throat. 'I'm sure, Dr Goldmark, you're more than capable of handling a small group of twenty-one-year-olds, especially when earlier this morning you were no doubt breaking up a gang war.' She tried to move away, to put some distance between them, but she didn't want him to think his nearness, the way the heat from his torso was emanating through her back, warming her all the way through, was causing her mind to falter.

'It wasn't a war, it was just a fight. Anyway, how does Lydia's EEG look?'

Darla thrust the readout into his hands and shifted to pick up the case-notes, glad of the excuse to put a bit of distance between them. She flatly ignored the way her heart rate had increased at being so near him, or the way his spicy scent still seemed to surround her, or the way she was having far more difficultly focusing her thoughts than usual.

'Nothing out of the ordinary,' she replied.

'Do we have blood results yet?' He reluctantly shifted his gaze from watching Darla, interested to note she seemed a little bit jumpy. Was it because she was tired? Or had she felt that burst of sensual awareness exploding around both of them when he'd whispered near her ear? Benedict forced himself to look to Heather, needing a reply to his question in order to click his mind back into professional mode.

'Not yet,' Heather replied.

'Do you want to do a CT or MRI?' he queried, turning to look at Darla again. She looked tired, exhausted, worn out and yet still managed to carry off her 'director' posture with finesse. At least he'd had the opportunity to get a good six hours' sleep before his shift had started. How long had Darla managed to rest? Since uncovering her secret, of finding out she was an honourable woman, it had been difficult to remove thoughts of her from his mind. Even when he'd been sleeping, he was positive he'd dreamt of her because when his alarm had woken him, Darla had been his first thought.

His previous caution, thinking she was another woman like Carolina who used others for their own gain, had been dismissed. According to his brother, ACT NOW had been actively receiving women who needed help, women who had been sent by the angel, for the past twelve months. Surely that proved she was not out for glory. For reasons still unbeknownst to him, Darla wanted to keep her activities under wraps, which only fuelled his curiosity further. She was an enigmatic woman and one he could now enjoy getting to know a *little better. He knew she'd still keep him at a distance* but the fact that he not only knew her secret but intended to honour it might surely bond them in some new way.

She was talking to him now, answering his question, and whilst he was looking at her lips, watching them move, he really wasn't paying attention, which was very unlike him. *Get a grip, Goldmark.* He focused in on what she was saying, knowing both she and their patient deserved his full attention.

'Depends on bloods and urinalysis. I've paged the neurology registrar, who's currently in Theatre, but he's asked us to organise Lydia's transfer to CCU.' Darla held out the case-notes to him. 'Here's the report from the road accident. Four months ago, Lydia sustained a head injury.'

Benedict raised his eyebrows in surprise. 'Could be the cause of the seizure.'

Darla nodded in agreement. 'We'll monitor her with that in mind. For now it's best if Lydia rests, giving her body time to recover.'

'And speaking of rest…' Benedict closed Lydia's notes and levelled Darla with a look '…it's time you went home, Dr Fairlie.'

'I don't think I need you—'

'How do you expect to boss and administrate and care for patients when you're burning the candle at both ends? I'm your deputy. I'm here to take over and do what needs to be done.' Benedict edged closer as he spoke. 'Everyone else in this department may be a little afraid of you but not me. Go home, Darla. Get some sleep, or I'll have Security escort you off the premises.'

Darla gaped at him. 'You wouldn't dare!'

He grinned. 'No, you're right, I wouldn't. Still…' He placed a hand on her shoulder '…be sensible, Darla. Have a good night's sleep.'

There was a caring tone to his words and for one brief second Darla allowed herself to believe it was real. To believe that here was an honest man who genuinely cared for her, rather than what he might be able to get from her. Was it true? Was Benedict a man of worth? A man of honour? A man she could come to trust?

Feeling her throat choke over with a surprising burst of emotion, Darla merely nodded and without another word walked from the room.

Two nights later, Benedict was once again rostered on with ACT NOW, working with Bartholomew and

Jordanne. Throughout the night, Benedict was rather quiet, both his brother and friend remarking on the fact.

'I'm allowed to be quiet now and then,' he defended himself when quizzed.

'Yeah, but why?' Bart asked.

Benedict tapped the side of his head. 'I've got a lot to think about.'

Jordanne looked at him closely for a moment before a wide smile broke over her face. 'Ah—it's a woman. You've met a woman and she's starting to tie you in knots.' She nodded. 'I remember that feeling. Oh, when Alex and I first met, the sparks were definitely flying.' Jordanne sighed and clasped her hands to her chest. 'For our first real date he took me to Mt Stromlo Observatory. What a magical night that was.' She shook her head. 'It was such a pity when the observatory burnt down in those terrible fires but at least we have our memories.' Jordanne blinked once, twice, clearing her thoughts from the past before fixing them squarely on Benedict. 'So…who's the lucky woman?'

'Are you really preoccupied with a woman, bro?' Bart grinned. 'Another Goldmark man bites the apple, eh?'

'Just because you've sworn to remain a bachelor,' Benedict countered, 'it doesn't mean the rest of us are following in your footsteps.'

'Aha!' Jordanne crowed. 'It *is* a woman that has you in a tizz.' She patted Benedict on the back. 'Well, good for you, mate.'

Bart continued to watch his brother, his smile turning into a concerned frown. 'What?' Benedict asked.

'It's not Carolina again, is it?'

'No,' Jordanne answered before Benedict could get a word in. 'It wouldn't be. That deceptive vixen took us all in. No, Ben isn't *that* stupid. Are you, Ben? It's not Carolina again, is it?'

Benedict laughed at Jordanne's complete turnaround. 'No, it's not Carolina. I've at last learnt to be cautious.'

'She was so sweet and kind and charming and all the while she was trying to work her way into marrying you, into conning you to open joint bank accounts together, to buy a house in both your names.'

Benedict shook his head, remembering. 'I was so close, too. So close to proposing to her, to signing the papers for the bank account, and we'd even started house-hunting.' He closed his eyes and shook his head. 'I was such a fool.'

'Hey—live and learn, buddy. So who's the lucky woman on your mind now? Must be someone special with the way you seem so preoccupied.'

'I'm *not* preoccupied.'

'You poured orange juice on your breakfast cereal, mate.' Bart laughed and Jordanne joined in.

'I'm just tired, that's all. Working at the hospital, volunteering here. I'm not used to it, especially after the more leisurely paced life I was living in Tarparnii,' Benedict offered, hoping desperately to throw both of them off the scent. 'In that glorious jungle, although the clinics are completely gruelling, there's generally quite a bit of time for rest and relaxation. Besides, the countryside is lush and green and—' He stopped as Jordanne sighed.

'Keep talking,' she said, resting her elbows on the table and propping her head up on her hands. 'I love that place. Alex and I are going back in another six months but just for a holiday this time. All of our children love it there.'

Benedict tidied up the van, almost wishing for an

emergency because he could feel his brother's sharp gaze boring into him. He'd been successful in distracting Jordanne but Bart knew him far too well.

'Yep, it's a woman,' Bart crowed. 'He's trying to change the subject.'

Benedict shook his head. 'I'm going to get some coffee,' he mumbled, needing to get some air before his brother pulled the truth from him. The truth was he was finding it nigh on impossible to stop thinking about Darla. He hadn't known her for that long but his mind was preoccupied with questions, wanting to discover more about her. Why was she so brisk and controlling in A and E, with her power suits and her hair all done up tight? Yet when she was out on the streets, she wore jeans and jumpers and hoodies and had her glorious hair flowing loose and free?

She was definitely good at her job, there was no doubt about that, but for some strange reason she seemed to prefer keeping her distance from the rest of the A and E staff. They all respected her but a few times he'd heard several members whining and muttering beneath their breath about her being too controlling. She helped people, both at the hospital and out here on the streets, yet she didn't seem at all interested in joining ACT NOW.

Was that because she liked to maintain control? At the hospital it was becoming increasingly difficult not to want to tease her. To see that glint in her eyes when he pushed her almost a step too far. When she nearly lost that tight grip on control and her brown eyes would flash with warning, her irises darkening as she glared at him. Her perfect lips would purse tightly as her exasperation blended with unwanted delight. Sometimes he had the impression she liked his teasing yet at other times he was sure if he kept on, she'd well and truly snap.

Outside the first-aid van, Benedict grabbed a coffee from the catering van then stood staring out at the darkened streets. The April morning cold didn't seem to affect him as he admitted to himself just how drawn he was to his new boss.

He closed his eyes for a moment, telling himself he needed to pull back, to remain professional and put some distance between himself and Darla. However, even thinking about leaving her alone caused his brow to furrow, especially when he knew she was out most nights, roaming these very streets. Her goals were admirable, wanting to help women, persuading them to seek a more permanent solution to their problems. He appreciated her drive to help those less fortunate than herself but it simply wasn't safe for her to go roaming the streets alone.

Benedict clenched his jaw and opened his eyes, struck with an overwhelming and powerful need to protect Darla. He knew she was out there, right now. He could almost feel her, just as he had the other day when he'd been standing close and she'd turned her head to look at him. If he'd leaned down, just a touch, their lips would have met. What would have happened next?

'She'd probably have walloped you across the face,' he muttered as he stood gazing out into the dark night.

There were all types of unstable people out at this time of early morning. She was probably somewhere, talking to a woman, urging her to seek help. Why was it she was filled with such a powerful desire to help? Usually if people wanted to help, they joined agencies such as ACT NOW, but not Darla. It was clear through her actions she preferred the one-on-one approach and only to women.

Why was that? Had something happened to her during her childhood? Bad experiences when she was young? Her determination was clear. He'd seen that on her face the instant he'd realised she was the angel, but what had sparked that determination?

For him, having his parents die when he was only thirteen years old had secured Benedict's need to be out here supporting ACT NOW in their good works. Lorelai and her father, BJ, as well as the rest of the township of Oodnaminaby, had been there to support the Goldmark boys as they'd all grieved. They'd offered help and advice with loving hearts. Even though it had been a time of complete tragedy and utter desolation, it had bonded them closer as a family and Benedict had long since told his older brothers, especially Edward, that he appreciated the sacrifices they'd made on his behalf.

He'd had loving people around him during the darkest moments of his life. Even when things had exploded with Carolina, Benedict had gone home to Ood and been welcomed by his family. He'd been blessed and he wanted to pass it on. If working with ACT NOW meant he could help even just one teenage boy find that same sense of security, to let them know they weren't alone, that they weren't useless and to help them see the world wasn't as unjust as they thought, then he'd be satisfied.

Benedict understood Darla's driving need and perhaps that was what had attracted him to her in the first place. She was beautiful, brisk and brilliant. He wondered if she was ever able to follow up on any of the women she'd helped. To see how well they were doing thanks to her encouragement. Did she ever see them

once they were involved in their life-changing programmes?

As one of the doctors working with ACT NOW,
Benedict had the opportunity to follow up with people
he met on these long and lonely nights. Over the years
he'd made lasting friendships with a lot of them, like
Eamon who had come to ACT NOW two years ago,
homeless and addicted to drugs and alcohol, but was
now clean, sober and working at *Delicioso*. There was
Keith, who at fifteen had come to ACT NOW after
being physically abused by his father and now, three
years later, was working with them to help other teenagers who found themselves in a similar situation.

Even Paloma and little baby Frankie were doing well.
While detox was mentally, emotionally and physically
painful, Paloma was determined to see it through and
this morning, when he'd dropped around to the care
house to check on their progress, she'd told him that
when she was better, she wanted to help other women
like herself.

He'd been eager to share this news with Darla but
when he'd arrived at the hospital he'd been informed by
her secretary, Syd, that Darla was in meetings all day
and wouldn't be available until very late.

As Benedict sipped his coffee, he heard a noise coming from further up the dark street. His body tensed as
he listened, wondering if whoever was coming towards
them was friend or foe. When he heard the sound of
a young child's cry, he quickly finished his coffee and
tapped on the door of the medical van. 'We're up,' he
called.

'I'll get the soup ready,' Keith announced from the
catering van.

Jordanne came outside, shrugging into her coat.

'Where?' she asked, and looked in the direction Benedict indicated. 'Looks like a young mother with three children.'

'I see our mysterious angel has been hard at work again tonight,' Bart murmured. 'I wish we knew who she was so we could at least say thank you.'

'I don't think it's thanks she wants,' Benedict murmured as Jordanne went up the street to greet the woman, desperate to appear friendly without startling her. 'She just wants to see these women turn their lives around.' And he decided that for his next date with Darla he'd show her just how effective she'd been.

Of course, he couldn't tell her it was a date. She'd probably level him with one of her brisk stares before walking away, her back straight, her shoulders even. He smiled at the mental image in his mind.

'*The angel* sent me,' was all the woman said, her body language indicating she wasn't too sure she was doing the right thing.

Benedict smiled and nodded. 'That's what angels do. They show you the way.' And perhaps Darla was showing him the way to learn more about her. What was it that made an educated woman like Darla risk life and limb to go out night after night to help these women? Oh, yes, she was one intriguing woman and now that he'd decided on his next plan of action, he turned his full attention to helping the young woman Darla had sent their way.

It was another five days before Benedict was able to put his plan into action. He'd studied the rosters carefully and on Thursday afternoon noted both he and Darla finished their shifts at six o'clock in the evening. Perfect timing. He'd already spoken to the house man-

ager where Paloma and Frankie were doing exceptionally well to see if it was all right to bring a colleague
around for a visit. He could just imagine Darla's happy
face when she saw all those women she'd helped, to
see the fruits of her labour, to know that she had been
instrumental in changing their lives—for the better.

At the end of the day he found her in her office, locking files away and keeping everything neat and tidy.

'Wow. It's actually a *wooden* desk.' He nodded, completely impressed. 'When I had this office, I was never
sure whether it was wood or plastic or made of glass
because the paperwork was piled so high, I could never
scratch the surface.'

'The paperwork isn't so bad, Benedict.' Darla
couldn't help giving in to the small smile she would
ordinarily try to hide from her colleagues. It was important she maintain her distance but with Benedict
that distance didn't seem to happen. He had a way of
invading her comfort zone, of barging his way in and
refusing to take no for an answer. Part of her wanted
to run away from him, as fast as she could, whilst the
other part was impressed he wasn't intimidated by her,
like other men.

He was more than capable of holding down a difficult job such as the one she was in and despite how
he might jest of his time in the 'top job', when she'd
taken over the position, she'd found the files up to date
and neatly organised. He cared about those less fortunate than him, volunteering and getting his hands dirty
rather than being the sort of man who did nothing more
than donate money now and then. He was a good doctor, the way she'd seen him care about their patients,
the way he put them at ease or gently extracted perti-
nent information.

In short, he was ideal and she'd idly wondered how on earth he could still be single. She'd read his personnel file, just to double-check her information. Why she'd done that was a constant topic of debate within her mind but for now she was interested to discover why he was loitering in her office when he should be going home.

'What do you want?' She picked up her large satchel and started putting thick folders inside.

'Still haven't heard about the job yet?'

'No. I had my "official" interview yesterday.' She shook her head. 'Can't they see I'm the right person for this job? Why do I have to go through this rigmarole every time?' The last phrase was muttered under her breath but Benedict heard.

'Every time?'

She looked at him, ignoring his question. 'What do you want, Benedict?'

He pointed to the files. 'A little light reading for tonight?'

'Yes. Don't change the subject. I need to leave almost straight away.'

Benedict raised his eyebrows at this information. 'Do you have a hot date?'

'No, but—'

He relaxed. 'Well, you do now.'

Her hands stilled and she glared at him. 'Pardon?'

'Come on. Get that bag packed. I need to take you somewhere. Won't take long and I'll even promise to feed you, but only if you're on your best behaviour.' He came over to her desk and put the remaining file into her satchel before picking it up.

'Benedict. No. I'm tired. I've had a hectic week and—' Before she could utter another word, he'd placed one finger over her lips, startling her into silence. He leaned a little closer and looked into her eyes.

'I know you're tired and that you need sleep. I understand. This won't take long and it *is* important.' His gaze flicked to encompass her mouth where his finger lay. He quickly dropped his hand and shoved it into his pocket, the other gripping her satchel a little too firmly. What was it about this woman that seemed to draw him in? She had the ability to make all rational thought and the world around them disappear into oblivion, especially when he was this close to her.

It appeared she wasn't going to be able to wriggle her way out of whatever he had planned, which only proved just how exhausted she was. Ordinarily, she'd scowl at such high-handed behaviour but as she'd had a difficult time schooling her thoughts where Benedict was concerned, right now she felt it was easier to simply go with the flow. The sooner she appeased him, the sooner he'd take her home.

'All right.' She sighed as she picked up her keys and headed the long way around her desk, making every effort to avoid being close to him again. 'I'll follow you in my car.'

'Actually, I don't have a car yet. Keep meaning to buy one but haven't found the time. We'll need to take yours.'

'What about the—?'

'Sports car? That's my brother's.'

'Um…' She thought for a moment. 'Bartholomew, right? I've met him at the heads of departments meeting.'

'No. The car is Hamilton's. He's the youngest. Just finishing medical school.'

'How can he afford such a car?'

'By scrimping and saving. He's doing well.'

Glad of the neutral topic, Darla ensured her office door was locked before walking out of the hospital, learning more about Benedict and his brothers.

'Proud of your brother?'

'Very. Ham is the youngest of the five. Edward is the oldest. Peter and Bart are twins. They're seven years older than me so between the three of them they simply took over when our parents died.'

Darla shook her head 'That must have been hard for you.'

'I thought so at the time, but now, seeing what some of these teenagers have to put up with from their parents and why they feel it's safer to live on the streets than at home, I can see I had it very easy. Surrounded by love.'

Darla sighed, her voice soft. 'That sounds nice.'

They climbed into her car, buckled up and as she pulled out of the doctors' car park she asked him to tell her more about his childhood. As she drove, Benedict shared some of his favourite anecdotes, amazing Darla at the way he could easily talk about his memories. He told her about the last camping trip he'd had with his father, going up to Mt Kosciuszko, the highest peak in Australia. He regaled her with some of the crazy stories from his recent trip to Tarparnii and it was then she learned he'd been to the Pacific island nation many times, first starting when he'd been a medical student.

'We have…extended family there, I guess you could call it. My brother-in-law, Woody, was initially married to a Tarparnian woman before she became sick and passed away. Then, Woody being Woody, he simply assumed responsibility for the rest of her family, ensuring he didn't bring dishonour to her mother and sisters. So I guess you can say there's a strong connection but we call each other "family".' He pointed to the road. 'Turn right at the next set of traffic lights.'

'Wait a second,' Darla said. 'I thought you said you only had brothers. How can you have a brother-in-law?'

'Woody? He's married to Lorelai. Lore is our surrogate sister. Her mother died when she was a young girl and my mother stepped into the breach. After my own mother's death Lorelai was really the only permanent female fixture in my life…well, until my brother Peter married Annabelle. Oh, and Woody's sister, Honey, is married to Edward.' He waved his hands in the air. 'It's all fiddly and complicated and…' he shrugged '…family-like.'

Darla slowed the car and put her indicator on, waiting to turn right. It was odd but hearing him speak made her wish for a family like his. All jumbled up and intertwined and happy, yet it seemed that she was always in the side lane, waiting to turn in the right direction but never managing to get to her destination.

'It sounds nice.' Her words were soft as the lights turned green and they continued on their way. Benedict looked at her as she cleared her throat and she couldn't believe how emotional she felt right now. It had been years since she'd sat down and allowed herself to wallow in misery at her unfortunate life but hearing Benedict talk so openly, displaying a clear love for his entire family, she couldn't help the strong surge of envy that passed through her.

'Slow down and take the next left. Third house down and we're there.'

Darla slowed the car and soon she'd brought it to a halt outside the house he'd indicated. 'So where are we and why?'

'It's almost time to tell you.' He opened the door and climbed out, coming around to her side to open the door for her, surprised when he startled her.

'What are you doing?'

He frowned. 'Opening your door for you. Helping you.'

'I don't need help,' she growled. And she didn't need him being nice to her either. Her life had been fine before Benedict had waltzed in and started turning it upside down, shaking things around and not seeming to care if bits and pieces came loose.

'You've forced me onto his wild-goose chase when all I want to do is go home and sleep for a few hours before head—'

'You're going back out tonight? Do you go every night?'

'I have to. What if tonight's the night some woman is ready to turn her life around? I can't allow that opportunity to pass by.' Darla stomped around to the footpath and indicated the house. 'So come on. What's this all about?'

Benedict's answer was to come and stand beside her, casually take her hand in his and then literally lead her up the garden path.

'Benedict?' she warned.

'Trust me,' he returned.

'No.' She shook her head for emphasis. 'I don't trust anyone.'

They stopped on the threshold and he looked down into her face. Tenderly, he raised one hand and cupped her cheek, his thumb gently brushing away the lone tear that was trying not to fall at one corner of her eyelashes. 'I'm really sorry to hear that,' he whispered.

CHAPTER SIX

EVEN though he hadn't knocked, the door opened and Benedict immediately dropped his hand back to his side, the tender moment with Darla broken.

'She is here. She is here. Oh, Dr Ben. Thank you so much for bring our *angel* to see us!' Paloma said, and before he knew what was happening, she'd reached out and pulled Darla to her in a warm, embracing hug. 'Thank you, angel. You saved my life.'

'Paloma!'

Benedict could hear the surprise in Darla's voice but it wasn't as bright and as cheerful and as happy as he'd thought it would be. He stayed back a step, watching as the other six women in the house came forward to greet her. The women hugged and thanked Darla for all she'd done for them, for helping them to see the light, for getting them on the straight and narrow, and the more they thanked her, the more Darla seemed to lock her smile in place and edge away from them.

'So that's the elusive angel,' Wanda, the house mother, stated.

'Uh...yeah.' It was then Benedict realised he might have blown Darla's cover. After all, if she'd wanted the workers with ACT NOW to know who she was, she would have told them months ago. 'But best keep that knowledge to yourself,' he muttered to Wanda. 'At least for now.'

Wanda held up her hands. 'If she wants to keep on playing super-hero, saving women and keeping her identity secret, that's fine by me. What's important are the women who need help.'

Benedict nodded, a little relieved to see Darla kneeling on the floor, interacting with one of the children. There was a smile on her face but it was a polite one, a stiff one, and again he was struck with the niggling sensation that he'd done the wrong thing in bringing her here.

'Oh, Dr Ben,' Paloma said, coming up to him and putting her arms around his waist. 'It is very wonderful. The angel, she says she is proud of me, that she is happy I am doing so well and that Frankie is looking more healthy.' Paloma pulled away and pointed to where Frankie was lying on the floor, gazing up at a toy frame, his little arms and legs kicking happily in the air. 'I promise the angel we will keep going, even though it is very hard sometimes. We *will* be clean, me and Frankie, and we *will* start the new life, the better life.'

At Paloma's words Benedict's doubts began to vanish. Even if Darla was a tad uncomfortable being here, he had to remember this wasn't about either of them. This visit was to strengthen these brave women, to show them there were people in this world willing to fight for them, to support them in their daily challenges and be proud of them when they accomplished more than they'd originally set out to do.

Thanks to Darla, little Frankie was not only going to get all those drugs out of his system and grow to be a healthy boy but he'd have a mother who was willing to work hard at providing a better future for him. Surely that gave her a sense of pride?

They stayed for fifteen minutes, both he and Darla talking to the women, playing with the children and encouraging them all to continue. The more he glanced at Darla, the more he sensed something was wrong, and when she announced it was time they were off because she had paperwork to complete, she gave a brief wave goodbye and was out the front door like a flash.

'Darla?' Benedict said a quick goodbye as well before hurrying out after her. 'Darla? What's wrong?'

'Why should anything be wrong?' she snapped, using that brisk, efficient tone he remembered from his first day at work. Darla tried to pull her car keys from her pocket but for some reason they kept getting stuck. In frustration, she stopped and placed both hands over her face. She hadn't wanted to lose control. She'd been trying so hard to remain calm, to not get angry, to be supportive of the women she'd helped, but the memories had swamped her the instant she'd set foot inside the house.

'Darla, what's wrong?' Benedict walked over and placed both hands on her shoulders, belatedly realising she was trembling. She instantly shrugged him away and took a few steps towards her car.

'Leave me alone,' she mumbled from beneath her hands.

'Pardon?'

Darla dropped her hands, anger, annoyance and anguish in her tone. 'I said, leave me alone.' Her tone was soft, almost too soft, as though she was so incredibly mad at him that all her temper-filled energy was being carefully suppressed. 'How dare you do something like this to me?'

'Something like what?' he asked, treading carefully and wishing to goodness he'd had more sisters instead of brothers. 'Bringing you to see a few women who were so desperate to thank you for everything you've done for them?' He spread his arms wide, still unsure what he'd done wrong.

'I don't want their thanks,' she told him.

'But surely you wanted to see how well they were doing? I saw that look on your face when I told you Paloma had come to see us at ACT NOW and that we'd been able to get her into a programme. I could see that you were happy to know the outcome.'

Darla glared at him as though he was incredibly stupid. 'It's not *seeing* the women that bothers me. Yes, I'm happy they've accepted help. Yes, I'm happy they're all doing exceptionally well, but that's not the point.'

Benedict spread his arms wide, completely perplexed. 'Then what *is* the point?'

She looked at him in disbelief, then shook her head. 'Forget it.' Darla turned and stalked to the car, walking around to the driver's side. Benedict followed.

'No. I won't forget it. I've obviously done something wrong and if you won't tell me what it is, how will I know not to do it again?'

Forcing herself to take calming breaths, Darla reached into her pocket and successfully pulled out her keys, eager to just get in her car and drive away, even though she was still trembling with repressed emotion. Going into that house, seeing those women there, the children… She leaned one hand on the car and closed her eyes against the images.

'Too many memories,' she whispered.

'What memories?'

Her eyes snapped open, not realising Benedict was

so close. She took a step back and pressed the button remote to unlock her car. 'It's nothing.'

'Darla.'

'Get out of my way, please?'

'Darla. Talk to me.'

'Why are you always blocking my way?' She reached out a hand to open the driver's door and again he noticed she was trembling.

'You're in no condition to drive,' he noted.

'Then you drive.' She surprised him further by tossing him the keys and stomping around to the passenger side, climbing in and shutting the door before he had time to compute what was happening.

Benedict opened the door and adjusted the seat. 'Sorry, but my long legs need a bit more room than yours.' He sat down and closed the door after him, both of them ensconced in the small, secluded cabin. Benedict didn't start the engine but instead turned to face her. 'Darla, I've obviously done something wrong, something to upset you, and I apologise—profusely— but how can I promise never to do it again if I don't know what it is I've done?'

'Why are you so interested in me?' The question sprang from her lips, as though her mind simply couldn't contain her curiosity any longer. 'Why?' she demanded again. 'From the moment we met, it's as though you've dogged my every move. Why? What is it you want from me?'

Benedict stared at her for a few seconds, his eyebrows raised at her questions. He could see she was trying to change the subject and he wasn't sure why. He wasn't sure of anything right now but he realised as he looked into her eyes that he owed her the whole truth, or at least the truth as far as he understood it. Darla wasn't like any woman he'd met before, which made her special…*very* special.

'I want your…time.' He shrugged, feeling exposed and a little self-conscious at this admission. 'I don't understand it myself, but from the moment we met I've had this burning need to spend time with you.'

'But *why*?' she implored.

'I don't know.' Benedict held his hands out. 'I like you. I think you're funny. You're intriguing. You're incredibly beautiful and talented and great with the patients and brilliant at your job.' The words seemed to tumble from his mouth, rushing over each other in eagerness to get out, to let Darla know that she wasn't like any other woman. 'You're unique.' He shrugged. 'I like unique.'

'You think I'm funny?'

Benedict smiled at her response. 'Out of all that, you only care about funny?'

'No one's ever told me I'm funny before.' She paused. 'You don't mean funny as in strange?'

'No.' He smiled brightly at her. 'You make me laugh, Darla. Your humour isn't silly, it's intelligent.' Feeling bold, he reached out and took one of her hands in his, pleased to see the trembling wasn't as bad as before. Whatever had riled her up was still present, he could feel it, but he was also beginning to discover there was even more to Darla Fairlie than met the eye and if he was going to uncover what that might be, he first needed to earn her trust.

'You run the A and E department with grace and elegance and you do a much better job of it than I ever did. You deserve that job.' She opened her mouth to protest and he quickly continued. 'And I'm not just saying that to be polite. I really mean it, Darla.'

She shook her head, as though she was finding it increasingly difficult to accept what he was saying. Benedict watched her response closely. She seemed annoyed when he tried to do something nice and embarrassed when he gave her compliments. Why?

'Darla, how many people have ever given you compliments before?'

'I don't believe in compliments.'

'That's not what I asked. I can see it makes you feel uncomfortable when I say nice things to you. Nice things you *deserve*.' The instant the words were out of his mouth, it was as though someone had switched on a light-bulb. 'Ah…that's why you were upset just now. That's why you were withdrawn when seeing the women. Their gratitude makes you feel uncomfortable.'

Benedict nodded as though things were finally starting to make a bit more sense. 'You help them because you feel you must but you don't want any thanks for it.' He nodded again. 'I guess that's also why you're an excellent A and E director. Patients come in, we patch them up and move them either to surgery, the ward, or they go home. No long-term care.'

Benedict was looking at her as though he'd managed to put another piece of the puzzle into place—the puzzle that was *her* life. Why was he so interested in her? Why couldn't he simply be like other colleagues who came to work, did what she told them to do and left her alone? She'd worked incredibly hard to erect firm barriers around her life so how could Benedict Goldmark waltz right in and start knocking them down?

'Why is it that you prefer to remain on the periphery?' he asked, and she felt like holding up her hands to hold him back, to keep him away from breaking down another wall. Her heart was starting to beat a little faster and she wasn't quite sure whether it was due to his nearness or the fact that he might just uncover the truth about her, because once he *did* uncover the truth, he wouldn't want anything to do with her. Wasn't that what she wanted? For Benedict to leave her alone? She tried to look away, to look down at their hands, past his shoulder, out the window into the early night surrounding them…but she couldn't. Blue eyes continued to bore into her soul as he verbalised his thoughts.

'Why is it that you work twice as hard as anyone else I've ever met? You're not burning the candle at both ends, you're burning a fuse, and you don't seem to care if it destroys you. Why?' He paused and peered closely at her for a moment, desperate to see further into her life. Then he pulled back, straightening up a little, but didn't release her hands. 'And why is it you now look like a startled rabbit? As though I'm trying to hunt you down and capture you?'

'Aren't you?'

'No.' Benedict raised her hand to his lips and brushed a soft kiss to her skin. 'I don't want to capture you, Darla. I simply want to know you better. I don't care about your past or the burdens you're carrying. We all have burdens but it does appear to me that whatever you felt in that house just now is related to your past. I don't know. It's just a hunch.' He cupped her hand with his other one. 'If you want to talk, just want to get it out, to unload, then I'm here for you. I'll listen.'

Darla pursed her lips together, feeling tears prick behind her eyes at his gentleness. She worked hard to control her breathing, to return her heart rate back to normal. 'What if I don't want to talk? What if I want to continue carrying my burdens on my own?' She tried to straighten her shoulders but it was difficult to do when he was holding her hand in his. Difficult to concentrate on anything when his thumb was gently caressing her skin. Difficult to forget the pact she'd made with herself all those long years ago never to trust or rely on anyone but herself.

'Then I'll loan you a forklift so you don't have to carry all that weight by yourself.' He was rewarded with a very small twitch of her lips into a smile. 'Seriously, though, Darla, your past is only one part of who you are. I'm interested in *you*. I want to get to know *you*.'

Darla listened to what he was saying, looked at the way he was gently caressing her hand. He'd asked for her time and he wanted to know more about her. She knew she was walking a tightrope but for the moment she at least had a safety net beneath. Things would never get serious with a man like Benedict Goldmark. She wouldn't let them. She would remain in control. So why couldn't she at least enjoy a small level of friendly companionship?

'Thirty-five A, West Fullarton Way,' she stated.

'Pardon?' Benedict looked at her as though she'd just spoke jibberish.

'It's my address.'

'Oh.' The grip on her hand, slackened a bit, as though he'd been expecting a completely different answer. Then it clicked. Darla wanted him to take her home. She was allowing him to do that for her. 'Oh!' His smile widened and he gently released her hand before turning to adjust the seat a tad more and then start the engine. 'Right. Home.'

'And I'm hungry,' she stated as they both pulled on their seat belts. 'You can buy me pizza.'

His smile was wide. 'Can I now?'

'Yes.' Darla's own smile became more pronounced

as Benedict pulled the car away from the kerb, away from the house that had seemed to swamp her with oppression. It wasn't Benedict's fault and it certainly wasn't the fault of the women who were staying there. Her stomach had growled and she'd realised she was hungry and tired. Having Benedict driving her home and enjoying a pizza with him were nice, calm activities that would help ease the tension she could feel tugging across her shoulders.

If Benedict held true to his statements that he wasn't interested in her past, that he wasn't going to try and pry into her life, then perhaps it was all right to give him the one thing he'd asked for—some of her time. Besides, at the moment she felt like a bit of light-hearted company and Benedict was just the man to provide it.

Within the hour, they were sitting on the floor of Darla's duplex, eating pizza.

'Why do you have so little furniture?' Benedict asked as he shifted around again, trying to get comfortable.

'I don't need much and nine times out of ten I'm usually only here to sleep.' It was on the tip of her tongue to tell him she had more furniture now than she'd had growing up. 'Besides, I'm still only *acting* director of A and E. If they appoint someone else to the role, I'll have to up and move. Again.'

'You've moved around a lot?' Benedict tried to sound calm, nonchalant, not wanting to scare her. Darla had relaxed somewhat since they'd arrived here and he didn't want her to startle her into silence.

'Uh…a bit. Melbourne. Sydney. Here.'

'That's not too bad. I lived all my life in one big country house until I came to Canberra to go to medical school and even then I still lived with my brothers.'

'You don't want to get a place of your own?'

'I had started looking…a while ago…before I went to Tarparnii.'

'And why did you go to Tarparnii for such a long time? You were director of A and E, a coveted position for a man so young, and then you up and leave? Something must have happened.'

Benedict shifted his position, sitting crossed-legged opposite her. 'Have you been checking up on me, Dr Fairlie? Reading my file?'

Darla felt a little uncomfortable that he'd rumbled her so quickly but she squared her shoulders, determined not to feel guilty. 'Of course I read your file. You're the new deputy director.'

Benedict stared at her for a moment before a slow smile spread across his face. 'Good answer.'

'So? Why did you leave?'

'The age-old answer, I'm afraid—a woman.'

'A woman? Really?'

'She tricked me, burned me and spurned me. Ripped my heart out and ate it—just for pleasure.' Benedict exhaled slowly, his smile completely gone. 'I needed to get away.'

'You ran away?'

'Yep, and I'm not ashamed to admit it. I needed space. I needed to be with people who loved me, people I could trust.' He nodded. 'Tarparnii was the best place to go because I could think things through supported by wise and wonderful people, as well as continuing to help out and provide medical care for those who need it.'

'It sounds lovely.'

'It is. You should go. Do a stint with PMA. You'll love it there.'

Darla shrugged a shoulder. 'I have work here. Important work. Helping women on the streets. Helping them to realise there's a better life for them, that they don't need to put up with living a second-rate life, that there is a life without abuse.'

Her words were vehement, strong, determined, and Benedict's previous hunch that she'd somehow been affected by this dark and desolate world increased. 'Understood,' he commented softly. 'But your work shouldn't define you. Being a doctor is just a job, Darla. An important one, no doubt, but no more important than the garbage collectors cleaning up our streets or the teachers educating young children or the mother who just wants the best for her child.'

He knew it was the wrong thing to say the instant her lips pursed together, making a tight line. 'I know you don't want to hear this. I know you're probably so used to everyone cowering at the sight of the great ice fairy and doing what you tell them but that doesn't work with me. I'm not trying to tell you what to do—'

'Oh, really?' she muttered, but knew he'd heard.

'Or what to think or how to live your life—'

'You could have fooled me.'

'But instead to help you see there is more to your life than just being a doctor, than just being the angel.'

'No, there isn't.'

'You work and you work, Darla,' he implored. 'But where do you live?'

She spread her arms wide to indicate the house. Benedict smiled sadly. 'This is just bricks and mortar.' He placed one hand over his heart, his eyes sad, his words imploring. 'Where is your heart, Darla? Why have you boxed it up and hidden it away?'

'That's… It has nothing to…do…'

'Who hurt you?'

'Too many people. All right?' She stood and crossed her arms firmly over her chest before stalking to the window, looking out at the dark and lonely night. It was how she felt. Dark and lonely. It was how she'd felt for years. Dark and lonely. It was how she'd always thought she would feel, so much so that she'd actually started getting used to it...hadn't she?

Now here was Benedict, asking her probing questions, digging into her life, into her past, even though he'd said he wasn't interested. Anger and pain, stronger than she'd thought possible, ripped through her. He'd lied to her. She shouldn't be surprised. Everyone lied. Always. Why had she somehow expected Benedict to be different? Why had she even contemplated being able to trust him?

'And this is you? Not prying into my past?' She didn't turn and face him, trying desperately to get her emotions under control.

'I said I didn't care about your past. A past is a past. You can't go back and change it but neither can you live there, and I'll admit,' he said, rising to his feet but making no effort to move closer, 'I'm curious about you, naturally, but the only reason I'd want to know about your past right now is because something at that women's shelter spooked you. From the moment you walked in, your back was ramrod straight. You not only looked uncomfortable with the gratitude offered by those women but you looked ill because of it. That concerned me then and it still concerns me now. Darla, whatever happened to you in the past caused those emotions to resurface tonight. *That's* what I care about because it's clearly affecting you right now, in the present.'

'So you want me to...what? Open up to you? Talk

about my past?' She turned to face him but kept her arms folded as though she needed protection from his probing questions.

'You seem to be living by a code of silence that you've no doubt inflicted on yourself. Perhaps, tonight, it's time to break that silence. Talk about your past so whenever someone else says "Thank you", and believe me they will, you won't feel upset.'

Darla listened to his words, her heart wanting to tell him, wanting to trust him, wanting to let go of the secret shame she'd carried around for most her life. She rubbed her hands on her upper arms, trying to resist the urge to turn and walk away, to ignore him completely.

Could she tell him? Was he really sincere? The fact that he wasn't afraid of her, that he didn't kowtow to her, that he didn't hide from the truth, were good things. Surely she could break her rules just this once and open up to him? Her heart started to hammer against her chest, the blood thrumming in her ears, perspiration peppering her hands and her brow. Could she do this? Open up to someone? Could she trust?

She'd tried it before—three times with three different men—and each and every time she'd been let down. It didn't seem to matter whether she'd been a geeky, gangly teenager or a medical student or even a qualified professional, the men she'd trusted had let her down, breaking her heart and forcing her back into her cocoon once more.

Now here was Benedict. Waiting and watching. Not making a sound in case he scared her off. He was patient, he was kind and he didn't pretend to be something he wasn't. He hadn't returned from Tarparnii and demanded his job back. Instead he'd weighed up his options and decided the top job wasn't for him any more.

He'd remained true to himself. Surely that was a good sign? Surely that showed he was honourable?

Benedict stayed silent, watching her closely. He could see her internal struggle and he fervently hoped she'd power through it rather than retreating once more.

My mother was a drug addict. My mother was a drug addict. The words spun round and round in her head. That was all she'd need to say to him. Benedict was an incredibly smart man and he'd quickly connect the dots. *My mother was a drug addict. Come on, Darla. Say them.*

Benedict didn't speak but instead walked towards her, reaching out to place a hand reassuringly on her upper arm.

Darla flinched, but only slightly, at the gentle touch. It was nice and reassuring and what a normal man would do to a normal woman who had captured his interest.

Could she do this? Could she tell the truth to the man who'd called her funny and beautiful and intriguing? Was it possible she could break free from the chains that had bound her for far too many years? *My mother was a drug addict. My mother was a drug addict.*

'My mother was a drug addict.' There. Although the words had come out in a rush, they were out and she sighed with relief, the fear, the tension, the stigma that went along with such a declaration flowing from her.

'Thank you—for trusting me. That couldn't have been easy to say, Darla.' His words were soft, gentle, encompassing. He brushed a lock of hair out of her eyes and tucked it back behind her ear, caressing her cheek with his fingertips. His gaze dipped to her mouth, her neck, her ear and back to her mouth again. 'What you must have gone through.' He shook his head, looking into her eyes once more, seeing the pain she'd kept locked away and hidden for far too long.

'Those children…tonight…in that house.' She breathed in deeply and forced herself to slowly let it go. 'That was me. Before I started school, I'd been in many different foster-homes while my mum went into rehab and tried to get clean. When she completed the programme, they'd return me to her. I was the child who always wore second-hand clothes, who couldn't understand why other children didn't want to play with me. *I was the one who suffered. I was the one who* was shunted from here to there, who was locked away, pushed aside…discarded.' Her voice broke on the word and she silently berated herself for becoming so emotional. She closed her eyes for a second and was surprised when a tear broke free of its bonds and slid down her cheek.

Benedict tenderly brushed it away with his thumb and when she looked into his eyes she was flabbergasted to discover *his* eyes glistening with unshed tears…tears for her.

'Oh, Darla. What you must have gone through.'

Her heart was hammering wildly against her chest and she wasn't quite sure whether it was from talking openly about her past or due to Benedict's nearness. He was such a nice man. So caring. So accepting, or at least that was how he appeared.

Could she trust him? She'd opened up to him, told him the truth about her mother, and still he was here, looking at her as though she were the most beautiful woman on the face of this earth. Did he really think that? Was she really that beautiful? That intriguing? That funny?

She wanted to be. She desperately wanted to be and

as he continued to gently stroke her cheek, the heat from his touch sending shockwaves of pleasure through her, such as she'd never felt before, Darla couldn't control the burning need she had to do something reckless. She wanted, just for once, to be out of control, to lose herself, to forget about her past, her present and her future.

She wanted to *feel*. To be like every other normal woman. She wanted to know what it felt like to have the lips of a handsome man on hers. A man who wasn't trying to force himself onto her but who seemed willing to hang back, allowing her to make all the moves, to take her own time, to learn to trust.

Was it possible? Could she really trust him, not only with the truth of her past but with the emotions of her heart?

Swallowing over her dry throat and dipping her gaze to look from his deep blue eyes to his sexy lips, Darla knew she needed to simply *do* rather than rationalise and think. *Just do. Just do.* And before she could allow any other thought into her mind, she leaned forward and pressed her lips firmly to Benedict's.

CHAPTER SEVEN

BENEDICT wasn't at all sure how it had happened—but it had. As much as he wanted to fight it, Darla was an amazing woman who was somehow becoming important to him. Was it because of her caring and giving nature, her desire to help other women and their children, or was it simply because she'd taken the chance and trusted him?

Could he, in turn, now let himself trust her? She was so different from Carolina. Darla was the genuine article, not someone who lived a life of lies and deception. Darla didn't seek a crown for the work she undertook, she simply wanted to help, to make a real difference in the lives of those less fortunate, and that positive, almost obsessive desire had sprung from a place of pain, a place of tragedy, a place of personal knowledge.

She was quite a woman and the more he learned about her, the more he seemed to be unable to control this strange need to protect her. To ensure she didn't burn out, that her fuse wasn't extinguished in the dark and dangerous world she walked through every night, and as he focused on the way the sweetness from her lips was fuelling the raging fire deep within him, he found it even more difficult to keep the kiss light and testing rather than fierce and unresisting. Ever since they'd met, he'd wanted to know what it would be like to kiss Darla and now he was finding out just how mind-numbingly incredible it was.

As he kissed her plump mouth, Ben felt the hint of a deep-seated longing that had been denied for far too long. He wanted to slide his arms around her, to have her as close to him as possible whilst plundering the depths of her delicious mouth, but he sensed that taking things slowly was the only way to go.

This woman was special and as such she deserved to be cherished, to feel secure in the new emotions they were presently exploring. He had no real idea what she'd been through but even with the small part of her past she'd shared, he could well imagine how much pain she'd suffered at the hands of others.

This uncontrollable need to hold her, to gather her close, to protect her surged through him again but once more he forced himself to tread lightly, to focus on the smallest sensations and to dwell in them. He eased back and pressed a few butterfly kisses to her cheeks. The softness of her perfect skin blending with the saltiness of her tears made for a heady combination of desire mixed with determination.

There was no sound outside, no cars, no birds, no kids playing in the street. No clocks ticking inside or anything else to disturb this perfect moment. Nothing seemed to exist but the two of them and Darla wanted it to continue for ever, to lose herself in this one moment where nothing bad could ever touch her.

She closed her eyes and lifted her chin to allow him greater access to her. His soft petal-fresh kisses were sweet and tender and she swallowed over the tantalising need for more growing deep down within. How could Benedict be so willing, so eager to kiss a blazing trail of delight from her cheek to her ear and down her neck? Why wasn't he repulsed by her declaration? Why hadn't he run a mile? Why was he still here, creating absolute havoc with her equilibrium?

Had she finally made the right decision? Confided in the right person? He'd said he wasn't interested in her past, that it didn't matter except where it had an impact on her present, and as he hadn't run screaming from the room, perhaps he'd really meant it. Was it possible for her to continue to confide in him? To *continue to* allow herself to feel this way for a man she barely knew? All she could think about at the moment was having his mouth pressed firmly to hers once more instead of enduring the sensual torture he was inflicting with his perfect little kisses.

Lacing her fingers through his hair, she urged his head upwards before instinctively seeking out his mouth, pressing hers firmly to his. The way he was making her feel, all warm and special and sexy, gave her the sensations of falling without knowing if there was a safety net below, waiting to catch her. She needed to take charge, to be in control of what was happening between them, because then she knew she wouldn't fall. Yes, she was attracted to Benedict. Yes, he was proving himself to be a man of worth, someone she could possibly draw closer to and, yes, she knew even in admitting that to herself, she might be in danger of releasing her tight grip on the reality she'd built around herself. If she took control now, if she kissed him as both of them longed to be connected, she'd feel much calmer.

Gently parting her lips, she pressed them to his. Benedict's answer was to groan with delight. Slipping her tongue out to tantalise his mouth had him winding his arms about her waist, drawing her as close as possible. Darla couldn't help but revel in just how perfectly he was responding to her cues, at how his intense reaction only seemed to fuel the powerful need deep within her, and for one split second she wasn't at all sure which one of them was really in control.

Need continued to build, to force its way to the surface, and as he held her close, his mouth still creating sweet havoc with her senses, she was amazed at the repressed desire she could sense within him. Here, in his arms, she could really forget everything. Her past, her present and her future. Being in Benedict's arms gave her the opportunity to live in bliss, where only the two of them existed…and nothing else.

When she opened her mouth even wider, desperate for more, desperate to search through these wild emotions she'd never really felt before, she was astonished when he eased away. The motion was only ever so slight but with her fingers still threaded through his thick, dark hair, she felt the imperceptible movement.

'Darla,' he murmured against her lips, but she wasn't having any of it. He'd managed to get her to open up, to trust him, to *feel*, and now he was trying to pull away, to break the bubble she'd created around them? He kissed her again, once, twice, but she could still feel him drawing away, his hand sliding down her back to rest at her waist. 'Easy. There's plenty of time, love.'

Love? She broke her mouth free from his, annoyed and angry that he'd pulled her back to reality. She'd been more than happy to live in a fantasy world, even if it was only for a short while. 'I am not your *love*. I'm nobody's *love*. Never have been, never will be.' The bitterness in her words surprised them both and within the next second she'd pushed right away from him and turned back to the window, hugging her arms close in an effort to combat the sudden coolness as well as to protect herself. The sounds of the world around them returned and she closed her eyes, the ticking of her kitchen clock much slower than her pounding heart rate. How dare he fluster her! How dare he kiss her with such intensity, such abandon and then take it away, as though he knew what was right for her!

'Darla.' Benedict took a step towards her.

'Don't.' Her word stopped him in the same way as being hit with a sledgehammer. 'I don't want to hear platitudes or explanations or anything. All right?'

Benedict stayed where he was and shoved his hands into his trouser pockets. 'Sure.' Was Darla trying to push him away? Keep him at bay? Had he got too close? When she'd started to deepen the kiss, he'd wanted nothing more than to follow her on that journey, but through some grain of logical thought still running around in his mind he'd also realised she might be trying to lose herself in a temporary embrace…and he'd suddenly realised that maybe he didn't want this thing *between himself and Darla to be temporary at all.*

He cared about her. Even as he stared at her standing at the window, her back to him, her entire posture screaming for him to leave her alone, he knew she'd somehow worked her way into his life and that alone should be scaring him witless. She wasn't Carolina. He knew that, he accepted that, but she was a woman who had a lot of things on her mind, things to sort out. Did he really want to get involved with her? To help her navigate the rocky waters through her past and into a new life? There was no doubt he was concerned for her, that he wanted to protect her, but was he equipped to do that?

She was definitely feisty. He'd give her that and at times she seemed to be drawing him close with one hand and then pushing him away with the other. Could he handle her mood swings? Would he be doing either of them any good? He'd only just managed to make some sense out of his own past problems. Was he ready to be there for Darla? Give himself to her completely without fear? No matter how much she pushed and pulled him in different directions?

Dragging in a calming breath and pushing his multitude of questions to the side, Benedict stooped and tidied up the remnants of their pizza meal, carrying the rubbish into her kitchen.

'Leave it,' she called, just wanting him to go. She'd made a big enough fool of herself and now all she wanted was to be left alone. She'd all but thrown herself at Benedict and then, when he'd refused her advances, she'd been left feeling betrayed and hurt. It wasn't a new sensation. She'd felt it before but she'd thought Benedict was different. He'd said she was beautiful. He'd said she was funny and intelligent. Surely with the way he'd caressed her cheek, with the way he'd spread little tiny kisses over her skin, that it meant he'd *wanted* her. Right?

'It's no trouble,' he returned. She heard him turn on the tap and wondered what on earth he was doing. It was strange to have someone else in her little home, let alone a man. 'Do you want a cup of tea?'

'No. Thank you,' she added belatedly. She may be annoyed and confused but that didn't give her any cause to be more rude to him than she'd already been.

'Mind if I have one?' He'd come back into the room and she turned to find him leaning against the doorjamb.

'Yes, I do.' Darla sighed and shoved her hands through her hair, wishing she hadn't taken it out. She felt more in control when her hair was up, when she wore her power suits, when she had her armour on. 'I think it's best if you go. I'm tired and I want to get at least a few hours' sleep before I head out tonight.'

He nodded. 'What time are you planning on going?'

'About two o'clock.'

He nodded. 'Between two and five. That's when the most carnage seems to happen.'

'Yes.' She adjusted her arms, recrossing them firmly over her chest.

'Is that the way it was when you were growing up?' The question was soft.

Darla glared at him, trying to convey her annoyance at the mention of her past. 'Yes.' The word was tinged with impatience. If he persisted in pursuing this line of questioning then she'd *make* him leave.

Benedict straightened up, slowly walking towards her. 'It must have been so difficult, so confusing, so painful for you.'

Darla continued to glare, continued to mentally try to hold him at bay, but, unlike every other male she'd ever met, Benedict didn't seem to be picking up on her signals. When he placed his hands on her shoulders, her arms suddenly became like lead weights and dropped to her sides, the anger and frustration draining out of her.

'I'm very stubborn, Darla.' His tone was gentle and intimate but there was a hint of determination mixed in as well. 'My brothers say it's one of my worst and best traits. When I sink my teeth into something…' Before he could stop himself he bent his head and captured her lips in a startling kiss, his teeth gently nipping at her lower lip. Darla gasped with surprised delight and stared into his eyes as he straightened just as quickly. 'I don't let go.' His gaze dipped to encompass her slightly parted lips, fighting his natural urges, before meeting her wide brown eyes once again. 'I like you, Darla. *A lot*. I also respect you, both as a medical professional and a woman. I don't know what sort of relationships you've had with men in the past but I'm here to tell you that I'm different.'

Benedict brushed his fingers over her cheek. 'Something dynamic is happening between us. I have no idea what exactly and it's scary but it's happening, whether we like it or not.' He paused, his breath fanning out over her face, caressing her. She could feel his own uncertainty and remembered him saying he'd gone to Tarparnii after the break-up of a bad relationship. She swallowed, unable to move, unable to look away, unable to stop herself from wanting him.

'Moving forward, especially into uncharted waters, is a huge step,' he continued. 'And I don't want to stand still, Darla. I don't want to let what might be the best opportunity of my life pass me by because I was too afraid to try. I want to try, to move forward too.' He leaned down and she gasped, thinking he might kiss her once more, but instead he brought his lips near her ear and whispered softly, 'I hope you're ready to try too.'

With that, he straightened once more and lowered his hands before turning and walking to the door. He gave her one of those smiles that churned the already excitable butterflies in her stomach, making her knees go weak. 'Sleep sweet, fairy princess, and stay safe.' With a wink he disappeared, closing the door behind him.

Darla stood where she was, unable to move her legs,

unable to think clearly. She raised a hand to her forehead and rubbed her eyes, not at all sure what was happening. Ever since Benedict had walked into A and E,
he'd confounded her, turning her nice, neat and ordered
world upside down and inside out.

When she closed her eyes, all she could see were
images of Benedict, memories of the way he'd kissed
her, held her, gazed into her eyes as though she was incredibly special. Opening her eyes, she shook her head.
How on earth was she supposed to sleep now?

'Ambulance is on its way in,' Heather told Benedict as
she put down the phone. He was sitting at the A and E
nurses' station, writing up a set of case-notes.

'What have we got, Heather?'

'Darla.'

Benedict was instantly alert, turning his head
sharply to give the nursing sister his undivided attention. '*Darla*? My Darla? What's wrong? What's happened? Is she all right?' He tried desperately to ignore
the pounding of his heart as a million different scenarios
of Darla hurt, bruised, battered and bleeding flooded
through his mind.

'"*My* Darla"?' Heather's smile was wide and it was
only then Benedict realised what he'd actually said.
'That's a very telling statement, Ben.'

He glanced quickly around them, wondering if anyone else had overheard Heather's comment. Thankfully,
though, as it was almost five o'clock in the morning,
there weren't as many staff around as during the day
shift.

'It's fine,' Heather continued. 'I won't say a word,
except that it's great to see you moving on with your life
after Car—' She stopped. 'Well…anyway…' Heather

looked down at the piece of paper and read from it. 'Darla's the one who called. She's in the ambulance with a patient, a woman in her late thirties. Suspected drug overdose.'

'That's not going to be easy for her,' he muttered, feeling his heart rate slowly returning to a more normal rhythm.

'Pardon?' Heather asked.

He shook his head. 'Nothing. ETA?'

Heather tipped her head to the side and listened, the sound of ambulance sirens drawing closer. 'Ah…that sounds like your Darla now, ex-boss.'

Benedict rolled his eyes as he stood. 'Very funny,' he remarked, and the two of them walked towards the ambulance receiving bay.

'How's it going?'

Benedict looked cautiously at Heather, a little unsure about what she meant. He didn't want to answer and say anything wrong that might upset Darla. They'd only shared a few kisses and whilst she had been all he could think about since it had happened, he wasn't ready for the entire A and E staff to be gossiping about his love life—again. Everyone in the hospital seemed to know what Carolina had done to him and he wasn't looking to be the centre of their water-cooler rumour-mill sessions any time soon. 'How's *what* going?' he checked.

'Working as deputy. You used to be the boss and now you're not. It can't be easy, coming back to your old department and answering to someone else.'

'Darla's a good administrator.' He shrugged. 'I'm more than happy for her to take the job.'

'Even when she's *your* Darla?'

They stood just inside the doors that led to the ambulance bay, waiting for the vehicle to turn into the hospital grounds. Benedict exhaled and pushed a hand through his hair. 'Listen, Heather, please don't—'

Heather grinned. 'It's fine, Ben. I won't say a word. I can't promise not to tease you a little now and then but…' She pretended to lock her lips and throw away the key. 'My lips are sealed,' she mumbled as the ambulance came to a stop.

'Thanks,' he replied as they headed outside.

'Benedict?' Darla said when he opened the rear doors. 'What are you doing here?'

'Covering for Matt because his kids are sick. What have we got?' he asked as they manoeuvred the stretcher from the ambulance into TR1.

'Tina, thirty-seven-year-old woman, ingested unknown substance. Found unconscious. Vitals aren't good.' As Darla continued to give her statistics, they transferred Tina onto the hospital barouche. The paramedics headed out with their stretcher and Heather started cutting away Tina's clothes. Benedict worked alongside Darla, not only doing all they could to stabilise their patient but also keeping a close eye on his boss. He could already hear the tension in her tone mixed with worry and frustration.

'Heart rate's dropping,' she called, checking the monitor.

'Get ready to intubate.'

'She's crashing. Charge defibrillators,' Darla returned.

On and on they worked. The atmosphere surrounding them was one of darkness and Benedict felt a sudden chill slide down his spine. It was a sensation he'd felt on many occasions over the years and he knew what it meant. He was surprised, though, when Darla took a quick look over her shoulder, as though she could feel it, too.

In the next instant a long beeping sound came from the ECG.

'She's in V-fib,' Heather announced, removing all the leads.

Darla immediately picked up the defibrillator paddles. 'Charge to one-sixty.'

'Charging,' Heather returned.

'Clear!'

Darla administered the shock and waited for what seemed like an eternity but in reality was only a few seconds. Benedict checked Tina's pulse.

'Nothing.'

'One-eighty,' she said, and waited for Heather's confirmation of the new setting before administering the second shock.

'Nothing,' Benedict said again, his gaze flicking between Darla and the patient.

'Charge to two hundred,' she said. She administered another shock.

'Darla, I'm sorry,' Benedict said after a moment, removing his fingers from Tina's carotid pulse.

'No. Epinephrine. Draw up—'

'No.' Benedict came around her and removed the paddles from her hands. 'Pupils are fixed and dilated. She's gone.'

'No. No. She can't die. She can't be gone.' Darla started cardiopulmonary resuscitation, her words eager and frantic. 'This is wrong. I'm supposed to save her. I'm supposed to do this. This is what I do. She can't die!'

Benedict quickly handed the paddles to Heather then

placed his hands on Darla's shoulders, but she shrugged him off as she continued counting.

'Oxygen, *stat*.'

'Darla,' Benedict urged.

'No. This is not happening again,' Darla ground out. 'Come on. Come on, Tina.'

Benedict could do nothing else except put his arms around Darla's waist and physically lift her up and away from the body. 'It's over, Darla. I'm calling it.'

'No.' She twisted, trying to get free of his hold, but it was too much for her. She pummelled her fists against his chest. 'No.'

'Time of death, oh-five thirty-two.'

Darla was still upset, still lashing out at him, although he could feel the fight starting to drain out of her. He pulled her closer into his arms, stroking her back. 'You did everything you could.'

'No, I didn't.' Her body was starting to shake and he could feel she was crying. 'I *didn't*.' With that, she spun from his arms and stalked out of the room, leaving Heather and a few very startled nurses wondering what was wrong with their boss.

'Ben?' Heather queried.

Benedict turned to look at her. 'Are you all right here? Can you manage?'

'Er…yes, but—'

'Thanks.' With that, he headed out of the room, wanting to catch Darla before she completely disappeared. He walked into the main A and E corridor but there was no sign of her. Where could she possibly have disappeared to so quickly? It was then he heard a faint click, the sound of a door closing nearby, and he headed in the direction of her office. He swiped his pass-card through the lock opening the door into Syd's office. As he stood there, outside Darla's door, he could hear soft, muffled sounds coming from within. His heart turned over with empathy.

Without hesitation he swiped the pass-card through the lock and slowly entered her office. The lights were off, the room still dark, even though outside the sun was just beginning to rise. Carefully, he made his way around to her desk, thinking she'd be sitting in her chair, but when he reached it, he found it empty. He listened and then realised the crying was coming from the far corner of the room.

With his eyesight now adjusting to the dark, he quickly made his way to where he could now see her sitting on the floor, hugging her knees close, her head buried as she sobbed.

'Oh, Darla,' he murmured, but it wasn't until he crouched next to her and touched her shoulder that she even realised he was in the room. She jumped almost half out of her skin.

'Leave me alone!'

'You don't mean that.' He sat down beside her and rubbed his hand gently on her back.

'Yes, I do. Just go.'

'No. This is not a good time for you to be alone, Darla. It's OK to lean on me.'

She shook her head and sniffed. 'No, it's not. I don't lean on anyone. I don't rely on anyone. I don't trust anyone. Only me. Only me.' Tears continued to stream down her face and Benedict quickly pulled a clean handkerchief from his pocket and pressed it into her hands.

'Not any more. I'm here. I'm not going anywhere.' Benedict continued to simply sit there, rubbing her back and offering all the support he could. He didn't tell her not to cry. He didn't tell her she was being foolish, overreacting. He simply sat there while she cried and although she was perplexed at his behaviour, unable to understand why any man would want to sit beside a woman who was wailing like a banshee, she couldn't deny his presence made her feel infinitely better.

'I couldn't save her,' she said after a little while, her tears beginning to subside.

'You tried.'

'I didn't do enough.'

'You did everything you could.'

'I should have tried harder.'

Something in her tone, the vehemence, the anger, the frustration, tugged at his mind. Why did she feel so responsible for what had happened to Tina? If her mother had been an addict, surely she would have seen…

Benedict stopped rubbing her back for a moment and Darla slowly raised her head to look at him. It was when he looked into her eyes that he realised she wasn't talking about Tina. No. She was talking about her mother.

CHAPTER EIGHT

'DARLA?'

'I couldn't save her.' She was looking at him but he could tell she wasn't seeing him. Her mind had slipped back into her past. He sat still, his hand resting on her back as he waited for her to talk.

'She'd overdosed before but each time I'd managed to call the ambulance in time.' She shook her head slightly. 'Not this time.' Darla's tone was soft and quiet, only invaded by the occasional hiccup as her tears began to dry.

'After school I'd gone to the library to do some more homework, trying desperately to get ahead. I'd sit in that library and I'd work hard, desperate to pull myself out of the cesspit that was my life. There weren't going to be any hand-outs, any miracles. I had to rely on myself and no one else. I was determined.' She sighed and closed her eyes.

'I came home from the library and I knew…I could just sense it. As soon as I opened the door something was…different. There was this sort of…presence in the apartment.' She screwed her eyes tight and shook her head as though wanting to rid her mind of the memory once and for all.

'Death. I'd never really smelt it or felt it before but

this time it settled over me like a lead blanket, its rancid stench filling my lungs. I couldn't breathe properly and I started stumbling around the place, my heart racing as I searched frantically for her, alarm bells ringing in my ears.'

A lone tear slid down her cheek and Benedict only barely resisted the urge to wipe it away. Touching her, shifting, moving from exactly where he was might stop her from talking, from reliving a traumatic event from her past, which had clearly sculpted her life. He wondered if Darla had spoken to anyone about this before but even if she had, it would have been years ago.

'She was lying on the bathroom floor. Needle still in her arm. Eyes open. Pupils dilated. I ran to her. I called her name. Mum! *Mum!*' The urgency in her tone brought a lump to Benedict's throat, one he found would not shift no matter how many times he swallowed.

'I checked the pulse in her neck. It was faint but there. I took the needle from her arm and raced to the phone, only to find it wasn't connected. She hadn't paid the bill, again. I went next door and asked old Mrs Fowl to call an ambulance then raced back. I called to Mum, I slapped her face, grabbed a towel and wetted it with cold water and put it on her face.' Darla's words were fast, tripping over each other in her effort to explain the urgency. 'I made sure she was on her side, in the recovery position, so if she vomited, she wouldn't drown. I did everything I could. *Everything I could!*' She hiccupped again and shook her head. 'It wasn't enough.'

She opened her eyes and let the tears drop to her cheeks as she tried to blink them away. 'She arrested in the ambulance and they managed to revive her…but not for long. At the hospital, I stood in that treatment room. In the corner. Off to the side. Nobody saw me.

They were all too busy doing what they could to save her.' She blinked, sniffed then raised her eyes to meet Benedict's for the first time since she'd started talking. 'It played out exactly as it did with Tina. The V-fib, the fixed and dilated pupils.' She shook her head again. 'I was sixteen and I stood in that treatment room and watched my mother die.'

Her tone was filled with complete desolation and despair and Benedict could take it no longer. He shifted around, settling himself firmly on the floor, leaning up against the wall before pulling Darla onto his lap and into his arms, holding her close. She didn't start crying again but she did put her arms around his neck, holding onto him so tight he hoped she'd never let go.

They sat like that for a while and then Darla shifted her face, leaning it more comfortably against his chest, listening to the steady rhythm of his heart. She couldn't believe how incredible it felt to have him hold her, to simply sit still and be. Never had she had this, feeling so secure and protected. It was her idea of heaven.

'Mum would always tell me,' she began softly, 'that I was a useless waste of space. Once, when she was drinking vodka and snorting cocaine, she told me she'd tried to have an abortion.' Darla cleared her throat and mimicked in a shriller pitch. '"Ya father was a loser. I'm a loser and you're a loser. I didn't want no baby and Runsie knew a doctor, he said, who could get rid of unwanted babies, but the idiot did it wrong and you were still there. Ya leech and you've been a leech since the day you was born."'

Benedict was shocked with what she was saying, anger towards her mother burning in his eyes, bile rising in his throat. He couldn't even speak, couldn't console her, he was so furious. Instead, he tightened his hold on her, wanting her to always feel safe with him.

'She only kept me around because the government paid child support. She'd use that money for her booze and drugs. How I lived through those first few years, I have no idea. I've been told I was in foster-care on and off for quite some time but they always sent me back to her. She was my mother and she would clean herself up just enough that they'd give me back—because that way she had her meal ticket again.

'At the age of seven she was sending me out to buy her drugs and if there were ever any raids around our neighbourhood, she'd hide her stash inside my tatty old teddy bear and make me hold it. "You scream your head off if the cops ever try to take it from you," she'd say. It worked every time and if I didn't scream loud enough, she'd pinch me when they weren't looking.'

As she continued talking, Benedict made a concentrated effort to relax his jaw because his head was really starting to pound with anger. 'Darla,' he murmured, unable to keep silent any longer. He rested his head against hers. 'I'm so sorry for what they did to you.' What she'd said also explained the drive she had for helping others who found themselves in similar situations to the one she'd grown up with. 'I wish I could help you. I want to take away the pain, to protect you from ever getting hurt again.'

Darla lifted her head and looked at him. 'You can't protect me, Benedict. Only I can.'

'Don't say that.'

'Why not? It's true. I've had to learn to fend for myself, to work hard, to make my own way in the world. At the age of sixteen, I was left all alone. No parents, no siblings, not even any friends, and yet I managed to stay under the government's radar, avoid being put into yet another foster-home and fend for myself. I studied hard, determined to get into medical school, working all sorts of jobs and taking out loans to pay for my tuition. I did it. By myself. With no help from anyone.'

Her tears and the emotions that had initially tipped her over the edge were starting to disappear and in their place appeared the strong, determined and incredibly stubborn woman who was starting to become more important to him than he'd dared to realise.

Darla shifted in his arms and he loosened his hold on her, not wanting her to feel hemmed in by his comforting embrace. She stayed where she was for another moment, as though she really did want to remain exactly where she was. He watched her internal struggle before she finally shifted off his lap and stood, walking over to her desk.

'Uh…thanks.'

'For?' Benedict asked as he levered himself upright and stretched his arms overhead to awaken stiff muscles. As he stretched, his shirt rose and the band of his denim jeans dipped, exposing a small section of his abdomen. Darla's gaze was unwittingly drawn to the movement, to the sight of his firm stomach muscles hidden beneath his clothes. Didn't the man have any idea just how crazy he could make her feel when he held her close, protected her whilst she blubbered all over his shirt and then excited her with the merest glimpse of his hard body hidden beneath his clothes?

When she didn't answer his question, he looked at her and was secretly delighted when he caught her staring at him. Darla had been ogling him. Surely this was a good sign, especially after the kisses they'd shared? She was still interested in him or, at least, he hoped so.

'Uh…for…um…you know…being supportive.' She momentarily closed her eyes against her stammering, unable to believe the way this man could fluster her so easily.

Benedict's slow smile spread across his lips, causing his eyes to twinkle. 'You are more than welcome.'

'No. Don't, Benedict.'

'Don't what?'

'Don't look at me like that.'

'Like what?'

'All cute and nice and gorgeous, especially when I'm embarrassed.'

'Embarrassed about what?' Darla's answer was to fix him with a look of incredulity. 'For crying? For getting upset? For opening up?' Benedict shook his head. 'Don't be.'

'I have to be.'

'Why?'

'Don't you have any idea what you do to me?' Darla placed both hands on her blotter and he could see she was struggling to find some semblance of calm. 'Where I was raised, men only ever wanted one thing from a woman and even then they took it rather than waiting for it to be given.'

Benedict's eyes widened at this news. 'Darla. Has a man ever—?'

'No,' she quickly answered. 'Well…almost once but thankfully my mother hit him over the head with a frying pan.'

'How old were you?'

'Thirteen.' She crossed her arms in front of her and rubbed her upper arms. Benedict wanted desperately to take her in his arms again, to hold her, to protect her, but he could also read the 'Keep Out' sign she'd erected and knew, if he was to continue earning her trust, he'd have to respect that.

'After that, my mother took to locking me in my room, especially when she had a guy coming around. "It's for your own protection," she'd say, and then hide the key.' Darla shook her head. 'One time I was locked in there for two days because she was so high on drugs she'd forgotten to unlock the door and let me out.'

Benedict's heart wrenched with pain at her words and he clenched his hands at his sides, determined to respect her wishes and keep his distance. It couldn't be easy for her to confess such things to him but he appreciated this sliver of trust she was giving him.

'The next time she was passed out I found the key, stole some of her drug money and went to the shops and had a key cut.'

'Smart.'

'That's right. I had to learn to be smart, to out-thwart her and all the deadbeats who would hang around our place. Any money I found lying around I'd steal and when I had enough saved up, I'd buy food. I grew up quickly. I did the shopping, I tidied the house, I learned self-defence. I had to clothe myself in mental bullet-proof armour if I was going to survive, and I did.

'I may not have had a mother who loved me but because of her I did what needed to be done. No one else was going to do it. It was up to me.' She paused for a second, then angled her head to the side. 'Although I have to say, the day I truly understood that my mother didn't love me was perhaps the worst day ever. All children want to be loved, and in the beginning that's why I did whatever she told me to do. I wanted to win her *approval. Then one day, about six months after the in*cident where she'd hit the man with the frying pan, I began to understand that she hadn't done that to *protect* me, she'd knocked him out because she was *jealous* of me. My body was maturing, it was young, untouched, and hers was the complete opposite. She locked me away because she couldn't stand the thought of her lovers wanting *me* when they should have been wanting her.'

Darla couldn't believe that tears were once more pricking behind her eyes. Hadn't she cried them all out yet? She swallowed over the lump in her throat and worked hard to ignore the heaviness of her heart. 'She didn't love me. My mother didn't love me. She *never* loved me. She kept me around because I made her life easier. She was paid money from the government, I cooked and cleaned. I ensured she had clean clothes to wear, food to eat and a roof over our heads. All she cared about was herself, and once I'd managed to get that through my thick skull I started pulling those walls around me, hiding inside them, and they provided protection from outside attacks. I was safe so long as I relied on myself and no one else. It's why I prefer being an A and E doctor, why I go out onto the streets. I want to help people as no one ever helped me. They can at least have their angel to cling to. I had no one.' Her voice cracked on the last words and she quickly shook her head and cleared her throat.

'You do now.'

'What?'

'You have someone now. You have me.' Benedict edged forward, coming to stand right in front of her desk, but didn't make any move to touch her. 'I believe in you, Darla. I believe in the work you're doing, both on the streets and here at the hospital. You're a remarkable woman, like no one I've ever met before, and I completely admire you, but don't for one further second think you are alone. Not any more.' Benedict raked his hand through his hair and looked down at her.

'I don't have a clue what you've done to me, Darla, how you've managed to draw me in with your natural charm and intelligence, but you have. I've tried to fight it but I can't any more. And I know you may think my words are shallow, that my head is easily turned by a pretty face, that I'm as typical as every other male in the world, but I'm not. I wasn't looking for this attraction either. The last thing I wanted was to be involved with *anyone*. But it's there and I'm not about to ignore it.' He looked straight into her big brown eyes to ensure what he was about to say rang as true as possible because he meant every word.

'However, given what you've just shared, I want you to know you have nothing to fear from me. I want you to believe I'm someone you *can* trust and someone who *values* you. I won't rush you, Darla. I want to spend time with you, for us to keep discovering each other, to be open and honest, to celebrate and commiserate together. I will hold your hand, gaze longingly into your eyes, and be bowled over by your smile, but I will also be a polite and courteous gentleman at all times.' He placed his right hand over his heart. 'And that's a promise.'

Darla tried not to tremble at his words, at the way his rich deep tones washed over her, calming her, filling her with hope. Was this for real? Was it possible that she might actually have found a man who was genuine, honest and true? She'd opened up to him a lot and that in itself showed her he was worthy of at least trying to earn her trust. He'd held her when she'd cried. He'd offered comfort and support and the way he'd made her feel when she'd been safely cocooned in his protective embrace had been heavenly. Still, the battle between head and heart continued to war within her and she nodded once at his words before straightening her shoulders and lifting her chin.

'Don't promise, Benedict. Prove it.'

A slow smile spread over his face, lighting his eyes and melting her heart. 'I intend to.'

Benedict held her gaze and she could see he was completely serious. It was intense and powerful and the emotions coursing through her made Darla feel exposed, vulnerable. She didn't like it but at the same time she was almost desperate to once again experience the warmth of his arms about her. Throughout her life she'd learned to rely solely on herself, not wanting anyone to see her vulnerability. Yet not more than five minutes ago she'd been sitting on Benedict's lap, with his arms firmly around her as she'd talked of her past. Even now, as her gaze flickered over him, she could see wet patches on his shirt where her tears had fallen.

She wanted desperately to trust him, to believe what he'd said was true, and now she'd challenged him to prove it. Had she gone completely insane? She looked away from his hypnotic eyes, focusing on the new files Syd had put into her in-box. She went to gather them up and then noticed the little red light flashing on her telephone, indicating she had a voice message. That was odd. It was a Saturday morning and usually, if there was an emergency, she'd be contacted on her cellphone. It didn't matter that today was officially her day off as she'd planned to come in anyway and get a jump start on some paperwork.

'Leave the files,' Benedict said, watching her every move. 'It's Saturday. You're not rostered on. You've had an emotionally draining night and morning and you've been taking enough files home to sink a battleship.'

'There's a message,' Darla said, pointing to the phone, and quickly picked up the receiver, pressing the button to replay the message.

'All right, but after that I'm taking you ho—'

'Shh.' Darla held up her hand and Benedict noticed her eyes start to widen as she listened. The message was obviously short as it wasn't a moment later that she replaced the receiver and sat down in her chair.

'Well? What was it?' he asked when she didn't speak. He walked around the desk to come stand beside her chair. 'Darla?'

'I got the job.'

'That's fantastic. I always knew you would. Congratulations!'

'I got the job.' She uttered the words as though she was in complete shock. 'This time I did it.' She shrugged, the reality of her situation still sinking in. 'I *really did it*.'

'This time?' he queried as he leaned against the desk, legs out long, hands on the table beside him.

Darla closed her eyes as though savouring the moment. 'Before I came here, I was in Sydney, working at A and E at Sydney General. I was acting director there and had a very good chance of getting the directorship.' She opened her eyes and looked at him. 'One of my colleagues, Colin, was also going for the job. We'd been colleagues for years, built up a healthy competition, and I'd thought he was someone I could perhaps one day come to trust—I mean *really* trust.'

'Like you trust me?' He couldn't help giving her a playful wink and was rewarded with a half-smile.

'Shut up,' she returned gently, before standing up and

walking over to the fern in the corner of her office. She reached out and touched the green leaves.

'Anyway, after years of working together, of spending our free time together, of him declaring he wanted our friendship to evolve into something more, something real, something romantic…' she dropped her hand and turned to face Benedict '…he stabbed me in the back.'

'What happened?' Benedict stayed where he was, resisting the urge to haul her into his arms.

'Well, the fact that we'd both applied for the same job was starting to cause tension between us. Colin suggested that we both withdraw and allow someone else to take the job, thereby choosing our relationship over work. One other person from a hospital in Brisbane had also applied for the job and after much discussion we decided to let it go. That our relationship was more important than a job.'

'Let me guess, Colin didn't withdraw his application?'

'Got it in one. Afterwards, he was confused as to why we couldn't continue with our relationship, why I didn't want anything to do with him.'

Benedict nodded as though all those times she'd asked him whether he really wanted the top job finally made sense. She'd thought he'd been going to change his mind. 'He'd lied to you.'

'Just like every other man in my life. Foster-fathers, social workers, drug dealers, boys at school, men at medical school, professional colleagues. They always want something, Benedict. Always.' She started to pace back and forth. 'In high school, about a year before my mother died, there was this new guy who came to the school and we hit it off straight away. He was smart, like me. We would both hide in the library at lunchtime, studying, reading, keeping out of the way of playground ridicule. I was young, naive and thought perhaps here was someone I could trust, but after a while he started coming less and less to the library. He started changing, fitting in with the "cool" crowd, and by the end of the year he'd completely snubbed me.'

'But teenage boys are like that, Darla. They're fickle and filled with raging hormones. You shouldn't take it personally.'

'Oh, no? Well, at one stage I confronted him. Asked him why he didn't seem to want to be my friend any more, and he told me he didn't hang around with drug addicts.'

'What?'

'Yep. He'd listened to the gossips. Listened to the *rumours flying around about me instead of coming* to me and asking me directly. So that was lesson one. Lesson two didn't happen until my final year of medical school when I once again let down my guard and started dating a fellow student. I'd told myself I was different now. My mother had been dead for years, I'd managed to work hard, to get into medical school, and I was doing very well. I was a different person now and I could handle the opposite sex.' She shook her head. 'He was a charmer. So much so that he ended up dating three girls—at once. When the other two found out, they didn't seem to care, but for me—'

'He'd broken your trust.'

'He'd lied to me and used me. It was the same pattern I'd seen with all men over time.' She stopped pacing and stood in the middle of her office, her arms spread wide. 'So you can see, Benedict, why I can't simply take you at your word. You say I'm different. You say I'm remarkable, that I'm worth it. You say that you won't rush me, that I can trust you, and that's why I need you to prove it.'

'I need to pay for every other man's sins,' he stated, wanting to show her he understood.

'Yes.'

'I accept that challenge, fairy princess, and we'll start right now.' He walked over and took her hand gently in his. 'Come on.'

'Wait.' She pulled her hand free. 'What are you doing?'

'I'm taking you out to celebrate.'

'Celebrate?'

'Darla! You just got the job of your dreams. This needs a celebration. A *big* celebration.'

'And I suppose you have something in mind?' She placed her hands on her hips and glared at him.

'I do.' He stepped closer, leaning down to whisper in her ear. Darla closed her eyes, forcing herself to ignore the spicy scent of him, ignore the comforting warmth emanating from him, ignore the way she wanted to turn her head to ensure their lips met. 'The best celebration ever,' he continued, his breath fanning her neck. 'Apple pie.'

'What?' She pulled back. 'Is that your new romantic nickname for me or—?'

Benedict laughed and the sound warmed her through and through. 'Darla, you're never boring, I'll give you that. No, I mean let's go celebrate with the best apple pie you've ever eaten.' This time he held out his hand and waited ever so patiently for her to put her hand in his. She looked at her desk, at the work sitting there, then she looked at his face, then back to his hand.

'You deserve this. You deserve to celebrate. This

is big news, Darla, and it requires a big celebration in return.'

'Apple pie is a big celebration?'

His only answer was a slow, soft nodding of his head. 'Come on,' he urged. 'We have to start somewhere.'

He was right. She'd already let down her guard, not only telling him about her past, her mother and the men who had previously broken her trust but showing him just how vulnerable she really was beneath the hard protective layers she'd pulled around her over the years… and he hadn't done an about-face and run away.

She had to start somewhere. Benedict was a good man. He'd listened, he'd been patient, he hadn't pressured her. Could she take the chance? Take a step forward into a world she'd only dreamt about? A world where she was a normal woman, with a normal job and a normal boyfriend? *We* have to start somewhere. He was in this with her. He was taking a chance as well, putting himself back out there after a bad relationship. Could she prove to Benedict that he could trust her too? Risk his heart once more?

'OK' came her tentative reply as she placed her hand in his. 'Pie it is.'

CHAPTER NINE

AT THE end of his shift, they took a taxi back to where Darla had parked her car.

'Haven't you got a car yet?' she asked, rolling her eyes when he shook his head. 'OK. Where's this great pie place?'

'Uh…why don't you go home, shower first, get all refreshed before celebrating?'

She seemed mildly relieved. 'Really?'

'Of course.' He opened the driver's door for her. 'I'll come pick you up in…' He looked at his watch. It was almost eight o'clock in the morning. He did a few quick mental calculations. 'About forty-five minutes? Sound good?' Darla nodded and Benedict leaned forward and pressed a quick kiss to her cheek. 'OK. I'll see you then.' He waited for her to climb behind the wheel and then shut the door. She quickly rolled down the window.

'What are you going to do?'

'Uh…I'll go shower and change, too.'

'I can drop you at your house. According to your personnel file, you don't live far from my place.'

'Thanks, but it's fine. I have a few other things to organise,' he returned.

'Like what?'

'Like how I'm supposed to surprise my girlfriend

when she keeps asking questions?' He shook his head but his smile was bright. 'Go home. See you in just under an hour.' And with a wink he turned and started jogging down the street, leaving Darla sitting in her car, stunned.

'Girlfriend?'

Forty-six minutes later, Benedict rang her doorbell and Darla, fresh from her shower and dressed in a comfortable pair of jeans, boots and a pale blue shirt, answered the door. Her hair wasn't completely dry so she'd left it loose and Benedict simply stood on the other side of the threshold, struck dumb at the sight of her.

'Aren't you going to come in?' she asked, stepping back to allow him access.

'You look beautiful.' He closed his eyes for a moment as though needing to steel himself before looking at her again. 'This chivalry thing is going to be harder than I thought,' he muttered, but she heard and couldn't stop the bubble of delight that zipped through her.

'Good,' she replied, and as he still hadn't moved she swept her arm in front of her. 'You're not coming in?'

'Uh…' Benedict shoved both hands into his pockets to stop himself from reaching out to touch her, to draw her close to him, to kiss her gorgeous mouth. 'I don't mind waiting in the car. It might be safer, at least until I can get my hormones under control,' he replied with a sheepish grin.

'Oh.' Darla was surprised to find her cheeks feeling warm at his words. He really did think she was beautiful. She could see it in his eyes and the knowledge made her feel incredibly special. 'OK, then. I'll get you the keys.'

'No. I meant my car.' He jerked a thumb over his shoulder.

'You mean Hamilton's car?'

'No. Mine. I just went and bought one.'

'What?'

'I bought one,' he repeated. 'Go. Get ready. I'll be waiting.' He turned and walked towards the white sedan parked in her driveway. Darla leaned out the door and realised he was telling the truth. He'd just gone out and bought a car! Stunned, she quickly made sure all her windows were locked and picked up her bag and jacket before slipping her sunglasses on and heading out.

When Benedict saw her, he quickly came around to the passenger door and opened it for her.

'Thank you.'

He winked. 'Chivalry, right?'

Her answer was a brilliant smile as she settled herself in the car. Benedict came around to the driver's side and climbed in, both of them buckling their seat belts before he started the engine. 'Sounds great,' she said.

'Do you know much about cars?' he asked as he reversed.

'No. Not really.'

'Neither do I. So long as they get me from A to B without breaking down, I'm happy.'

She laughed then asked, 'So where's this secret apple-pie shop?'

'Actually, it's a bit of a drive but as neither of us are rostered on today and as we're celebrating, I thought a drive would be nice.'

Darla could feel her apprehension starting to increase at this change in events. She wasn't a big fan of surprises but had to remind herself that she was stepping into the unknown. The way Benedict made her feel, all happy, mixed up and delightedly confused, was a good thing. She'd opened up to him in a way she'd never thought she could open to *anyone*. Perhaps she should try something new? Follow his lead.

'Are you all right with that?' he asked when she didn't say anything. 'Because if you're not, if you're not ready for surprises, then we can make other plans.'

'No.' She turned to face him.

'Er…no, you're not all right or…?'

'Don't make other plans. It's good for me to…step outside my very comfortable comfort zone.'

Benedict's smile was bright at her words and he reached over and took her hand in his, bringing it to his lips to kiss it. 'It really is the best pie I've ever tasted.'

'Then my life, and my gastronomic delight, are in your capable hands.' Darla settled her head back against the headrest and sighed, feeling a contentment like she'd never felt before.

Benedict slowed the car as they neared the town of Batlow where the apples were grown, cooked and made into the best pie in the country. He glanced across at Darla, and smiled at the sight of her sleeping peacefully in the seat beside him. They'd made it to the motorway, heading out of Canberra towards Tumut, which was the small town where he'd gone to school, before exhaustion had claimed her. She'd slept soundly for over an hour and now as he decreased speed yet again she began to stir.

'Hello,' he murmured as he brought the car to a stop, parking on the side of the road near the memorial park. Darla gazed at him, her eyes still fuzzy.

'Hi.' She smiled.

'You've had a good sleep.'

At his words Darla suddenly realised where she was. She shifted so quickly in her seat that the seat belt restrained her. 'What? Where are we?' She looked around, remembering she was in a car, a car with Benedict, a car she'd fallen asleep in. She closed her eyes as mortification washed over her.

'We're in Batlow and, by the looks of things, it's going to be a great turnout.'

'What?' She opened her eyes and looked at the view outside the windows. There were people all around, quite a lot of people actually, and cars seemed to be parked everywhere. There were families and children and laughter and sunshine and happiness and... normalcy.

'Benedict, I fell asleep!'

'I know. I was there.'

'But...you shouldn't have let me.'

'Why not? You were obviously exhausted.'

'But I don't—' She stopped as the words she wanted to say would sound ridiculous on her tongue.

'Don't what?' he prompted as he unclipped both their seat belts.

'I don't...sleep in front of people.'

'Oh. Well, it's just as well I'm not people.' With a wide grin he exited the car and quickly came around to her side, opening the door for her. 'You might need your jacket. It's a little cooler here than in Canberra.'

Pushing aside her embarrassment, Darla gathered up her handbag and jacket before allowing him to help her from the car. 'The last thing I remember was setting your radio stations,' she murmured.

'And you found one that played nice soothing jazz. So soothing you dozed off.' He shrugged. 'You've nothing to be worried about, Darla.' His words were light, fresh and held a hint of teasing. 'You didn't snore.'

She opened her eyes wide, glaring at him, but he only laughed in response and took her hand in his. 'Come on. Lots to do and explore and pie to eat.'

'What *is* this? I thought we were going to a little café somewhere.'

'I like to be original for first dates.'

'This is a date?'

'No. This is the Batlow annual *apple* pie fair. The *date* fair isn't held until October.'

'Really?'

'No. I'm making it up. Come on. I'm hungry.'

She wasn't sure why but she allowed him to lead her towards the showgrounds where there were stalls and tables and chairs and music and laughter. She was also surprised at the number of people who seemed to greet Benedict as though they were old friends.

'Oh, you came, you came, you came!' A woman with long honey-coloured hair came running up to Benedict, her arms out wide. Benedict instantly dropped Darla's hand and caught the woman in a fierce hug, even spinning her round. Once her feet were firmly back on the ground, she planted a big kiss on his cheek. 'I'm so happy to see you. You look great.'

Darla stared at the woman and started to wonder whether there was more going on here than Benedict had let on. Who was she? Why had she greeted him in such a familiar fashion? Wasn't she a bit old to be twirled around like a child?

'Thanks. It's good to see you, too. It's been too long.'

The woman gave his arm a playful nudge. 'Over twelve months. Still, you're back.'

'I am.' Benedict placed his hand in the small of

Darla's back. 'Darla, I'd like you to meet my exuberant sister-in-law, Honeysuckle.'

Darla released a breath she hadn't realised she'd been holding and smiled at Benedict's sister-in-law. This woman was family and she already knew how important family was to Benedict. She held out her hand. 'Pleased to meet you.'

'Oh, we don't bother with that here,' Honey remarked, waving Darla's hand away and pulling her close into a warm embrace. Darla stared at Benedict over Honey's shoulder, her eyes wide. Benedict's reply to her unspoken question was to shrug as though to say 'That's Honey'.

'Where's Edward?' Benedict asked, looking around for his brother.

Honey released Darla. 'Over at the face-painting stand with the children, although we all know it's going to be washed off with the apple bobbing later today but it's all in good fun.' Her exuberance was like nothing Darla had seen before.

'And the baby?' Benedict continued as they walked slowly towards the face-painting stand. 'Where's my beautiful new niece?'

'Eddie has her in the papoose. I've been here since before sunrise, baking pies, so I can guarantee they're fresh. Oh, hey…' Honey was distracted by someone else and waved wildly. 'Sorry. Need to keep going. Next year I've promised Eddie I *won't* be on the organising committee.'

'Sure, sure,' Benedict joked. 'I've heard that one before, Hon.'

She grinned at him before looking to Darla. 'It was great to meet you,' she replied. 'I'll catch up with you both later.' And as fast as she'd come, she was off, absorbed in the crowd of people milling their way between stalls.

'So...I take it you live around here?'

Benedict nodded. 'Oodnaminaby's about half an hour from here by the main roads but twenty on the back roads, but you can only drive them in the warmer months. In winter, they're closed due to the snow.'

'This is the first time you've been back since returning from Tarparnii?'

'Yes.'

'Why didn't you mention this?'

'Because it's part of your celebration surprise.'

'To introduce me to your family?'

He shrugged and slipped his hand back into hers, realising the enormity of her question. 'That's a by-product. Truly, Darla. You'll love the apple pies, and then, if you want, I'll even pay for you to have your face painted.'

Darla stared up at him as though he'd gone completely bonkers but she found his eyes alive with life, his smile wide with happiness, and both of them were highly infectious. 'You're crazy,' she said with a little laugh.

Benedict nodded. 'Better you find out now.' With that, he steered her towards the pie stands, where they joined one of the long queues. Finally, they were sitting at a table, about to have their first tasting of pie.

'Wait.' Benedict stopped her and held his fork up in the air. 'A toast.'

'With forks?'

'Why not?' He cleared his throat. 'Congratulations on your new job, *Director* Fairlie. You deserve it.'

'Thank you,' she responded, and grinned when he tapped his fork against hers, then started eating his pie.

He closed his eyes and savoured the delight. Darla took her first bite.

'Was I right, or was I right?' he asked and Darla swallowed her mouthful, nodding.

'It's…delicious.'

'It's *heavenly*,' he said, and she laughed.

'This is lovely, Benedict. A great idea for a celebration even if it wasn't what I was initially expecting.'

'Surprise,' he said softly, and reached across the table to take her hand in his. He laced their fingers together and smiled at her. 'Thanks for letting me in, Darla. I know it hasn't been easy but I appreciate it.'

Darla stared across the table at him, her gaze dipping from his eyes to his lips. She wanted him to lean across, to capture her mouth in one of the glorious kisses they'd shared before…but he didn't. Instead he winked and smiled and she could see he was using incredible restraint. He had to learn to trust completely again too. He'd promised not to rush her, to let her set the pace for the romantic emotions surging between them, proving that he was definitely someone she could come to trust.

Hours later, after a day of looking at the different craft stalls, laughing as people actually bobbed for apples in large barrels of water and seeing Benedict give shoulder rides to a few of his nieces and nephews, Darla was starting to feel rather exhausted. Honey had invited them back for dinner and although Darla wanted to start the journey back to Canberra fairly soon, she was also curious to see the home where Benedict had grown up.

'At least have a good meal before you head off,' Honey had said. 'Or you're more than welcome to stay the night if you choose. We're in no hurry for you to rush off,' she'd remarked, her gaze encompassing both of them. 'After all, Ben, it's still your family home.'

'Do you want to go?' he'd asked Darla, even though she could see quite clearly that he would love to have a few more hours with his siblings. During the day, and between bites of apple pie, she'd been introduced to Peter and his wife Annabelle and their two boys, as well as to Benedict's surrogate sister Lorelai and her husband Woody and their two girls. It had been interesting to meet Peter and Edward, noting the clear genetic heritage the three brothers shared. Dark hair and blue eyes were the order of the day yet all of them possessed their own unique qualities.

'Of course. I'd love to stay for dinner. After all, this is my celebration day.'

His eyes had twinkled with delight and his mouth had beamed into a bright smile. 'Yes, it is.' Then he'd surprised her by bowing from the waist. 'Thank you, Darla.'

The Goldmark house in Oodnaminaby was what Darla had always pictured as the perfect family home. Two storeys, filled with photographs and pictures and toys and people and kids intermingling everywhere. Honey and Edward's latest addition to the clan, three-month-old Susan, was cradled securely in Benedict's arms.

'How are you holding up?' he asked Darla as Susan gurgled up at him, safe and secure in the knowledge she was loved unconditionally.

'It's…loud,' she said, and he smiled.

'We do tend to get a bit rowdy. It's even worse with Bart and Ham here.'

'Do you get together often?'

He nodded. 'A few times a year at least. Special occasions, Christmas, New Year.' He shrugged. 'It all depends on shifts.'

A loud clanging sound came from the kitchen and Susan jumped in his arms. A moment later a frown furrowed her cute little brow and he could tell she was about to start crying. 'Why don't we go out into the garden?' He looked at Darla. 'Care to join Susan and me for a pre-dinner stroll?' He cradled Susan carefully in one arm and offered the other to Darla.

'I'd love to,' she said as she slipped her hand into the crook of his elbow. They slipped through the kitchen and out the back door, heading towards the back garden. There was a small building to one side and opposite it the most beautiful little garden Darla had ever seen.

'That's the old coach house,' he remarked, indicating the building. 'It took my father years to restore. My mother would complain that it was taking him too long and he'd say, "Well, I can only work on it in my spare time so if you want it finished sooner, roster me some more spare time."' Benedict smiled as he recalled his father's words. 'They worked together, they raised a family together and they died together, and they did it all with love.' He studied the building for a moment before turning and walking down the few steps of a small neatly trimmed garden. There were pretty flowers on one side and native shrubs on the other and in the dimming light Darla saw a small stone bench with words engraved on it.

'"Hannah and Cameron",' she read out loud.

'This was my mum's garden. Her sanctuary where she could come and have five minutes' peace. She designed and planted it but over the years, whenever we had something to discuss with her, or a problem we couldn't solve, she'd bring us out into the garden, get us doing some weeding and then just as she'd gently pull the weeds from the ground, she'd pull the weeds from our lives.' Benedict stood, looking out at the setting sun. Darla sat down on the bench and watched him. Little Susan had stopped fussing and had closed her eyes, quite content with the world.

'Do you miss her?' The question was soft.

'Yeah. Probably more than I miss my dad. She was busy. What woman wouldn't be with five boys, a husband and a busy country practice? But she always made time for us. Each and every one. No matter what. She'd sit on the grass and she'd pull weeds, waiting patiently for us to talk out whatever was on our minds.'

'So if she was here now,' Darla asked, knowing she was branching into uncharted waters but unable to stop herself, 'what would you say?'

Benedict smiled. 'I'd tell her all about you. About how you work too hard. How you help restore people's hope when they think that it's gone for ever. I'd tell her about how you make me laugh, about the way your whole face lights up when you're happy. I'd tell her how you've managed to restore my faith in the opposite sex by proving you're a woman of worth.'

'Why was your faith broken, Benedict? What happened to make you go to Tarparnii?'

'You mean you haven't heard the hospital gossip?'

'I don't listen to it.'

'Of course you don't. See, Susan?' he said to his niece. 'A woman of worth.' Benedict looked at Darla and exhaled slowly. Now was the time to tell her everything and put the past to rest. 'Her name was Carolina and, quite frankly, she lied and deceived me at every turn. We'd known each other for a few years but after a while our friendship started to become more personal, but as it turns out, Carolina wasn't really interested in *me*. The only reason I'd made her radar was because I'd been promoted to A and E director. She was a gold-digger, latching onto me in the hope that I'd give her everything she wanted. She pretended to be someone she wasn't. She would tell me what a great nurse she was and how she'd really helped a lot of her patients with their emotional issues. She built herself up to be so great, I believed her. She even started volunteering with ACT NOW, always telling me how much she really wanted to help the homeless… But it was all false. All she wanted was my signature to open a joint bank account before she could clean me out. We'd even started looking at homes to buy and I'd planned on asking her to marry me.'

'So what happened to break the spell? To open your eyes?'

'One night, at ACT NOW, there was a riot. I mean, a really bad one, and the rioters turned their attention onto us. They were outside the ACT NOW vans and started rocking the medical van to and fro, with both Carolina and myself inside. The van was tipped and Carolina sustained a fracture to her clavicle, humerus, ulna and tibia, as well as a mild concussion. Basically, she was so mad at me, mad that because of me, because she'd been pretending to like that sort of work, she'd been injured.'

'The rose-coloured glasses came off?'

'Smashed to smithereens,' he agreed. 'I couldn't believe it. The woman I'd thought I loved wasn't real. She was fictitious and not only that, she was deceitful. She was in hospital for a week because of the concussion and she blamed me for her injuries. She even threatened to sue me, but none of it was my fault so she really didn't have a leg to stand on—literally.'

'So you went to Tarparnii?'

'Not straight away. At first I threw myself into my work, becoming demanding and critical of my staff. I was hurt, bitter, and alienated quite a few people. I avoided coming home because I knew Edward would no doubt lecture me on my behaviour and he would have been right, too. Then, when I finally did come home, exhausted and burnt out, Edward didn't say a thing. Instead, he unleashed his secret weapon.'

'What's that?'

'Honeysuckle *and* Lorelai. The two women in the world I knew I could trust. Lorelai was twenty when my mum died and while she was good at supporting and caring, it was Honey who could really pull those weeds the way Mum used to. Between the two of them I didn't stand a chance. Honey suggested Tarparnii and within two weeks I'd applied and been granted a sabbatical and was on a plane heading overseas.'

He came and sat down next to her on the bench seat, carefully shifting a sleeping Susan to his other arm.

'I'm sorry you were hurt,' Darla said softly.

'More my pride than anything. Turns out she didn't do as much permanent damage as I'd originally thought.'

'That's good news.'

'Is it?' Benedict shifted and looked at her, their faces close. His gaze dipped to look at her lips and even though the light was fading fast, he could still see every contour of her beautiful face, simply because he'd memorised it.

'Yes.'

'Darla, I want to kiss you.'

'I'm right here,' she murmured, feeling his glorious warmth surround her, feeling her heart hammering wildly against her ribs due to his nearness, feeling light-headed and ready to take a chance.

'I know. Your senses are drugging me, enticing me, urging me forward...' He leaned closer, gazing at her parted lips, their breath mingling with delight. 'But I can't.'

'You can't?' She was unable to hide the hint of desperation in her tone.

'I promised. I want you to trust me, Darla. It's even more important to me now than it was this morning and I'm not going to break that trust, even if it drives me slowly around the twist.'

CHAPTER TEN

IT WAS almost midnight when Benedict pulled up outside Darla's apartment and once again she was sleeping soundly in the seat next to him. Even when he switched off the engine, she still remained asleep, indicating just how exhausted she was.

He was fairly sure she was planning to head out to the streets at two o'clock in the morning, even though she'd probably do herself more good by actually getting one good night's sleep. Working all day and then being the angel every night would soon take its toll on her and he didn't want her collapsing from exhaustion, which was where he could see she was heading. At least he'd managed to get her away from the constant grind today. He smiled as he recalled the way she'd interacted with his family. She'd been shy and reserved at first but during dinner she'd slowly started to come out of her shell.

She'd offered to stack the dishwasher and tidy the kitchen with Edward whilst Benedict had helped Honey with the bedtime routine. Lorelai, Woody and their two girls had left first, with Peter and Annabelle staying around a bit longer as their two boys were older.

'They're all so wonderful,' she'd told him as they'd

waved goodbye to start the two-hour drive back to Canberra.

'I'm glad you like them.'

'I do. I'd always dreamed of a family like that but I never thought I'd get to really experience what it would be like.' Then she'd surprised him by taking his hand in hers and giving it a quick squeeze. 'Thank you, Benedict. Today has really felt like a celebration.'

'I'm glad.' He'd lifted her hand to his lips and kissed it. Now as he looked at her sleeping there, her breathing calm and even, Benedict could feel himself slipping further and further towards loving her. It overwhelmed him. When he'd returned from Tarparnii, starting a relationship with any woman had been the last thing on his mind and yet somehow Darla had managed to infiltrate his life and show him just how bright life could be. His past was his past, just as Darla's was hers. Sure, it could sculpt their future but only in a positive way and he felt that with today's activities, with the way she'd handled meeting the rest of his family, it was certainly a step in the right direction. Things were finally changing. He could finally move forward in his life.

'Darla.' He whispered her name and gently rubbed her shoulder but received no response. 'Darla.' He tried again, a little louder, and this time managed to rouse her but only for half a second. She really was dead to the world. He thought for a moment, then reached down to the floor near her feet where she'd put her handbag. 'Sorry,' he murmured as he opened it and peered inside, easily locating her keys. Leaving her in the car, he quickly went and unlocked her door, taking the liberty to go into her room and turn down her bed before returning to the passenger side of the car and carefully opening the door.

He unclipped her seat belt but still she slept on. 'Come on, gorgeous,' he whispered as he managed to scoop her from the seat, carrying her into the house and placing her gently on the bed. Next, he removed her shoes and covered her with the blankets, ensuring the heater was on low to keep her warm through the clear, crisp night. She'd had an emotionally draining day and it had definitely caught up with her.

Benedict stood and watched her for a moment, her blonde hair splayed out on the pillow. She was stunning, both inside and out. She'd been through so much and yet here she was director of a busy A and E department, working hard to fulfil her dreams. He hoped he was part of her dreams because she was definitely part of his. Not only his dreams but his hopes and goals for the future. Tenderly, he brushed a few strands of hair back from her face, then bent and pressed a kiss to her cheek. 'Sleep sweet, my Darla,' he murmured, before heading out, ensuring her house was securely locked before he left.

Darla slowly stretched and breathed out, feeling more content and relaxed than she had in a very long time. There was a smile on her lips and a lightness to her heart and she knew why—Benedict. She reflected on the glorious dreams she'd just had, ones where the two of them walked hand in hand over a grassy oval, sounds of the apple-pie fair all around them, a child between them, holding their hands and jumping around with excitement. Her mind continued to filter through the dream, realising it wasn't one Benedict's nieces or nephews that was between them but *their own child*—a daughter with blonde hair like her mother and blue eyes like her father.

Darla sat bolt upright at the thought, eyes snapping

open. She'd been dreaming about living the fairy-tale life with Benedict. He'd been her husband, the little girl had been their daughter and they'd been taking her for the first time to the apple-pie festival, meeting the rest of Benedict's family for a day of fun.

She covered her face with her hands. 'No. No. No. You are *not* to think of a future like that. There *is* no future like that for you. It's just a silly, childish dream. One you've yearned for all your life but you know it'll never happen. You're not meant for a normal life, Darla Fairlie. You're meant to quietly reach out and save others. Quietly helping those who need your help. Marriage and children are *not* your future. Benedict is just a man and men *always* let you down. Be strong. Steer clear. Focus.'

Her words were stern, her mind dictating to her heart the way it was going to be. Her mind had protected her throughout the years whilst her heart had been the one to leap forward and take what she'd thought were chances at happiness…yet all of them had failed.

But Benedict is different, her heart whispered.

No. Her head was adamant and with a satisfied nod she dropped her hands and glanced at the clock. *'Eight-thirty!'* With horror, Darla flicked back the bedcovers and only then realised she was fully dressed. Startled, she stood in the middle of her room, desperately trying to remember what had happened last night. She remembered being in the car, driving away from the best day she'd ever had in her life, Benedict beside her, the radio playing quietly in the background and then…nothing. She couldn't remember arriving home or going to bed.

Shaking her head, she hurried to the bathroom where she showered and dressed. By nine o'clock she was stalking through the entrance doors to the hospital, heading straight to the A and E nurses' station to check *on things*. Her step faltered when she saw Benedict sitting at the desk, alone, writing up case-notes.

'Hello, gorgeous,' he greeted her when he looked up and saw her standing there.

'Shh,' she hissed, and glanced around lest anyone had heard him.

'It's all right. The department's very quiet at the moment. A calm and comfortable typical-Sunday-morning quiet, rather than an eerie quiet-before-the-storm type of quiet,' he clarified, and stood, intending to lean forward to press a quick kiss to her cheek. Darla placed a hand on his chest, stopping him before he could follow through.

'Not here,' she said between gritted teeth. 'My office. Now.'

Benedict raised his eyebrows with delight. 'Well, if you insist, boss. I'll just finish this and be right with you,' he said, indicating the notes. Darla nodded once and headed to her office, fuming on the inside and wondering why she still couldn't get through to Benedict that she was angry.

She left her office door open but as soon as he appeared, she walked around him, keeping her distance and shutting the door before she turned to glare at him, hands on her hips, *foot tapping impatiently*.

'What happened?'

Benedict had been about to take her hand in his, hoping she'd let him draw her close for a cuddle. He hadn't been able to stop thinking about her, dreaming about her, wanting her to be with him always, and after yesterday he'd sort of hoped that she might feel the same way. Still, he'd promised not to rush her and it was clear she had a bee in her bonnet. 'What happened when?'

'Last night. This morning.'

'I don't know, Darla. I drove you home, carried you to your bed and left you to sleep.'

'You turned my alarm off.'

'I didn't touch your clock.' He was starting to become concerned. 'What's this all about?'

'It's about me sleeping until eight-thirty this morning!'

'You did? That's great.' He took a step towards her but she held up her hand again.

'Great? No, it's not.'

'It's not?'

'Of course it's not. You should have woken me when we arrived home.'

'Sweetheart, I tried, but you were exhaust—'

'I didn't get up and go to the streets!' she blurted, not caring if she raised her voice. He'd already said there was hardly anyone in the department and right now she didn't even care about that. She had important work to do and she'd failed to do it. She was a horrible person.

'If you'd woken me, I would have been able to set my alarm, to shower before I went to bed, to be ready for when my alarm went off. I could have gone to the streets, I could have talked to more women, I could have saved them.'

'Darla. It's one night and you were exhausted.'

'I don't care about that.'

'I do.' He stepped forward and placed both hands on her shoulders but the instant he made contact she shrugged away from him. 'Darla, you can't expect to go out each and every morning.'

'Yes, I can. I've done it for years now.'

'And how many of those mornings have you come

up empty-handed? Unable to get through to people?' he asked.

'That's not the point.'

'Yes, it is. You can't be expected to get through to people every night, and I'm not saying you don't have to keep on persevering and trying because you do, but neither are *you* supposed to be single-handedly saving the world, Darla. There are other people out there who are also helping, like the volunteers with ACT NOW, who are as concerned as you about the state of affairs. Granted, half of us don't have your first-hand knowledge of the situation but a lot of them do. You do amazing work, no one's denying that. You've helped so many women both here and, no doubt, in other States where you've lived. You really are an angel to them, Darla, but you're also human and as such *you* have needs, and one of them is to look after yourself.'

'I don't care about me.'

'Well, I do. I care that you've been working yourself too hard ever since we first met. I'm also guessing yesterday was the first time you've taken time out since arriving in Canberra.'

'You forced me to do it.'

'Because I could see you needed it.'

'I don't need you to tell me what to do, Dr Goldmark. Everything in my world was fine until *you* came along and wrecked it.' She pointed her finger at him. 'I was working at the hospital, I was helping people on the streets in the mornings. I was coping fine and now you…you come along and take me away for apple pie, to meet your family, to show me a world that's real and not just a fairy-tale. You show me how wonderful families can be but it's all a farce. Real life is tough. It's hard. It's hurtful and destructive.' She stabbed herself in the chest with her finger. 'I know this for a fact. There is no happily ever after. There is no "happy families". Not for me. Not ever.' Darla turned her back to him, knowing it didn't matter what she said, she'd never be able to make him understand.

Benedict remained silent for a while before saying softly, 'I said I wouldn't rush you, Darla, and I won't.' Then, to her surprise, she heard the quiet click of the door opening and a moment later another click as it closed behind him. She stood there for a whole two minutes, her back to the door, refusing to allow the tears to fall. It was better this way.

Benedict had been a distraction. A lovely, warm and encompassing distraction but she had a job to do and that job didn't leave any room for distractions. Pain continued to pierce her heart and she pursed her lips together, desperate to fight the overwhelming sense of sorrow flooding through her. She'd pushed him away. It had been the right thing to do. Distance. Focus. Self-control. That was the way to go.

So why did it feel as though she was dying inside?

Darla made herself a cup of tea and was just sipping it when her phone rang. Frowning, she picked it up, hoping it wasn't an emergency at the hospital. It was almost two o'clock in the morning and she was about to head out to the streets. As she'd missed her rounds yesterday, she was eager to get started. 'Dr Fairlie,' she answered.

'Ah, good. You're up.'

'Benedict?'

'Yes. I didn't want to ring your doorbell or knock in case I startled you. I thought calling was the best option and it turns out I was right.'

'What are you talking about? Is there an emergency

at the hospital? Has something gone wrong? Are you all right?' The last one came out before she could stop it.

'Concerned for my well-being, fairy princess? I'm pleased to hear it. No, there's nothing wrong.'

Darla tried not to be affected by the deepness of his voice, the way it sounded like warm chocolate. She sighed and tried to control her thoughts, remembering she'd been mad at him, that she'd pushed him away, shoved him right out of her life. 'Then why are you calling me at this hour?'

'I'm at your front door,' he stated simply.

Darla frowned at her phone, pulling it away from her ear and glaring at it. Was she still sleeping? Dreaming? Why on earth would Benedict be outside her house at two o'clock in the morning?

She returned the phone to her ear, positive he was delusional. 'Benedict. You're making no sense.'

'Look. I'll prove it.' The next instant, Darla could hear knocking at her front door and even though he'd told her he was there, the sound still startled her.

'Benedict!'

'Yes?'

'Is that really you? This isn't just some weird, spooky coinciden—'

'Oh, my giddy aunt. Will you open the door, Darla?'

She walked to the door, cellphone still to her ear. She kept the chain on the door as she opened it slightly, her eyes widening as she saw him standing there. Quickly, she closed the door, removed the chain and opened the door completely.

'Blimey. It's like Fort Knox—but that's good.' He nodded as he disconnected the call and slipped his phone into his jacket pocket. 'Hello.' He stepped forward and pressed a kiss to her cheek before she even knew which way was up.

She was dressed in old denim jeans and a comfortable jumper with decent walking shoes on her feet. Her beautiful blonde hair was pulled back into a ponytail with a single band. He knew she was trying to downplay her appearance, to blend into the background, and he wasn't quite sure whether to tell her she hadn't succeeded. She was far too stunning, no matter what she wore, to be overlooked, and it was *that* concern for her safety that had prompted him to be standing in front of her right now.

Darla blinked once then twice and gave her head a little shake. 'What are you doing here?' she blurted.

'I'm here to help.'

'But I'm mad at you. I pushed you away. I—'

'Vented your frustrations,' he interrupted. 'I know, I was there.' He tapped his wrist. 'It's almost two o'clock. Ready?'

'No. Stop. I don't understand. *Why* are you here?'

'I'm here to help.'

'Help?'

'You know…heading out to the streets? Doing your *angel* thing. I thought I could give you a lift. Or we can go in your car. I'm not fussed.'

'But I was angry at you. I yelled at you,' she reiterated. 'You're not supposed to want to be around me any more.'

Benedict slowly shook his head, a small smile on his lips. His actions only caused her eyes to widen and a fire to light in her belly.

'Don't you dare laugh at me, Benedict Goldmark.'

'I'm not laughing, fairy princess. Don't you have any idea how gorgeous you are when you're angry?'

She threw her hands in the air and turned to go and collect her jacket. 'You're impossible,' she muttered. When she returned, she found him leaning against the doorjamb, thumbs in the pockets of his jeans, looking casual and relaxed and as sexy as anything. She swallowed over the instant flood of desire that seemed to course through her every time she saw him.

'Go away,' she tried, but he simply shook his head.

'You can be angry at me all you like. You can vent and rant and rave but it doesn't change the way I feel about you.'

'It doesn't?'

She seemed genuinely shocked at that and it gave Benedict a big insight into just how much she really hadn't been able to trust anyone in the past. 'Couples fight. Couples argue. Couples sort things out and then make up.'

'There's nothing to sort out,' she said, frowning as she picked up her keys. 'You and me? We're not a couple. There is no future for us. OK? I am not your girlfriend. You are not my bo—' She stopped and swallowed over the word.

'Boyfriend,' he finished calmly. 'And I want to be more than just your boyfriend. Something far more permanent.'

'A thorn in my side?' she quipped as she pushed past him and headed towards her car, knowing he would close the door behind him. She couldn't deny he looked good, wonderful in fact, and to hear him saying he still wanted to be around her was more than she'd ever expected. Right from day one she'd been unable to control him, unable to freeze him out, unable to resist his hypnotic eyes, his smooth tone and his gorgeous lips.

He was quick and slid into the passenger seat beside

her as she started the engine. 'I hope you have success tonight,' he said softly.

'Stop that.' She glared at him for a moment before putting the car into Reverse.

'Stop what? Hoping that tonight you're able to get through to a woman who needs you? A woman who has lost all hope?'

'I thought you didn't want me going out onto the streets.'

'I've never said that. I've said you shouldn't feel obliged to do it *every* night or else you run the risk of damaging your health. I'll also admit to being a little concerned with you being out in such neighbourhoods alone but—' he quickly continued when she took a breath to interrupt '—I appreciate that you can no doubt spot trouble before it happens. Still, I'm concerned.'

Darla closed her mouth and refused to speak to him until she'd parked the car. 'Don't follow me,' she said as she climbed out, pulling her jacket around her. 'I can look after myself. I know how to fly under the radar. I know about hunger and cold and a burning emptiness deep inside. I know that taking drugs is the coward's way of solving problems and I know that if you come with me right now, you're going to thwart any chances I might have in making a connection and getting someone off the wrong path and onto the right one.' Darla was bristling as she finished talking. Hands on her hips, back straight, chin held high.

Benedict stood in front of her and nodded, placing his hands on her shoulders. 'Just…be safe. OK?' He rested his forehead against hers, his heart churning with an intense surge of love, and he couldn't stop himself from telling her. 'I love you, Darla.'

Darla closed her eyes for a moment, her heart celebrating and breaking all at the same time. She breathed him in then, as she exhaled, she pulled back, stepping away from his embrace. 'Don't. Don't love me, Benedict.' She shook her head sadly. 'I'm no good for you.' With that, she turned and sprinted up the street, away from him.

Benedict couldn't believe how busy they were at the ACT NOW van. Both Jordanne and Hamilton were rostered on with him and the catering van had actually called in extra staff.

'It's a Wednesday night,' Hamilton stated in disbelief as he pulled off one pair of gloves and pulled on another. 'This is ridiculous.' Throughout their shift the van had been so congested that at times they'd had to go outside just to change their minds.

'No.' Benedict shook his head, caution in his tone. 'I've seen this before. This hive of activity. These small spats where people are hurt and require medical attention. There's unrest. Something big has happened somewhere and it's causing a lot of disturbance. We all need to be on guard.'

'When was the last time you saw this?' Jordanne asked as she restocked one of the cupboards.

'On one of the worst nights of my life.' Benedict's words were soft.

'The night Carolina was hurt?' Jordanne guessed.

'Yes.' Benedict checked the clock. He knew Darla was out there. He could just sense it. Ever since the other morning when she'd walked away from him, telling him not to love her, he'd been trying to leave her alone, to give her some space. He was almost positive she felt the same way about him as he did about her. She had to. If she didn't, he thought this time he might really die of a broken heart. *She was a good, hardworking, honest* woman and he knew she was scared of moving out of the past and into the hope for a new future.

As the angel, she gave advice and hope to those who were in a terrible place, locked in a world of no escape, but she couldn't see that she, too, was still locked into the past, allowing who she'd been while she was growing up to dictate who she needed to be in the future. She wanted the fairy-tale family, as she called it. He'd seen it in her eyes the day they'd gone to the apple-pie fair but she was too scared to take a chance, to risk everything in case she plummeted back into the depths of despair. He had to give her time but he honestly didn't know how much longer he could wait for her to come to her senses. He loved her. She loved him. Surely it *was* that simple?

Concerned, Benedict walked to the door and peered out the van, hoping to see Darla walking towards him, safe and sound, but all he saw were another group of young men heading in their direction, two or three guys, carrying their buddy, who was obviously injured.

'Next round,' Benedict said, after scanning the area once more. Where was she? Which one of these streets was she in? Who was she talking to tonight? Was she safe?

Benedict focused and with Jordanne's orthopaedic expertise they managed to patch the injured man up as well as they could. 'I'm sure you've dislocated your shoulder,' Jordanne stated as she looked at the tattoo of a large, ferocious-looking grizzly bear on the man's arm. 'And you'll need to go to hospital for X-rays to confirm the diagnosis before we can relocate it.'

'Nah. It always pops out,' the guy growled between gritted teeth. 'Put it back.'

'If the head of the bone is fractured, then putting it back in won't do any goo—'

The man bared his teeth, cutting short what Jordanne was going to say. The man in question was about six feet five inches but built like a tank. His arms, neck and upper chest were heavily tattooed and his head was shaved. 'Put it back.'

'I've got this, Jordanne,' Benedict said, and with Hamilton holding the man steady Benedict carefully manipulated the bone back into its socket. The patient didn't yell but instead clenched his teeth and was breathing hard.

Once the bone was back in place, the man started breathing more normally but Benedict could see the pain written on his face. Jordanne checked the shoulder was relocated correctly before prescribing some analgesics.

'Don't want no pills. I don't do drugs any more. Not even paracetamol. I need to get back out there. Lead my gang.'

'Gang?' Benedict's eyebrows hit his hairline. He didn't like the sound of that and once more he scanned outside the vans for any sign of Darla.

'We need to protect them,' one of the men said.

'They're on *our* turf. We got the right to defend it.'

'And I guess we'll just patch you all up and send you back out to risk getting killed again,' Benedict returned, holding the large man's gaze, never wavering. The man didn't look away either but a moment later he surprised them all by grinning.

'You're all right, mate.'

Another young guy who had come with the group of

men stuck his head in the van door, agitation clear in his tone. 'Bear. We gotta go. *Now.* The cops are here.'

Bear, the large tattooed man, stood and looked Benedict, Jordanne and Hamilton in the eyes. 'We'll try and keep you safe, too,' he said firmly.

Within a matter of minutes the van was cleared and Hamilton was setting up for the next round. 'If they're about to fight...'

'We're going to need a lot of back-up,' Jordanne finished. Benedict was looking out the door again. 'What's wrong?'

'Darla,' Benedict replied absent-mindedly. 'She's out there. Somewhere.'

'Why? What on earth is she doing out on the streets at this hour of the morning?' Hamilton asked, completely perplexed.

'She...does...a...' Benedict stopped and tried again. 'She...uh...' How to say it without giving away Darla's secret?

'Oh, my word.' Jordanne gasped, dawning realising in her eyes. 'Blonde hair. Brown eyes. She's *the angel.*'

Benedict closed his eyes for a moment but didn't deny it. Instead he reached for his jacket. 'I need to go and find her, to make sure she's all right, because if anything happens to her...' He trailed off, unable to finish the sentence as his gut was twisted with pain and his mind was flooded with a blinding fury such as he'd never felt before.

Jordanne took one look at him, then nodded. 'Go. Ham and I will be fine here, especially as I'm calling our other team members as well as the authorities to let them know the situation.'

'Good, and put the A and E retrieval team on

standby,' Benedict added as he picked up his phone and put it in his pocket.

'Hey, bro. Do you know where to start looking? It's starting to get wild out there.'

'I have an idea.'

Hamilton nodded. 'Stay safe.'

'Likewise,' he murmured with a brisk nod, before stepping from the van and pulling the collar of his jacket up high. He headed towards the street where she usually parked her car, figuring he'd follow the direction she usually went. It wasn't much but it was something.

His shoes echoed on the quiet road, hands shoved into the pockets of his jeans, gaze constantly scanning the area for any sign of her. Where was she? The panic he'd tried hard to control in the van started to wage war within him and he found himself muttering, 'Where are you?' over and over.

It wasn't right for a woman to go traipsing around the streets at such a time of the morning. He didn't care what sort of upbringing she'd had, he didn't care if she held a black belt in karate, it simply wasn't right. She could get hurt, or worse.

'No.' He stopped that thought as he turned down a darkened street. She couldn't be hurt. In his mind he needed to think of her being strong and vibrant because even the slightest thought that she might be lying in the gutter somewhere, hurt, robbed and all alone, turned his mind to mush.

He needed to see for himself that she was all right. Once he'd ascertained that fact, she'd no doubt yell at him about being too overbearing and tell him yet again not to bother loving her. Well, she didn't have a choice in the matter. He loved her and that was all there was to it.

As he turned down an even smaller, even darker side street, still intent on his goal, it was a few minutes before he noticed the group of dark shadows nearby.

'Hey! You!' one of them called, a deep, growling voice. 'Get outta here! This ain't no time for a stroll.'

Benedict frowned. He'd heard that voice before. Another sound echoed behind him and he turned around to find another group of dark shadows coming down the street towards him. He spun again, belatedly realising that due to his focus on finding Darla he'd walked down the wrong street.

'I said get outta here,' the voice growled again.

'Bear?' Benedict was astonished.

'Benedict?' It was Darla's voice. He heard Darla's voice and he spun in the direction he'd thought it had come from. She was all right. She was OK. Alive. Good. Relief flooded through him and a smile lit his face.

The next moment he felt a blinding pain in the back of his head and then his legs seemed unable to hold him up. With white spots flickering before his eyes, he tried to figure out what was going on. Where was Darla? He tried to call her name but he didn't seem able to talk. Pain continued to pound through his head and more shot up his arm. Then everything went black.

CHAPTER ELEVEN

'BENEDICT? Benedict?'

Darla was beside herself as she applied a cold compress to the back of Benedict's head. 'Can't this thing go faster?' she said to the ambulance driver. 'Benedict? Come on. Wake up. I really need you to wake up.'

She clutched his hand in hers, squeezing it tight, desperate for him to open his eyes, to look at her, to let her see that he was all right. He *had* to be all right. He just *had* to be. When she'd seen him go down, hit from behind, her heart had seemed to stop.

For a split second she hadn't known what to do. In all her life, no matter how bad things had been when she'd been growing up, she'd always had a thought, a plan, a course of action. It was how she'd controlled things for so long. Always planning. Always thinking. Always wanting to do whatever she could to find some control.

Then Benedict had been hit. He'd been assaulted by the gang who'd been trying to get to a group of women sheltering in a house. Bear and his gang had been protecting them but Bear had been too late to protect Benedict.

'Benedict?' she called again, tears blurring her vision as the ambulance finally pulled into the hospital. She'd made them call ahead. She'd made them tell the A and E team exactly who was in this ambulance. Everyone *in the department loved Benedict…she most of all.*

She *loved* him. She could admit it to herself now. She *loved* this man. This impossible, protective, crazy man. He'd somehow managed to break down her defences, he'd accepted her for who she was, and he'd wanted to spend as much time with her as possible.

'Benedict?' she said again, but he remained unconscious. He was wheeled into TR1, with Darla barking out orders to her team, calling for tests and X-rays, and all the while she found it impossible to let go of his hand, even when he was transferred to the hospital barouche.

'Benedict?' she whispered and leaned close. 'Come on. Wake up. I need you…and I don't need anybody.'

The hustle and bustle in the room around her seemed to slow to a snail's pace, everything fading to a blur as she looked down into his handsome face. 'Come on,' she tried again, and this time, not caring in the least who saw, she bent and brushed her lips across his. '*Please?*'

'Darla?' Her name was a choked, dry whisper, barely audible.

'Benedict?' Relief started to flood through her. '*You're OK. Oh, thank God.*' She closed her eyes and bowed her head for a moment, wanting to rest it on his shoulder, to put her arms around him, to feel his comforting warmth, but she knew he needed treatment. 'You had me worried.'

'Really? Worried? About me?' He tried to open his eyes but quickly frowned and squinted at the bright lights in the room. 'What happened?'

She straightened up. 'You don't remember?'

'We're ready to take him to Radiology now, Dr Fairlie,' Matrice said.

'Good. Let's go,' she returned, and still holding his hand walked alongside the barouche. As they went along the corridor, Benedict closed his eyes to block out the brightness from the overhead lights. 'Benedict?' she called again.

'I'm here,' he said, his voice a little stronger. 'And I'm glad to see you're OK. You had me worried.'

'Worried?'

'There was a gang war. I couldn't find you.'

Darla momentarily closed her eyes as she began to realise exactly why Benedict had been in that street in the first place. He'd been looking for *her*. Guilt immediately swamped her. He'd been worried about her. He'd come looking for her and he'd been hurt in the process. What was happening to him now was all her fault.

While she waited for him to have X-rays taken, she buried her head in her hands and closed her eyes. It was all her fault. Benedict had been hurt because of her and she vowed it would never happen again.

'Dr Fairlie?' The radiographer spoke quietly and Darla dropped her hands and turned to face the young woman. 'Did you want to see the image on the screen? From what I can see, everything looks fine.'

Darla peered closely at the screen, which displayed the digital image of Benedict's skull. 'It looks clean. Everything's good. No fractures.' Darla straightened and let out a deep breath. 'He's going to be fine.' Tears started to prick behind her eyes and she sniffed, unable to control her rising emotions at this good news.

'Are you all right, Dr Fairlie?' The radiographer was both shocked and startled by this open display of emotion from the ice fairy.

'Uh.' Darla cleared her throat. 'I'm going to my office. Can someone call me when he's back in A and E, please?' She sniffed again, annoyed with herself for losing control and especially in front of a staff member.

'Of course.' There was empathy in the woman's voice accompanied by a small smile. 'I'll make sure of it.'

The woman's kindness threatened to overwhelm Darla and she quickly turned and walked with as much dignity as she could muster towards her office. She pulled her hospital pass-card from her pocket and swiped it through the lock. In another moment she was standing in her office, the door closed behind her, the silent darkness surrounding her.

Benedict was going to be all right. No fracture. No permanent damage, and he also appeared to have excellent recall of events. He was going to be all right. The first sob almost shocked her but as it was closely followed by another, she gave in and allowed herself to cry.

Leaning against the wall, she slowly slumped down to the floor, the picture of him standing there in the street running through her mind. The shock, the fear, the terror at seeing a dark shadow come up behind him before it attacked. She closed her eyes tighter, desperate to block out the image as her body was racked with another spasm of pain.

'Oh, Benedict,' she murmured. She hugged her knees to her chest, unable to believe how much she was hurting. She'd known she had serious feelings for the man but now she could clearly recognise and admit to herself that she was in love with him. There were no two ways about it. She loved Benedict Goldmark.

Somehow the man had managed to get beneath her skin, to infiltrate her carefully constructed walls and make her care about him. She'd fought it. She'd tried to keep her distance but he hadn't let her. He'd been all *cute and charming and gorgeous and…and…*

'And I have to let you go,' she whispered into the dark. 'No fairy-tales for Darla Fairlie.' Loving him wasn't part of her plan. Becoming involved with Benedict's life would only cause them both more pain in the long run and she loved him too much to let that happen.

'I'm fine,' Benedict implored as his brothers fussed over him like two old women. 'Seriously. A few stitches and I'm fine. See?' He showed them both the back of his head where a sterile white bandage covered the ten sutures in his head. 'It's not the first time I've had sutures.'

'True,' Bart relented, and Hamilton sat down, lounging in the chair beside the bed. 'It's a hard habit to break—caring for my brothers.'

'I'm not asking you to break it, bro, just tone it down. You're as bad as Mum used to be.'

Bart grinned. 'I'll take that as a compliment.'

'Now, tell me, Ham, what happened after I was knocked out? Is everything settled now? Did the police manage to get everything under control? Jordanne? *Is she all right?*'

He looked through the glassed walls of his private room into the ward, as though expecting their friend to immediately materialise. Secretly, he also knew he was searching for Darla. Where was she? When he'd returned from Radiology back to A and E she'd come into the treatment room to check on him but this time, instead of being the woman who had held his hand and kissed him ever so tenderly, she was the ice fairy once more. He scanned the nurses' station but there was no sign of her. Where was she?

'Everything's sorted. Jordanne's fine. By the time the police were in position it was basically all over. That guy who dislocated his shoulder—Bear—was the leader of the gang protecting a group of women who were sheltering in one of the houses in the street. Bear brought in three from his gang for us to fix and told us how sorry he was you'd been hurt.' Hamilton nodded. 'He's a good guy. Rough as guts but a good guy none-theless.'

Ward Sister walked into the private room and stood there, crossing her arms over her chest and tapping her foot. 'What are the two of you still doing here?'

'Talking to our brother?' Hamilton offered.

'Bringing him some clothes,' Bart said at the same time.

'He's had enough excitement for the moment and has to rest. Come along. Bartholomew, I'm sure you have a ward round to attend and, Hamilton, you look as though you could use a shower and some sleep. Off you go. Leave your brother in peace so he can rest.'

'I don't know why I have to stay,' Benedict grumbled. 'I'm perfectly all right.'

'I don't care what you say, Ben, it's doctor's or-ders and they state quite clearly that you're to be kept in for observation for the next twenty-four hours at least,' Ward Sister returned in her usual brisk manner. Benedict frowned. Usually he was able to charm the woman, to get a smile from her, to get her to bend the rules a little here and there, but not now. She was ada-mant that he was not only to stay in bed until he was properly discharged by his admitting doctor but also that his brothers needed to leave in order to allow him to get some rest.

'You're not a colleague now, Benedict,' Sister continued, as though she could read his mind. 'You're my patient. This is my ward and you will obey me.' She turned to glare at Bart and Hamilton. 'And you two—go.'

'OK. OK.' Hamilton held up his hands in defence. 'We'll let the poor old soul rest.'

'Thank you. Now I need to see to the breakfasts.' She bustled the brothers out and then closed the blinds to the room. 'Get some rest, Ben.'

'Yes, Sister,' he replied meekly as he closed his eyes. He was sure he wasn't tired, sure he would be wide awake and completely bored before the breakfast trolley had made its rounds, but with the room now nice and dark and relatively quiet Benedict found his eyes becoming heavier.

The next time he opened his eyes, for a moment, he wasn't sure where he was. Lying still, he slowly took in his surroundings. He was in the hospital. As a patient. The events leading up to him being there flooded through his mind and as he shifted slightly, he tried not to wince in pain.

'Try and stay still.' A sweet, angelic voice spoke from somewhere on his right and he had to force himself to slowly turn his head. There she was. The angel. *His* angel.

'Darla?'

'I'm here.'

'What time is it?'

'Just after two in the afternoon. You've been sleeping *quite nicely*.'

'Where were you?' he asked.

'In my office, catching up on some paperwork. That little melee brought us quite a few casualties but, thankfully, there were no fatalities.'

'No, I mean before. On the streets. I couldn't find you and I was so worried and concerned and—'

'Shh.' She leaned forward and placed a finger gently on his lips. 'You're fine. I'm fine. That's all that matters now.' It wasn't until she went to remove her hand that she realised just how close she was to the man she loved. What was it about him that simply drew her in? How was she supposed to resist him, especially now when he was lying in a hospital bed with sutures in his skull?

'Darla.'

Benedict somehow looked directly into her soul, his magnetic allure drawing her closer as he continued to hypnotise her with his soothing voice and come-hither eyes. The urge to follow was overpowering and when he reached out to tuck a loose tendril of hair back behind her ear, she was completely captivated.

She loved him. He loved her. He'd said he wouldn't pressure her. He'd said he'd allow her to take her time and she knew that he would continue to keep his distance if she asked. Right now, she didn't want him to and realised it would be nothing to close the distance between them. Following through on her selfish urge, Darla leaned closer and within the next moment had pressed her mouth firmly to his.

She closed her eyes and sighed at the touch, not realising how much she'd missed feeling these sensations, the ones she only felt when Benedict was kissing her. This time, though, there was something different about the way he kissed her, about the way he cradled the back of her head with his hand, his fingers instantly working her hair from her sensible ponytail. His mouth was more familiar, his touch more intense, and his previously reined-in hunger was bursting forth.

He wanted to show her, to let her feel just how important she was to him. Her lips were parting, accepting his advances as he continued to devour the deliciousness of this incredible woman. Step by step, moment by moment. She kept pace with him, appearing to want him just as much as he wanted her. It was what he'd been waiting for, the realisation that they were made for each other.

When he groaned, she instantly pulled back, breathing hard as she frantically scanned his face. 'What's wrong? Did I hurt you? I'm sorry, Benedict. I didn't mean to get you hurt. Do you want some analgesics?' Her words ran over each other, fear and trepidation flooding through her.

'I'm fine,' he muttered quickly, before urging her lips back to where they belonged—against his own. 'Darla. Darla. You are so beautiful, so caring and warm,' he murmured against her mouth between kisses. 'I can't stop loving you.'

'You must,' she implored.

'No. I can't and I won't.'

Darla straightened up and moved away from the bed. Benedict reached for her hand but she was able to avoid his touch.

'Darla, I'm sorry if that scares you but it's the truth. I can't hide it from you any more.'

'Yes, you can.' She was astonished to find her legs trembling as though they were made of jelly. 'Hide it. Quash it. Forget it.' She shook her head. 'Don't love me, Benedict. It doesn't work.'

'What doesn't work?' he asked, raising his voice

slightly in complete exasperation. A moment later he scowled at the sudden pounding in his head.

'Will you stay calm?' she scolded, worry in her tone. 'You'll give yourself an even bigger headache.'

'I don't care.'

Darla picked up the small container of tablets that had been left by his bed and handed them to him, before pouring a glass of water. 'Take these.'

'I'm fine.'

'I'm your doctor and you'll take them.' Darla stood over him and he knew she wouldn't let him move on, explain himself, make her understand just how important she was to him until he did as he was told.

'You know, you could discharge me. I can convalesce at home quite easily.'

'But you wouldn't stay still,' Darla countered, replacing the glass back on the bedside table once he'd done as he was told.

'So you're keeping me in for extended observation because you don't think I'll follow your orders?'

'I *know* you wouldn't.' Darla stepped back from the bed and crossed her arms. She stared at him and Benedict stared right back, trying to read her, trying to figure out why she didn't want him to love her.

'You want me where you can monitor me,' he stated.

'Yes.'

'Because you care about me.'

Darla's gaze flickered for a moment but she eventually nodded her head.

'But you don't care about me enough to accept the love I have for you?' His words were quieter this time and she sucked in a breath, squaring her shoulders and standing firm beneath his gentle scrutiny.

'Why, Darla?' he asked softly. 'Why aren't I allowed to love you?'

'Because it will only bring heartache and pain to us both.' She turned and took a step towards the door. 'Go back to sleep.'

'If you leave now, I'll get out of this bed and follow you,' he threatened. Darla looked at him over her shoulder and saw he was lifting the bedcovers. She didn't want him walking about the hospital, not just yet. She wanted him to recover, to be safe, to be secure, and she could only ensure that by keeping him under her watchful eye until she was positive he was really OK. He was slowly moving his legs beneath the covers, getting ready to swing them out.

'All right,' she said, and turned back to face him, her arms still crossed in an effort to protect herself from his delicious gaze.

'Thank you.' He indicated the chair. 'Won't you sit down?'

'I'm fine standing.'

'OK. So, why am I not allowed to love you, Darla?'

She smiled at his words and rolled her eyes. 'Straight to the point.'

'I don't see any reason to beat about the bush. I've *confessed my love, you've rejected it. I think I'm enti*tled to know why, considering I'm fairly sure you love me back.'

'Arrogance,' she muttered.

'Yep.' He didn't waver, didn't lower his eyes, just kept looking at her, firm and sure in his words.

'Why? How could you possibly be in love with me?' Her voice was soft and he could hear the apprehension in her tone.

Benedict's eyes widened as the words rushed out of

her mouth, all her insecurities on display for him to see.
'Darla.' He held out his hand. 'Come here.'

'No.'

Benedict dropped his hand. 'OK. Then why don't
you sit down and tell me why you think you shouldn't
be loved?'

'Because I'm not worthy of it.' She spread her arms
wide, exasperation powering through her. 'Because I'm
not a nice person. If you knew half the things I've done
in my past…' She rubbed a hand across her forehead,
fear in her eyes.

'That's the past. It doesn't matter.'

'No, Benedict. My past is a part of me and I know
when you find out, you'll stop loving me. Your love for
me is a lie but you can't see it. It's why I can't be around
you, why you need to forget me.'

Benedict held out his hand again and shifted over to
make room for her to sit beside him. 'Please come here.
Please?'

Closing her eyes for a moment, she knew the time
had finally come to let go of this man. She would tell
him the truth, she would be open and honest, answering all his questions, and then he would see she was no
good…and leave. Even the thought of him not being in
her life brought a stabbing pain to her heart.

Opening her eyes, she dragged in a breath and then
nodded then slowly walked towards him. She accepted
his hand and sat on the side of his bed.

'Thank you. Now, what is it you've been hiding for
far too long?'

'Me. I've been hiding me.'

'Hiding behind your past?'

'Yes. You've called me on it before, Benedict, and
I've managed to keep you at bay, but when you say you

love me, I don't have any defences left. I've been fighting my past for so long that if I let go of it…what am I supposed to cling to?'

'Us. You cling to us.' Benedict brushed a hand across her cheek. 'Let go of the past, Darla. Come with me into the present so we can build a wonderful future together. I can promise to be there for you, I can offer you my heart and my love, but it's up to you to accept it.'

'That's the point, Benedict. I don't know if I can.'

'But do you want to?'

Yes.' The word was filled with vehement conviction.

'Then do it. Take that chance, Darla. Take the chance with me. Hand in hand we'll walk together.' He pulled her close, wrapping his arms around her. Darla shifted to untangle her legs and belatedly realised she was lying down beside him, his arms firm about her shaky body.

'I want to hold you in my arms and protect you. I want to make sure that no one else *ever* hurts you again. I want to show you how easy you are to love, how important you are not only as a person but as a desirable woman.' He dropped a kiss to the top of her head and held her, wanting his actions to mirror his words. *'Darla, I love you. Can you at least accept that?'*

'Yes.'

'Can you accept that even if you want me to stop, I can't. You are *it*.' He shrugged his shoulders. 'There is no other woman I will ever love as much as I love you. There is no other woman who can make me as happy as you do. I watched my parents have a happy and healthy marriage and even in death they were still together. Morbid as it sounds, that's always brought me comfort. My brothers Peter and Edward, as well as Lorelai, have all found long and lasting loves and that's what I want for us. I choose to be with you for the rest of my life and I desperately hope you want the same.'

Tenderly, he stroked her hair, brushing it from her face so he could look down into the deep brown eyes of the woman he adored. 'I love you, Darla. Nothing is ever going to change that. Do you believe me?'

'I want to,' she whispered. 'I really want to, Benedict.'

'Do you love me?'

Darla opened her mouth to say the words, knowing he could see it clearly reflected in her eyes, but there were also many years of locking her heart and emotions away that still needed to be overcome.

Benedict chuckled when she didn't respond and again Darla was perplexed. He never seemed to respond in the way she expected. 'All right, then, how about this? Blink one long blink if you love me.'

Darla immediately blinked her eyes, opening them to gaze into his.

'That's what I thought,' he murmured as he lowered his mouth to brush a tantalising and seductive kiss across her lips. 'Now, how about one long blink if you really want to spend the rest of your life with me?'

Darla bit her lip, hesitating only because with everything she'd endured during her life this was the scariest thing she'd ever done. She closed her eyes, sighed deeply, then opened them to look into the kind, caring and caressing eyes of the man of her dreams. She was rewarded with another, sweet and glorious kiss, this one a little longer than before.

'I want to marry you, my darling Darla. We'll take things slowly and steadily, savouring every new step together. Does that sound good?'

Darla nodded and gave one long blink at the same time. Benedict brought his mouth to hers, lingering, taking his time and letting her know he was serious about taking it slowly. Slowly and sensually. Darla deserved to be cherished and he was just the man to do it.

Without warning, she jerked back and glared at him, her eyes wide with terror. 'What about children?' she gasped. 'What if you want them and I don't? What if I accidentally get pregnant? What if I can't have children at all? Benedict?'

'Slow…and…steady,' he said softly, punctuating his words with kisses. 'I come from a big family, Darla, with my siblings presently populating like rabbits.' He chuckled as he said the words. 'If we decide not to have a family, there will always be plenty of nieces and nephews to spoil.'

'Really?'

'I will never lie to you, Darla. With you in my life, I am a happy and contented man. I also understand how important your work is. The way you help those women is a gift and one that should be nurtured. I'll do whatever I can to assist *the angel*.' He winked at her.

'Oh, Benedict.' Darla sighed and relaxed back into his arms. 'I knew you were trouble from the first moment we met.'

'Trouble?'

She kissed his mouth and laughed, feeling lighthearted and free for the first time in her life. Benedict hadn't been permanently hurt. He loved her. He wanted to marry her, to be with her, to help her. He accepted her for who she was and what she could give. Never in her life had she ever thought she could be *this* happy. Benedict had integrated himself into her life, into her heart, and she'd never been more pleased with the trouble he'd caused her. 'Trouble,' she confirmed.

'Is that a good thing?' he asked, still a little uncertain.

Darla laughed, feeling the shackles of her past float away as she moved towards her future. Benedict. The man of her dreams. 'Is that a good thing?' She echoed his words as she leaned forward to kiss him once more. 'Most definitely.'

EPILOGUE

A FEW weeks later they headed back to Oodnaminaby for little Susan's christening.

'I'm nervous,' Darla confessed when they were about five minutes away from the Ood turn-off.

'Nervous? Why?' he asked, glancing across at her. 'You've met my siblings before and they all love you.'

'Yes but we're…you know…more than we were before.'

'I think the word you're looking for is *engaged*.'

'Yes, we're engaged.' She forced herself to say the word. Every morning it was a constant challenge for her to accept this new life she'd been granted. She had a man who adored her and wanted to spend the rest of his life with her. Through him she was being given the big fairy-tale family she'd always dreamed about. She was incredibly happy yet at the same time she was having difficulty in accepting all these blessings.

After Benedict had been discharged from the hospital, before he'd even returned home, he'd insisted they head to a jewellery store to buy her ring. Darla had been scared and thrilled and excited and nervous all at the same time.

'This is you not rushing things?' she'd asked as they'd stood outside the store.

'I just don't want you to change your mind,' he'd confessed, showing her his insecurity. 'I want you to choose the ring, to have something *you* love, rather than what I might choose. If you don't want to wear it straight away, you don't have to. If you don't want to tell people straight away, you don't have to. Just so long as you and I know, that's all that matters.'

So they'd looked at rings and, quite to her own surprise, Darla found the most perfect engagement ring. It was white gold with a single, solitary diamond in a bezel setting. In fact, it had been Benedict who had pointed it out. 'I think this one would look perfect on your fingers. Stunning and elegant. Just like you.' He'd pressed a kiss to her lips, then winked.

The shop assistant had handed it to Benedict who had slipped it onto her finger. It had looked perfect, too perfect, and for one split second Darla had started to panic again. She'd glanced up at Benedict, who had merely smiled encouragingly, his eyes projecting a mix of security and tranquillity that had miraculously allayed all her fears.

She'd looked back at the ring, then nodded. 'This is the one.'

'Would you like to wear it?' the sales assistant had asked. Again, Darla had looked at Benedict, unsure what he wanted. Did he want her to wear it? Would he be offended if she took it off and kept it in a box?

'We'll take it in the box,' he'd stated, not breaking eye contact with her. After they'd left the shop, they'd driven to his favourite bakery where he'd introduced her to his friend Tom. Over coffee and her favourite blueberry muffin, he'd presented her with the box.

'Darla, I want you to take your time. This is only a symbol of my love. It can't capture the surging torrent of eternal love coursing through me but so long as you know I am yours, for ever, that's all I need.'

Furiously blinking back tears, she'd accepted his vow and the box. Right now she had the box in her jacket pocket, her ringless fingers held warmly in his. He indicated to turn off to Ood and all too soon he brought the car to a stop outside his family home. He switched off the ignition and turned to face her. 'Don't be nervous, my darling Darla. This is good. This is right. This is meant to be.'

'I know.'

'Come on,' he urged, and unclipped their seat belts. 'The longer we sit out here, the more we risk them all trooping out to see what's taking us so long.' He leaned over and lovingly kissed her lips, before climbing out and coming around to the open her door. He took her hand in his again and as they walked up the driveway, Darla marvelled at the large two-storey house surrounded by the beautiful colours of late autumn. It was perfect.

They went up the front steps and in through the door, Darla feeling strange at not knocking. The first thing that hit her as they entered was the noise. Children running and laughing, voices, both male and female, all talking over each other. The sweet smells of home cooking coming from the kitchen and the widest smile ever on Benedict's face.

This was Benedict's home and this time she would be here with his entire family. Last time, for the apple-pie fair, Hamilton and Bartholomew had still been in Canberra and Lorelai's father had been at work. Now everyone was here and everyone would be wanting to know the status of her relationship with Benedict. She tried not to feel pressured and the ring box felt like a lead weight in her jacket pocket.

'Ben! Darla! Finally.' Honeysuckle ran towards them both, her arms out wide as she embraced them. 'What took you so long?

No sooner had Honey welcomed her than Darla found herself embraced in another hug, this time by Benedict's surrogate sister, Lorelai. After Lorelai came Peter's wife Annabelle, then Darla was introduced to BJ and was surprised when even he embraced her with a warm hug.

'Welcome to the family,' he'd stated with a wink.

'Benedict?' Darla had looked at her fiancé in surprise. 'You told them?' she whispered.

BJ obviously heard her remark because he laughed. 'Oh, Darla. Your feelings for Ben are written all over your face. It's clear the two of you are in love.' With that, he was distracted by his granddaughter, leaving Darla completely stunned.

'Is it?' she asked Benedict. 'Is it written all over my face?'

He smiled. 'I hope so. This is family, Darla. You're safe here. Just relax and enjoy the ride.'

And what a ride it was! It was a loud, vibrant and energetic household and at times more than a little overwhelming. After a few hours, with Benedict standing at the dishwasher, chatting to his brother Edward as they stacked it with yet another load of plates, Darla slipped out the back door, needing just a brief moment of peace.

She headed out to the little garden, pleased to find it empty. Sitting down on the small bench, she closed her eyes and drew in a few calming breaths. It was what she'd wanted, the fairy-tale family, and she was

sure she'd get used to it in time. It was all happening.
All her dreams were coming true and as she opened
her eyes and looked out over the lovely township of
Oodnaminaby, she knew, even though it was completely
overwhelming at times, it was the best thing that had
ever happened to her. *Benedict* was the best thing that
had ever happened to her.

Slowly, she withdrew the box from her pocket and
took out the ring. She held it between her forefingers
and thumbs, watching the different colours in the diamond as the afternoon sun's rays reflected through it.

'I thought I'd find you here.' Benedict's soft words
floated around her as he walked down the small steps
that led to the garden.

'This place is beautiful.' Darla didn't move. She was
still holding the ring but allowing her gaze to encompass the surrounding garden.

'I love it. We all do. It makes us feel close to Mum. I
can still picture her out here. Planting, weeding, drawing secrets from me.'

'She sounds wonderful.'

Benedict nodded. 'She was. She was a doctor. She
was a mother. She was a helper. She was a friend. She
was amazing and you, my darling Darla, remind me a
lot of her.' Benedict came and sat down beside her.

'I do?'

'Yes. Maybe not in looks because she had dark hair,
but in personality most definitely.'

'Do you think she would have—?'

'Liked you?' he finished when she broke off.
'Without a doubt.'

They sat in silence for a few minutes before Darla
suddenly stood and turned to face him, surprising

Benedict further when she went down on one knee. 'What are you doing?' he asked.

'Shh.'

'Right.'

Darla took a moment to gather her thoughts before she held out the ring to him. 'Please hold it with me.' He did as she suggested, the two of them holding the engagement ring between them. She cleared her throat. 'Benedict…' She paused and blinked her eyes in one slow, long blink. 'I…'

He waited.

'I…'

He silently urged her on, wanting her to overcome her fear of completely trusting another person. During the past few weeks she'd been accepting of his touches and kisses and quiet talks as they'd discussed their plans for the future. He'd known she'd say the words when she was ready and it appeared now was the time.

'I…love you.' She breathed a sigh of relief then laughed as silly tears came into her eyes. 'Oh, my goodness, I *love* you. I love you. I love you. *I love you!*' She laughed again. 'I had no idea I would feel *this* free. I love you, Benedict Goldmark. I love you so much and I want desperately to be your wife. Your lover, your friend, your soulmate. I want to bear witness to your life, to all those little intimate moments you'll share with no one else but me. I want to be together for a very long time, to grow old, to continue helping others throughout our lifetime.'

Darla heaved another enormous sigh, then looked from Benedict to the ring. 'Please place this on my finger so everyone will know it's a token of the love we share.'

'With pleasure,' he murmured, and slipped the ring

onto the third finger on her left hand. 'I love you, Darla. So very much.'

'And I love you.' With that, he pulled her to her feet, standing beside her and wrapping his big protective arms about her, drawing her close and pressing his mouth to hers in a true and honest kiss that would bind their lives together—for ever.

* * * * *

NO. 1 DAD
IN TEXAS

BY
DIANNE DRAKE

MILLS
BOON

To Chris, one of the people I love most.
You make the world a better place.

First published in Great Britain 2012
by Mills & Boon, an imprint of Harlequin (UK) Limited.
Harlequin (UK) Limited, Eton House, 18-24 Paradise Road,
Richmond, Surrey TW9 1SR

© Dianne Despain 2012

ISBN: 978 0 263 89171 3

Harlequin (UK) policy is to use papers that are natural, renewable and recyclable products and made from wood grown in sustainable forests. The logging and manufacturing process conform to the legal environmental regulations of the country of origin.

Printed and bound in Spain
by Blackprint CPI, Barcelona

She glanced over at him, simply studied him for a fraction of a second, then, without a word, turned her attention back to the dirt road and the never-ending expanse of nothingness stretching out in front of them.

But in that fraction of a second he felt… There weren't any words to describe it, really. Except she'd looked not into his soul but through it, and it shook him. Shook him bad.

"For us," he conceded. "And for our son. I really want to make this work, Belle. We may not be married, but Michael needs consistency from us…together."

Dear Reader

When I approached my editor with an idea to write a story featuring a child with Asperger's Syndrome Mills & Boon® stood behind me solidly—for which I'm grateful. Asperger's has become popularised in fiction lately. I knew some of the overall facts, but after I began the deep research I needed for this book what I discovered was that every piece of information written about Asperger's Syndrome is basically the same: a laundry list of traits.

Then I met Chris who, with his Asperger's Syndrome, pretty much defies everything on the experts' list. And Chris is where the idea for my story went—from that laundry list of traits to the real face of Asperger's Syndrome. Musician, composer, poet, computer tech, athlete, scholar…you won't find those on the lists, but that's who Chris is—as well as a guy who absolutely makes direct eye contact and has a wicked, funny sense of humour. While he's not the character Michael I created, Chris inspired me to find that little boy—and, amazingly, what I discovered is that my Michael is pretty much like every other seven-year-old boy.

I think we tend to believe the lists, no matter what the situation or diagnosed condition. But Michael is an athlete, a computer genius, he loves bugs, plays games, has a passion for pizza, and the desperate wish of his heart is that his mom and dad will get back together. He's a kid with a plan.

Michael is also a kid with parents who love him more than anything in the world, and who are both trying hard to give him the support he'll need in the struggles he'll face in life. It's through Michael's eyes they finally see themselves.

As always, wishing you health and happiness.

Dianne Drake

www.DianneDrake.com

CHAPTER ONE

"ANYONE else?" Dr. Belle Carter called out to the ten or so ranch hands standing around, gawking at her. She was used to men gawking, but not like this bunch was doing. They were queasy, some of them wobbling on their feet, grabbing on to furniture, hugging walls. If there was a particular shade of color common to the sickly lot presently resisting her, she'd call it gray-green. But food poisoning did that, even in slight cases. Today, the old *E. coli* bug had struck down half the crew who worked on the Chachalaca Creek Ranch outside Big Badger, Texas. She'd suspected bad bean sprouts on the salad were the culprit when she'd sent the first samples *to the lab for tests, though she was actually quite en-*couraged over a bunch of cowboys eating salads and not big, thick steaks or pork chops. Until all those cowboys let her take a look, she wasn't going to be sure about anything, though. "If you've still got any of the symptoms I've just described, or talked about the other times I was out here, you'd better tell me now. If you don't, it's going to knock you down, maybe for up to ten days. That's a promise." She held up a large bottle of pills, rattled it for effect. "Anti-nausea pills, if you're interested." Which nobody was. This was her third trip

out here for this, and her last, if they continued to shun
her the way they were doing.

"It's hard getting used to a new doc in town," Maudie
Tucker, her nurse, said under her breath as she pulled
Belle back from the men. "These boys are used to the
way Doc Nelson used to do it, and having a lady doc
makes them jumpy. They don't trust you yet."

They didn't trust her? That was clear. But they were
sick, and in most cases sickness would override distrust.
Not here apparently, and she was about to be bested by
a bacterial gastric upset. "But Doc Nelson eloped with
his thirty-five-years-his-junior receptionist, and I'm the
only doctor within a hundred miles, so it's get used to
the lady doctor or ride out the illness without my help,"
she whispered back, sympathetic to the men's plight and
at the same time annoyed, watching them lope and drag
themselves in single file into the next room over—the
game room. Just to get away from her. As if she couldn't
follow them and perform their exams on the pool table
if she had to.

"It'll take them some time to adjust," Maudie replied.
"Folks around here are cautious, but they'll get used to
you—eventually."

"Eventually's not good enough. They're sick right
now." Belle loved Maudie to pieces. She'd come with
the medical practice, boasted forty-two years of hard-
boiled nursing, and if she could she'd mother every
one of Big Badger's citizens. Today, though, mothering wouldn't work. But a firm hand would, and she
doubted Maudie had it in her to be firm with any of the
ranch hands. "Which means they take the pills or…"
She shrugged. "Some of them will probably get sicker,
incur more time off work, and have to face the conse-
quences when I explain to the ranch owner that they

refused treatment—treatment he hired me to give." It also meant she was going to be the one to take a hard line here, if she intended on getting somewhere with the men. So she was going to chase them down, examine them, and treat them, whether or not they liked it. Good thing she was used to taking a hard line. Dr. Belle Carter, family practice specialist, had developed pretty thick skin over the course. Had had to, with what she'd gone through to get to this point in her life—tackling med school years later than many of her classmates, being a single mother, marriage to a man who'd spent most of their wedded years somewhere else. Married, past tense, naturally.

So today, with ten moderately sick people trying desperately to run away from her in their sluggardly sick gait, six appointments back at the office this afternoon, and flu vaccinations to give out later at the Salt Creek Ranch, she was extra-busy, and time was something she didn't have much of because at the end of it all she'd promised most of her evening to her son, Michael, and that was a promise she didn't want to break. He was the reason she was doing this, and doing it the hard way.

"My purpose here, my only purpose, is to have a look at each and every one of them, check their vital signs to make sure nothing else is going on and assess for dehydration or worsening symptoms, then treat what I find. It's a simple thing. Or it should be, if they'd let me do my job."

"Need some help?" a familiar voice asked from the doorway. "I don't have my medical bag with me this trip, but I can certainly help you with some of the process."

Anger was her first reaction to that voice. Then her heart skipped a beat. Then her lungs clutched, but only for a fraction of a second as when she caught her breath again she was right back at anger.

"What are you doing here, Cade?" she hissed, trying hard not to let the ranch hands overhear, even though every last one of them had now exited the room. "It's not your weekend. In fact, it's not even a weekend. So why are you here, bothering me, while I'm trying to do my job?"

"I'm here because I missed my favorite person in the world."

She swallowed hard, fighting to regain control as all the ranch hands in the other room, no matter how sick, were watching her, gauging her reaction, probably trying to find some argument to use against her when they were called out for refusing treatment. She sucked in a deep breath, squared her shoulders, steadied herself, and said, with all the calmness she could muster, "He's in school." Three words, so much effort. But Cade took effort.

Oh, they had an amicable situation where Michael was concerned. No one looking on could say otherwise. Twice a month Cade flew from Chicago to Texas to visit his son, and he never missed a date, never made excuses. He was diligent in that, something she actually admired in the man. In fact, she'd seen Cade more often in the two months she and Michael had lived in Texas than she had the last two months they'd lived a block down the street from him. He'd never missed his visitation then either. But in that situation it had been easier to avoid Cade, which she did as often as she could.

Now, though, with Cade showing up on her doorstep so often, coming from so far away, avoiding him wasn't all that easy. "And I don't need help taking care of my patients." Finally, now that the first flush of anger was under control, and nothing was skipping, clutching, or doing anything abnormal to her physiology, she turned to face him. "How did you know where to find me anyway?"

He looked straight at Maudie, who was blushing all kinds of red, and smiled. "I have a few friends here in Big Badger, Texas."

Dr. Cade Carter could sweet-talk the needles right off a prickly old cactus. He was a charmer, all right. Nothing about him had changed in that respect, and Maudie Tucker was the living proof. "Well, in case your friend didn't tell you, I've got a busy day ahead of me and I don't have time to waste standing here talking to you. But since you're here, for who knows what reason, you can see Michael after school. I'll call Virginia and let her know you'll be picking him up." Virginia Ellison, retired librarian, was Michael's caregiver, and the only person in Big Badger she really trusted with her son.

"Except it's not just Michael I came to see. Normally, when I'm here on my visitation weekends, there's not enough time or you're too busy. But we need to talk, Belle. There are some things I want to say, want to tell you, that don't fit into the regular schedule, and I was hoping…" He shrugged. "It's important. That's all I'm saying."

Now her heart skipped a beat again, and not in a good way. She'd had years of disappointments, one after another, from this man, and she was conditioned for it. But not here, not now, and that's all she could think this would be. Cade changing something, Cade doing something that would affect her life. The divorce, five years ago, had ended all the letdowns and she didn't want to go back to that. Not even for a minute. Yet it felt like that's exactly where Cade was trying to drag her now.

Except nearly ten years of having Cade Carter in her life had taught her how to dig her heels in. But those same years of Cade Carter had also taught her just how vulnerable she could be to him, if she let herself.

"I'm working, Cade. Whatever you want, we'll do it later when I'm ready. And in the meantime, leave me alone."

"Fine, later. When you're ready. But in the meantime, it looks to me like you could use another doctor here."

She glanced into the next room at her patients, who all seemed to have lost interest in the interchange between Cade and herself, then took two steps closer to Cade. Gritted her teeth. Whispered, "Don't do this to me in front of my patients, Cade Carter. Do not undermine my abilities by implying that I can't do my job without your help. So get out of here and leave me alone."

"I was just offering," he said, not budging.

Just offering. But what was he really offering here? That's what had her stumped. They'd been divorced five years now, and she'd been relieved to see it end when it had. Sure, it had been sad, in so many ways. Especially because of Michael. But she couldn't have survived with Cade. She'd needed more, he'd needed less. "Fine. We'll talk later. Whatever kind of bad news you're going to spring on me can wait until I've finished my day."

"I never meant to do that to you, you know?"

"Do what?"

"Make you think the worst of me. Or anticipate that anything I have to say to you is bad news."

"I don't think the worst of you, Cade. But we were married, remember? I got used to having the worst of you."

"And sometimes the best." He cocked a half-smile,

stepped back, tipped his cowboy hat at her. "Later," he said, then turned and walked off.

"Surprised you'd let him get away," Maudie commented, watching him almost as hard as Belle was.

"You can't keep someone who doesn't want to be kept, Maudie," she said, turning back to the group of men she'd come to treat. Now, though, her mind was on Cade. Good dad. First-rate surgeon. And the last person she'd expected to see when he wasn't scheduled for a weekend with Michael. But Cade was up to something. She knew it, felt it, didn't know what it was, and that's what she had to get her mind off right now.

"OK, everybody," Belle said, fighting to refocus on her patients. "Here's the deal. I've got a kid to support. He's seven. I don't have a lot of time to spend with him, and the longer it takes here, the less time Michael and I are going to have. So you can fight me on this, refuse to let me check you, but it's affecting my son. Any of you have children you'd like to spend more time with, or mothers who'd love spending more time with you? Because if you do, then you'll understand what I'm talking about, and get in line so I can get this done as quickly as possible."

"Ah, the sentimental touch. Well done," Maudie joked as, one by one, the men started to trickle forward.

Belle laughed. "Whatever it takes." She wondered what it would take with Cade. Surely he wanted something she didn't want to give. Quite the opposite from their marriage, where she'd wanted something he hadn't wanted to give. Definitely, whatever it takes, she thought to herself.

Two hours later Belle was pleased with the results of her morning. All but three ranch hands had eventually fallen in line. This evening, once the nausea pills took effect, all but three ranch hands would feel better. Had she gained any respect from these men? Nah. She wasn't that deluded. They'd sympathized either as a father or a son. It was good enough for now. Battle number one went to the lady doctor. Battle number two coming up, though, with Cade? No, she didn't know for sure there was going to be a battle between them, but she was clearly feeling something in the pit of her stomach, and it made her nervous, as the only thing she could think that Cade would want was Michael.

"Didn't mean to put you in a spot," Cade said, as Belle stepped out of her car.

"That's an apology?"

"If you need one then, yes, it's an apology."

He was leaning up against the entrance to her office, standing in the shade, cowboy hat tipped low over his face. Admittedly, he still took away her breath. A sexier, better-looking man God had never put on the face of this earth, and she responded to that in huge ways. Dark brown hair just slightly wavy, slate-gray eyes. Tall, muscled physique of a god. She'd responded to it too quickly all those years ago, jumping into his bed the first opportunity she'd had, then into marriage at approximately the same irresponsible speed. "What's with the hat?" She'd never seen him in a cowboy hat before today, but it did him justice. If anything, it made him look sexier.

"When in Texas." He tilted the brim back. Stared her in the eye. "Since you're raising my son to be a cowboy now."

"Apology accepted, but don't ever do that to me again, Cade," she warned, brushing by him to unlock the door. "I'm having a hard enough time as it is, establishing myself here in the wake of the legendary Dr. Nelson, and I don't need you stepping in to help me, or whatever it was you were trying to do out there on the Chachalaca. And why are you here anyway? You just left three days ago, and you're not due back for—"

"Nine more days, which is why I'm here now. Nine days is a long time. Too long."

That feeling in the pit of her stomach turned into a hard knot as the hint of a custody battle took on stronger overtones. Cade had never fought her on her being custodial parent, so why now? "Meaning?" she asked, struggling not to sound as apprehensive as she felt.

"Meaning I don't get enough time with Michael. He's growing up, and every other weekend isn't working for me. You've been gone two months, Belle, and the arrangement is driving me crazy. So I decided to take a few weeks off my practice and hang around Big Badger, see what's rocking his world these days. Discover things I can't discover in my allotted few hours of visitation."

"Why now, Cade? It's been this way for five years, so why now?"

"Because I'm getting older."

She shook her head. "That's not it."

"Maybe there's not one certain 'it', Belle. Maybe I just want to be included more."

Like he'd wanted to be included in their marriage, but hardly ever showed up for it? Like he'd wanted to be included in so many of the other milestones they should have been celebrating as a family, only Cade had always, conveniently, been missing from them? Cade had been the consummate husband in absentia, so why this? And why now? "You're not sick, are you? A terminal illness, or something life-threatening?"

He chuckled. "You always were straight to the point but, no, I'm not sick. Does that disappoint you?"

"Believe it or not, Cade, I don't hate you. Never have, and unless you give me cause, like taking Michael away from me, I never will."

"Is that what you think? That I'm here to take Michael away from you?"

"Seems logical, doesn't it? Things are going along fine then, out of the blue, you're here, telling me you want to make changes. So is that what it's about, Cade? Do you want to take Michael away from me?"

"What I want, what I've always wanted, is what's best for him. That's you, Belle. I wouldn't take him away from you, and I'm sorry you'd think I would." He shook his head. "That's the second time I've apologized for causing you to think the worst of me. It's not how I want it to be between us, you know."

She was relieved. Still curious, since Cade was acting so out of character. But very relieved. "I know, and neither do I. And for what it's worth, I really didn't think you would take him from me. We've had our bad moments, Cade, but I didn't think you'd do that. It's just that you showing up here the way you have makes me uncomfortable. I don't know what to expect."

"And in your life you always like to know what to expect." It was said with no malicious intent whatsoever.

"It's who I am." And part of the reason their marriage had failed. Cade never had understood that in her. "So anyway, I know you miss Michael, but what's the real reason you're here?"

"That is the real reason. Can't it be just that simple?"

She shook her head, then gestured for him to follow her through to the exam rooms and into her private office, trying not to think about how Cade was still on the verge of something that, try as she did to fight it, made her feel anxious. "So, on a whim, you can just walk away from your surgical practice?" she asked, shutting the door behind her and grappling for something, anything, to steady her nerves. A deep breath, a sturdy wall to lean on. Amicable divorce, yes, amicable parenting arrangements, yes. But there was nothing amicable about the way she was feeling as this was all about Cade wanting to change her life again, no matter how simple he claimed this matter of his was going to be. "You can just decide you don't want to work then fly to Texas for a day or two?"

"Actually, like I said a minute ago, I'm here for a few weeks. That's one of the advantages of being co-owner of a growing surgical practice. You get to make the rules. And since there are always a dozen or so other surgeons to cover for me, I decided I needed—well, you can believe what you want, but I came to spend some time with Michael."

"Really? A few weeks?" This was making less and less sense by the minute. "You're going to stay in Big Badger for a few weeks?" Normally, Cade was one step shy of arrogance, but she didn't see that in his eyes. They were the eyes that kept him hidden, blocked the light from his soul. Not now, though. Cade was not only serious about staying here, he was emotionally invested in it.

"Seriously, Belle, is wanting more time with my son such a bad thing?"

Under most circumstances, no. And she didn't know what to think about this now. Except she'd seen that flicker of emotion in his eyes just then. Brief, but definitely there. The same flicker of emotion she'd seen the day Michael had been born, same flicker she'd seen the day she'd told Cade that Michael had been diagnosed with Asperger's syndrome. Cade Carter kept most of himself hidden, but not always. And those unhidden moments were always genuine. She knew that with all her heart. "OK, I understand that you're not going to tell me everything, and I don't have time to stand here and try arguing it out of you. I do think you want to see Michael, and for now I'm going to leave it at that. But later, Cade. We're going to deal with this—this whatever it is—whether or not you like it."

"I swear, it's all about Michael," he said, putting on the old Cade grin. The charmer grin that had got her into trouble in the first place. "And since we have an open agreement about him—"

"Before you make any more plans, I've made arrangements for him in Austin for the next three weeks. It's a good program. It's gained lots of awards for its advances in autism, and is headed by a doctor who's internationally known for her work."

"Which he doesn't need to go to now that I'm here to spend that time with him."

"But it's arranged."

"And I don't remember you asking me about it."

"OK, maybe I should have asked, like you should have asked before just showing up here unannounced. But a month ago, when I told you I wanted to talk to you about a program I'd found for him, you said you'd get back to me. Said that to me each of the three other times I tried talking to you about it. Remember that?"

He drew in a stiff breath. "I was busy."

"I was, too." Now the charm had dissolved, and they were back to the same old problems. "But I made the time to investigate the program, and made the time to

try and get you to listen to me about it. But you weren't
listening at all, were you? That's why you're here now.
Because you didn't hear a word I said, sort of like the
way it was when we were married." There was no dis-
puting they both wanted what was best for their son,
but that's where the co-operation stopped. Cade had
his ideas, which were, basically, more love and more
involvement could cure anything. She had hers, which
were to find her son the best available programs for
children with Asperger's syndrome. That didn't pre-
clude more love and more involvement. It merely gave
Michael one more shot at having a better life. "So I hope
you bought a round-trip ticket, because if you hurry,
you can be back in Chicago by tonight."

"Unenroll him. I want to spend the next few weeks
with him."

"No, I'm not going to unenroll him. You've got
Michael six straight weeks at the end of summer, and
that's all you're getting, so deal with it. Go home, leave
me alone." Arrangements had already been made for
Cade to take Michael back to Chicago with him, which
she didn't like but which she hoped would be good for
her son. Unlike Cade, she had no intention of stepping
in and trying to upset things. Michael's life was a pre-
carious balance, and he didn't need the disruption.

"And what I've been telling you is that six weeks
aren't enough, Belle. I miss him. It's driving me crazy,
knowing I can't see Michael whenever I want to. Getting
him for three-day weekends every other week and every
other holiday isn't cutting it. And half that time is spent
in transit, flying down here to be with him and flying
back to be home on time for my Monday morning sur-
geries. And, really, how much time do I get to spend
with him when I'm here? Have you ever thought about

it, Belle? Three, maybe four hours total, adjusting to
his schedule and routines, as well as his attention span?
Which is why I want to spend the whole summer with
him, and not just part of it." He drew in a ragged breath.
"I need to connect better with my boy and teach him to
connect better with me."

She did have to admit Cade was the one who got
cheated, especially as she was the one who'd moved
from Chicago to Big Badger, breaking up a perfectly
good custody arrangement, one much more conducive
to Cade's situation. But he was the Texas boy after all.
The cowboy who'd spent every day of their marriage
talking about how great Texas was, how he wanted to
move back someday, how it was the best place in the
country to raise kids.

Well, she'd listened. More than that, she'd believed.
So now here she was, raising their kid in Texas. And
here Cade wasn't, except for his every-other-week vis-
itations. "Look, it's only a three-week program, Cade.
You can have the three weeks after it's over, here in Big
Badger, though. And that would still give you more time
than we'd originally planned."

"But I want more than that," he repeated, stubbornly.

"Without notice."

"Because there was no notice to give. I decided to do
this…" he glanced at his watch "…ten hours ago. Ten
hours, Belle. I changed my life in the last ten hours because I miss my son. And I think spending the next few
weeks with me will be better for Michael than sending
him off into some program."

Even if it was an excellent program, letting Michael
spend time with his dad was the better situation. No argument there. And having Cade here would be wonderful for Michael. Still, one of the reasons she'd chosen

to move to godforsaken Big Badger was to be close to Dr. Amanda Robinson. Sure, the town had made her an offer she couldn't refuse, but it was one of three amazing offers that had come at her. The decision had come down to Amanda's excellent reputation in autism. She worked miracles with kids no one expected miracles from, and to be so close to all that was why she was working in a town that didn't want a lady doctor, and being on call to a bunch of hostile ranch hands. Yet nothing Amanda could or would do would substitute for the fact that Michael needed his father, and that's what ultimately changed Belle's mind. Not Cade's need, but Michael's. "OK. If you're really going to stay here, I'll pull him out of the program. But there's a three-day trip he's been begging to go on, and I'm not cancelling that, no matter what you say. Dr. Robinson is doing good things for Michael and I don't want to cause problems with that."

"You think that highly of the good doctor's program?"

"I do. Michael needs that kind of professional guidance and I need that kind of personal support. With Amanda, we get both."

"Good. Then I can live with that."

But could she? Big Badger was a small town, there wasn't much to do here. And she could envision herself bumping into Cade every time she turned around for the next six weeks. Bumps she didn't want to be making. "It's not about what you can live with," she snapped. "It's about what's best for Michael. Dr. Robinson's part of it, but you're a bigger part." He'd spent their married life staying away, and she'd got used to it. Got used to the distances in their divorce, too, and she wasn't sure what having him around all the time was going to do to her. But for Michael... "And you're not staying with me."

"Didn't intend to. I took a room at the boarding house. Paid for the full six weeks."

He smiled, arched ridiculously sexy eyebrows—the whole Cade effect that had always been her downfall.

"Cade Carter, staying in a boarding house and not some luxurious hotel suite?" Belle raised her eyebrows over that one, because it told her, whatever his reason, he was dead serious about spending more time with Michael.

"Find me a luxurious hotel in Big Badger, and I'll check in."

"And you're still not going to tell me what this is really about?" There wasn't a casual explanation. Knowing Cade, there couldn't be. But Cade honestly loved Michael, even though Michael didn't give much back to his dad. So maybe it was about Cade feeling excluded or unloved? Certainly, that's how she would feel if Michael was as unresponsive to her as he was to Cade. So she hoped that was the simple explanation after all.

But there'd been a time when she'd hoped so many things about Cade, and look where that had got her.

"I can tell you a thousand times a day for the next six weeks. My being here is about spending more time with Michael. That's all, Belladonna."

Nope. She knew Cade, and she didn't buy it. But, as they said, forewarned was forearmed. Only she didn't know against what. "Fine. You've got your extra six weeks. And don't call me Belladonna." Meaning beautiful woman, or deadly nightshade, take your pick. It used to be his pet name for her, used when he'd wanted to get his way. Which he'd just done, hadn't he?

The charmer grin grew larger as Cade tilted his hat back down over his eyes. "Anybody ever tell you you're a real pushover, Belle Carter?"

Nobody had to tell her. When it came to Cade Carter, she always had been. Looked like that hadn't changed too much either. "All the time," she said, opening her office door and gesturing him to leave. "All the time."

Belle watched him amble down the hall and out the back office door, admiring that same swagger she'd always admired. "So, what are you up to, Cade?" she asked, under her breath, as she shrugged into her white lab coat and headed off to see her first patient of the afternoon. "What are you really up to?" And how was she going to stay resistant to it? That was the big question.

"How would you like to spend more time with your dad this summer, Michael?" Kicking her shoes to the other side of the room, Belle dropped back onto the sofa and lay there, flat on her back, staring up at the ceiling. "Michael," she said again, without glancing over. She knew what he was doing. Playing video games. The love of his life. Lately, though, he hadn't been playing them so much as creating one of his own, doing preliminary sketches, working out the story details. "Did you hear me? I asked if you'd like to spend more time with your dad this summer."

"Yeah," Michael said, his rapt attention still fixed on his game.

"Well, he's here. In Big Badger." Not that telling him would make a difference, but he did process the information. Just not always on the spot. "And he wants to spend the summer with you. So you'll have to start thinking about all the things you'd like to do with him, maybe make a list. OK?"

"Yeah," he said.

Belle was sure he was simply telling her what she wanted to hear, and paying absolutely no attention to her at the same time. Complex mind. So complex that it scared her sometimes. Most of the time, though, she didn't think about it. Because to Michael she was only Mom, doing the mom things she was supposed to do. Like making dinner. Her next chore. "What do you want to eat?" she asked him, then added, before he answered, "Not pizza. We've had that two night in a row now. So, what else?"

"Pizza," he said anyway.

She wasn't sure if that was because pizza was truly his favorite food or if it was simply what came to mind first, turning it into the easiest way to respond to her yet still stay focused on what he was doing. "No pizza," she said emphatically.

"OK." He turned to her, grinning. "Fried chicken, mashed potatoes without lumps with white gravy without lumps, corn on the cob and homemade biscuits. *With honey.*"

Belle moaned, then laughed. He did this on purpose—his sense of humor. Michael knew she couldn't cook, at least not that kind of meal. And he teased her about it. "You mean hamburgers, don't you? On the grill?"

"Can I cook them?" he asked.

"Do pigs fly?" she asked, teasing him.

"Only in another universe, Mom," he said, then turned back to his game.

"When you say something cute like that, you know what I'm going to have to do, don't you?"

"No!" he squealed, curling himself into a ball. "Not that!"

Belle rolled off the couch then crawled on hands and knees across the floor to Michael, who was rolling away from her. "Yes, that! The cuddle game. You know how much I love the cuddle game." Her cuddle game was a form of hug therapy used on children who had an aversion to being touched, like Michael had had when he'd been younger. It was one of several sensory issues she'd been dealing with, along with loud noises and some bright colors. It had taken Belle years to get him to the point where accepting physical affection was a pleasant experience for him. Sometimes, even now, she wasn't sure if it was or if he was merely putting on an act to placate her. Either way, it didn't matter. A few minutes to cuddle her son meant everything. Everything.

"Can he come to dinner?" Michael asked, before Belle had even gotten all the way over to him.

Of all things, that was the one question that stopped her dead, threw that bucket of water on the cuddle game. Could Cade come to dinner? Her first response was, *When pigs fly!* She didn't want to spend the evening with Cade. Didn't particularly even want to be in the same room with him. But this was Michael asking. Michael, who never asked for anything except more RAM for his computer. "Well, I have a better idea than that. Why don't I call your dad and see if he'll come take you out for pizza?" Which was exactly what she did, when Michael's attention, once again, returned to his game.

"He wants pizza, he wants you," she said to Cade, when he answered his phone. "And what's with the pickup truck I saw you in earlier?" A sleek, low-riding sports car was more his style.

"Had to rent something."

"Well, Michael's never been in a pickup truck so I don't know if that's going to work. You can leave it here and borrow my car."

"Or I can leave your car right where it is and take him in the truck. Or would the two of you rather meet me somewhere?"

"I prefer the sound of a boys' night out, while I take a long, hot bath and finish that mystery novel I've been trying to finish for the last month." A night that might have, under different circumstances, been perfect. Tonight, though, the image of a cozy little family of three eating pizza together popped into her thoughts, making her feel, well, not sad for the present so much as sad for the things they'd had in the past. It seemed like such a long time ago. So far away it was difficult trying to remember when they'd been happy. They had been, though. In the early years, when Michael had still been a baby and she had been plunking along through medical school a little at a time, trying to balance motherhood and career. Good times for a while. So many hopes and dreams. Bright futures in the planning. But with a supportive husband for only such a short while before he'd started retreating. "Oh, and I've told Michael you're going to be here for a while, and to get a list ready of things he wants to do with you. And before you tell me there's nothing he wants to do with you, you're wrong. There are a lot of things. You have to be patient, getting him to tell you."

"But he will," Cade replied. "Isn't that what you always tell me? Be patient, and he'll do it. Except he never does, Belle. Never does."

He did, though. Cade simply wasn't very good at picking up on the subtle signs. The irony was that that was a typical Asperger's symptom. Only thing was, while Michael had Asperger's, Cade did not. And it was Cade's lack in that area that was, in part, responsible for the death of their marriage. "Then work on it. And, please, not video games and computers. He gets enough of that in his day-to-day life, and he really needs something else."

"In Big Badger, Texas? What else is there, Belle? You pretty much came to the end of the earth with this *job, and I can't see this place being exactly stimulating* for a child."

"In Big Badger, Texas, you have to use your imagination. Get used to it, Cade. You're the one who chose to spend six weeks here." She thought she heard a groan on the other end of the phone. She smiled. "Pick him up in an hour. And make sure he wears his seat belt in that truck. He's in a new phase where the seat belt bothers him, and he'll take it off if he thinks you're not watching. So watch him!"

"Anybody ever tell you to lighten up?"

"Anybody ever tell you that we're divorced and I'm none of your business any more?" Still smiling, she clicked off. But rather than being angry, she was wondering if having Cade around for a while might be good. Definitely for Michael, but maybe a little bit for her, too? Funny thing was, since the moment she'd heard his voice out there on the Chachalaca, she'd had this peculiar feeling in the pit of her stomach. Suddenly, it was gone.

CHAPTER TWO

OK, so maybe it wasn't the smartest thing he'd ever done, taking a leave of absence and coming to Texas. Not the most thought-out either, since he'd done it on the spur of the moment. But, damn it, he missed Michael. For all the rough patches in their relationship, and there were plenty of them, his kid was his life, and he hated it that he couldn't see him any time, like he'd done before Belle had moved to Big Badger.

It was about his brother Robbie, too. It was his birthday today. That was another regret, realizing how much he'd missed. And guilt. Feeling it more acutely as the years rolled on. Recognizing he was well on that track with Michael, too.

So he'd endure Big Badger for a few weeks, see what he really wanted to do after that, and the trade-off for the things he hadn't figured out yet was extra time to spend with Michael while he was traveling through yet another undecided phase of his life. Maybe, just maybe, he'd find a way to relate to his son better or, at the very least, get Michael to respond to him.

Spending time with Belle was also something he'd given a lot of thought to. He'd caused the divorce. There was no other way to look at it. She'd needed a husband, and he'd needed—well, he still didn't know the answer to that, did he? But whatever it was, he owed Belle in a big way for the letdown of a husband he'd been, and while he couldn't make that up to her, he could make some amends by being a better father.

How? He wasn't sure. There weren't many options open to him. But somewhere inside those next six weeks, maybe he'd prove himself to Michael, and also to Belle, by showing how he was more than the father who simply appeared at the door to pick up his kid every couple of weeks. What would he get from Belle in return? He didn't have a clue, but he was willing to take anything. Michael needed that. So did he. Because those were some feelings he had to resolve as well while he was here.

Tall order to fulfill—better dad, better ex-husband. To move forward, though, that was his agenda, otherwise he'd have to step away from them altogether, for Michael's sake, he told himself. Whatever he did, it had to be for Michael's sake. And for Belle's. Because, God knew, he didn't deserve anything for his own sake.

"So, what kind of pizza do you want?" he asked Michael, as they headed to the truck.

"Mom coming?" Michael asked, trailing along behind Cade by a good ten large steps.

"Mom's tired tonight. So it's only going to be the two of us." Not the best choice of words apparently, because once Michael heard them he stopped, then turned around and headed back to Belle's front door. A purposeful march, and a very obvious one. Michael wanted his mother, not his dad. Understanding that, Cade felt his heart fall.

"I'll get her," Michael said.

"But she doesn't want to come." Neither did Michael.

"That's OK. She likes pizza, too. Just not every night."

With that, Michael disappeared back into the house, leaving Cade standing alone on the sidewalk. Feeling rotten. Inadequate. Feeling like an idiot for not knowing what to do now. Should he go after Michael, insist that pizza was only for the two of them? Ask Belle to come along to make the situation better? These were the things that eluded him, the things he should know how to manage. But didn't.

"See, this is the way it always is," he said, clearly frustrated when Belle appeared at the door with Michael in hand.

"I explained it, and now Michael understands that I'm not part of the pizza party tonight. He was just afraid that I might not fix myself anything for dinner."

It was more than that. It was Michael showing concern for his mother in a way Cade had never seen. Or had never felt from Michael himself. It was a proud moment, *seeing that in his son*, yet a profoundly sad one as well. To Belle's credit, though, for being such a good mother to Michael. "And will you?"

Belle shook her head. "Too tired. I'll grab an apple, maybe some yogurt, and I'll be good." She scooted Michael out the door, then took a step back. "So you two have fun tonight. And I'll see you in a couple of hours."

"Sure you don't want to come with us?" Cade called.

"Sure," she said, shutting the door.

This time she locked it. Cade heard the bolt latch. "OK, then. It really is just the two of us." And a whole summer ahead, with more of this. On top of which, he was going to be with Belle. Now, that was going to be the bigger challenge. Belle Elise Foster Carter—the best of his life while he was the worst of hers. Yes, she was definitely going to be the biggest challenge he was going to face in Big Badger, Texas.

"So tell me about school," Cade said, handing a slice of pizza, pepperoni only, over to his son.

"It's OK," Michael replied, his attention fixed squarely on a floor-sized video game in the corner of the restaurant—a road-race game meant for kids twice his age.

"Is math still your favorite subject?"

"Um, yes."

"Still like your science classes?"

"Uh-huh."

It was clear Michael was more interested in the game than his dad, and Cade understood that. Still, it was frustrating not being able to hold his son's attention for more than a fraction of a second, basically losing out to a game, and he was fighting to keep in his nettled sigh. Belle had the relationship with Michael he wanted. He was glad for her. But it bothered the hell out of him that, no matter how hard he tried with Michael, he was *barely on his son's radar. "Want to go play?" he finally* asked, giving in to the obvious.

Michael nodded his head and, for a second, glanced at Cade. His expression was…happy? Did he see happiness in his son's eyes, or was that merely wishful *thinking? As quickly as Michael looked over, though,* he looked away. Right back at the video game.

"After you finish your pizza," Cade said. "Deal?"

Michael nodded. "Deal." Then he crammed the rest of his pizza into his mouth, so much so his cheeks bulged as he tried to chew it and swallow. Finally, his mouth cleared, he held out his hand to Cade. "Money, please."

"How much?" Cade asked, not expecting an answer.

"It's a dollar a game. Can I play ten games? Because that would be ten dollars."

Explained very seriously. But it was the most Michael had said all evening and for that Cade rewarded him with ten dollars. For a moment it crossed his mind to go play the game with Michael, but he knew that would cause his son more frustration than he could deal with, so he twisted his chair to watch, then leaned back to make himself more comfortable. "I'll save you some pizza for later," he said, before Michael scampered off.

"Thanks, Dad," he said, clutching the handful of dollar bills like they were a lifesaving elixir.

Cade blinked his surprise. "You're welcome. Oh, and, Michael…" he called, as Michael was already halfway across the room. "Have fun."

"It was nice, hearing him call you Dad," Belle said, settling into the chair next to Cade.

"Thought you were staying home."

"Turns out I can't."

"Because you don't think I can take good care of our son?" he asked. "Because you want to see, in action, how you're the good mom and I'm the bad dad?"

Immediately, Belle bristled. "Don't go there, Cade. I didn't come down here to fight with you. I've got to go out to the Chachalaca again, to see a couple of the holdouts. The ranch owner threatened them with their jobs and now they're willing to let the lady doc treat them. So don't hassle me. This is my fourth time out there, and I'm not happy about it."

"I could go," he offered. "Seriously. You could take

the rest of the night off, maybe stay here and finish the pizza, and I could go out to the Chachalaca."

"Trying to make amends is nice, Cade, and I appreciate it. But duty calls, and this duty is mine. What I was wondering, though, is when you take Michael home later on, would you mind staying there with him until I get back? If you can't, that's fine. I can call Virginia Ellison, and she'll be glad—"

"Not a problem," he said, sliding the pizza box over toward Belle. "If it gets too late, I'll sleep on the couch. Care for a slice to take with you?"

She laughed. "Between you and me, I really hate pizza. But Michael loves it, and sometimes it's the only thing I can get him to eat."

He pulled the pizza back and took a large slice for himself, one dripping with pizza sauce and cheese. "You're the one who worked with him on calling me Dad, aren't you?"

"I know it's difficult for you, not getting to see him more, then when you do it takes him so long to warm up to you. So I thought—"

He held up his hand to stop her, then swallowed the bite in his mouth. "I appreciate it, even if it doesn't come naturally to him. And what I just said about you coming here to watch me be the bad dad..." He sighed. "You are the good mom, you know. Sometimes when I see that, and see how Michael responds to you—it bothers me, Belle. And it bothers me that you had to teach my son to call me Dad. I loved hearing him say it, but I would have loved it even more if it had been spontaneous."

"I think it was. Normally, I prompt him before your weekends. Just mention it once or twice. But this isn't one of your weekends, and what's happening now is totally off Michael's routine. So I didn't prompt him."

Cade smiled, but didn't respond, because he knew Belle was wrong. It was her work that had brought about Michael's efforts. More than that, it made him feel terrible that, even in divorce, Belle cared more about his feelings than he'd ever cared about hers while they'd been married.

"Anyway..." She scooted back her chair to leave, then turned and waved to Michael, who took a moment to glance up from his game in progress. "I've got to go. *So I'm going to go tell Michael where I'll be while you* polish off all that pizza, because he's too caught up in his game to want any more of it." She stepped away, stopped, then turned back to him. "You still got the six-pack?" Referring to his rock-hard abs.

The question totally surprised him. And intrigued him. "Why?"

"Just a warning about what can come from too many nights in the pizza parlor. And if Michael has his way with you, you'll be here every night." She smiled. "It would be a pity to mess up one of the good things about you, Cade."

"Sounds like you almost care."

"You had nice abs. That's all I'm saying." Then, finally, she walked away.

He watched, didn't budge an inch to stand and be polite, or even walk along with her over to Michael. Belle, with her honey-blonde hair and sassy green eyes. And a sway to her hips that begged his stare. She was sexy as hell. Always had been, always would be. That's what caught him first glance, but what reeled him in was her intelligence, and her overall zest for life. Belle did life in a big way, bigger than anybody he'd ever met in his life. So straightforward about it, too, like she'd been just then. She still remembered liking his abs? He wasn't sure how to take it. Maybe as a compliment, maybe as a warning, like she'd said.

Or maybe—nah, he wasn't going there. He had friends who'd told him sex with the ex after the divorce was awesome. Maybe it was, he didn't know. But Belle wasn't the type. And, truly, he'd never even thought about it until just now. Well, maybe he had thought about it a time or two. But not seriously. And what she'd said about his abs—that was Belle being her straightforward self, giving him a warning and letting him know, in her own way, he was going to get a lot of time with Michael. Yes, that's what she'd meant. He was sure of it. Positive. Well, almost positive.

Still thinking about Belle as she lingered a moment to watch Michael's game, he knew now what he'd always known—nobody compared. Nobody even came close. In fact, the skinny list of women he'd considered dating from time to time were either so boring, bland, or so inane, trite, or shallow he never got around to the asking-out stage. Truth was, he hadn't dated because nobody seemed—well, like Belle. Not that he'd ever date her again, or do anything else with her, because he'd messed that up in the worst way a man could mess up the best thing in his life. But in a woman he needed personality and drive and, so far, he hadn't found that in any way that suited him other than in Belle, and that didn't count any more.

Which was fine, for now, as he wasn't in any hurry to settle down again. Of course, some people, Belle specifically, would argue he'd never settled down in the first place. "Look," he said, jumping into her path as she whooshed by him on her way out the door, "I don't want to fight. OK? It seems like we're always fighting, or just on the verge of it, and I don't want us doing that."

"Neither do I, but we're so good at it," she said, smiling. "I'd hate to give up on a good thing."

He chuckled, in spite of himself. "That's the thing I fell in love with, you know?"

"What?" she asked. "That I defend myself? That I stand up to you, face-to-face, and punch back?"

"Well, that could be part of the charm—for someone else. But what drew me to you was your fire. Just not so much of it. Anyway, that accusation a few minutes ago—it was a cheap shot. Totally uncalled-for, and I'm sorry. But sometimes—"

"Look, I do understand. It's not easy being Michael's dad, and it's probably not easy being my ex—although I'm not sure why it isn't, because I think I'm pretty easy to get along with." This time her smile was a tease. "Anyway, I've got to make my house call and these ranch hands aren't happy about it, so I just want to get out there and get it over with. Michael knows you're going to spend the evening with him, and that I might be late. He understands. So…" She shrugged, then hurried out the restaurant door, leaving Cade to watch her until she climbed into her car and drove away.

Yep, she certainly had fire. And if he was not mistaken, the flames had shot up a notch or two since they'd divorced. It was not unattractive in her, he decided as he ambled over to Michael and watched him trounce the evildoers in his game. Trounce, like a pro.

Damn, if his kid wasn't good at it! "So, Michael. Want to show me what you're doing?"

Michael didn't take his eyes off the screen, didn't even miss a shot. "Um, no."

The sting of that one word rocked him back a couple of steps. But that's as far as he went. Then he stood his ground, the way Belle would, and watched his son accomplish the highest score ever achieved on that particular game machine without breaking a sweat. How the hell was he ever going to make the score with Michael, with or without sweat?

That was the question he'd been asking himself for years. It was also the question for which he couldn't find an answer.

Then it hit him. Michael had called him Dad. Maybe prompted, maybe not. But—Dad. The most beautiful word he'd ever heard. So maybe there wasn't an answer to his question, except patience. And time.

The big problem, though, was distance, and there was no way to get around that.

He looked so innocent sleeping. So beautiful. She'd always thought that. And in their last year together, after so much struggling, she'd thought it was a pity he didn't sleep more often, because when he woke up, life changed. Fighting, bitterness—the emptiness of long, lonely hours by herself. Cade had caused her the kind of unhappiness she'd never thought would be part of her life. Yet she understood. Part of it came with his frustration over Michael. It hurt him, being ignored by a son he loved so deeply. But part of it was his absence, which was something she'd never understood and which, in retrospect, she wished she'd pursued with him until he'd explained it. His need, or lust, to leave had started mere weeks after they'd pronounced their vows, and had only got worse with time. She'd hoped it was a phase, some kind of life adjustment she just didn't understand. But it hadn't been, and when she'd asked him to explain, to help her understand, she'd been met with Cade's characteristic wall of resistance. So after a while, being rebuffed every time she asked, she quit asking, essentially giving up as it was clear that she was moving forward with her life and her husband was moving away.

Oh, sure. Cade had his causes—causes she admired. Sadly, at the time, his family hadn't seemed one of them. Maybe it was because she was strong and he'd believed she could hold things together in his absence. Maybe he found more satisfaction helping others than he did helping his family. All these years later she still didn't know why. But now she didn't dwell on it so much because her choice to move on without him, or get left behind, had been a good one.

Yet he still looked so innocent, sleeping. Like the man she'd fallen in love with all those years ago.

Belle smiled as she studied him. Michael looked so much like him. Same gray eyes, same dark brown hair, wavy with a little bit of curl. Same crooked smile. Except neither Michael nor Cade smiled much, which was a pity. Because it was a beautiful smile. One she'd wanted to capture in a family photo back when they'd been a family.

"It's late," Cade mumbled in his sleepy voice.

The sleepy voice—another thing she used to love. It was a little thick, a little gruff. "Going on to midnight."

"Does it happen often?" he asked, propping himself up on one elbow.

"What? Me running around and leaving Michael here with a babysitter? Is that what you're asking me, Cade? Do I neglect my son on a regular nightly basis?" She hadn't meant to take offense, but sometimes Cade provoked that in her. Usually without much effort. Like now, when she was thinking about the things she'd planned with him—things she'd never have.

He stretched, sat up. Stretched again. "Actually, I

wasn't thinking about Michael. It's you I was concerned about, being the only doctor for miles."

"More like a hundred miles." She backed off the anger immediately.

"Which doesn't mean much, since it's Texas miles, and there's not much civilization from here to there."

"Sorry. I didn't mean to get so—"

"Defensive?" he asked.

She tossed her jacket over the back of the couch and stashed her medical bag in the coat closet on the top shelf. "That's what we do to each other, isn't it? Get defensive at first sight." She turned to face him. "You were right earlier about not fighting. I don't like being this way either, Cade. It gets easy to do, like a habit, and I don't want Michael seeing it."

"Then we'll have to make sure we don't."

"Agreed. No more fighting," she said, kicking off her shoes then dropping down into the overstuffed chair near the stairs. Said with a sly grin, "But clarify this for me, will you? Does the ban on fighting include low blows, subtle innuendoes, and casual jabs? And this means both of us, doesn't it? It's not like I have to quit fighting with you, but you still get to fight with me, is it?"

Cade chuckled. "You always came out swinging with the best of them. We did have our good moments, though, didn't we?"

"Enough that I could probably count them on both hands."

"OK, I'm going to count that as a casual jab, but it came damned close to being a low blow," he warned her, smiling. "Which means you owe me."

"There's a penalty system connected to this truce? Do I need to have my lawyers go over the terms of the contract?" It was said with neither inflection nor expression.

"See, that's the thing. Most people would take what you said as a serious comment because you don't even crack a smile. But I know the sign, Belle."

"What sign?"

"The arched left eyebrow."

"I do not!" she said, feigning indignance.

"There it goes again, arching up, just for a split second. Subtle, but, oh, so readable."

"*OK, so maybe I underestimated the number of good moments we had together. Does that get me off the hook for the penalty?*"

"Eyebrow up again. And no. You're not off the hook."

"Try collecting," she challenged, shoving herself out of the chair and heading for the stairs.

This time it was Cade's turn to arch an eyebrow.

It wasn't the largest medical office, but it was modern—twenty years ago. Belle preferred to think of it as practical. She loved it, every last tongue depressor and cotton swab. She also loved the quaint little waiting room where non-communicable patients sat nearly knee to knee, and the ten-year-old TV was permanently on the rerun channel. On a positive note, Belle did make sure the magazine subscriptions were up-to-date, and the coffee in the coffee-pot was refreshed every hour. Oh, and tea for the tea-drinkers. A couple of her old-timer patients had suggested that a little additive to the tea and coffee would be nice, and she'd assumed whiskey. But she hadn't dignified the hints with a response, and truly hoped her predecessor hadn't indulged in the practice.

Today was a busy day, and her receptionist, Ellen Anderson, another employee inherited along with the practice, was nearly frantic answering the phone, serving drinks, and sorting through patient charts for insurance billing information. In Big Badger, it seemed like people required medical attention in droves. One day they trickled in, the next day they flocked. She couldn't figure it out, and those she asked were pretty noncommittal on the subject. So this was a droves day, and Belle was ushering them in and out as fast as she could, given the nature of the various complaints.

"So, Mr. Biddle, you've had gout before?"

"Expect I did, Doctor. Some time last year, late in the spring, if I recall."

"And did Dr. Nelson give you any specific instructions on how to take care of yourself?" Emmett Biddle's gout was limited to his left big toe. "Diet, how much to drink, that sort of thing?"

"He did mention drinking water, I believe."

Polite man, age seventy-nine. Sharp. Still a cowboy. In fact, he'd ridden in on his horse today. Tied it to the hitching post, which happened to come along with the medical office. *Impractical, she'd thought at first, but* Emmett Biddle wasn't the first one to saddle up and come to an appointment on horseback. "And restrict or cut out your alcohol consumption?"

"Don't recall that, ma'am."

The twinkle in his eyes suggested otherwise. "Well, here's what I'd like you to do. Drink eight to sixteen cups of fluid each day—half that has to be water, and the other half cannot be alcohol. In fact, avoid alcohol. Or limit it to one small drink a day if you have to have it. Eat a moderate amount of protein, preferably from healthy sources, such as low-fat or fat-free dairy—" She would have said "tofu" next, but there was no way Emmett Biddle was a tofu-eating kind of a man, so she skipped that. "Eggs and peanut butter are good, too. Also, limit your daily intake of meat, fish, and poultry to no more than six ounces."

"Six ounces is only one big bite of steak, ma'am. What am I going to survive on if I can't have my steak?"

"You can have it, just not as much."

"Sissy portions," Emmett grumbled as he slid off the table and picked up his cowboy boot, then bent down to tug it on. "Not fitting for a man to eat sissy portions."

"You should probably try soft shoes, too, like a pair of athletic shoes." Sandals worked, too, but she didn't see Emmett in sandals. Texas men don't wear sissy shoes, he'd probably tell her. "And here's a prescription for an anti-inflammatory. Follow the directions on the bottle—one pill a day, with food." But not steak, she wanted to say.

"It'll help with the pain? 'Cause it's getting so I can barely walk. And getting up on my horse is kind of hard nowadays, too."

"It will help, but if you don't follow my advice, you're going to keep on having trouble. And it could get worse." She scribbled something in the chart, then opened the exam-room door. "I want to see you back here in two weeks. I'll have another prescription for something you can take long term to help prevent the flare-ups. But nutrition, Mr. Biddle, plays an important part in controlling your gout."

"My nutrition is fine, young lady. It's kept me healthy seventy-nine years, with an occasional cold, and I'm not changing it for a toe ache."

She hadn't thought he would. Didn't really blame him either. At his age Emmett deserved to do what he wanted. "Two weeks, Mr. Biddle. Don't forget to make an appointment."

She wasn't sure what kind of noise he made on his way out, something between a grunt and a snort, but with a very clear message that she probably wouldn't be seeing Emmett Biddle, once the medication worked, until his next flare-up.

"Gout?" Cade questioned. He was standing in the doorway to her private office, taking up most of the space within it.

An imposing figure of a man, Belle thought as she stopped short of squeezing by him. "Patient confidentiality," she responded. "What do you want, Cade?"

He shrugged. "Just passing time until Michael's out of school. Thought I'd stop by and see if you needed any help."

"As in helping as a doctor?" Judging by his eyes, he seemed sincere enough. But Cade came within a hair's breadth of loathing general practice. At least, he used to. "Is that what you're offering?" she asked, not sure what to expect.

"If you need it. No pressure, though, Belle. I know this is your practice, and I'm sure you run it the way *you see fit, but if you need help while I'm here*—sure. I can do that when I'm not with Michael."

That was a surprise. Cade seemed almost humble. Something new, in her experience. Admittedly, part of the initial Cade Carter charm had been his cockiness. She'd been attracted. But life had changed, their situations had changed, and his old cockiness didn't work for her the way it once had. After she'd had Michael, she'd needed mellow and supportive. Almost what she was seeing now in Cade. "Well, I'm pretty busy most of the time. Between my practice and taking care of a number of ranches—house calls—it keeps me moving. But can you handle what you used to call mundane work, like gout?"

"Then it *was* gout. I thought so, by the way he limped."

"That diagnosis coming from a surgeon?"

"We surgeons do come into contact with other medical problems from time to time."

"And you surgeons, according to the surgeon I used to be married to, don't particularly care to deal with anything non-surgical." She took a step closer, taking care not to get too close. "So can you really handle this, Cade? Because I could use help. But I don't want it to become an issue between us, since we already have enough of those going on."

"How about split the work? You get more time with Michael, I still get my time with Michael. We all win. It's not an issue, Belle."

"Do you have cowboy boots with you?" He'd had them back in Chicago. He'd always joked something about taking the cowboy out of Texas but not taking Texas out of the cowboy. Suddenly she could picture *those boots* paired with some nice tight jeans and a T-shirt that hugged his abs. Rugged. All man. Probably not the way she should be thinking about her ex, though. Still…

"I never come to Texas without them."

She smiled. "Well, go and put them on and I'll put you to work."

"The cowboy look. Is that for you, or for—?"

"For image, Cade. That's all. Just for the image. Now move. I need to get into my office."

With that, he tipped his imaginary hat, then stepped aside. "I don't suppose you've ever given in to the boots, have you?"

Instead of answering, Belle simply shook her head.

"When you get back, I'll have three patients for you. Then we're going to take a ride out to Ruda del Monte. We've got about a dozen hands there, with a few assorted other employees, and I have a contract to do physical exams on all of them. Thought maybe now that I have help, we could get started this afternoon." She smiled. "You still up for it, Cade?"

"See you in twenty minutes, Belle," he said, then spun around and swaggered away.

She couldn't help watching that swagger until it turned the corner and disappeared. So, what was she doing, letting Cade work with her? It was crazy. She had huge misgivings. But she also had a modest case of tingles. And that's what worried her the most. Especially as, for the past five years, she'd been under the impression she was impervious.

"What a nice young man, that Doc Cade is," Mrs. Kitty Peabody commented as she stepped into the hall, preparing to leave the office. "I'm glad someone's come to work with you. You needed the help. So is he your boss, dear?" she asked, blinking innocently as she looked up at Belle.

Belle bit the inside of her lips, trying hard to plaster some facsimile of a smile to her face. "No, he's not my boss. He's my—" No need to air the dirty family laundry. "He's my temp. He's in town on business for the next few weeks, and he needed a place to work, so I took him in."

"That's a casual jab, if ever I've heard one," Cade whispered in Belle's ear as he stepped up behind her. He turned to Mrs. Peabody. "We were married to each other, years ago. She had a hard time getting over me."

"Definitely a low blow," Belle said, out of the corner of her mouth.

"I can see why she would," Mrs. Peabody said to Cade. "If I were fifty years younger…"

Cade stepped forward and wrapped his arm around the woman's shoulder. "If you were fifty years younger, I'd be sitting on your front-porch swing right now—you do have a front-porch swing, don't you, Mrs. Peabody?"

The old woman raised her fingertips to her lips and giggled. "No, but if you want to come visit, I'll have my grandson hang one."

"You tell me when it's up, and I'll be the one to take the maiden swing." He shot a free and easy wink in Belle's direction as he escorted the woman to the reception area, while Belle stood there, staring, amazed.

"Who are you?" she asked a minute later when Cade came ambling back down the hallway. "And what did you do with Cade Michael Carter?"

"I'm simply a doctor who's trying to get along with his partner."

"Except I'm not your partner, Cade."

"That's right. I'm your temp, the one who showed up on your doorstep, begging for work."

Said with the biggest, brightest grin she'd seen since she'd, well, divorced him. "You're different," she commented, moving past him, on her way into the exam room to look after three-year-old Bonnie Thompson, a little girl who was prone to getting hives.

"In a good way?" he asked.

"Guess time will tell," she said, grabbing Bonnie's chart from the rack on the door then stepping into the exam room. Once inside, it took her a full ten seconds to find her focus before she turned into a doctor again. "So, Mrs. Thompson, did you make that list of foods, soaps, and things Bonnie commonly comes in contact with, and when, then note the time of her outbreaks?"

The girl's mother shrugged. "That takes a lot of time, Doctor. I have three other children, and my husband is on the road half the time. I wanted to. Even bought a notebook, and started, but…"

She held the notebook out for Belle to see. First page, marked day one. No entry other than oatmeal, orange juice. Not much to go on. "Does Bonnie drink orange juice every day?" she asked, picking up the child's arm to look at the red welts popping up below her elbow.

"Yes. In the morning. She loves it!"

"Bonnie," Belle said, "will you pull up your shirt so I can look at your tummy?"

Bonnie obliged quickly, and Belle found exactly what she expected to find. More welts. The same with the child's back and bottom. Not severe, not infected. But definitely hives that seemed to come and go at will. "For now, keep her off orange juice. And I know I've asked you to switch detergents, but this time I want you to double-wash Bonnie's clothes separately, first in a detergent without fragrance or brighteners, then the second time in clear water."

"Did I mention that I have three other children to take care of?" the woman asked, almost irately.

"You did, and I sympathize. But unless you want Bonnie to keep itching, we're going to have to get aggressive about finding out what's causing her allergy."

"Dr. Nelson gave her pills," Mrs. Thompson replied.

"And I've prescribed medication as well. But she can't go on taking it forever. So I want to find the cause of the problem so we can avoid it altogether."

"What about some kind of test? Wouldn't that be better than guessing?"

Guessing often played a part in medical diagnosis but Mrs. Thompson didn't want to hear that. Of course, Belle hadn't wanted to hear guesses either when Michael had been undergoing his diagnosis. "The tests are expensive, Mrs. Thompson, and unless something has changed, you have no medical insurance. If you want to pay out of pocket, that's fine. I'll have Ellen schedule an appointment with an allergist. Or you can do it the way I've suggested, which may take a little longer but in most cases can give us the same diagnosis." In the meantime, she didn't have time to waste arguing with a mother who didn't want the inconvenience of a little extra effort. It angered Belle. Really, truly angered her. Because if there was such an easy, simple fix for Michael, she'd be all over it in a second. No questions, no resentments, no holding back. But hives and Asperger's were two entirely different things and, in most cases, hives could be cured.

"Why the scowl?" Cade asked, as he hung up his borrowed white coat.

Belle shrugged. "I guess I don't get it sometimes. One of my patients, a little girl with an unspecified allergy, is getting hives. She's not sick, they're not causing her any problems, and I'm keeping them under control with a couple of different meds. But her mother—"

"Let me guess. Not a mother-of-the-year candidate."

"She's a good mother, but she doesn't do enough. Seems put out when I give her suggestions. Wants an easier way out."

"In other words, not up to your mothering standards?"

"I'm not an über-mom, if that's what you're getting at." She handed her last patient chart to Ellen to file away, then picked up her medical bag, ready to hit the road. "But if there was something I could give to Michael to fix the problems he has, I'd move heaven and earth to give it a try."

"I know you would," Cade said, donning his cowboy hat then tipping the brim at Maudie, who practically melted when he followed it up with a wink. "But trust me. Not all mothers have that higher purpose. There are some mothers who weren't meant to be. One of nature's practical jokes, I think. But you're the kind of mother every child should have." Said in all sincerity. "The kind I wish…" His voice trailed off, and he ended the sentence with a sigh.

"Your flattery scares me, Cade," Belle said, wondering where that comment had come from. And that sigh, as well as the look in Cade's eyes when he'd made it—did she see sadness there?

"Then you're out of practice," Maudie quipped, breaking up the serious moment and clearly aligning with Cade as she scooted by on her way to the supply closet. "Because most people would be pleased with a compliment from someone like Dr. Carter."

"Cade, please," Cade said. "No need to stand on formalities here."

For the second time Maudie almost melted. Her normally steely eyes turned mushy, and her thin lips unfolded into a generous smile. In fact, she was so smitten with the man she was nearly batting her eyelashes at him. Quite unlike anything Belle had ever witnessed in her office nurse until Cade. Now she was concerned. More than that, she was suspicious. What in the world was Cade up to, ingratiating himself that way in a place he didn't need to ingratiate himself?

It made her wonder. Made her think. But at the end of it all she still didn't know. And that made her worry.

CHAPTER THREE

"How many miles do you travel, on average?" Cade asked, settling back into the passenger's seat of Belle's beat-up car. Old model, lots of dents and rust. It was a constant source of irritation to him since he'd been offering to buy her a new vehicle for the past two years. But she was as stubborn as she was pretty, and there was no budging on her refusal. She would buy another vehicle when she could afford to pay for it herself. And she was always quick to tell him that beat-up didn't mean it wasn't dependable. Well, in spite of her bullheaded refusal, he kept the option open to her, because of Michael.

"My farthest ranch is the Chachalaca, which is a hundred-mile round trip. Today we're only going out about twenty-five miles."

"Hope they pay you for the inconvenience," he said, tipping his black cowboy hat down over his eyes.

"I'm paid adequately, not that it's any of your business."

"Enough to get you better wheels? Because I'm still concerned about that, Belle. For you, for Michael, when he's with you. You need something better than this bucket of rust."

"This bucket of rust is fine. I had the mechanic check

it a couple weeks ago when I put on new tires, and he said other than the fact that it doesn't look good, it's OK. So don't try the emotional blackmail stunt by dragging Michael into this, because it's not going to work. There's nothing wrong with my car, and Michael's perfectly safe riding in it."

"Until it stalls out in the middle of nowhere and you've got to contend not only with a stalled car but with Michael's anxieties. And you know that's going *to happen, Belle. Maybe not this week, or even next* month, but eventually the car's going to die a gruesome death and I sure as hell don't want my son in it when it does."

"Your son? Did you forget that he's my son, too?"

"Actually, that's probably the thing I've been thinking about most lately. How he's your son, but he never quite makes it over to being my son." He didn't resent Belle, but he'd been spending too many sleepless nights lately, *trying to figure out what to do.* Pacing the floor. Standing, staring out the window, sometimes for an hour or more, lost in his thoughts. Going out for middle-of-the-night walks, hoping to exhaust himself. Making unnecessary night rounds on his surgical patients in the hospital simply to occupy time. Unfortunately, his efforts never got him any answers, and they didn't help him sleep. In fact, the harder he tried to find those answers, the more confused he became.

"It's not the way I want it, Cade. It's just the way it is—right now. But Michael will change. It takes time."

"I know that. But it's frustrating coming down here twice a month and seeing how everything is exactly the same as it was the last time I visited, and the time before that. Which means I simply have to accept the situation for what it is, or try harder. Or differently. And I know that. So I'll quit bugging you about your car when I quit worrying, which won't be until after you have better wheels under you. At least give me that much satisfaction."

She laughed. "You want satisfaction? OK, once a week. But that's all you're getting from me. You can bug me about my car once a week. And as far as Michael goes, I like the idea of trying differently. I do that, all the time. Every day, in fact. And sometimes I see these amazing advances, then sometimes I see—well, nothing. But Michael's very open to new things, even though he might not show it the way you'd expect. Also, it may take him a little longer to fit them into his normal routine, yet once he does, he can become very enthusiastic if it's something he enjoys. So maybe, instead of trying to fit yourself into his regular niche differently, you should think about creating one that's just for the two of you. You know, develop something new where Michael has to depend on you for guidance."

Turning the corner, they headed off the main highway down a dirt road where the next twenty miles of scenery could only be described as bare, with an occasional clump of sagebrush. He loved Texas, even with its sparse scenery. It had an honesty that made sense to him. Maybe that's why he loved it. Probably why he missed it, too. But he'd never considered coming back on a permanent basis. Too many painful memories to deal with. Too many unhappy things he didn't want to look back on in his life.

Yet Michael was here, so every other week, rain or shine, hell or high water, he packed an overnight bag, hopped a plane, and here is where he landed, regrets and all. Here as in Texas, not here as in sitting next to Belle—and a nice sitting it was, he did have to admit.

Somehow, over the years, he'd forgotten how absolutely wonderful she smelled, like flowers and sunshine. He missed that, actually. Missed a lot about her, and while they shared custody, the obligatory parental hand-off when he came to get Michael rarely involved her in any substantial way. Oh, she'd greet him at the door, be cordial—hardly ever let him into her house, though. And words between them were few and far between unless there was something to discuss about their son.

Other than that, he didn't know what was going on in her life. Did she have good friends in Big Badger? Or a serious relationship? Did she even date, or was she reclusive? Was she happy now?

Cade tried picturing her with someone other than him—maybe this Dr. Robinson she thought so highly of. Had the personal support this Dr. Robinson gave Belle turned into something more? He thought about it for a moment, wasn't sure how he felt about it. "So, what would your Dr. Robinson suggest I might try with Michael?" he asked, still trying to picture the guy, hoping to God that Robinson was grandfatherly and not someone with the abs Belle seemed to like.

"Honestly, I don't know. Maybe something not even remotely close to anything he does, or likes now."

"Maybe I should talk to him myself, see what he suggests."

"Who, Michael?"

"No. Dr. Robinson."

A strange smile crept to Belle's lips. "First thing, Dr. Robinson is a great advocate of making the discoveries yourself. The merit in that is the journey. And second thing, Dr. Robinson's first name is Amanda."

Cade smiled uncomfortably. OK, so maybe he had that one coming. Still, he did wonder about Belle's social life. Especially certain aspects of it. After all, any man connected to Belle would be connected to his son, so that made it his right to know. At least, that's what he was telling himself and, halfway, trying to believe. "So, what kind of new interest do you think Michael might enjoy? Something athletic? I've never had the impression he likes sports very much." Not the best recovery from his almost-gaffe, but the only one he could come up with. Had Belle seen through what might have looked like a little bit of jealousy? Even though that's not what he'd really intended, that little smile on her lips caused him to blush.

"Did you just want to come right out and ask me?"

"What?" he asked, even though he knew exactly what.

"If I'm involved with anybody."

"If it affects Michael, I'd have the right to know."

"Maybe you would, maybe you wouldn't." Her smile broadened. "But I suppose you'll never know if you don't ask the question."

"What if I just said that I trust you to make the right decisions about the people you bring into Michael's life?"

"Not good enough, Cade. You're dying to ask. Admit it."

"I'm curious, yes."

"Curious enough to just ask me if I'm involved?"

"Are you?"

"See. That wasn't so bad, was it?"

"It won't be once you tell me, so we can end this conversation." She was enjoying this, enjoying seeing him squirm. Being pretty bold about it, too. Part of that straightforwardness he usually liked but was finding a little vexing at the moment.

"OK, no. Nobody. Not involved. No time. Not even sure there's anyone in Big Badger who would be my type."

"And your type would be…?"

"You were, once. Don't know any more. So anyway," she continued without missing a beat, "Michael likes soccer. Plays on the junior league at school. Started off as a midfielder, then they moved him to goalie because he has incredible focus on the ball—never loses sight of it. Oh, and he likes horseback riding, too, when I have the time to take him…which isn't often enough. And hiking. One of his favorite things in the world is hiking out into the wilderness and just—well, I guess the best way to describe it is observe the things around him. Michael has this uncanny eye for spotting things nobody else would even notice."

Well, now he knew about her relationship status. Wasn't sure how he felt about it one way or another, but at least he knew. "I knew someone like that once. He could sit and watch a bug for hours. Or the movement of leaves in the wind. The smallest details fascinated him. There was this one time when he was watching this cloud formation…" He stopped, swallowed hard, regrouped. "Why haven't you told me any of these things about my—our—son?"

"You never asked. Since you are now, I think your visits with him have gotten into a bit of a routine—go get pizza, get ice cream, go see a movie, play video games. And I'm not faulting you for that, Cade. But don't blame me for you not getting to know what your son likes. All you had to do was ask me, or ask Michael. He might not tell you the first time, or even the tenth time, but eventually he would tell you. For that matter, have you ever asked him what he wants to do when you visit? He will have opinions, but he's not going to come right out and say them."

Cade exhaled a deep breath. She was right, of course, every single, frustrating, insightful word she said. Which pointed out how miserably he failed at the thing that meant the most to him—being a dad. Well, he had six weeks to work on it, six weeks to change things or, at least, make the situation better. And six weeks where pizza, ice cream, movies and video games weren't going to be enough. "I think I have an idea," he said. "Not sure it would work, but—"

"Sometimes, Cade," Belle interrupted, "it's not so much about what you do with him as it is the fact that you're with him. That's what's important, and I think Michael would probably enjoy quality time over all your trivial pursuits. And I'm not faulting you for those. I know it's tough being a part-time parent."

Suddenly, his anger flared. His back went rigid. He tipped his hat off his face for a direct confrontation. "I'm never a part-time parent, Belle. When you still lived in Chicago, I bought a condo one block from your apartment to make sure I could see Michael, and stay involved with him as much as possible. But you're the one who took my son and moved over a thousand miles away. You're the one who took away my involvement, who limited me. But that doesn't make me a part-time parent, because I'm his father twenty-four hours a day. The father, by the way, who was never told that his son was a hell of a soccer goalie."

"When was the last time you asked me what Michael was involved in, Cade? You come here, spend your weekends trying to do your best with him, and I know you're angry because it doesn't always work out the way you want it to, or the way you think it should, but..." She shook her head fiercely. "Don't blame me for moving. I have a life, too. Something that you never seemed to recognize when we were married—where my time was soon taken up with caring for a house, a husband, and a baby. I had to let opportunities pass me by but then I got my shot, Cade, and it was here. I'm sorry you don't get enough time with Michael because of that, but that's the way it worked out. We live here now, this is our home, and Michael's adjusting. And if I forgot to mention that our son is one hell of a goalie, or that he's pretty good on the back of a horse, maybe it's because I'm the only doctor within a hundred miles, I'm on call every hour of every day of the week, I have custodial care of our son and manage to be a pretty involved mom, and I get by on four hours of sleep a night, if I'm lucky. And this isn't arguing, by the way. It's me expressing my point of view in an exasperated manner."

Damn, this wasn't the way he'd wanted it to go. What he'd thought he was getting into when he committed himself to spending the next six weeks here, well, he wasn't sure. Maybe as little as trying to make peace with Belle, again. All the way down here he kept telling himself it was for Michael's sake. But one look at her, and he knew it was for his sake as well. They shared a son. They shouldn't be fighting or expressing exasperated points of view. But put them together in the same room, the same car, even the same town, and that's what happened. They came out swinging. There were huge emotions involved. Yet he didn't believe there was any hatred mixed in there. Had never believed it. More like it was a breakdown of everything they'd once believed in. A flame had died out. "I know it's tough, and I'm sorry. And you're welcome to your exasperated point of view, but I'm entitled to mine as well. OK?"

"OK," she said, backing off the raging heat of the moment. "And I know I get a little defensive—mostly with you."

He chuckled. "We always did have a way with bringing out the worst in each other, didn't we?"

"And the best, sometimes."

"Sometimes…" Cade sighed, relaxing back into the seat. Sometimes had been pretty great, but it was difficult wading through the rest of it to find the good. "Not enough times, though. That was our problem, I think. The best was awesome, but we couldn't find it often enough. And I'm not blaming you, Belle. You tried, and I didn't."

"It takes two, Cade. Either way it goes, it takes two." She glanced over at him, simply studied him for a fraction of a second, then laughed. "But if you want to own most of the responsibility for our breakdown, that's OK with me."

She turned her attention back to the dirt road and the never-ending expanse of nothingness stretching out in front of them. But in that fraction of a second when she'd looked at him, he'd felt…there weren't any words to describe it, really, except she'd looked not into his soul but through it, and it shook him. Shook him badly. "OK with me, too," he conceded. But seriously. "For our son. Because I really want to make this work, Belle. We may not be married, but Michael needs consistency from us, together. You know. A united front."

"He needs us to be the adults, you mean?"

"The adults. And there was a time when those adults in question could actually stand to be in the same room together."

"I can stand being in the room with you, Cade. And that's not just about Michael."

He was surprised to hear that. So surprised, in fact, that he tilted his hat down, almost covering his whole face, and smiled the rest of the way to Ruda del Monte.

"So how many of these physicals do we have to do?" he asked, reaching into the back seat to grab a medical bag.

"Twenty. With the *E. coli* outbreak over at the Chachalaca, I've had several calls from other ranch managers who are worried about their hands. Ruda del Monte is actually the first ranch that's doing something about it pre-emptively, but I have an idea that within the week I'll have another five or six ranches join in. Especially if we see symptoms popping up anywhere else."

"This *E. coli*, it's spreading?" He slammed shut the car door and walked around to the driver's side, and waited there while Belle grabbed her medical bag and shrugged into her white coat—something he thought looked totally out of place, given the circumstances. But, then, so did her tan linen slacks, her blue silk blouse, and her string of pearls. Damn, if she didn't look good but, damn, if she didn't look out of place on a working ranch. His first instinct was that he was going to have to teach her the finer points of Texas style, but his second instinct reminded him she wasn't his to teach. Sometimes it was hard remembering those distinctions. "Any symptoms in town?"

"A few. The county health officials told me it was salad ingredients, and I took their word for it. Our grocery supplier here also supplies a number of the ranches, so that makes sense. But the thing is, the outbreak isn't widespread, so…"

"So you're wondering, what?" he asked, falling into step with her.

She shrugged. "Why is it contained when everybody's eating from the same source? Shouldn't there be more people sick? Anyway, the county health department is testing for it, which means for now the only thing we can do is treat the people when they're sick. So far, we've been lucky. All the symptoms I've seen have been mild."

He thought about it for a moment. As a surgeon, this was totally out of his league, but he did recall outbreaks known to have been caused by broccoli, lettuce, bean sprouts. So the salad theory made sense. Except Belle wasn't convinced, and if there was one thing about Belle he knew beyond a doubt, she was one hell of a doctor. More than that, she had the finest instinct he'd ever seen in medicine. So if she didn't believe it was the salad, neither did he. "Then the physicals are just cursory?"

She nodded. "Maybe. I have an idea there may be more to it since there was some urgency to the call. But the foreman denied anything was wrong with any of his hands, so until I know differently I'm going to have to take him at his word. Right now, I'm going to take a basic look, ask some questions." Smiling, "Earn my monthly retainer."

"Oh, I guess I didn't realize you're getting into concierge medicine out here." Payment meant to keep a doctor on retainer, much like many corporations paid to keep their lawyers on retainer, whether or not they used their professional services.

"I guess you could call it that. I prefer to think of it as the smartest way to recruit a good doctor. And before you ask, all the ranches have me on retainer. And they're honoring my terms, because I'm saving to buy the medical practice from the town, to make it my own. The town bought it from Doc Nelson when he needed the money for his new life—a young wife and a beach condo can get pretty expensive, I hear. Anyway, the town's made it perfectly clear they don't want to be in the medicine business for long, so the practice is mine to buy back from the town if I want it. And I do, because I need permanent roots for Michael and me, a real home, and it's going to be in Big Badger. So my goal is to have the practice bought and paid for inside three years."

Cade shook his head, whistled a low whistle. "That's going to take some effort."

"You don't think I can do it?"

"Quite the opposite. But I guess I thought you'd get over it and eventually come back to Chicago."

"Get over what? My need to be independent?"

"Your need to stay as far away from me as possible."

Rather than getting angry, Belle laughed out loud. "You're really full of yourself, do you know that? My coming here has nothing to do with you and everything to do with me." She pointed in the direction of the side door. "And so you'll know, you were as insignificant to me in Chicago as you are to me here." Then, she smiled sweetly. "Getting more so every day."

"Remember those last few miserable months of marriage, when we were both consumed with trying to figure out what we were going to do?"

"Definitely miserable months."

He cocked an amused eyebrow. "You didn't have to agree so quickly."

"What's true is true, though."

He pondered that for a moment, shrugged, then grinned. "Anyway, I was trying hard to figure out what I ever saw in you in the first place."

"That's harsh."

"What's true is true, though," he mimicked. "And I finally remembered. You were incredible, Belle. Smart, funny, with a barbed tongue that could slit you open at a hundred paces..."

"I'll take that as a compliment," she said, bending slightly at the waist to bow to him. "Whether or not you meant it as one."

"Oh, I meant it to be a compliment. One of the things I loved most about you was your sharp wit. You always had an answer for everything, and God pity the person who crossed you, because your answers could get lethal. Sometimes I liked to stand back and watch you in action."

"When you say in action, I'm assuming you mean something to do with my sharp wit and my lethal answers." She met his stare directly, and challenged it head-on. "That's what you liked?"

Damn, she was sexy when she stared at him that way. Someone else might have found it intimidating, but he found it to be another of the things he missed about Belle. It was a growing list, one he was surprised he had in him. Close proximity, he decided. And maybe a little unfinished business between them. That's all it could be. "Did back then. Still do." Too bad they weren't able to stay focused on the good things, but those last months had turned into a nightmare. She had been justifiably angry, he had been unjustifiably defensive. Not some of his finest moments, and he didn't like thinking about that time in his life—their lives. So he jumped straight into safe territory. "Before we go in, how do we divide up our patients here? Or do we?"

"Well, if this place turns out to be like the Chachalaca, we won't have to worry about dividing anything. They'll flock to you. Probably trample everybody in their way getting out of my line to go and stand in yours."

"Yet you want to settle here?"

She shrugged. "They'll get used to me—in ten or twenty years." That last was said almost under her breath.

"Well, if you want to endear yourself, lose the pearls and the silk blouse. Buy yourself a good pair of boots, some nice, tight-fitting jeans and a T-shirt, maybe even a hat like mine." He tipped the brim up for her. "Try to fit in, not set yourself apart. It'll go a long way." OK, so he hadn't meant to get involved, but he couldn't help himself. It was Belle after all. And while she wasn't exactly in over her head, she was up to her neck and didn't even know it. Besides, it was only advice. In the truest Belle Carter fashion, she'd probably ignore it anyway.

"And you know this because…"

"Because I was born and raised in Texas. I'm one of them."

"Yet you married a woman who wore silk and pearls."

"Temporarily lost my way." Blinded by love for a little while. "But I got over it." Not as much as he'd thought, he was fast discovering.

"Want to know one of the things I miss most about you?" she asked, on her way to the door.

"What?"

She didn't answer. Instead, she opened the door, walked through, and shut it in his face.

"Well, damn!" he said, smiling.

"Anything unusual?" she asked Cade an hour later.

"Two with mild symptoms, like you suspected." He

handed her the notes he'd made. "And one with a problem of a personal nature."

"Personal nature."

He wiggled mischievous eyebrows at her. "Let's just
say that I prescribed him an enhancement medication,
and leave it at that."

"I did a thorough physical on every one of these
men a month ago, and nobody…" She stopped, nodded.
"Because I'm a woman first, then a doctor. At least, to
them."

"It's a man thing, so don't take it personally."

"If I had time, I might. But I've also got two with
symptoms, and another one who's laid up in the bunkhouse, not able to come down here to the ranch office.
He's telling the manager there's nothing wrong with him
as he bends over in knots with cramps. And to be honest
about this, I'm getting a little concerned. After I get the
test results back, I'm going to have maybe twenty confirmed cases of *E. coli* between the ranches and town,
and this has only been going on for four days."

"But the common denominator is still the salad fix-
ings. They had it for dinner a couple of days ago. I've
got the cook rounding up samples to send to the lab…
I'm assuming you'll want to send them to the lab. Or
am I overstepping my bounds as a doctor?"

She smiled. "As a surgeon, you're brilliant. As a diag-
nostician and purveyor of sexual enhancement drugs,
you're pretty good, too. And, yes, send it to the lab. I'm
sending everything I can get my hands on right now.
Oh, and look, Cade, for what it's worth, I'm glad you're
here. We had our bad times, but I've always thought you
were the best doctor I've ever seen."

"Except for you. That's what you're thinking, isn't it?"

She wrinkled her nose at him. "Of course that's what

I'm thinking. Anyway, I'm on my way to the bunkhouse to see what we've got there."

"With the serious cramps, think *E.coli* could have resulted in hemolytic uremic syndrome?" A condition resulting from the abnormal destruction of red blood cells, known to clog the filtering system in the kidneys, which could lead to kidney failure, even death.

"Depends on a lot of factors. Especially his overall health. I'd given that some thought, but normally you don't see that kind of complication for eight to ten days after onset. You could be on to something, though. Maybe he got into the contaminant before the others did, or he has some kind of underlying condition that brought it on sooner." She picked up her pace on the way to the bunkhouse, pleased to see that Cade was going with her. Not that she couldn't handle this on her own, because she could. And she intended to, maybe even for the rest of her medical career. Still, he was nice to have around, even temporarily, and he did give her a little boost of confidence, which she'd never, ever let him know. "Don't know what we're looking for, but all my patient notes for everyone on the ranch are available right here." She held up her electronic pad.

"I'm impressed."

"Actually, so am I. It was Michael's suggestion. First day in the office, he looked at the old file system, hit a few computer keys and saw what we had available there, and told me I had to update if I wanted to be efficient. 'Mom, you've got to understand that good medicine is about the technology, too.'"

"That's what my son said?" he said, his voice full of pride.

"That's what our son said. So I hired a tech to come

make changes. Michael wanted to do them himself, by the way."

"You didn't let him?"

"He's seven. He may have the capability, but he needs to be seven, not an adult. Anyway, going electronic is a slow, ongoing process. But that's changing, and I now have, as they say, connectivity. So I'm uploading all my ranch files first." She pointed up to the sky. "My own link to a satellite that links to my computer that links to my patient files, or something like that."

"Amazing kid."

No arguments there. Michael was amazing, and it was time for his parents to be a little more amazing as well. "So, Mr. Ralston, can you tell me how you're feeling?" she asked. Even before she was all the way across the room to Dean Ralston's bedside, she knew the answer to her question. He was confused. It registered in his eyes. And he was pale. There were also small bruises around his nose and mouth. Face and hands swollen. All bad signs.

Without a word, she looked at Cade, who was already pulling out his cellphone. "Who do I call?" he whispered.

"We dispatch out of Laredo, which is a long way away. Why don't I do that while you take his vital signs? And I'll also go get an IV set up."

Within minutes she had a rescue helicopter on its way, but its estimated time of arrival was something close to an hour, which didn't make her happy.

"Blood pressure's critical," Cade whispered when she came back to the bedside. "And unless I'm mistaken, I think he's had a stroke."

"Then you were right about the hemolytic uremic syndrome. It shouldn't have happened so soon, but it did."

"This man's an alcoholic, Belle." He opened the bottom compartment to Dean Ralston's bedside stand, to reveal a dozen or more mostly empty bottles of alcohol. "That's his underlying medical condition, and probably the reason this hit him so hard, so fast."

"The things we do to ourselves," she said, as she tried locating a good vein for an IV needle. Turned out that wasn't so easy. His veins were shot, she couldn't find a suitable site anywhere. "I think I'm going to have to go with a subclavian," she finally said. "Not my favorite thing to do."

"How about I go find something to jack up the end of the bed for you?" A measure to prevent the possibility of an air embolism.

"While you're at it, ask the foreman if Mr. Ralston has anybody we should notify." She would have asked her patient, but he wasn't responsive at all. His eyes fluttered open, more a nerve twitch than anything else. For all intents and purposes, Dean Ralston was well on his way to slipping into a coma. And they'd told her it was stomach cramps! Well, they were wrong, and their aversion to calling a female doctor until it was almost too late for this poor man was going to be costly. "Mr. Ralston," she said, her voice deliberately loud, "I need to get an IV line in you. It's going to be up near your collarbone. We're also going to take you to the hospital in a few minutes. I believe you're having complications from some kind of food poisoning." Mild understatement. This man was critically ill and, given her limitations out here, she wasn't sure of his prognosis. Which now turned a mild *E. coli* outbreak into a serious one.

The next few minutes went textbook perfect. Cade, with the assistance of a couple of ranch hands, put the foot end of the bed up on bricks, while Belle placed a rolled towel between Ralston's shoulder blades to make his clavicles more prominent. Cade located the obvious landmarks for the IV insertion, while Belle anesthetized the area and swabbed it down with antiseptic. Then Cade inserted the IV line with the swift skill of a surgeon, while Belle attached the line to the bag. Cade readied a sterile dressing for the site, while Belle taped it into place. A perfect medical union, to anybody who cared to look. And all of it done without a spoken word between them, like they'd been working together as a cohesive team for years when, in fact, this was their very first time.

Thinking about how good they were together, good naturally, made her shiver. That's what concerned her when they readied their patient for transport to the hospital. It's what still concerned her when the helicopter lifted off. And concerned her even more an hour later, when she dropped Cade off at his boarding house. How could they be so perfectly in sync in a medical situation, but totally out of sync with everything else?

It didn't make sense. In all honesty, though, she didn't want it to. Cade needed to be an afterthought in her life. She'd finally put him in that place, and she wanted him to stay there. Problem was, that wasn't happening. In fact, if anything, this situation with him seemed to be going in the opposite direction.

"Not good," she was muttering two hours later, preparing grilled cheese sandwiches for the three of them as Cade had stopped by to visit with Michael.

"What's not good?" Cade asked, stepping up behind her. Dangerously close.

"The way I think I'm going to burn your sandwich."

"Burned by Belle Carter, could be interesting," he

said, now pressed so close she could smell every drop of his potency.

She spun around to face him, and found herself caught in an impossible position—step forward into him, or backwards into the stove. Either way, she was the one who was about to get burned. Rather than allowing that to happen, Belle raised the spatula, shoved it at his chest, then sidestepped him. "Burned by Cade Carter, been there, done that." With that she walked with all the composure she could muster until she got up the stairs to her bedroom, where she locked the door behind her and gave way to wobbly knees that barely managed to carry her across the room to her bed. Then, for the next ten minutes, she stared at the ceiling, too scared to think or breathe properly. Most of all, too scared to admit to herself that one step more and burned sandwiches would have been the least of her problems. The very least.

CHAPTER FOUR

"ONE night. That's all I'm asking for. Just one night to go camping with Michael, and it's not even going to be very far from here, Belle. Close enough that I can have him home in twenty minutes, if I have to."

"I guess my biggest concern is that he's never been camping." And she wasn't sure now was a good time to start. It took time to get Michael ready for new experiences, and while camping was something he might enjoy, at least she hoped he would, it was also something they shouldn't just spring on him. "Spontaneity isn't exactly part of Michael's comfort zone, Cade, and I haven't had time to, well, get him ready for camping. You know, like a trial run. Take him out into the wilderness for a couple hours, maybe two or three times, so he can get used to his surroundings. Spend a night in a tent in the back yard. He's very adaptable, and eager to learn new things, and also get involved in activities he's never done before, but at his own pace. You know, taking it deliberately." People singled that out as a characteristic of Asperger's, but she often wondered if it wouldn't be better if everybody slowed down a bit, and took life a little more deliberately. There was a time it had been called caution. Now it appeared on a list of traits used to identify a condition.

"One night is preparation. I'd like to take him out for a two- or three-day stretch at some point. Maybe even longer if he likes it. His choice, of course. But since *you're so worried about doing it tonight, you could al*ways come with us, if that would ease your mind."

Going camping with Cade and Michael? Maybe she was the one who needed the preparation time, because the thought of it made her uncomfortable. No, actually, it scared her to death. Spending a night in that kind of cozy proximity to Cade was a big part of that fear, owing to the way she'd felt all through their grilled cheese sandwiches the night before, as well as the fact that she'd never been camping in her life. Never slept outside, not even pretend camping in the back yard when she'd been a little girl. Then there was Michael's reaction, and who knew what that was going to be? OK, all of it gave her cause for worry, she'd admit it. But the thing that unsettled her the most was wondering why, after all these years, Cade was causing these strange feelings in her. It defied any explanation she could come up with. "How? I can't simply walk away from my practice. I'm the only—"

He held out his hand to stop her. "You have connectivity, remember? And like I said, we're not going far. Just out to the Ruda del Monte. There's an amazing area out in the back acreage and the owner, Jake Gibbons—who's a real nice guy—appreciates the way you take care of his ranch hands. Anyway, Jake gave me permission to use it any time I want."

"Just like that, he gave you permission?" How did Cade charm everybody in his path? Jake Gibbons was a grouch. An unadulterated, dyed-in-the-wool grouch, who had flat-out told her he didn't like the idea of a woman doctoring his men. Yet Cade had called him a real nice guy.

"Yep. Open-ended permission, and he said if I need supplies, to stop by and ask his foreman. So we're set for about everything a camper could want. And if any emergencies come up, you can come right back to town," he continued. "Besides that, I gave Maudie a set of walkie-talkies, just for more connectivity." He shrugged. "She's already agreed to take the call for anything minor that comes in."

"First Jake Gibbons, then you sweet-talked my nurse?" The charmed-by-Cade list was growing. Sure, he'd amazed her with that charm all those years ago when they'd met, and if she was still amazed by its effect, which she wasn't admitting to, she might be a little miffed that he succeeded where she, well—she wouldn't call it failed so much as stalled.

"She's a pushover."

"Because you flirted with her."

He grinned. Tilted his hat back and arched wickedly sexy eyebrows at her. "Because I asked her. And smiled when I did it. She told me you never smile, Belle. So I suggested that you might come back smiling after a night of camping with your son. It could go a long way in your relationship with…everybody." He shrugged. "And Maudie sure seemed supportive to me. Very nice, too."

OK, so she was a little miffed. Why deny it? After trying for two months to fit in here, without success, Cade had waltzed right in and done it immediately. One smile, one smooth word, and everybody loved him. While her they merely tolerated. The thing was, Belle was more than miffed, she was envious. Having that kind of rapport with people, she couldn't even imagine what it would be like. Dr. Cade Carter, he's the nice one. And Dr. Belle Carter, she's the serious one. Search a list of synonyms for serious and you got grave, persevering, severe, somber, even unplayful. Unplayful! She'd actually heard people say these things about her, though. And not just once or twice. "Well, supportive or not, we can't go camping, Cade. Don't you understand? Michael and I don't get to do things on the spur of the moment like other people do."

"But have you tried lately? He's growing up, Belle. His interests are changing, he's taking on new challenges. You have to allow him room for all that growth or at least give him the opportunity to see how it works. Then let him succeed or fail on his own, without you trying to shelter him from everything."

"I do allow him room. It's just that…" She exhaled a frustrated breath. Cade's view of the world was always rosy, always give it a try and it will work out, while she was practical or pragmatic. That was probably the biggest difference between them, the one that had rendered the final split. There were times when she'd have loved living in Cade's world, sharing his rose-colored glasses, believing that things would work out simply because you wanted them to, but reality always superseded. Yet who was she to deny Cade his tinted outlook, or Michael his opportunity to prove her wrong on so many levels? So it was off to camp with the two of them and, for Michael's sake, even for Cade's, she hoped this camp-out succeeded.

More than that, she wanted it to be fun for them. Michael deserved that with his father, and while she didn't care so much about what Cade deserved, there was still a part of her that believed he deserved that with his son. "OK, I'll ask him. But you'll have to abide by his decision. That's the best I can do."

"Then I'm going to ask you again. Come with us, Belle. The three of us, camping together. Maybe we're not the family we used to be, but we can make it work for one night. Otherwise you're going to be miserable, wondering what's happening. You'll stay up all night, pacing the floor." He winked. "Probably come sneaking out to the camp at three in the morning to make sure everything's fine. Then pace some more when you get home. So why not skip all the intermediary steps, pack an overnight bag, and come with us? It's already arranged."

Yes, it was arranged. But she didn't always trust Cade's arrangements. That suspicion sprang from years of his arrangements when they'd been married. *I'll only be gone a week. I'll call you every day. I promise I'll stay home for a while.* Yes, she was aware of his arrangements, and they didn't always work out. In fact, they didn't work out most of the time. "Then what I'm assuming is that you want me there so you can prove me wrong, and I can see it firsthand."

"You are wrong," he said, his voice so gentle it was barely more than a whisper. "But not about the things you think I think."

His voice, the way it was so quiet, so seductive, gave her goose-bumps. Always did. She rubbed her arms, trying to get rid of the chill, hoping he didn't notice. "You, um…you don't get to make assumptions, Cade." She was fighting to stay focused on the camping trip, not on the way Cade could still affect her simply by the way he spoke. "That's what killed us in the first place. You assumed everything would work out, then left me there alone to make it happen while you went off and did whatever you wanted. And you took me for granted, almost every day of our married life, because there were things that needed to be fixed, things I couldn't fix alone, that you assumed I would, or could." OK, now she was back in the moment. Past Cade's effect and on to the issues at hand. Belle drew in a ragged breath, fighting not to get angry. There had been enough of that in the past, and she was a different person now. She hoped Cade was, too, but she didn't really know yet. "Look, I know you love Michael, and I know that relationship is difficult for you. But you're here to work it out with your son, not with your ex-wife. So spare me the assumptions and we'll get along fine. And while you're at it, don't make plans for me again, then proceed to the arrangements and assume I'll be fine with it. I'm not. Not on any level."

"You've changed," he said.

"I had to, if I wanted to survive. It's what you caused." And in many ways she was grateful, because she was better for it. But getting to this point had been so hard.

"Well, I don't know how to respond to that."

"You don't have to. I'm living the life I want, I'm happy. That it came about as a result of our divorce is unfortunate, because it would have been nice having the things I wanted inside our marriage. But none of that matters now. You're here because of Michael, and that's all there is between us—our son. Nothing else, Cade. Nothing else." But was that really true? Last week she'd have said an unequivocal yes. Today she wondered.

"Well, since this is about our son, I think he'd probably like to have his mother go camping with him. And that's not an assumption. Just a guess."

"But the question is, would his mother like to go camping?"

"I'll take care of you, Belle, if that's what you're worried about."

"Even though you know I'm not the outdoors type?"

"Because I know you're not the outdoors type."

It could work. She didn't take Friday afternoon office calls, all of her ranch work was caught up, paperwork was completed. And she was available for emergencies certainly. Still, she cleared Friday afternoons to spend with Michael—a trip to the park, or the library, or maybe the movies. What they did was always Michael's choice, and that was as spontaneous as their lives ever got. So camping?

"Look, Belle. For what it's worth, and not to make you angry, but you're the one who seems to have a problem with spontaneity, so why don't you simply ask him if he wants to go camping, like you said you would, and go from there? One step at a time. And if this is about you and me camping together, I'll respect the distance, keep to my side of the line, whatever you want. For Michael."

He was trying. She couldn't fault Cade there. He was being everything he should be. "Fine, I'll talk to him on the way home from school, and see what he wants to do. Then I'll decide what I want to do after that."

"How about we talk to him?"

Another thing to worry about, since Michael wasn't quite responsive to Cade. But Cade was insistent, it was also his right as Michael's father, so she agreed. Reluctantly, though. And thirty minutes later Cade and Belle stood outside the main entrance to Big Badger Elementary, waiting for their son to come out, while inside, Michael looked out the window at the two of them huddled together, talking, and smiled a smile they didn't see.

"So that's what I'd like to do this afternoon and tonight," Cade said to Michael, who was fidgeting with his backpack while Belle paced in circles around the picnic table on the school playground. "I used to camp when I was a kid. Haven't done it in a long time, but I think we can have fun. So do you want to go?" Thus far, Michael hadn't done so much as glance at him, and Cade truly didn't know if he was even listening. "You know, give it a try, see if you like it?" Then when Michael responded with a single nod of his head, Cade wasn't sure what to make of it. "Is that a yes?"

Michael nodded again. "Yes, that's a yes."

Belle stopped dead in her tracks and stared at Cade, who stared right back at her. "And you don't mind if I come along, too?" she asked.

"I don't mind," Michael said, quite seriously. "But if you're afraid of tarantulas, recluse spiders, black widows, and scorpions, you'll have to sleep in the car."

Cade paused for a moment, the look on his face completely unreadable, then suddenly he burst out laughing. "She's afraid of common houseflies, too," he said.

"I know," Michael replied. "And grasshoppers, and bees, and moths."

"I am not afraid of moths!" Belle chimed in.

"Then why do you always scream when you see one?" Michael countered, chancing a quick, mischievous look at her to gauge her reaction.

"I don't scream. I just—well, sometimes I gasp if I'm startled."

"Scream," he contradicted. "Not gasp. And if we build a fire when we're camping, it will attract moths. Then you'll scream."

Michael was teasing Belle. Cade saw it, and was surprised as it was a side of his son he hadn't known existed. And the whole bug thing…that nearly brought a lump to his throat, thinking back to those summer days with his little brother. Days he wished to God he could get back and do better. "I'd like to build a fire, and cook our dinner over it. And, Belle…" He looked directly at her, and winked. "You're welcome to sit with Michael and me near the fire, but you've got to control yourself."

"Control myself?" she asked, playing along.

"Control yourself, Mom," Michael answered in place of Cade. "Moths won't hurt you. Although studies show that they're not bothered by high-pitched sounds, so if you have to scream, it won't hurt their hearing."

"How do you know that, Michael?" she asked, utterly surprised.

He shrugged, completely indifferent to her reaction. "I read it somewhere."

She looked at Cade again. "And it stayed with him."

"Because I like bugs, Mom. You know that!"

Another lump came to Cade's throat, caused by even more painful memories from some other time. "Do you know what entomology is?" Cade asked, struggling to recover.

Michael looked perplexed for a moment, then shook his head.

"Entomology is the study of insects. An entomologist is a specialist who makes his or her career out of studying insects." His son liked bugs and that made him pretty typical of most boys his age. It also made him so much like Robbie, Cade didn't know how to deal with it. "What's your favorite insect?" he asked, his voice shaky.

Michael scrunched his face into a frown for a second, thinking. Then his eyes lit up, and he smiled. "Moths!"

"I think your two are ganging up on me," Belle said, her attention totally focused on Cade.

"Maybe because you deserve it, Belle," Cade responded. He'd caught her stare, saw the question in her eyes. Felt the guilt over it. But what was done was done. Leaving Belle out of something important in his life all those years ago was something else he couldn't take back or undo.

"Yeah," Michael echoed. "Because you deserve it."

And just like that Cade's bond with Michael started to form. All these years, and all it took was a moth. It choked him up, actually. So much so he had to turn away to blink back the tears for Michael, tears for Robbie. Tears for himself and what he'd lost.

She hadn't seen much of Texas, yet. There weren't enough hours in her day to do everything she wanted. Hardly enough to do what she had to do, and if she had extra time, sightseeing certainly was not at the top of Belle's list of priorities. But this was a pleasant place to camp, she did have to admit, and, thankfully, close enough for her connectivity, so she didn't feel completely guilty, or nervous.

Cade had chosen a little patch of land on the back half of a ranch that surely looked desolate, compared to the front half, something totally removed from the structure of civilization, but not so much that she felt isolated and not at all what she'd expected. Barren was what came to mind first, when she thought about Texas

in general. Wide open spaces, naked land, nothing green
unless she carted along a tossed salad. Yet this—it was
breathtaking. A lush, rocky little area, with lots of trees
and grass, and a pristine stream running through the
middle of it. And the sky…oh, my gosh, the sky. It was
an eternal azure blue, so pretty all she wanted to do was
lie down and look up at it, for hours, or days.

No, this was definitely not the Texas she'd thought
she'd be getting on this little outing. In fact, this place
Cade had picked out was so nice, she daydreamed of a
house here. Maybe a sprawling ranch-style up on the
rise overlooking this perfect little valley. Something
high enough to get the full view of the area yet secluded
enough so as not to be seen from any of the dirt roads
or vantage points nearby.

For now, that was all wishful thinking. She was
barely scraping by, paying rent on the two-bedroom
Southwestern bungalow sitting adjacent to her office,
running her medical practice, squirreling away every
spare penny to buy it. Still, she could hope for more.
Hope for her ranch-style home on a scenic bluff someday. Somewhere sumptuous, like this. "Guess I didn't
expect anything so beautiful," she said, dropping her
just-bought pup tent on the ground, then falling to her
knees next to it. "Except for a couple of the major cities,
and Big Badger, I haven't really seen much of Texas."

"It's a beautiful state, Belle. People get the wrong
impression all the time, but we have scenery here that's
as pretty as anything you'll find anywhere else in the
world."

She smiled, tickled by his response to her naivety.
More than that, amazed by the feelings of home that
still ran deep in him. She'd never seen that side of him
before. "Watch it, Cade. You're beginning to sound like

you could live here again. You know, big-city doctor re-
turns to his country roots." She wasn't sure Cade could
actually do that, though. He loved his conveniences and
out here they were few and far between. "Not that you'd
ever do that, would you?" she asked.

But he didn't answer. Instead, he simply stared off
into the wide open spaces. Stared so long it made her
uncomfortable. "You wouldn't actually—" she began,
but he cut her off.

"You never know," he said.

Cade, back in Texas? That was something she
wouldn't have anticipated. "You're not thinking about
it, are you?"

He turned to face her. "What I'm thinking about are
the pup tents, and getting them pitched before dark."

Something was definitely going on with him.
Something she didn't know, or understand. Was it the
real reason for his spur-of-the-moment decision to take
a leave of absence from his practice and come here? The
real reason for some of the changes, or differences, she
was seeing in him? "Starting a fire would be good, too,
since I'd like to fix something to eat before it gets dark."

"Can I cook the hot dogs?" Michael asked, suddenly
animated, as the cricket he'd been stalking was totally
forgotten. "All by myself?"

Cade deferred to Belle for that answer by tipping his
hat and nodding at her.

She answered, "Before we can cook hot dogs, we
need to set up a camp, then go find the right kind of
sticks to put the hot dogs on. Which chore do you want,
Michael?"

"Sticks."

"Long ones," she said. "Not too big around, since

the hot dog has got to slip down over the end of it. How about you find them, and your dad can come cut them?"

"No knife?" Michael asked. "I wanted to cut the sticks."

Belle shook her head. Saw the sullenness creeping into her son already. His intelligence might be way above the norm, but there was always the fine line of his age, and seven was too young to do half the things he wanted to do, and knew he could do. "No knife, just like at home. But maybe if your dad goes with you, he can show you how to cut the sticks with a pocket knife, so you'll know for when you're older."

"Or clippers," Cade said, pulling a hand-held pair from his hip pocket then handing them to Michael. "Safety catch, easy to use, great for hot dog sticks." He grinned. "Belle, while you put up both tents—"

"Both tents?"

"Can't help it. Michael and I have other chores to do." He glanced at his son, who was back on his hands and knees again, looking at another bug.

"Then I'll put up the tents. But I think you're on the stick detail by yourself."

"You never insist on anything when he gets distracted like that, do you?" Cade asked, fighting to keep in the annoyance that had suddenly flared. But it wasn't about Michael, or even Belle. It was about himself, and so many lost opportunities. Sure, there were any number of things he could teach his son, but would he be here when Michael got to put that learning to practical use? Would he be here to experience the pride that came of his son's accomplishments? "You just—" There was no point finishing the sentence because he wasn't going to drag his son into this. Instead, he slapped both his hands against his thighs, and spun to walk way.

But Belle grabbed him by the arm and held on. "Look, I don't know what this is about, and it's obvious you don't think it's any of my business. But in case it's me, or leftover feelings about us, I just want you to know that no matter what's happened between us, I've gotten through most of the hard feelings and I'm really not against you the way I used to be." She let go of his arm. "And if it's about Michael, he doesn't mean to *shut you out, Cade. That's just the way he is sometimes.* Nothing personal."

"I appreciate that. And what I said about never insisting—"

"With Michael, you learn to pick your battles. In the whole scheme of things, that wasn't one of them."

"But what is, Belle?" he asked, stopping but not turning round to face her. "And how do we decide what's worth it, and what's not? Because I don't know."

She glanced down at Michael, who was making friends with some black, multi-legged thing sprinting through the dirt. "Sometimes it's a guess, sometimes intuition. And as often as not it's just about the mood I'm in."

He chuckled. "What? Is that Belle Carter confessing she doesn't have all the answers?"

She leaned in closer to him, then whispered, "That's Belle Carter confessing that most of the time she doesn't have any of the answers, she just fakes it." She straightened back up. "And if you repeat that to anybody, especially to Maudie, I'll cut your cowboy hat to shreds."

"Not my hat!" he exclaimed.

In one quick motion, Belle snatched the hat off Cade's head, then put it on and patted it into place. "And what I said about not being against you—I meant it, Cade. I'm not." With that, she turned and sashayed away.

And, oh, what a sashay it was. One the likes of which he'd never seen on any woman, lady doc or cowboy, anywhere before. And one he wasn't likely to forget any time soon.

"He's exhausted," Belle said, settling down across the campfire from Cade. "Went to sleep the instant he crawled into the sleeping bag." Much to her surprise. Normally, Michael was a bit of a problem at bedtime. He always had more things he wanted to do, play one more set in a game, read one more chapter in a book, watch one more television show. An active mind never ready to settle down. But tonight she was pleased. Camping agreed with him. And so far it hadn't been so bad on her either.

"You enjoying yourself?" Cade asked.

"I think I am. It's nice being away from responsibility, even if it's only for a few minutes. It's been a long time since I could just step out of myself for a little while. Even now, having you here, sharing responsibility for Michael, it means a lot to me."

"I feel guilty as hell because I can't do more to help you. And guilty as hell because I never seem to succeed with Michael the way I want to, no matter how hard I try."

"You don't need to feel guilty about me. I'm good on my own. As for Michael, maybe you should try not trying so hard. You know, let up a little. Quit forcing yourself to succeed the way you want to and try succeeding with Michael the way he wants it. Because Michael does have opinions and likes and dislikes, just like the rest of us do. But he responds differently, so sometimes you're better off letting him adjust however he wants to rather than imposing your own parameters on that adjustment."

"I do that?"

"Yep. You did it with me when we were married, always trying to make me fit into your box, your set of definitions and boundaries. So you do it without thinking. Besides that, it's part of trying to be a good parent, I think. You know, wanting your child to try to fit inside your own boundaries, hoping he'll turn out to be a smaller version of you. And I'm as guilty of that as you are. The thing is, I know I have to make allowances for Michael's Asperger's, and there are times it's tough because for me the conflict—my own personal conflict—is always about letting him find his own way or me finding it for him. As his mom, I want to find it for him, to make his life easier. But that's my need coming out, not his."

"And my need is to find any way to parent him."

"From your heart, Cade. That's where you start. Instead of beating yourself up because you don't think you do it good enough, maybe stop trying to make all the little details fit into a nice, tidy little puzzle and accept the fact that sometimes the pieces fit together even if they're not quite in the right place. It may distort the picture you're trying to create, or it may make it more interesting, depending on the way you look at the world." She gazed up at the black sky, and sighed. "Anyway, if it's of any consolation, I'm glad I came out here with you two, even with the bugs. But I think I'm going to head back to town early tomorrow, probably before Michael gets up in the morning. If you don't mind."

"Not on my account, I hope."

"Actually, on my account. Like I said, I don't get a lot of time for myself, and barring medical emergencies it would be nice to have a few hours just to…" She smiled. "Soak in the tub. Maybe get my hair cut. Buy a new pair of shoes and not have to worry about Michael, because I know he's safe with his dad."

"I've missed you, Belle."

She picked up a stick and poked at the fire, sending wisps of smoke and red-lit ash up into the night-time sky. "I know how that feels," she said. "I spent too much of my time missing you, but maybe that's the way it was meant to be. I think we started at the wrong place, Cade." She looked across at him, remembering all the reasons she'd loved him. And there were more than there were reasons not to love him. But the reasons not to love him had been so overwhelming. "I don't regret it, though. I think you and me, as a couple, through the good and bad of it, gave me a different balance than I would have had if we hadn't been together."

"A good balance?"

"The best." She tossed the stick aside, and stood up. "Being divorced isn't bad. I love my life the way it is now. Wouldn't trade it for anything. When we were married, I wasn't…happy. Not the way I wanted to be, or expected that I could be. Part of that was you, part of that was me. Probably because we were suited in some ways yet in so many ways we weren't, and those were the ways that mattered most. Then when Michael came along, and after he was diagnosed, I had choices to make, lots of them. I was finishing medical school, trying to decide what kind of medical practice I wanted, coming to grips with what I'd have to do for Michael. It was tough on me, and you weren't there for a lot of it. In the end, though, the only real choice I knew I had to make was to find a life that made me happy, because I couldn't be the kind of mother Michael needed if I wasn't."

"And you're happy without me. You don't even know how lousy that makes me feel when I hear you say something like that."

She smiled. "But I am happy. Happier than I've ever been. Not because we're not together any more, but because of me. All I ever wanted, Cade, was a home, a child, a good medical practice. I told you that when we got married, and kept telling you, over and over. But you never seemed to hear it. Then when you accepted that surgical post in Thailand without even discussing it with me, then the one after that in Chicago— Anyway, I've got everything I want now, and I doubt there are very many people who can make the same claim."

"It was six months. Thailand was six months, then I was coming back."

"And I'm glad it worked out for you. So please be glad this is working out for me, because this is where we're settling, just the two of us."

"Then marriage doesn't figure into that happiness equation somewhere in your future?"

"Once burned—and the thing is, marriage isn't the cure-all for everything that ails you. What I've discovered is that I do life pretty good without it. So why rock that proverbial boat?"

"Maybe because if you rock the boat often enough, some time there might be a ripple effect that will rock your world. And you deserve that, Belle."

"You rocked my world once, Cade. Then turned it into an earthquake. This time around, I like the ground a little more solid underneath my feet. But you know what? I've missed you, too." Tall, handsome, maybe even better than he'd been when they'd met, she wondered if any other man could ever affect her the way Cade had then, and even now. A long time ago she'd decided no one could, and lived with that. Taking a step closer, she stood on tiptoe and brushed a tender kiss to his lips. "I've definitely missed you. Anyway, it's time to turn in, and hope there aren't any little creatures crawling into my sleeping bag."

"Goodnight, Belle," he said, raising his hands to his lips as he watched her walk to her tent.

Inside the tent, Michael let the door flap drop back into place then made a fast lunge for his sleeping bag. He'd barely wiggled in when Belle crawled into the tent and stretched out on her bag. Even though she looked over at him, in the dark she didn't see the grin that had spread ear to ear the moment he'd seen his mom kiss his dad. A grin that hadn't faded the least little bit as he lay there in the dark, thinking about it. She also didn't see the little hand tucked down beside him in his sleeping bag, the one with crossed fingers.

Like he'd needed that kiss! Sleep had been elusive lately anyway, and now there was no way it was going to happen tonight. Not for quite a while anyway. Because Belle had kissed him. "Damn," he muttered, kicking dirt into the fire. It didn't mean anything. He knew that. Didn't delude himself into thinking there was any significance in it whatsoever. Still, one little kiss and he was a mess.

Rather than hanging around the campsite and risking doing something that would disturb Belle or Michael, Cade wandered down the path to the creek, well within sight of the camp. He sat down on the bank and, with the light of the moon casting a perfect silvery beam down on him, watched the water churn over the rock bed. The water itself was pure, a vital source of life. And the rock bed impeded its progress. Yet the water got through it anyway. Found its path along its course without much struggle. In some ways, his life was that rock bed, he thought. An impediment to good, a hindrance to a vital life source. One way or another, that's what he'd been doing for the better part of his life—living outside his life, not fitting in. Impeding the progress. First, there had been Robbie. Then Belle, and even Michael.

Sure, maybe there was a little bit of self-pity mixed into his emotions, but mostly he was just...frustrated. And tired of the struggle. Not sure if he could move from the outside back in, though. So that's why the nights turned into his enemy so often. They were filled with the memories he couldn't put away. Filled with the struggles that got put aside for other things during the day, but always seemed to find their way back after dark.

"I have nights like this every now and then," Belle said, sitting down on the creek bank next to him. "You can't sleep and the night seems eternally long. So you pace or read a book or listen to music, hoping something will do the trick. Yet an hour later, two hours later, three hours later nothing has changed, and you're alone with your thoughts, and the things that frustrate and scare you."

"The things you can't change in your life," he said, scooting over a little to accommodate her.

"*Some things you can't change. And some things* probably shouldn't be changed. Most things I think you can, though, if you want the changes bad enough."

"Like the divorce. I didn't want it, Belle. Fought like hell to hang on."

"But too late. Because that was the change I wanted. The thing you couldn't change and the thing I wanted badly enough to change. It's what we had to do, Cade."

"That's what I keep telling myself on nights like this. The thing is, I wasn't cut out for marriage, but I sure as hell wasn't cut out for divorce either."

Belle laughed. "Then I'd say you're caught in quite the conundrum."

"How did you know I was out here?"

"I didn't. But after I lay down, I discovered I wasn't in the mood to sleep either. So I came down here because it's so…peaceful." She pulled her feet up and unlaced her shoes. "Care to go wading with me?" she asked, glancing back at the campsite to make sure Michael wasn't stirring the way his parents were.

"There could be bugs in that water. Since the only light we've got is the moon, you might not be able to see them."

"I'll take my chances," she said slipping her feet into the water. Then sighing. "Haven't done this since I was a child. Used to be afraid to do it, actually. We had this little creek that ran out behind our house, and it was full of these little crawdads, as we called them. Technically, I think they're called crayfish. Anyway, they have claws, and I was scared to death of getting my toes pinched. Thing was, it really didn't even hurt when they got you. But I missed out on some good wading because of my fears." She kicked a little water, then bent down and scooped some into her hands and splashed it at Cade. "Coming in?"

"Oh, yeah," he said, his voice suddenly full of the devil. "And you'd better watch out because there are much more dangerous things in this creek other than *the crawdads.*" He pulled off his boots, tossed aside his hat, and jumped into the water with full force, and the first thing he did was splash Belle back. "You know, I'm good at this. We had a little creek behind our house, too, and…" But by the time Robbie had been old enough to enjoy playing in that creek, Cade had already moved on to other things. Try as he might, he couldn't recall a time when he'd waded with Robbie or even splashed around with him.

"Cade? Where are you? You wandered off."

He shook his head to shake off the melancholia. "I'm right here, getting ready to soak you," he said, then grabbed hold of Belle's hand and pulled her over to him.

She fought to get free, but not too much. "What are you going to do?" she asked cautiously.

"What makes you think I'm going to do anything?" He held on a little tighter, not enough to hurt but enough to ensure she wasn't getting away without a struggle. Playing just like a kid would, he thought. And all his broodings seemed to magically splash away, too. Because of Belle? he wondered.

"I think the question should be, what would make me think you're not going to do something, Cade Carter? Because you know you will."

He thought about it, but only for a second, then without the slightest bit of warning let go of her hand, wrapped both his arms around Belle, pulled her tight to his chest, then dunked them both into the water. It wasn't deep, didn't cover them, and it wasn't cold. But the shock of it caused her to gasp. When she did, he let go of her, and that's when the battle began. She splashed him, he splashed her. And laughed… Cade couldn't remember laughing so much since, well, he couldn't remember when. "This is crazy," he sputtered, making a lunge for her hand to pull her under again.

She escaped him, and had enough time to reverse his plan by grabbing hold of his hand and pulling him under the water. But her reverse was met by his, and the next thing she knew, she was sprawled on top of Cade in six inches of water, precariously close to him. Awkwardly close to him. He saw it in her face, saw the change from happy and playful to—it wasn't fear. Maybe surprise? Or trepidation?

Whatever it was, it caused her to push off him, and didn't allow him to stop her. But he stayed there in the water as she scrambled for the bank. He fully expected her to pick up her shoes and run straight back to her tent. But she didn't. She simply stood there and looked at him for a moment. "What?" he finally asked, standing up now that the moment was truly over.

"Just thinking about the good times."

"Does that come with an asterisk? One that indicates, at the bottom of the page, that thinking about the bad times comes next?"

"Not really. Sometimes it's nice to remember only the things we did the right way and pretend the rest of it never happened. Anyway, I'll wake you up in the morning so you can look after Michael when I leave. And, Cade…thank you."

It might have been the moment they would have kissed had they been lovers. He wasn't even sure that Belle would reject him if he tried. Right now, though, he liked the friendship. Maybe that's what they'd missed the first time—the friendship. Anyway, he had an idea that friendship would be the nice, soft pillow he needed to help him sleep tonight. So he waded out of the creek, put on his boots, picked up his hat, and carried his soggy self back to his tent. For the first time in years, sleeping alone wasn't going to feel quite so…alone.

Seeing his parents heading back up the trail, one by one, Michael scurried up the trail to get to the tent before his mother did. When she finally entered, he was fully involved in the best fake sleep of his life. Fingers on both hands crossed this time.

"Interested in trying something new?" Cade asked. The morning had been rough. Belle left early, as she'd said she would, and Michael was in a bad mood. He wasn't saying why, but Cade could only guess that he'd expected his mother there, not his father, when he woke up. For that, he couldn't blame the kid. Sometimes life's surprises weren't the easiest to deal with.

"I want to go home now," Michael said, in his best matter-of-fact voice. "Right now, please. I want to go home."

Like he hadn't heard that a hundred times this past half-hour. "There's something I want to show you, first."

Michael shook his head vehemently. "It's time to go home."

How did you fight against that? Belle probably knew, and since his connectivity out here was as good as hers, he thought about calling her. Pulled his cellphone from his pocket, started to dial. Then what? he asked himself. Admit defeat? Tell her she'd been right all along, that this camping trip was a bad idea, and not realizing that made him a bad father? Hell, no, he wouldn't admit it. Wouldn't admit anything to her. "We will. But we're going on a hike first," he said, stuffing his phone back in his pocket. "Maybe we'll find some interesting bugs."

"I wouldn't mind looking for a whirligig beetle." Michael's eyes lit up with sudden interest. "They live in the plants along the water, and like to go swimming."

"Then maybe we can find one in the stream." And start the second phase of this camping trip.

"Can we go now?" Michael asked anxiously. "Before breakfast?"

Now he was willing to stay through breakfast? Sure, it was a little step, but little steps led to bigger ones. "Sounds like the best time to me. Oh, and grab that black bag sitting over there next to my backpack. There's something in it I want to show you."

"A present?" he asked, his interest definitely piqued.

"Yes, if you like it."

"A video game?"

Cade shook his head. "Better than a video game."

"I don't think so," Michael replied, hefting the bag then simply holding it, looking at it from all angles. Studying its contours, its fabric, its strap. "Unless it's two video games."

"Take a look inside," Cade said, then literally caught himself holding his breath. He wanted this to work so badly.

Slowly, with the patience of a saint, Michael unzipped the bag, inch by everlasting inch, studying the zipper teeth as they parted, occasionally re-zipping part of the bag then taking the same course again. Only after nearly a minute of zipping and unzipping, when he reached the end of that journey, did he finally look inside. "It's a camera!" Michael said, grabbing it out and looking almost excited about it. "Is for me?" he asked.

"Sure is. I thought you might like to take photos of the things that interest you—bugs, for example. That whirling beetle, if we find one."

"Whirligig," Michael corrected as he studied the camera for a moment, clicked the button that extended the lens, then held the camera up to his eye to look through the viewfinder.

"*OK, whirligig. So how about we go* down to the creek and see what we can find?"

Michael looked at his dad through the camera, saw him come into focus, saw the way his dad looked at him, not smiling. Maybe his dad was sad, the way his mother was sometimes. Last night, though, they'd looked happy, playing in the creek. Too bad he hadn't had the camera then.

"Ready, Dad," Michael said, then snapped a photo. "Now let's go find some bugs."

CHAPTER FIVE

"It's a bee sting," Belle said, looking at the red welts on Cade's arm. "Actually, about a dozen of them. What happened?"

"A hornet, not a bee," he said defensively. "And there are thirteen, to be exact."

"I'm afraid to ask," she said, pulling a tube of topical corticosteroid from her supply closet then turning back to face him, "but how?"

"There was a hornets' nest in the garage eaves at the boarding house, and—"

"Let me guess. You were being your ever-charming self, trying to appeal to the admiring masses by volunteering to get rid of it." Applying a measure of the ointment to a swab, she dabbed it to the first welt on Cade's forearm. "Did you even check to see if it was an active hornets' nest?"

"You always do that, don't you, Belle? Even after all this time, you still jump to conclusions—the worst conclusions when it comes to something, anything, about me."

"Well, I think I have reason." Raising her eyes to meet his, she cut him with her glance. A look meant to challenge. Or wound. "Because you always left Michael and me when a good cause came your way. What else am I supposed to think?"

"I wasn't ready to settle down, Belle. No excuses. I was a bad husband. All that responsibility scared me. I admitted it to you then, and I'll admit it to you now. Married life wasn't—wasn't what I'd expected it to be. And I struggled."

"You struggled, and I jumped to the conclusion that you were a bad husband when—let's see. Was it the first, second, or maybe the third time you went your merry way in the world without even mentioning it to me? Remember that, Cade? I'd wake up in the morning, find a note on your pillow saying you've gone to Cambodia or Haiti. Good humanitarian causes, but you never checked to see what kind of humanitarian needs your wife and son had. So I guess jumping to the worst conclusion about you has become a Pavlovian response because you conditioned it in me." She returned her attention to treating his welts. "I'm sorry, Cade. I don't *want to be bitter about this any more, but sometimes it* pops out."

He chuckled. "You still hold your own with the best of them, Belladonna. That's one of the things I always admired most about you. You're a force."

"Who doesn't always want to be reckoned with," she added. "And for me to jump to the conclusion that you tried to help someone isn't assuming the worst. That's who you are, and sometimes I think I'm a little envious of it. You never asked me to go, Cade. Not once. And I might have, before Michael came along, to do the same work that caught you up, get to know you that way, and maybe even to see what it was that took you away from me. But you always left, half the time never bothering to tell me, and you can't even begin to know how that feels, always getting left behind."

"Because I was stupid, immature…" he said, gritting his teeth against the sting. "I'm sorry we didn't talk more while we were married, because I didn't know you would have gone."

"To save my marriage, I would have gone. And I think we talked. We simply didn't say the right words at the right times. Anyway, your stings—how did the hornets beat you? That's not me judging you now, Cade. I want to know."

"You want to know because you think it's going to be embarrassing."

They made eye contact once more, only this time there was laughter in her eyes. "Maybe you deserve some embarrassment."

"Well, sorry to disappoint you, but Mr. Parker was up on the ladder, teetering. He's too old be climbing around like that, so I—"

"You traded places." Said with modest appreciation. "Which is a good thing, Cade."

"Good or not, let me tell you, for someone in his upper seventies, he runs like a man half his age. When I knocked that nest down, and at least a million angry hornets came screaming out of it—"

"Wouldn't there have been an easier way?" Spraying them would have been easier, but that's something Cade would never do…never intentionally kill any creature. Not even one with a stinger meant for him. His gentleness was one of the first things she'd adored about him.

"Maybe. But my idea was to dislodge their nest, agitate them, and hope they'd scatter. Which they did, actually." He paused. Cringed. "Straight into the house."

"What?"

"Open kitchen window."

"By way of your arm first." Thirteen stings had to hurt and Cade was lucky he wasn't allergic, or this could have turned serious. Still, the mental image of Cade versus the hornets—there was a time she would have wished this on him. Not any more. Truth was, she liked him better in divorce than she had in marriage. He'd matured, and mellowed. It fit him well.

"Better me than Mr. Parker, I guess," he said, wincing each time she dabbed a different welt. "Although I've got to tell you, Mrs. Parker was angrier than the hornets at both her husband and me."

"Did you get all the hornets out of her house?"

"Hornets seem to beget hornets, I think. They're everywhere. So the Parkers have gone to Dallas to stay with their daughter for a couple of days, while someone here tries to smoke them out of the house. Apparently, the better way to go about this whole thing would have been to wait until night, when they're dormant, close all the house windows, then build a fire underneath the nest. They don't like smoke, so they would have left without much drama. Something about beating the nest with a stick didn't put them in a very good mood, I suppose." He tried grinning, but winced instead.

"But no one else got stung, did they?"

"Nope. Just me."

Belle cringed. "I'm sorry, Cade. I'm sorry about doubting you, sorry I automatically thought the worst, and I'm sorry this happened. You were trying to do a good deed, and—"

"And you haven't seen the ones on my back yet. They got me through my shirt, Belle. Those little beggars ganged up on me. Had a huge grudge to carry out."

"There's more?"

"Don't know how many. But my back's on fire. Hurts worse than my arm, which hurts pretty damned bad."

"Then take your shirt off," she said, returning to the supply cabinet for more swabs. "And just in case, I think I'm going to give you a shot of antihistamine."

"Or whiskey," he muttered, beginning to unbutton his blue chambray shirt ever so gingerly.

"Since when did you start drinking?" He had his share of faults, but the common vices weren't included in those. Cade took care of his body, something she'd appreciated when they were married, something she was afraid she was still going to appreciate once she turned around.

"Since right about now—the same time you're probably going to want to start drinking."

She turned to face him, kept her eyes purposely fixed on his. "What's that supposed to mean?"

"Since the boarding house is temporarily closed down, you know that spare room above your garage?"

"No." She shook her head. Thought about it. Shook her head again. "No way. You can't possibly think you're going to…"

"But you're not using it, are you? And wasn't it an efficiency apartment at one time? So it's got a bathroom. All I need is a bed, or a cot, and I'll be fine. It'll be good for Michael, too."

"Good for Michael? How do you figure?"

"I'll be closer to him, so we'll have more time—"

She thrust out her hand to stop him. "This isn't about Michael. It's about me. And I don't want to live with you, Cade. Did it once, remember? And it didn't work out well."

"Me staying in the room over your detached garage, which is all the way to the back of your property, a whole yard away from your house, is hardly living to-gether. Besides, if you don't take me in, I'm going to have to go to Newman for a room, and that's a twenty-minute drive one way. Everything here in Big Badger, which is ten rooms at the Fourth Street Motel, is booked for the next few days. Of course, when my back isn't so sore, I can go and camp at the Ruda del Monte."

"Spare me," she said, slapping the swab packets down on the exam table. "You can stay, but that doesn't give you house privileges. I'm serious about that. You can't just come and go in my life as you please. And that includes my house, even if you are living in my garage—wounded."

He dropped his shirt on the exam table. "Fine. I'll respect that. Oh, and that antihistamine shot? I'm going to pass. I want to see a few patients before I go home today, and the antihistamine will make me groggy."

"You don't have to do that. I can see them for you."

"I know you can, but so can I." He grinned, then groaned when she treated a particularly angry welt. "Besides, if I don't keep myself busy, all I'm going to do is sit around and grumble about feeling miserable."

"Well, the offer will stay open if you start feeling worse. Same goes for an antihistamine. You know where the syringes are, and how much to take if you change your mind. And, Cade, really. You don't have to push yourself. You're not having an allergic reaction to the stings, which is good, but you've got so many of them—"

"I appreciate the concern, Belle. I know you as-sumed, well—when you said I was trying to ingratiate myself with the masses was a little harsh, but some-times that's been the easiest thing for me to do, rather than face up to what I needed to."

"And all the time we were together, you never told me why. Maybe that's the saddest thing of all, Cade. We were married, yet we weren't." Belle actually gasped when she saw the mess his back was in. Seventeen welts in all, when she counted. "OK, I understand why you don't want the antihistamine right now, but do you want something for pain? A small dose with codeine take the edge off?" she asked.

"Oh, so you're feeling sorry for me now?" he asked, fighting back a gasp of his own as her fingers skimmed lightly over each sting.

Yes, she was. She was definitely feeling sorry for him trying to make himself comfortable on that cot in the garage apartment. Suddenly, an image of Cade sprawled across her bed flashed before her eyes and she tried hard to blink it away before it took hold. "How about I offer you one night, two at the most, in a real bed? It'll be more comfortable for you than a cot."

"I wasn't complaining about the garage."

"Maybe not, but you haven't seen your back, and no way that cot's going to work. So you can have my bed, and I'll take—"

"The left side, if you want it. I won't cross the line, promise."

"I sleep on the right side now. And I don't care if you cross the line because I'll be downstairs, on the couch." Safe. OK, so maybe the offer was tempting. She'd always liked waking up next to him, feeling so safe, so connected, even when their connection had been starting to break. But now? Cade wasn't serious about the offer. Or did he think they could simply crawl into bed together to find some of what they'd lost? Whichever, the mere suggestion of something that wasn't them any more tweaked her nerves as it made her think about things that could never happen, and things she didn't want to know she still wished for. "You should have stayed in Chicago, Cade," she snapped. "You could have stuck to the original plan, stayed at your job, spent six weeks with Michael at the end of summer like we'd agreed on, and none of this would have happened."

"I was stung by some hornets. It's not the end of the world, Belle."

Maybe not the end of the world, but it was beginning to feel like she was being stung. And just when she'd thought she was impervious.

"I'm concerned about the growing number of *E. coli* cases," Belle said, dropping down into the chair next to Cade, who was busy jotting notes into a patient chart. He was sitting on a wooden stool, not looking any too comfortable about it. But at least his back wasn't touching anything. Neither was his arm. It was a small lounge, though, the best she could do considering space constraints. She'd turned one of the supply closets into a staff lounge and crammed in one small love seat, a table with a coffee-maker, microwave oven, and a mini-fridge. Inventive use of minimal space. Or, at least, that's what she'd thought until she had to sit knee to knee with Cade. And touching knees, even through his denim and her linen, gave her a little jolt. "Another of the ranches called in with a couple of sick ranch hands. Maybe a couple more, the manager wasn't sure. Ranch owner and his family are fine so far, though. So I'm going out to have a look in about an hour."

"But you've sent everything you can find to the lab and no results?"

"No results. And, actually, I'm using two different labs to make sure I'm getting consistent results. The thing is, Cade, I have enough cases now to call it an outbreak, which I don't want to do because that will cause a panic. I'm new here, people don't trust me yet, especially the men, and if I get more aggressive, make that official call to the state health department for help, you know how the scenario will play itself out. Alerting the public to be cautious, I'm the hero if it is a real outbreak and the villain if it's not. There's no gray area in that, and since I haven't found a source yet, it's not responsible to sound the alarm when I can't even tell them if they should avoid bean sprouts, lettuce, well water, or dirt in general."

"Well, you're right about that. It's better to err on the side of caution rather than cause a mass panic. But that's only going to go on for so long, then you'll be called irresponsible no matter which way it turns out." He shut his chart, set it aside, and twisted to face her. "I think it's cattle related, Belle. We're in the heart of cattle country, all the ranches around here raise cattle, and half the town residents are involved in the industry somehow."

"But I've had the local beef tested, several times, and...nothing."

"The thing is, without taking mass cultures of everything, and I mean everything around here—"

"We're stuck. More people get sick and I'm in deep trouble. Damned if you do, damned if you don't. But you've seen what happens when health warnings go out. You link the bacterium that's making everybody sick to the cattle, and the people will—well, I don't want to think about what they'll do. It could decimate the town's economy, though. People in panic mode, normal, rational people otherwise, will go to extremes, and I don't want to be responsible for that. The problem is, since

I've been sending samples to the county lab, as well as a private one, I'm not sure how much longer I can keep this quiet. The county health officials are on my side about discretion so far, and they've even had a couple of investigators kicking around to see what they can find. But at some point word's going to leak out no matter what happens. I mean, right now people think it's only a stomach bug going round, which is really what it is. But attach the word outbreak or endemic to it, which will happen when we go public, and we're in big trouble." She sighed heavily. "Either way, time's running out."

"For what it's worth, I think you're doing the right thing. It's a tough choice, Belle. I think the people here are luckier to have you than they know."

"Yeah, well, tell that to the lynch mob when they come to get me." She stood, then walked around Cade, stopping at the back of his chair. Gently, she lifted his shirt to have a look at his back. "Can I give you something yet?"

"Sympathy?"

She smiled. There were so many things about Cade that hadn't worked for her when they were married. Yet there were so many things that had worked, and still did. Overall, she was glad he was here, for Michael's sake. Maybe even a little for hers. "Goodnight, Cade. Will you lock up when you leave?"

"He might be hungry," Michael said, aiming his camera directly at his mother while she dumped the spaghetti into to colander to drain it.

Belle was glad he was taking such interest in his photography, but he must have snapped fifty shots of her fixing dinner, and fifty before that, when she was stretched out on the couch, barefooted, hair a mess, reading a medical article. "There are plenty of places in town where your father can get something to eat," she said, turning her back to Michael before he snapped another picture of her, one where she looked annoyed. Because she was annoyed. All these years later, and she was still letting Cade get to her. Too many thoughts about him, too many memories. "And I think he's pretty tired. I'm sure he's asleep by now."

"But his light's on," Michael argued.

Of course Cade's light was on, and here was her son wanting his dad to come for dinner. How could she refuse that? The answer was, she couldn't. "OK, go knock on his door. Tell him dinner will be ready in ten minutes, if he'd like to join us. Then come and help me set the table."

Without a word, Michael ran out the door and straight to the garage, pausing only a fraction of a second at the steps before bolting up them. He was so agile, so athletic, it made her proud. Especially when she thought back to the day when the specialist had told her what to anticipate from a child diagnosed with Asperger's syndrome. Certainly, physical ability hadn't been on the list of expectations. Rather, she'd been told to look for clumsiness. And look at him, a true seven-year-old athlete who didn't know what he was supposed to lack, or not achieve in life.

She watched as Michael banged on the door the first time, waited a moment, then knocked again. No answer. So he tried a third time, and by his fourth attempt Belle was out in the yard, on her way to the garage. "Michael," she yelled. "Maybe he's not home."

"But I heard his music."

Classical. Mozart. She hated Mozart. He'd always

thought she loved it, insisted that she did. But she preferred something more meaty, like Beethoven. Another one of their differences, as it turned out. And, Mozart was definitely blaring away in the apartment, which, for some unperceived reason, alerted her. Cold chills shot up her arms, and she immediately bolted into her house to grab her medical bag then ran right back into the yard. "Michael, would you go back into the house and make sure the front door is shut and locked?" She wasn't sure what she'd find once she got into the apartment, but she was sure she didn't want Michael finding it with her. "Then set the table for dinner, please." Hopefully, this was her being an alarmist, and Cade was off somewhere, having dinner. She was trying to think positively even though a second round of cold chills assaulted her.

"Can I see Dad, first?" he asked, turning to jiggle the doorknob.

"It's locked, sweetheart, so please don't try to open it." Belle jumped between Michael and the door, then pointed to the house. "Check the front door," she reminded him, then waited until he'd scampered away before she tried the apartment door, found it locked, then pulled out her master key and stuck it in the lock.

"Cade," she gasped when she was inside, and discovered his lifeless form on the floor next to the cot. She ran over to him and dropped to her knees. First instinct, find a pulse. It was there. Weak, thready, but beating away, thank God. Second thing, she put her ear to his chest to listen for breath sounds, heard clear gurgling and wheezing. "What did you do, Cade?" she choked, shoving back the coffee table to give her more room to assess his pupillary action. Good. Equal, reactive. No head trauma that she could discern. And a quick check from his neck down revealed no other kind of trauma.

She actually paused, like she expected a response from him. But that lasted only a second before she was back, examining, listening, observing. Looking for anything.

"It was locked," Michael said from the doorway. "What's wrong with him?"

It was too late to hide anything now. "He wasn't feeling well earlier today, and I haven't checked him enough to see what's wrong now," she said, not sure if she wanted Michael to see his father this way. But it couldn't be helped. Besides, Michael had been around any number of her patients and had never gotten squeamish. Somehow, she'd always thought he might be a doctor, even though his fascination was clearly for bugs.

"Is he sleeping?" he asked, his attention suddenly caught by some computer equipment stashed in the corner of the room. It was still boxed, as was an unassembled workstation next to it.

"You dad got stung by some hornets today, and—" Ten thousand scenarios clicked through her mind as she opened her medical bag. Delayed reaction to the stings, some kind of undetected cardiac problem. "And I think he may have taken a shot that made him go to sleep pretty quickly." She hoped it was an allergic reaction to the antihistamine—the drug that should have prevented an allergic reaction to the stings.

"Paper wasps," Michael corrected. "They make paper from dead wood and plant stems for their nests." He frowned. "But they don't usually sting unless someone attacks them first."

"Did you hear that, Cade? They don't usually sting unless someone attacks them first," she said, as she unlocked the medical bag with a key she wore on a chain around her neck—a precaution since she had an active, inquisitive child in the house. Then she grabbed out an epi pen—a pen filled with epinephrine, which would, in theory, stop the allergic reaction. "Please, hand me the stethoscope," she asked Michael once the shot was in.

"Can I listen to his heart after you do?" Michael asked, even though his eyes were fixed on his dad's computers.

"Maybe. You'll have to ask him, after I wake him up." His heart sounds were good. Wheezes decreasing, the gurgles going away. Airways relaxing now.

"OK," Michael responded. "Then can I set up his computer?"

"I think that sounds like a wonderful idea," she said, not even caring that Cade might have other plans for it. Right now she had an emergency to deal with, a seven-year-old child to distract, and a brand-new computer was the best thing she could think of for her son. She glanced quickly at Michael to make sure he was OK, then right back at Cade, who was already beginning to stir. His eyes were fluttering open and he was trying to shake his head, as if to shake away a fog.

"What happened?" he whispered, rather thickly.

"Did you take an antihistamine shot?" she whispered back.

"After I came home. Couldn't get comfortable, the stinging was increasing..."

"Then I think you're allergic to the antihistamine," she said, finally allowing herself to sit in a comfort-able position next to Cade rather than stooping over him. "Classic anaphylactic reaction. You responded well to epi, though." And he'd scared her to death. Jolted some feelings to the surface, too. Thoughts and feelings about her life without Cade in it somewhere. "And you're going to stay down for the next half-hour to make sure nothing else goes wrong."

"Where's Michael?" he asked, his voice finally returning.

"Putting together your computer equipment. I thought it was a suitable reward for saving your life."

"I did?" Michael asked, not even bothering to look at his parents he was so intent on studying the laptop computer he'd already pulled from the box.

"You did," Belle said, overwhelmed by so many emotions she was suddenly on the verge of tears. "And I'm so proud of you."

"Then can I still invite Dad to dinner?" he asked, as if what he'd done had been an everyday thing.

"Yes, you can." She turned her head sway to swipe at a stray tear that had fallen. Life without Cade? She didn't even want to think about it, didn't want to think why she was all caught up in this emotion either. It was a scare, that's all. Just a scare. Yet when she closed her eyes and didn't picture Cade there… "If he's up to eating."

"I'll be fine in a few minutes," Cade said, reaching over and taking hold of her hand. "Are you OK?" he whispered.

"I'm fine. But you almost weren't, Cade. Damn it, you almost weren't." Life was so fragile. As a doctor, she saw that all the time. But as Belle Carter, mother and ex-wife, maybe this was the first time she'd realized it in a deeply personal way. "I don't know what I'd have done if you…" Biting back the rest of her words, she held tighter to his hand as she swiped away more tears with her other hand. "Damn you, Cade Carter. Why did you do this to me?"

"What?"

Her answer was a tender kiss to his forehead. Not missed by Michael, who caught it on camera. Then came total silence. What was there to say other than the obvious? Her feelings were deeper than she'd thought. And that was something for which she had no words.

Thirty minutes later Cade felt up to eating. But more for the company than for the food. The whole ordeal had worn him out. The stings, the allergic reaction. He'd much rather have gone to bed, but he didn't want to disappoint Michael and, in a way, he wanted to be with his family for a while, even though they weren't really a family any more. Yet they were as close as it got for him, so he took a small portion of spaghetti, pushed it around on his plate, tried to force down a few bites, then looked helplessly at Belle as he pushed the plate away. "You always were a good cook."

"I never cooked," she said.

"Sure you did. Once or twice."

"And you remembered?"

"I remember the good times. We should have had more of them, then maybe I wouldn't feel so..." He glanced at Michael, who was cramming spaghetti into his mouth as fast as he could. "He's in a hurry?"

"He wants to get back up to your apartment and finish setting up your computer. Something about a router and connecting it to something else wireless." She shook her head. "I'm not sure."

"A wireless internet connection," Michael explained in all impatience, like everybody should know what he was talking about. "We can network him in with us, so he won't have to have a separate hook-up. And all I have to do is—"

"Finish your dinner," Belle interrupted. "Then your reading. Then go to bed. It's getting late, you've had a busy day, and your dad's computer can wait until to-morrow."

"But…" Michael started to protest, then stopped, shrugged, and pushed himself away from the table. "OK. I'll go read."

"You're finished eating?" Cade asked. Michael didn't answer, though. His mind was already somewhere else, probably racing on to the next adventure or the next challenge to solve. "He's obedient," he commented to Belle.

"At times. Then at other times he's a seven-year-old tornado, like every other child his age is occasionally. You can't keep him down, he won't mind, he's sullen, gets angry…"

"Sounds like me at his age. One minute sweetness and light, then the next—boom! Except I didn't have an Einstein intelligence to go with it." He stood, stepped away from the kitchen table, and pushed his chair back in.

"Michael's the one thing we did right, Cade. Even with all our mistakes, we have an amazing son."

"I can think of a couple of other good things we did, too. But Michael's definitely the best. So anyway—I appreciate you saving my life and all, but I'm exhausted, so I think it's time to get back to my apartment and get some sleep."

Belle laughed. "You're so casual about it. Thanks for saving my life, but…" She got up from the table, too. "Look, you've had a rough day. You deserve a real bed, so take mine. I'm good on the couch."

"You don't have to do this, you know."

"Sure I do. As your doctor, as the mother of your son—"

"As a friend?"

"Maybe. But does it ever really work when ex-spouses turn friends? Aren't there always some hard feelings buried somewhere, even though you profess an amicable divorce? So for tonight—"

"I'm sleeping in my doctor's bed. And for what it's worth, she's the best friend I've ever had."

Belle nodded, choosing to ignore the last part of that remark. "Well, your doctor didn't have time to put on clean sheets."

That didn't matter. Smelling Belle's scent on the sheets wasn't as good as having her there next to him, but it would definitely make his sleep come easier.

"One last thing. Did you know you have an antihistamine allergy? At your age, I'd have thought…"

"You thought I'd take something that would knock me down hard enough so I'd find my way to your bed?" A huge grin spread across his face.

"You almost died," she snapped. "It's nothing to joke about."

He shrugged. "What else is there to do?"

"Take it seriously. Wear a warning bracelet. Make sure that next time you almost die, you do it somewhere where our son isn't watching." She bit her lower lip. "Damn it, Cade! You scared me. When I opened that door and saw you there, on the floor…"

He walked around the table and stopped directly in front of her. So close, he could smell the slight hint of strawberry-scented shampoo in her hair. "It's nice to know you still care—a little bit."

Holding her ground, not backing away even an inch,

she looked up, met his stare. "This won't work, Cade," she said. "We won't work."

He cocked his head slightly, continuing to stare into the most beautiful green eyes he'd ever had the privilege of staring into. "They weren't who we are, Belle. Those two people back then, they were nothing like we are now."

"For once, we agree on something. But the two people who exist now are too wise for this, Cade. They've been through too much. Can't go back, can't move forward."

"But what about right now? Sometimes living in the moment isn't such a bad thing."

She didn't respond. Just held her ground, looking at him. Searching his eyes for an answer? Or asking a question? He didn't know. Which ultimately was the reason that made him step forward to find out. And in that sweep of mere inches it was like the air between them turned into a barrier…the barrier they needed to keep them separated. They'd always been so good at this, perfect in a way he'd never known perfection, and had never found since Belle. One kiss was all he wanted. A reminder of the memory. And he could feel the barrier shifting, feel it slipping away as he raised his hand to stroke her cheek, and she leaned her face into the cup of his hand. Shut her eyes. Sighed softly. Relaxed. Smiled.

Gently, very gently, he slipped his hand from her cheek to just below her jaw, then tipped her head back, but only slightly. Just enough to see her every feature—imperfections, perfections, everything he'd loved about that face flooded back to him. This was a Belle he knew so well, yet didn't know at all. A Belle he'd never before kissed, yet could almost savor the taste of her lips without even touching them, the lingering memory of that taste was so keen.

She wasn't stopping him. But she wasn't encouraging him either. His choice, entirely, to kiss her or step back. Feel yet another sting, or avoid that next pain altogether.

No choices here, though. Not for him. He wanted her, felt it crushing hard at him as he lowered his lips to hers and awaited her verdict.

Belle's verdict… She snaked her left hand around his neck and pulled his face down to her, while the fingers on her right hand tangled themselves in his hair. That touch had always given him chills. Caused him to gasp… And as he did, as his mouth parted ever so slightly, she pressed her tongue to his, which caused fire, pure fire to ignite him like he hadn't been ignited since the night of their divorce…one for the road, she'd called it.

"Belle," he murmured against her lips as she pulled herself into him, pressed the length of her body hard into his, demanding more, demanding everything.

There was nothing tentative here. The kiss grew more carnal, lips pressing even harder, tongues plunging even deeper, no dividing lines. The feel of her fingernails digging into the flesh of his neck, the bite of reality…damn, what was he doing? A question he asked himself again as she removed her hand from his neck and squeezed it in between them, pressed it to his chest, raked it from slightly below his shoulder to his pectoral, then…pushed him back. Hot, sweaty, aroused, half-dazed, he took that step, then exhaled a shudder. "Now what?" he asked, trying not to sound as ragged as he felt.

"Nothing. We were curious. We satisfied that curiosity. One moment, and it's over. We don't have to do it again."

Maybe that's what she wanted him to believe but, oh, those eyes said something entirely different. And he'd always been able to read her eyes. "Fine. One moment." He took another step back. "If that's what you want."

"We're not reconciling, Cade. If that's why you came to Texas, go home."

"Why I came to Texas," he murmured, smiling, "was for Michael."

Once again, she didn't respond. Just stared. And it occurred to him that Belle was a little mixed up about this. A little off balance. Well, she could join the club. This was about as off balance as he'd ever felt in his life, and that included the day she'd told him the marriage was over. He'd expected that. But not this. Not any of it. "Goodnight, Belle," he finally said, struggling with the idea that there was more below the surface. And there was, he was sure of it. But he wasn't in the mood to figure out what it was. Leftover feelings, new feelings, curiosity, as she'd said. It had been a hell of a day, from the wasp stings to the anaphylactic reaction to that damned kiss. Somewhere in all that mess, though, he was sure of one thing. As rough as his day had been, his night, snuggled alone between Belle's sheets, was going to be even rougher.

CHAPTER SIX

IT WAS the unsettling feeling waking her up that something wasn't right, as well as her mother's intuition that sent her running for Michael's bedroom first, only to find an empty bed. "Michael!" Belle called out, looking in his closet then under his bed. "Where are you?"

Michael didn't turn up in the bathroom, kitchen, or den, not in her bedroom with Cade either, she discovered when she peeked in, only to find her bed was empty as well. Where had he taken Michael? Without telling her?

The panic in her fast giving way to anger, Belle looked out the kitchen window and saw the garage apartment lit up at— She glanced at the wall clock. Two in the morning! Cade had taken Michael out at two and there was no doubt in her mind they were up there assembling the computer. It was so…so irresponsible of Cade to do that, to allow it, or enable it, whichever the case turned out to be. That was the thought that propelled her up the stairs and straight to Cade's door, which she shoved open rather than knocking.

Inside, looking as innocent as you please, father and son were sitting cross-legged on the floor, both absorbed in their individual projects—Michael with the laptop, clicking away on the keys, and Cade with a screwdriver in one hand and an instruction sheet in the other. It could have been a cozy scene under different circumstances, with father assembling a knock-together desk while son assembled computer peripherals and installed software. But not under these circumstances. "You're supposed to be in bed, Michael," she said, fighting to sound patient when everything inside her was boiling mad. "You know you're never…never allowed to get up in the middle of the night and leave the house unless it's an emergency, and we've talked about those. Do you understand me?"

It wasn't Michael who responded, though. "I couldn't sleep. Got up, decided not to disturb you, and came up here. Apparently our son had been here for a while, working."

"My son knows the rules," she said, stepping around the cartons on the floor, on her way over to Michael. When she got there, he finally looked up, picked up his camera, then clicked a picture of her, which made her even angrier, in turn causing her attempt to hold it in even more difficult. "And doing what he's doing right now is breaking one of them. So, Michael, please get up and come with me back to the house."

"But I'm almost finished," he argued, getting ready to click and shoot again. This time at Cade, though, who was putting on a properly stern face, even though his eyes were anything but stern.

"No, Michael. You are finished for tonight. Now get up and go back to the house. No arguments. Do you understand me?"

"Ten more minutes?" he asked. "That's all I need."

She didn't answer his question. Instead, she simply stood there, frowning that mother's frown every child knew, the one that told the child he'd better mind, or else. In this case, Michael knew what "or else" meant... two days without his video games. Not a cruel punishment by most parental standards, not even a harsh one, but it was effective on a seven-year-old boy who, too often, thought he should have adult privileges.

"OK," he grumbled, then stood. And snapped another picture of her, one that captured her mother's frown. "I'm going."

"Straight to bed," she said. "I'll be there in a minute to make sure that's where you are." This time she turned her frown on Cade, who was still sitting cross-legged on the floor, and her expression definitely had nothing to do with being a mother. "After I talk to your father."

"OK," he said again, then marched sullenly to the front door. But before he left, he turned back to Belle and Cade, snapped one last photo of the two of them, then stomped out the door and down the wooden steps, every last footstep sounding as loud as Michael could make them. On purpose.

"I suppose I should apologize," Cade said, pushing himself off the floor.

"I suppose you should," she snapped, her attention still centered on Michael while he stomped on across the yard and into the house. Finally, when he was in and the back door was shut, she whirled around to face Cade. "What were you thinking, Cade? Do you realize that by sitting here, aiding and abetting Michael, you've endorsed his actions? Or, at least, in his mind you have!"

"I was thinking that since my son had come up here to work on the computer in the middle of the night, I should probably stay with him since he's too young to be out here on his own, like he was."

"Did it occur to you to make him go back to bed? Or did you even remember that I'd specifically told him he wasn't going to work on the computer any more tonight?"

"Actually, I did. Then he told me that, technically, it was the morning of the next day. Not a logic I'd particularly cared to argue with him."

"In other words, he wins, I lose?" She shook her head vehemently. "Look, Cade. I know you don't get to be a full-time dad, but you can't pit Michael against me, which is what you just did. He's smarter than any kid has a right to be, and he can manipulate situations with the best of them. That's what happened here. Michael knew what he was supposed to be doing, but you're the one who caved." She took another look out the window to make sure Michael wasn't trying to sneak back, and saw that his bedroom light was on. So for now, he was on his way back to bed. She turned to Cade again. "We're in this together, and you're going to have to support me when I tell Michael to do something. If you can't, then find another place to stay tomorrow."

"You were always so sexy when you were angry, Belladonna," he said, nudging a couple of cartons away from the cot in the corner. "Still are. And for what it's worth, I'm sorry. I saw an opportunity, and took it. I know I should have made him go back to bed the second I found him here, but the excitement on his face... I don't get to see that very often. So if you want to be mad as hell at me for breaking your rules, there's nothing I can do about it. But it was worth it, and I won't do it again." He plunked himself down on the cot with a groan and turned over on his side. "Under the circumstances, I think I'll be safer spending the rest of the night out here. So now I'd like to make the most of what's left of it, because Bill Thompson is coming into the office at six to have me check his prostate and as I haven't done that kind of an exam in years, I need my sleep."

"At six?"

"Only time he could make it." He shrugged, winced, and smiled up at her. "Oh, and he said he likes having a man back in the office."

"Well, tell him not to get used to it." Belle spun away, and headed for the door. Halfway there she turned back to Cade. "Oh, and so you'll know, I'll be locking the house doors when I go in."

"Spare key?" he asked, trying to find a comfortable position.

She watched him wince as he settled in on the cot, thought about inviting him back to her bed, then give herself a mental kick. "Nope. No spare key." For her own good. "And tomorrow I'll be having electronic locks installed. Seems Michael is being tempted by outside forces."

"Or inside," he said, then shut his eyes and let out a ragged sigh.

And that was the problem. Cade wanted in and she didn't blame him. But getting into Michael's life more than he was also meant he was back in hers, and that's what she didn't want. Truth was, there were moments when she caught herself reacting the way she had the first time she'd ever laid eyes on him. Breathless, heart palpitations, trying to be cool, even cold about it. She liked to remember it as when surgery met internal medicine. He'd been a surgical resident, she'd been a medical student assigned to a rotation through his service and had seen, right off, how five other female students had practically swooned over him. And he'd loved it. Eaten it right up.

Well, not her. Sure, there was the attraction factor, but Cade...he was like this enigma. Very perplexing and contradictory. The ultimate surgeon, skilled, passionate, devoted. Yet not settled outside his medicine. The man she might want, yet the man she was pretty sure she didn't want. Consequently, her self-imposed coolness toward him had lasted for the duration of her service under him, and she'd had to fight every step of the way to keep herself from looking as silly as the other women had when they'd been around him, because Cade certainly did have his way.

First day off of Cade Carter's service, though, he'd asked her out and she'd jumped at the chance, then all that coolness had melted into a puddle. First night—a night to remember. But the thing even more memorable was, in spite of Cade's way, he had been genuine, and nice. His charm had oozed naturally. One date, one night, she'd been hooked.

For all his faults, and there were a few she'd learned over the years, Cade had never cheated on her . He could have. Opportunities had been thrown at him all the time. Yet that first night together he'd made her that promise, and it was the one promise he never broke. Oh, he'd cheated on her with life, going in more directions than she could keep up with, and in an ambition that had simply kept getting bigger and bigger until it had squeezed her out. But as a lover, then a husband, Cade had stayed faithful—something she'd never doubted in him. Even now, she remembered, with a little smugness, how she used to walk down the hospital halls, watching all the women swooning over him, all of them envious that he was hers.

So the problem Belle was facing now was that the things she'd found irresistible before hadn't changed, and the things she'd found positively infuriating had... for the better. The Cade Carter who existed now was the man she'd hoped she was getting nine years ago. But the Belle Carter who existed now wasn't the woman who, nine years ago, had wanted Cade beyond all reason. Their happily-ever-divorced status was changing because of proximity, and there wasn't a darned thing she could do about it. He wanted to be closer to his son, and Michael certainly needed that. She didn't, however. And maybe the true reason she didn't was because, deep down, she was beginning to discover that she really did.

For whatever it was worth, and she hoped not very much, Cade still had his way, and she was still swayed. But wiser. And wise always won over anything else in her life.

"Are you sure he's going to be OK?" Cade asked, watching the bus drive off with his son.

"It's three days, and Dr. Robinson is the best." Belle waved at the bus, even though Michael never looked out the window to wave back. He was too preoccupied with his hand-held electronic game.

"The best at what?"

"I already told you. She has impeccable credentials as a doctor of medicine for starters. Pediatrics. On top of that a doctorate in psychology, specializing in autism and specifically Asperger's syndrome. Amanda's done some of the leading research in the country and Michael responds well to her." Smiling, Belle patted Cade on the arm. "You've always accused me of being the overprotective one, and just listen to you. He's going to be gone for three days, Cade. You'll survive, which really isn't my biggest concern. And Michael will have a good time, which *is* my biggest concern. But what I'm counting on most is Amanda's evaluation for progress. She's watching his social interactions, by the way. Michael's typical of the social awkwardness associated with Asperger's and that's what we've been working on lately. You know, getting him to be more outgoing."

"Don't take this the wrong way, Belle, because I'm not challenging you, but was Michael OK with this camping trip, or is it something he's doing because you insisted?" Robbie hadn't been OK any of the times he'd been sent away. In fact, he'd run off more often than Cade probably ever knew about after Cade's mother had sent Robbie packing to one program or another. Groups homes, military school, private care facilities— you name it, and that's where she'd sent Robbie. In fact, dispatching his brother's upbringing to someone else had always been her priority, because she hadn't cared. Cold, heartless woman. She hadn't cared about him, hadn't cared about Robbie…

"Look, Cade. Insisting he do things outside his comfort zone is part of the process, but there's nothing to worry about. Michael does well with Amanda and what's more important, Amanda does well with him. Probably as well with her as he does with just about anybody other than…"

"You can say it, Belle. Other than you." He knew it was true, and the truth hurt. No matter how he wanted to deny it, or argue the fine points, he was a part-time father, and part-time fathering was a kick in the gut.

"I'm sorry but, yes. Other than me. You're in and out of Michael's life every other weekend, Cade, and flying down here the way you do—you prove yourself. It's a good thing. Something most fathers wouldn't, or couldn't, do. But Michael doesn't adapt to changes in his schedule very easily, so you don't get the best of him when you're here because he's in readjustment mode for most of that time, which is difficult for him."

Everything she said was true, like it or not. Belle was the full-time parent and he was the intrusion. Still, every other weekend wasn't enough, and that's why he was here. He had to figure out how to get more, how to be more. Had to figure out how not to be resentful of what he didn't have and Belle did. And there was no denying that, at times, he was resentful as hell. He'd caused the situation, he took full responsibility, but that didn't change the way he felt. His mistakes had cost him dearly, and it was killing him. "Look, do you want to go out to dinner tonight?" he asked, totally out of the blue.

"Are you asking me on a date?"

"Can't ex-spouses have a date every now and then?"

"They can, if one of them doesn't have evening call at one of the ranches. It's probably going to be a late night."

"And you don't eat on your late nights?"

"Well, there is this little roadhouse on the way out there. Good food, loud music. You could meet me there later."

"Or drive you to your evening call and help speed things along for you."

"With everything you've been through these past twenty-four hours, you don't have to do that, Cade."

"What if I want to?" He did want to, but he wasn't sure why. Maybe to spend some time alone with her? Actually, it was quite an appealing idea, the two of them together, no one else around. It had been years, and they used to be good at it.

Belle stepped back off the curb, took one long look down the road, even though Michael's bus was long out of sight, then nodded. "Well, I've got patients scheduled all afternoon, and you've probably got a fair portion of Big Badger's male population trekking in to see you, as they won't trek to see me, so how about we play it loose? You text me when you're done, or I'll text you when I'm done, and we'll go from there." She smiled. "Michael taught me to text, by the way."

Well, at least it wasn't a firm no. "We're working in the same office, Belle."

"But texting keeps it impersonal."

That it did. And there was no mistaking that she was sending him a clear message. But as she turned and walked away from him, he pulled out his cellphone and texted her a message that clearly wasn't impersonal. *From behind, you're still the best looking woman I've ever seen.* He watched her check her text, pause like she was thinking about it, then pick up her pace back to the office. "I mean it, Belle Carter," he shouted. "Always were, still are." It was certainly true, but he sure didn't know where he was going with it. Especially as Belle wanted none of it, or none of him.

"Three sick, seven fine. I don't get it. There's a contaminant source that's either picking or choosing its victims, or part of the population of Big Badger is involved in something the rest of the people here know nothing about. And we're not making any progress, because these people haven't eaten anything that resembles a salad." The exams were over, no one was critically ill, she'd written the prescriptions and handed out a few pill samples to tide them over until morning, and she was ready to end the day. Grab a bite to eat, go home, kick her shoes off, and spend the first night alone she'd had since she couldn't remember when. It sounded good. No, it sounded luxurious and she was keeping her fingers crossed there would be no night emergencies. "So let's go get dinner over with, and—"

"Is having dinner with me such a chore, Belle? We used to enjoy our evenings together."

"We used to be married, and we enjoyed our evenings together because we only got them once every couple of weeks, if we were lucky. And, no, it's not a chore. I just want to go home, be alone, and not have to worry about anything for a few hours." Belle's words were cut off by her cellphone ringing. Ten seconds later, after the blood had drained from her face, she clicked off and jumped into the truck. "Emergency in town, at the diner. One of the customers there is giving CPR…to Maudie."

"Damn," Cade muttered, on his way to the driver's side. He jumped in, hit the gas, and within a second they were on their way back to town, not sure what they'd find when they got there.

"She's healthy," Belle finally said. "Even for her age, she's strong. And normally if *E. coli* goes beyond the usual symptoms, it's on someone who's not healthy, or elderly. But Maudie is…robust."

"You're assuming it's what everybody else is getting, but maybe it's not."

He turned a sharp corner, which threw Belle almost into his lap. In fact, she was sprawled across him quite suggestively, like a woman whose only emergency was taking care of the man next to her. She extricated herself quickly from that awkward spot, although she didn't slide away from him nearly as quickly. In fact, she lingered there purposely, enjoying the way it felt pressed up against him as she was. Tingling with goose-bumps, not even trying to hide her shivers. Yes, there was a part of her that could have invited Cade back to her bed for more than just a comfortable night's sleep. She wasn't dead after all. Neither was her attraction for Cade. And she wasn't a prude. But Cade—it worried her that he might want more. Yet the thought didn't go away. "I, um…I forgot to fasten my seat belt," she said, remembering the times when she'd purposely forgotten to buckle up so she could ride this close to him, to feel his raw strength against her arm, her hip, the way she was doing now. It did send her back to the good times.

"Apparently," he said, his voice rough.

"Look, Cade. With Michael gone for the next few days, if you want to come up to the house and stay in his room…" OK, not her room. Close, though.

"Since I've got a few more weeks ahead of me here, I'm having a real bed delivered to the apartment tomorrow," he said. "But thanks for the offer. I wouldn't mind a door key, though. In case I need to borrow a pot, or pan."

An absolute, flat-out rejection. She'd offered the room across from her bedroom, he'd chosen the room above where she parked her car. She hadn't expected that, but maybe it was for the best. Leftover longings didn't translate into anything of substance, she knew that. So did Cade. But that didn't make his rejection sting any less. "Sure, I'll find the spare and slide it under your door later on." Said as she scooted back to her side of the truck cab and fastened her seat belt for the last three miles of their trip back to Big Badger—a trip without another word spoken between them.

He hadn't meant to turn her off cold, but that's what had happened. A little bump into his lap, a little press against his arm, and sleeping across the hall from her wasn't good enough. Having Belle so close—even now, as he pulled the truck into a parking spot behind the diner, all he could see was what he'd seen so many times before. The most beautiful, the most seductive woman he'd ever met. He couldn't do that to himself. Just couldn't do it. It would drive him crazy. In fact, he was wondering now if the garage apartment was too close. Time to brace up and remember he was here to establish a better relationship with Michael, and seducing Michael's mother wasn't part of that. Even though that's exactly what he wanted to do. "Do you know if an ambulance has been called? I didn't see one out front," he said, trying to put it all out of his head.

"Ambulance service here is…difficult. The only hospital nearby is in Newman, and it's more like a glorified clinic, with a few overnight observation beds. No emergency services, actually. So if we have something serious, we call an airlift like we did before with Dean Ralston. Maudie calls an airlift." She swallowed hard. "Which I'm sure hasn't happened yet."

"You need a hospital here," Cade said, grabbing his medical bag out from behind the seat, as well as the large, portable emergency kit with extended supplies that Belle carried with her on her trek out to the ranches. "Even a small one would be better than nothing."

"We need a lot of things, but what we have is one overworked doctor who's doing the best she can and struggling to buy her medical practice from a town that can't afford to run medical services on its own. So we deal with what we have to any way possible."

She was on his heel in the diner's back door and through the kitchen. Finally, in the dining room, they were greeted by a wall of people, all standing back as one of the servers, a young girl named Judie Lawson, huddled over Maudie, not attempting resuscitation but fanning her for a lack of anything else she knew how to do.

Judie saw Belle approach and immediately scooted away.

"I could use an IV setup," Cade said, dropping to the floor as Belle opened her emergency kit and started to pull out supplies.

"As soon as I get oxygen on her." Oxygen from a small emergency cylinder she always carried with her. Maudie looked bad. Pale. Not responsive. She glanced over at Cade, who was already midway through his first assessment. Admired the way he worked so fast, so efficiently. It's what she'd seen that first day on his service, and a huge part of what she'd loved in him.

"Pulse thready," he stated. "Respirations shallow." He glanced up at Belle. "Does she have a heart condition?"

Shaking her head, Belle pulled a large-bore line from her bag, and handed it over to him. "Not that I know of. At least, she's never said anything to me." Once Cade had inserted the IV, Belle attached a bag of normal saline to it then waited for Cade's next assessment, as he was listening to Maudie's chest again.

"No changes," he said, as Belle strapped the blood-pressure cuff to Maudie's arm.

She blew up the bulb, had a listen. "Sixty over palp." Meaning, deathly low.

"Has she shown any symptoms of *E. coli*?" Cade asked, almost in a whisper. "Because I'm wondering if this is about a heart…" He stopped, and looked at the vial Belle had fished from Maudie's pocket.

"Nitroglycerine," she said, opening the vial and shaking out a pill then putting it under Maudie's tongue to dissolve. It would improve blood flow to the heart as well as decrease the work of the heart. Something that, had she taken it at the onset of her chest pain, could have prevented this. "I don't suppose she had the chance to take a pill before this happened."

"Or didn't think it was important enough."

"She's my nurse, Cade. Maudie knows that the nitro is important, but never told me she had a heart condition, and that's what has me concerned. I should have known. She should have told me." Glancing over at Cade, who was on his phone to call for a helicopter, she went on, "She likes you better than she does me. I don't suppose she mentioned it to you, did she?"

"Not a word." After giving directions to the dispatcher, he snapped shut his cellphone then had another listen to Maudie's chest. "It's not quite so erratic. Not good, but better. Oh, and the helicopter's twenty minutes out. So I think we just hold where we are with her, unless something else happens. OK with you?"

Belle nodded. "Forty minutes getting her to a hospital—that's a long time, Cade. If they want to get a clot-buster in her, we're running out of time."

He reached over and squeezed her hand. "Don't beat yourself up about this, Belle. Maudie's going to be fine."

"She should have told me, Cade. But she's like everybody else here. They don't trust me. My own office nurse doesn't trust me." For the first time since she'd come to Big Badger, she was having serious doubts about staying. Nobody trusted her, the people in town were getting sicker every day with a contaminant she couldn't identify. And Maudie...

"You didn't cause it, Belle." Cade squeezed Belle's shoulder. "Give it time."

"Time," she muttered. "So why didn't you tell me, Maudie?" she asked the unconscious woman a couple minutes later, as she prepared to do another blood-pressure reading. No answer, of course, not that Belle expected one. But the reading was much better. Maudie was stabilizing, thank heavens. Now, if she could just get the rest of her life to stabilize as well.

CHAPTER SEVEN

THE first thing Belle did before she even rolled out of bed was call to check on Maudie. She'd called once during the night, learned Maudie was stable. This time, though, the news was a little more grave. Maudie was on her way to have an angioplasty, due to another cardiac episode having happened shortly after Belle had called earlier. "But she's stable?" she asked the attending physician.

"She doesn't want to be sidelined," Dr. Redmond told her. "Wants to get out of here and get back to work. Overall, I'd say she's hanging in pretty well. Once we get the procedure done—"

"And this condition. Long-standing?" Belle interrupted.

"Going on to two years."

Somewhere in the middle of the night, Belle had convinced herself that it was a relatively new condition to Maudie, and maybe not talking about it had been Maudie's way of coming to terms with it. But two years? "Well, tell Maudie I'll come up to see her as soon as I can. And Dr. Redmond, if there's anything she needs, or anything I can do, call me, will you?" After she hung up, Belle stayed flat on her back in bed, staring up at nothing in particular. An angioplasty was a common procedure, often a preventative for bigger problems, like full-out heart attacks. Specifically, an angioplasty opened blocked or narrowed coronary arteries and improved blood flow to the heart. Shortly, a small mesh tube would be placed in Maudie's artery to help keep it open. Then soon Maudie would be up and about, probably back to work, on restricted duty, in a week or two.

But it wasn't the angioplasty that bothered Belle. It was the fact that Maudie hadn't told her about her heart condition. Which got back to the same old thing. She wasn't being well received here. In other words, she was buying a medical practice in a town that didn't trust her medical services. It was troubling, especially since she was wagering her and Michael's futures here. More than that, it was frustrating.

For the first time since she'd come to Big Badger, an awful lot of misgivings about making this her permanent home were pelting her. Even the disdain of the men hadn't caused that, but discovering how her nurse didn't trust her enough to tell her she had angina pectoris, that shook her to the core. It made her look bad, gave the people here something else for speculation. If Maudie didn't trust Dr. Carter, what's wrong with Dr. Carter?

"But I want to stay," she said, finally pushing herself up then dropping both her feet to the floor. "I like it here, it's a good place for Michael." And she wasn't a quitter. Never had been, except on her marriage, and that handwriting had probably been on the wall long before she'd said "I do." She'd just ignored it.

Well, she could ponder it all she wanted but that didn't change the fact that she needed to get up and get her day going. A trip past the mirror on her way downstairs revealed a fright. No surprise there. Mussed hair, tired eyes—she looked exactly like she felt this morning, and she didn't care. No one was there to see her and by the time she got to her office, a little dab of makeup and some artful combing would put her in order. She wanted coffee right now, though, before she started anything. Lots of it. So she trudged out her bedroom and straight into the half-naked torso she hadn't seen half-naked in years.

"Why are you in my house?" she asked, startled to find him there. "Wearing nothing but boxer shorts?"

"Decided to take you up on the offer of a nice, soft bed for a couple days since mine is delayed in arrival." He stretched, twisted left, twisted right, showing off a pretty magnificent pectoralis major. Rather than thinking how that particular chest muscle received dual motor action by the medial pectoral nerve and the lateral pectoral nerve, the way a doctor should, all she could think was, Wow! Really, just—wow!

So with that thought in her head Belle glanced down at Cade's bare toes then up at the morning stubble on his chin, taking particular care to avoid the delicious landscape along the way. But remembering it, every solid, fine-looking inch of it. Dear God, make it stop! Then, huffing out an impatient sigh when it wouldn't, she shoved on past Cade and continued down the hall. "Put some clothes on, Cade. And stay out of my way," she called back, not turning around to look at him again.

He chuckled. "You never were a morning person, and the years haven't changed that."

"When did I lose the last shred of control over my life?" she asked, as she kept on trudging, trying not to think about what she'd encountered. But the harder she tried to blot it out, the more it seeped in, leaving her to wonder where ever had he got those muscles? He sure hadn't looked like that when they'd been married. Good, yes. But not great, the way he did now.

Twenty minutes later, fully invested in her second cup of coffee and a piece of buttered toast, with Cade finally out of her visual memory, Belle was beginning to feel like herself again. Normally, her mornings meant getting Michael up and making sure he got dressed, had breakfast, brushed his teeth, combed his hair. Then sending him on his way, either to school or to stay with Virginia Ellison, who'd raised her own autistic son and loved taking care of Michael. It all worked out perfectly. Michael had a great caregiver who loved him, Virginia was happy being needed again, and Belle had amazing peace of mind with the arrangement. All that was a large part of the reason she didn't want to leave here. Everything worked out.

Damn it! Big Badger was everything she needed. Yet this morning she was still hung over with the feeling that she wasn't what Big Badger needed, and that mattered more than what she wanted, as being a good doctor here was important—to her, to Michael, to the town. But how good could she be if the people wouldn't even let her try? In the scheme of things, that might be what ended up mattering the most.

"She came through it fine," Cade said, sitting down next to her on a stool at the breakfast bar.

"What?" Belle said, glumly.

"The angioplasty. I called to check on Maudie, and the procedure went well. I mean, I thought you were worried about her and that's why you're looking so… rough." He took the coffee mug Belle had pushed away, pulled the coffee-pot over to himself and poured himself a fresh cup, with the exception of the inch she'd left in the bottom. "Is there something else going on?"

"You!" she snapped. "That's what's going on." She gave him a quick appraisal, glad to see his jeans and T-shirt, yet a little sad he hadn't joined her in his boxers. He did look good, and when all else seemed to be going sour, having a nice view first thing in the morning should have started the day off better than it was starting. But Cade was only a temporary fix, not a solution to her problems. She sighed, and scooted the plate with the last piece of toast over at him, to go along with the coffee she'd left in the cup. Once, that kind of sharing had been intimate, normal. Now it seemed wasted. "You know, my life was fine, then you showed up and now you're drinking out of my coffee cup! My coffee cup, Cade. Like you had some proprietary right to it. That's what's going on."

"It's not about the coffee cup, Belle," he said sympathetically. "Don't even think it's about me showing up here, since I've shown up a couple times a month pretty regularly since you moved down here. So care to talk about it?"

She twisted to face him. "What I'd care to talk about is why you're really here. And why now? The rest of it, why half the town refuses to let me be their doctor, why my own office nurse doesn't trust me enough to tell me she has a serious heart condition..." Belle swiped angrily at her hair, pushing it back from her face. "Those aren't questions you can answer, and since you won't answer me about why, out of the blue, you have this need to be underfoot, there's nothing to talk about. Oh, and don't tell me it's about spending more time with Michael. Because that's just your excuse, Cade. I may not have got some of the important things right about you when I fell in love with you, but I do know when you're not being honest with me."

She pushed off the bar stool, but before she could get away, Cade grabbed hold of her arm. "Look, Belle. I know you're feeling like hell over the way the town's treating you. But you're replacing a man who took care of every last one of these people for over forty years. That's a hard legacy to inherit. The town advisory board thought you could do it, though, which is why they hired you and not somebody else. So maybe some of the people here aren't lining up at your door yet, but give it time. You've only been here two months. And in another forty years, when you're retiring, I promise they won't be too accepting of the newbie coming to replace you either." He grinned. "Because they're going to find out what I found out a long time ago. That you can't be replaced." He let go of her arm.

"Knock off the charm, Cade. I'm not in the mood for it this morning."

"Bad night?"

Bad morning, she thought, but didn't say it aloud. Finding Cade in her hall, then discovering she couldn't control her feelings about him—at least, some of her feelings—had started her day off with a thud. Then Maudie. And the *E. coli* outbreak that wasn't getting solved. All that on top of some realizations about her status here she didn't want to be realizing. Yes, it was a bad morning all the way around, and even a peek at Cade's magnificent muscles wasn't going to shake that mood out of her. "I didn't mean to take it out on you. Sorry. It's just that things are piling up on me. And I miss Michael. That's probably the worst of it."

"Yet you were willing to send him off to a program for three weeks?"

"Because that's what's best for him. Doesn't mean I wouldn't be miserable, though." And lonely, and depressed. As well as worried every minute of every day. "It's not easy letting go. I know he's only seven now, but I think about the time when he leaves, whether it's off to college or out to start his own life, and it…" Her voice trailed off as she visualized Michael as a grown man. Handsome, like his dad. But that look in his eyes, the one she saw every now and then—the one that said naive in the world. That's what scared her most for her son, what she worried about on those nights she couldn't sleep.

"He's going to be fine, Belle. You're going to get him ready to face the things he'll face, and you're going to help him become a man who will achieve his fullest potential." He laughed. "Dr. Michael Carter, world-renowned entomologist."

"Or Mike Carter, one of the wealthiest people in the world due to his game creations."

"Who has a bug hobby."

Belle smiled. "And parents who clip articles about him and stash them in scrapbooks." It was nice, sharing a dream with Cade. They'd done it when she'd been pregnant—talked about what their child would be when he or she grew up. Hopes and dreams. Futures to fulfill. "Remember when you wanted to name him Phineas?"

"Or you wanted to name her Calendula?"

"I did not!" she said, laughing. "It was Calen, after my mother, and Della after my grandmother. Calen Della Carter, if he'd been a girl."

"Why didn't we want to know the baby's gender?" Cade asked. "Do you even remember?"

"Because from the time I was a little girl—"

"Now I remember. It was your dream to hear the doctor say, 'Mrs. Carter, it's a—'"

"Mrs. Carter, it's a boy!" Belle supplied, shutting her

eyes to recall the moment of Michael's birth and she'd heard she had a son. A perfect, beautiful little boy with ten toes and ten fingers. "Remember how loud he was, like he was angry to be here?"

"Did a man proud, to hear his son come fighting his way into the world the way Michael did." Cade exhaled an audible sigh. "Except I was late."

"Late for eighteen hours of labor and the actual birth. But you got there right after."

"Which wasn't good enough." Suddenly, the nostalgic moment turned sour, and Cade stood up then headed for the door. "I always understood why you divorced me, Belle. I was mad as hell for a long time, but I did understand. And for what it's worth, I'm sorry I made the divorce as hard on you as I made the marriage. You deserved better than anything I ever gave you."

"You gave me Michael, Cade." She smiled. "That makes up for everything." Words spoken that he didn't hear, though, because by the time she'd said them, he'd slammed out the door. Punishing himself, Belle thought. For Michael, for the breakdown of their marriage, but there was something else, and Cade was the master of keeping himself in the shadows of evasion.

"Well, the good news is, everything I treated this morning was routine." Cade was sitting at her desk, in her rolling desk chair, with his feet propped up, looking like he belonged there. "Nothing out of the ordinary for a family practice."

"Like you'd know what's ordinary for a family practice," she said, shoving him all the way to the other side of the office.

"I'll admit, it's a challenge."

"It's a challenge and you're anxious to get back to your surgical practice. No?"

"Don't sound so hopeful about my leaving. Because working in a different type of medicine gives me a brand-new perspective. I don't really mind it."

"That's not going to get you on my good side," she warned, fighting back a smile. Cade was trying so hard to get along, it was almost endearing. Too bad he hadn't tried this hard when they'd been married.

"Then tell me what will?"

"I want that date tonight. Barring unforeseen emergencies, I've got a light schedule for the rest of the day, no evening calls on any of the ranches, and you owe me. So I want to collect." OK, where had that come from? Because those spontaneous words seemed to have popped right out of her before she'd thought about the implications of her asking him out.

He straightened up in the chair, looking more than a little surprised. "To what do I owe this sudden change of heart?"

Now she wondered if she should take back the invitation. She thought about it for a moment, landing on the fact that Cade wasn't bad company. There'd been times in the past when he'd been great company. So why not? "Calling it a change of heart is pretty optimistic. Let's say that I wouldn't mind an evening with good food, wine, and some adult conversation."

"Not to be confused with adult activity, I'm guessing."

Even though his little innuendo caused her heart to skip a beat, she didn't comment on it. "Can you still ride?"

"We're not talking a traditional restaurant, are we?"

"There's this little spot out on the Chachalaca. A bluff

overlooking the plains. Not pretty like where we went camping, but you can see forever from there, and I've always wondered what it would look like at sunset." She'd gone there once to treat a ranch hand for a rattle-snake bite, and had always longed to go back. But not with Michael. He was too young, the land too rough. Too many dangers to go there alone. But with Cade? Suddenly, her heart skipped another beat, as there were different kinds of dangers involved in going there with him. But her life was so routine. No variations. No way to step outside herself, not even for a minute. And this seemed so daring. A way to shake off the routine for a little while, and simply be Belle Carter, not doctor, not mother.

Cade stood, then bowed at the waist. "Your wish is my command."

"In the meantime…" she waved her spreadsheet of patients at him "…I've got one more patient." She glanced down at the page to see who was up next. Then laughed. Mr. Brent Gilmore. A man on her list! Maybe things were beginning to look up after all.

"Michael and I come out here occasionally. He has quite a way with animals—loves horses. And the people here at Chachalaca really like Michael so we can ride any time we want. We don't get to do it often enough be-cause of my schedule." Never enough time was the tough part about being a single mom.

"Here I am, the Texas native living in Chicago, and you, the princess of the greater metropolitan Toronto area living in Texas. How did this happen, Belle?"

"It happened when we met in San Francisco and ev-erything changed." In one swift motion she pulled her-self up onto Sally, the dappled gray mare she always rode, looking far more experienced at horseback riding than she was. "Love, marriage, child, divorce, the quest for a better life—that's how it happened."

The stallion chosen for Cade by the ranch foreman was midnight black. Stunning creature. Temperament of a pussy cat. And Cade pulled himself into the saddle like the experienced horseman he was. "Wow. I've missed this. When I was a kid, we had a couple of horses and my dad and I rode all the time. I took it for granted because it was simply part of what we did, nothing special. But it's been years and, damn, I miss Texas."

"Life moves in strange directions sometimes. My parents owned a pharmacy. I lived in an apartment upstairs with them, then in one with you. Then in a third-floor walk-up with Michael after you and I divorced. Always in a big city. I'd never even been to Texas until I moved here, but I think I'd miss it, too."

"It does move in strange directions," Cade said, patting his horse on the neck. "Speaking of direction, you lead. Because I have no idea where this perfect place is."

The perfect place. Belle thought about that as they ambled over the rocky trail for the next little while. To her, it wasn't a place so much as it was a state of mind, or even a state of being. Perfect meant being with Michael. One time it had meant Michael and Cade. And even now, when she pictured, in her mind, what was perfect, while Michael was front and center, she did catch a glimpse of Cade standing off to the side. Maybe it was habit. Maybe she'd never really taken the time to reframe her picture. Or maybe...

Cade back in the picture, and not off to the side? That was the thought she wouldn't allow in, because no matter how much it seemed right, the three of them together scared her. Could she weather another go with Cade only to find out it was wishful thinking that got her back into the position where she'd found herself the first time around? He seemed different. Seemed more earnest in wanting to settle down, yet she wasn't sure if she could believe that. Then what about Michael? What would it do to him if they did get back together and discovered nothing had really changed? Tossing Michael about in all this was the risk she wouldn't take. Refused to take. Because there was one big thing, and it was the wall she couldn't break down in Cade. There was still something on the other side. She knew it, felt it with every fiber of her being. Cade was keeping something back, and it was something that worried her. So no matter how her emotions played out here, she wasn't going to act on them because Cade had proved himself, but not enough.

It was a sad revelation. But even now, in the middle of her life without him, Cade had set the course and like she'd been doing for the past near-decade, she followed it. Only now their roads divided, and she had her own to take. Her choice, yes. But in so many ways his choice as well. After all, he was the one who'd constructed the divide.

OK, the logical arguments were all firmly rooted, her defenses were up. Her choices. This time the shots were hers to call. So why did she feel so sad about it?

Because she still loved him. That's why. You loved who you loved, and there was no getting over it. No getting over Cade. But she could get past him, and that's what she had to do. Only how?

That was the question for which she didn't have an answer. And for the first time since she'd moved here, Big Badger, Texas, didn't seem far enough away from

Chicago to save her. "So the view isn't what I'd call stunning, but what amazes me about this place is how far you can see. I'm a city girl, the farthest I've ever been able to see in my life is the next street over. But look at this, Cade. It's like it never ends out there. If you go as far as your vision will take you, you'll drop off the edge." Sort of the way she'd been feeling these past few days—dropped off the edge.

Here they were, standing on the bluff, preparing for a simple picnic, and he was actually nervous, looking out over the barren landscape with Belle, because all he wanted to do was watch her. It was like he couldn't get enough of her. That's the way it had been the first time he'd ever laid eyes on her. She'd been loitering in the back of a pack of a dozen or so fourth-year medical students, hanging on his every word, gawking at the medical machines, so enthralled—and not the way the other women in the group had been enthralled. They'd been caught up in him. Belle had been caught up in what he'd been teaching, which was what had caught him up in her. She'd wanted his knowledge, his experience. Every last scrap of it. And there he'd been, a little more than cocky because he was used to the way the other women reacted to him. Sure, he liked to think he'd been impervious, or aloof, or too dedicated to notice that kind of attention. But he was human. He'd not only noticed, he'd enjoyed.

Then there had been Belle, the one who hadn't been affected. A challenge to him, because she'd had this purpose, and it had showed on her in everything she did, turning those six weeks of working with that bunch of students into the longest six weeks of his life, trying to hold back.

No, he'd never dated students, never dated nurses he worked with, never dated colleagues. Actually, truth be told, he'd rarely ever dated, and definitely never got himself involved in anything more than a temporary situation—temporary and blessedly short. With Belle, though, he'd wanted her to look at him the way the others did. Wanted to break his own rules, ask her out, worship at her feet, whatever. Some of it had been because of her looks. Who was he kidding? She was the most drop-dead gorgeous woman he'd ever met. But she was more than looks, and as the days had gone on, he'd discovered that most of his leanings toward her had been because of her determination. Belle had been strong, she'd kept her head no matter what had been going on around her, and she had been smarter than just about any medical professional he'd ever met. Yet so…unobtainable.

So he'd spent six frustrating weeks knowing that, at the end of them, she'd rotate onto another service and he'd be a thing of the past. On that last day, though, he'd decided to give it a shot. She'd say yes, she'd say no. Either way, he had to know.

And did he find out! Then gone on to totally destroy his life and lose the best thing that had ever happened to him. "Life does seem much simpler out here, doesn't it?" he asked.

Belle turned to face him. "We usually make our own complications, Cade. If we want it simple, we can have it simple. If we want it complicated, it's ours to complicate."

"I could take that as an accusation, you know."

"And I could intend it as one, because you did complicate my life a long time ago, but it's really just a statement of fact. Or perspective. Anyway, I've brought a simple picnic, some cheese, fruit, crusty bread, wine. Not your everyday Texas fare, but if you'd like to get the blanket from my saddlebag and find a nice place for us to eat—"

"What's your perspective, Belle?" he asked, interrupting. "What's your perspective of you, me? Of us?"

"That's an odd question. I'm not sure you've ever asked me about, well, anything that matters to me. I mean, maybe you might have asked early on in our relationship, but if you did it got covered up by so many other things that I don't remember."

"We got covered up by so many other things," he said. "And I regret it."

"What's done is done. We didn't survive, and maybe that's my perspective. We didn't survive but I did, and I don't cry myself to sleep at night over things that will never be. Life moves on and you've got two choices— move with it, or let it go on without you. Michael's the one who shows me that every day. It's tough for him, being different, and so much of the time I see him trying to swim upstream. Kids tease him, he doesn't fit in for a number of reasons, yet he moves with it every day, facing the fight with a strength I don't understand, and couldn't duplicate if I tried. Our little boy is seven, with a lifelong condition that will carry him to amazing places and limit him in ways most people can't understand, and I survive every day because of him, because of what I see in him." She swiped a tear from her cheek. "That's my perspective, too. It's not simply one thing. It's—it's everything."

Without saying a word, Cade walked straight over to Belle and pulled her into his arms. She went willingly, and pressed herself to him the way she'd done all those years ago. He'd missed it, missed the feel of her, missed the emotional intimacy in such a simple thing. And he wanted it back. Wanted Belle back. Wanted his family back.

But how? Wanting something and knowing how to get it were two separate things. He wanted more deeply than he'd ever wanted in his life. Even so, he was further away from having what he wanted than he'd ever been in his life. And maybe that was because he was only just now beginning to understand how much he'd lost. Yet through his loss it was obvious Belle had gained so much. So he was the one to release her, to head for his horse, to find the picnic blanket. But before he reached it, his cellphone rang. Belle's rang at exactly the same time, and they both clicked on, listened...

"I'm on my way," she choked, looking at Cade, who was already looking up, waiting for the helicopter.

"A couple of the men from the Chachalaca are on their way out to pick up the horses," he said to her, then turned his back to speak quietly to Amanda Robinson on his cellphone. "How bad is it?" he asked urgently.

"Bad," she replied. "I sent him in by ambulance, and I'll be on my way as soon as I make sure the rest of the kids here in the camp are taken care of. But I think you'll be there before I get there."

The whir of the rotors overhead caused him to look up again. "Thanks." He clicked off the call, turned his back to Belle, and made another quick phone call, then went over to Belle and took her hand. "Dr. Robinson sent the helicopter. She called your service, they told her where we were," he shouted, as they ran to the flat stretch beyond the bluff, while the pilot sat the chopper down in a whirlwind of dust and waited for Cade and Belle to climb on board so he could take them to the hospital, where Michael had been admitted a while earlier, displaying the classic signs of *E. coli* infection, but with serious complications.

"I've been on the phone with the hospital. He's already there and they called for my permission to—to put him on dialysis, Cade," Belle managed to say as she strapped herself into the helicopter seat. "He's not…"

Cade strapped himself in next to, motioned for the pilot to take off. "Your Dr. Robinson caught it early, Belle. She recognized the symptoms."

"But he would have been sick when he went with her."

"Showing no symptoms."

"No symptoms, Cade? He never complains about anything. I sent him to school with a hundred-degree fever one day and didn't even know that he had a virus. The school nurse caught it because he was eating ice—ice to cool himself down. I'm a doctor, and I didn't even see that my own son was sick. And with this…" She visibly shuddered, then wrapped her arms around herself. "Everybody here's getting sick and I've been too concerned about saving some cows to do what I should have…"

Cade grabbed hold of Belle's arm and gave her a gentle shake. "Stop it!" he ordered. "You're not doing yourself any good taking the blame, and it's certainly not going to help Michael if you're in such a bad emotional state when he sees you in a little while."

"Sees me? He's not going to see me, Cade. Michael was admitted unconscious. The emergency doctor said he was so sick he went into a coma right after he got there, and I'm not there to…" Tears streamed down her face, and she sniffled. "To hold him when he needs me."

Cade tried putting his arm around her, but she shoved him away.

"Don't," she snarled. "Just—don't!"

"That's right. You're the one who gets to be the martyr, aren't you? Just shove me away and take it all on your shoulders."

"How dare you? You weren't even in the country when Michael was diagnosed with Asperger's syndrome. In fact, I didn't even know where you were. Hadn't heard from you in three weeks."

"I was in Cambodia, working in an amputee clinic. You knew where I was, if you'd wanted to call me. Or e-mail."

"In Cambodia. Did you ever tell me where, exactly? Did it ever occur to you that I couldn't call you there, or that e-mails didn't go through? It went both ways, Cade. You knew where your wife and son were if you'd wanted to call or e-mail them."

"And you punished me for it, Belle. Didn't tell me for weeks that my son had been tested for autism. No, you kept that to yourself, like I didn't have a right to know. Like I didn't love my son as much as you did."

"I was angry. I didn't want to deal with…you. With anything." She shut her eyes and laid her head back against the seat, allowing the jarring from the choppy ride to divert her emotions, past and present. "I know you love him as much as I do," she finally admitted. "But it always hurt, Cade, being so alone. You had the right to know, but I hated you for abandoning me when I needed you, and I was angry at God for Michael's diagnosis, and angry at myself for all the things I couldn't control. Like now, I'm so damn angry I don't know what to do. It's not fair." She balled fists and pounded her knees. "None of it is and I wasn't there to…"

"I'm scared, too," he said, taking her balled fist into

his hand and holding on for dear life. "And there's something I need to tell you now. Something I should have told you years ago, when we met, or when we married. But I didn't, and I'm apologizing now, because we can't fight about it with Michael so sick."

She drew in a ragged breath. "What you're about to tell me. Is that why you're really here?"

"No. I'm here for Michael. But it's—it's complicated."

"How, Cade?"

"I've asked someone to come help us. Called before we got on the helicopter. He's a public health doctor who's pretty much burned out for the moment. Taking this part of his life off. Spending most of his time now on a fishing boat, anchored at dock off the east coast of Texas, not fishing. But he's brilliant."

"And your brilliant, burned-out friend can help us how?"

"He's worked in some pretty difficult regions in the world, in the middle of some rough outbreaks—Africa, South America. He knows what to look for with something like the *E. coli* going around in Big Badger, and better than that he knows how to look. We need to find the source, need to find out how Michael..." He swallowed hard. "We can't protect Michael from it now, but we have to protect other children, protect everybody in town."

"You friend, if he's left medicine, then how, or why—?"

Cade held up his hand to stop her. "Jack may have some different insight into treatment as well, because that's what he does. He'll know what's best for Michael."

"You'll trust our son to this acquaintance of yours?" she snapped.

"Not to an acquaintance, Belle. To Michael's uncle."

She shook her head. Tried to process what he'd just said. "Michael's uncle? What are you talking about, Cade?"

"Something I should have talked about years ago."

"A brother? You have a brother? How could you not tell me, Cade?" She was too stunned to be angry.

"Half brother. We're estranged. Have been for a decade or more."

"Oh, so being estranged makes it all right, not telling me that my son has an uncle?"

"It's complicated, Belle. And now's not the time to get into this."

"Apparently, all those years we were married weren't the time either, were they? *Oh, Belle, by the way, let me tell you about my brother.* But it's so typical of you, isn't it? Excluding me from pretty much every aspect of your life?" Another case of someone not trusting her enough. The others were frustrating, but this one hurt. Except she couldn't process it now, let alone deal with it. So she twisted away from Cade and stared at nothing.

"He's on his way," Cade said, despite her withdrawal. "Going to meet us at the hospital. And so you'll know, he's not sociable. Probably not even friendly. But I want him working on Michael."

"Then I'll have to trust you on that, won't I? Trust being the key word here since apparently I'm expected to give it even though I don't get it from the people who matter in my life." Belle huffed out an annoyed breath. "You haven't changed at all, Cade. I thought, maybe— You know what? It doesn't matter what I think. To you, it never did."

"You're wrong," he said, almost under his breath.

She batted at the tears streaking down her cheeks. Angry tears mixed with tears of fear. "How can I not be wrong, Cade? Tell me, because I'd like to know when, in our marriage, something about me ever mattered to you."

"It was never you, Belle. I promise, the problem was never you."

"That's not good enough, because I was the one left alone, and left out. And you were the one who left me alone and left me out of God only knows what." She drew in a ragged breath then turned to him and saw the most excruciating agony on his face. It was a pain far deeper than anything she could cope with at the moment, so she turned away and thought about Michael, only Michael, for the rest of the ride.

Minutes later, as they exited the helicopter and prepared to face whatever they had to, Belle grabbed Cade by the arm and stopped him from running straight through the emergency-room doors. "We've got to stop this," she said to him. "The *E. coli*, we've got to stop it. Tell your brother, when he gets here, that he'll have access to anything he needs in Big Badger. And if he has treatment to recommend for Michael, I'll listen."

"We'll listen. Don't shut me out of this, Belle."

"It hurts, doesn't it?" she said, then let go of his arm and ran through the hospital doors.

Cade didn't go in right away, though. As much as he wanted to, Belle was right. It did hurt being left out. But that had been his choice, hadn't it?

"He looks like you," Jack said, stepping up to the observation window going into Michael's intensive-care room. "Better looking. Could pass for Robbie's twin, I think."

Cade spun to his brother. "This isn't about Robbie!" he snapped.

"No, it's about my nephew. Otherwise not speaking

to you for another decade would have been my pleasure." He stepped around Cade, pulled a stethoscope from his pocket, and headed toward the door. "Mind if I have a look at him?"

Rather than answering, Cade waved him ahead, then followed him into the room.

Belle looked up, but not at Cade. "You would be Jack Kenner, wouldn't you?"

"And you would be my ex-sister-in-law. The one I never knew I had."

Rather than answering, Belle did a quick assessment—large man, close to Cade's size. But there was no resemblance beyond that. Black hair. Dark brown eyes that saw no laughter. A mouth that never curved into a smile. Striking, but severe. Startlingly handsome, and with the same sadness or distance she saw in Cade's eyes from time to time. "Belle Carter," she said, standing then extending a hand to him. "And this is your nephew, Michael."

Jack stepped to the bedside, then simply stared down for a moment. Not breathing, not moving. Just looking. And Cade knew why. The resemblance to Robbie at that age was startling. He didn't notice it so much because he saw Michael on a regular basis and to him Michael looked like Michael. But to be confronted by the past in such an immense way, the way Jack was now, Cade felt bad for him. One more thing to add to the list. "He's had dialysis. They haven't figured why he went downhill so fast, but he's stabilizing."

Jack nodded. Drew in a ragged breath. "Any sign the kidneys are starting to kick in yet?"

"Not yet," Belle said.

Jack turned to face Belle. "Would you mind if I examine him?"

"I'd appreciate it. When Cade told me—"

"You didn't know I existed, did you? Married to the man, and he never bothered to tell you about us?"

She glanced over at Cade, whose full attention was devoted to Michael. "I expect Cade has his reasons," Belle said, surprised that she was defending Cade, and even more surprised that she wanted to defend him.

"You're one of them?" Jack asked. "Even after you're divorced?"

"One of whom?"

"The legions who fall at his feet."

"Actually, Jack, I was the legion who married him and had his child. And while it's none of your business, I want you to know that I don't fall at anybody's feet. Not Cade's, not yours. Nobody's."

Jack's answer was a low whistle and the slight arching of his eyebrows.

Admiration? Probably not. In all likelihood he was thanking the Fates he hadn't been the one to marry her, Belle decided, suddenly quite pleased with herself. "Oh, and I appreciate you coming to help. Cade speaks highly of your skills—"

"I don't give a damn what he speaks highly of," Jack interrupted, putting his stethoscope earpieces in. "I wanted to help the kid. We may not be blood, but…"

"What do you mean, not blood?" she gasped.

A sly smile crept to Dr. Jack Kenner's lips. "Seems my brother hasn't told you something else." With that, he bent down over Michael and placed the bell to his chest. "Now, if you two will excuse me, I want to make this between Michael and me. I'll let you know when I want you back in the room."

"You're kicking me out?" Belle snapped.

"Not kicking you out so much as asking you to leave.

I don't need all the negative energy in here while I'm trying to get to know my nephew. And you and Cade have enough negative energy going to melt the polar ice caps all the way from Texas."

Belle swallowed hard, then stood and bent over Michael, kissing him tenderly on the cheek. "I'll be right outside in the hall," she whispered to him. "Your Uncle Jack has come to have a look at you, Michael. He's a very good doctor and he's going to take care of you." She kissed him again, then righted herself and marched out of the room, straight past Jack, straight past Cade, who followed her out, then took his place next to her at the observation window.

"How is he not related to Michael, if he's your half brother?" she muttered at Cade.

"My mother married Gerald Kenner after she and my father divorced. Jack is Gerald's son, and my mother adopted him, making him my half brother legally, no blood relationship."

"You have a mother? Since you never talked about her, I always assumed— No, you know what? It doesn't matter what I assumed. This is all about Michael, and the rest of your secrets simply don't matter to me."

"Not secrets, Belle."

"How is the presence of another family I knew nothing about not a secret? Oh, wait! It's complicated, isn't it?"

"Do you want it now?" he asked. "The short version? Because it starts with a bad mother, who didn't want to be stuck with a lower-middle-class domestic life, so she left my dad and me, married up, got everything she wanted. Because that's it, Belle. My mother walked out. Said she didn't want to be saddled with—well, for starters, me. I heard her say that. 'Why do I have to be saddled with him?' Then she traded me in for a son who at least came with a pedigree and an old man with lots of money and status. So the reason I never mentioned it is because—what was the point?"

"I'm sorry," she said, her voice low. "You didn't deserve that, Cade, but I still don't understand…" She shifted her focus back to Michael, and to Jack, who'd sat down next to the bed, taken care of Michael's hand, and was simply talking to him. "Does he have children?"

"No. Never married. But he loves them."

"I can see that." She turned to Cade. "Look, for what it's worth, I'm glad you brought him here. Whatever you two have going between you doesn't matter, at least not right now. But I want to know, Cade. At some point, I want to know everything, because it's about Michael, too. His right to know. And I'll try and keep my ego out of it since—"

"I was wrong," Cade interrupted. "About everything. And I'm sorry, Belle. For more than you know." With that, she went back to sit at Michael's bedside, while Jack left the room and took his place in the hall next to Cade.

"You said your mother married up," Jack said, stopping at the window and looking back in. "I think you did, Cade. Belle deserved better than you."

"Finally, we agree on something. So, what about Michael?"

"Holding his own. Vital signs are stable, I'm cautiously optimistic that once we get the *E. coli* cured his kidney function will return. I've seen it happen like this before, seen good outcomes at the end of it. No reason to think otherwise for Michael."

"Thanks, Jack. For everything. After, well—after Robbie, I wasn't sure."

"Like you said, this isn't about Robbie. So tell me,

what kind of an idiot would let someone like your amazing country doctor get away? Oh, that's right, I already said idiot, didn't I? Which answers my question."

Cade chuckled. "I'd like to say it's good to see you, Jack, but it's not." His brother looked good, though. Rugged. A little tired. He certainly had a weathered look about him, one Cade didn't remember. But it had been ten years, and Jack had still been soft back them, struggling through medical school, struggling with Robbie's death. Time changed people. On the outside time had been good to Jack, but on the inside Cade didn't have a clue.

"You always were brutally honest, except about the things that counted."

"Want to go grab a beer?" Cade asked, for a lack of anything better to offer his brother. "There's a little pub across from the hospital, and right now I think Belle would be glad to get rid of the both of us."

"Sure. Why not? Then we can sit and look at each other across the table while we're not indulging in old memories."

"I sit at the bar. The only thing I'm going to look at is the TV above the bar."

"If that's the case, I'm in. And you're buying. It's the least you can do for interrupting my fishing."

"Fishing?" Cade quipped, as they headed off together down the hall.

Belle watched them from the door to Michael's room, wondering what the real story was.

While Cade and Jack were definitely not together, they weren't exactly apart either. Strange, she thought, going back to the chair next to the bed. Definitely strange. But, then, what, about her life lately hadn't been strange?

* * *

He'd been standing there for about an hour now, looking in on Michael, while Belle sat at the bedside, holding Michael's hand. Trying to figure out a way to approach her, or just to be part of that family. It's all he wanted. And everything he'd screwed up. One screw-up compounded by another.

"You're not in there?" Jack asked.

"I was. We've decided to take turns. She'll sit with him a while so I can rest, then I'll go in while she rests."

"Well, isn't that just the united front Michael's going to want from his parents when he wakes up?" Jack snapped.

Cade turned slowly to face his brother. "If I weren't so damned angry about things that matter, I'd take offense, maybe even pound your face in the way I did that day when you accused me of taking money from your wallet."

"But you did, didn't you? Twenty bucks. That you never paid back, by the way."

"That's beside the point. We were sixteen, it didn't count."

"Michael's hanging in there, Cade. The drug I managed to procure is working."

"How did you get it, Jack? It's still in clinical trials."

"Showing amazing results. Michael's going to be one of those results."

"But nobody can just get a clinical trial drug because they want it." Except, perhaps, his brother. "And I read that it's the most expensive drug ever manufactured. So give."

"Favors. I was owed, I collected. And if the European trials weren't so overwhelmingly successful, I wouldn't have. That's all there is to say, except Michael's primary-care physician is encouraged by Michael's progress. He's got urinary output again, which means his kidneys are working. His vital signs are still stable. He's unconscious, but that's because his body is fighting hard to throw off the infection. All of which means it's time for me to head out to Big Badger to see what the hell you've got going on there. And I wouldn't be leaving Michael if he wasn't doing better." He put his arm around Cade's shoulder and, surprisingly, Cade didn't shrug it off. "Look, I'm going to go in there for a few minutes and talk to Michael before I leave. And for what it's worth, if Belle needs me to see a few patients while I'm in Big Badger—"

"See patients? And just when I'd convinced her there's nothing redeemable in you."

"For you, there's not. But I've got a nephew who needs his parents to be here, so I've got to make that happen." He stepped away from Cade. "Now go get yourself a cup of coffee, and drag her with you, if that's what it takes." He nodded to Belle, who'd barely moved, even to switch positions, in the last hour. "I'm going to sit with him for a while and hope to God you two will go off somewhere and work out whatever it is you have to work out, because I sure as hell don't want my nephew waking up in the middle of it."

Cade sighed heavily, then nodded. "Just give me a minute with her, OK? She's not doing very well with this."

"And you are?" Jack asked, his voice uncharacteristically full of concern.

"Doesn't matter what I am, does it?" He stepped back from the observation window, then turned and walked into the room. But at the door, he stopped. Didn't turn to face Jack. Just stopped and lingered there as if he was thinking. "At some point, I think you and I need to talk."

Said to the air, though, because when he finally looked at Jack, Jack was on his way to the nurses' station.

"It's time to take a break," he said to Belle, stepping up behind her. "Jack said he'd like to sit here alone with Michael for a while and talk to him. So as soon as he gets back, how about we go get some coffee, or something to eat if you're hungry?"

"Not hungry," she said. "But I wouldn't mind stretching my legs if Jack wants to stay here for a few minutes." She looked up at Cade, "Look. In the helicopter, all those things I said—"

He shook his head, then forced a smile. "Don't remember you saying anything." Raising his hands to her shoulders, he began a gentle knead. "It's a lot to deal with, and nothing really counts but Michael getting better."

She melted into his touch. Relaxed for the first time in hours. "How could this have happened, Cade? I'm careful. Even though nothing I've had tested came back positive, I washed everything...double-washed. And now—" Her voice broke.

"He's holding his own right now. That drug Jack got hold of is working."

"Which isn't enough. He needs to be improving. Has to be improving." She twisted around to face him. "He's had dialysis, Cade. His kidneys are better now, but what if—what if Jack hadn't been able to work his miracle? And what am I going to do about the people in Big Badger? They need me, too, but I can't leave my son to go take care of them."

Cade stepped around to face her, then bent down.

"Shh," he said, reaching out and taking hold of both her hands. "It's all taken care of. Jack's going back there in a little while, and he's going to manage the practice for you."

"He'd do that?"

"His idea. Something about Michael needing us both here."

"He's a good man, Cade. I'm not even going to ask how he got the trial drug because I don't care. He did. That's all that matters. I didn't like him at first, and I was wrong. You are, too, if you still hate him. And while I don't know what's wrong between you two, you and Jack should…" She glanced over at Michael, studied the rise and fall of his chest. He was on oxygen, not a ventilator, so even that small movement reassured her Michael was still with her, even if, right now, the condition of his young body had taken his mind to another place. For safekeeping, was what she told herself. Michael's gone someplace for safekeeping. "You and Jack and Michael should spend time together as a family. Maybe go camping when Michael's up to it because he's going to need it, need that solidarity. I think Jack can be important to him. But I also think he can be important to Jack."

"You two ready for a break?" Jack asked from the doorway. His attention wasn't fixed on Belle or Cade, however. It was undivided, and only for Michael. "Because Michael and I've got some things to talk about." He walked over to the bed and looked down. Studied him for a moment, then nodded. "Lots of things, don't we, Michael?"

"Cafeteria?" Cade asked, once they'd left the room.

"I'd rather take a walk in the garden, if you don't mind. Step outside the hospital for a few minutes, breathe some real air. It gets a little confining in there." Instinctively, she looped her arm through Cade's the way they'd used to do when they'd been married. Back then it had been for the connection. She hadn't been able to get enough of him. Today, it was for the physical support because she wasn't sure her legs would carry her where she wanted to go. "Maybe on the way back in we could stop by Maudie's room for a minute. I hear she's going to be released tomorrow, and she's been sending messages, asking about Michael."

"She's really concerned, Belle."

"You saw her?"

"For a minute. She called me, so I ran upstairs to look in on her, and she's the same old Maudie. Loud, demanding, heart of gold. They've adjusted some of her medications, and she's going to be cleared for light duty in a week. Full duty in about a month—if you want her back."

"If I want her? What's that about? I never, ever said anything about—"

"She's past retirement age, Belle. That's why she didn't tell you about her heart condition. It wasn't because she didn't trust you. She was afraid that with her angina, on top of her age, you wouldn't want her as a nurse. That you'd hire someone half her age if you found out about her medical condition."

"Why would I want someone with half her experience? How would that be of benefit to my medical practice?" She breathed out a ragged breath. "Why didn't she ever tell me any of this, Cade? Am I that unapproachable?"

"It's not you, Belle. It's because it's not easy admitting our deepest fears, or talking about the things that hurt us most. Maudie doesn't need the income, she needs to be needed, and you're the one who has the power to change her life, to turn her into someone who's…unnecessary."

"So she'll talk to you and not to me. That's not the way it's supposed to work. But apparently I'm wrong about that. Nobody talks to me. Not you, not Maudie… Michael didn't even tell me he wasn't feeling well. I'm his mother, Cade, and he didn't—"

"Does it make it all better, torturing yourself this way?" he asked. "Because you can blame yourself over and over, say exactly the same words every time you do, but that won't change anything. Michael's sick, it's not your fault. You're not a bad mother because your son didn't tell you he was sick. And who knows, maybe he wasn't. Sometimes the symptoms hit so hard and fast you don't feel them coming on. Especially with some of the new strains of *E. coli* coming on the scene."

Moving through the garden, through the patches of prickly pear cacti blooming in various shades of yellow and gold and past the rows of lavender prairie verbena, they came to stop under a trellis draped with Carolina jasmine with its yellow blooms, and Confederate jasmine with its darker leaf and white blooms. The sight was magnificent but the scent… Belle shut her eyes and simply breathed it into her lungs, into her soul. "It would be nice, having a small hospital in Big Badger. One with a garden like this," she said, as she sat on the marble bench underneath the trellis. "Then people like Michael and Maudie wouldn't have to be so far from home when they're sick. Except Big Badger can't even really support a medical practice. If it weren't for the work I get from the ranches…" She paused, took in another deep, perfumed breath, then shook her head. "But none of that's important right now, is it? I should stay focused on Michael. Try to figure out if there's more I could be helping him with."

"You're giving him every bit of strength you have, Belle. That's all you can do."

"Is it?" she snapped. "If I hadn't brought him here to Texas, if I hadn't been trying so damned hard to prove that I could be as—as good a doctor as you are, then he'd be fine. But no! I had to uproot him from Chicago, move to a place I'd never even seen." She swiped at angry tears. "You don't know, Cade. You—you can't understand how I'm feeling right now. I'm so—"

"Numb?" he asked. "And angry, and scared? You want to hate someone, or something, but you don't know what or who? And if there were a wall in front of you, you'd like to put your fist through it, or kick through it, or fall against it and cry. Or run away? Or go to bed, pull the blankets up over your head, and pray you're not trapped in a nightmare? Most of all, you despise yourself for what you didn't see or know, or what you didn't do? And your heart is ripping in half, hurting so bad that you're not sure it's going to give up its next beat? Is that how you feel, Belle?"

She looked up at him, blinked back her tears. "I'm sorry, Cade. I know I'm not the only one who's feeling…" She shrugged.

"Well, you do come out of it the other end, Belle. For what it's worth, I've read to the back of the book already, and while I can't predict the exact detail of the plot, I do know the overall premise and you do get through it. You have to. There's not another choice."

It was said so bitterly it scared her. Even at his worst, Cade had never sounded like this. He was scared to death about Michael, but this cut deeper. She could sense it in him. "The exact detail is where Michael gets better. That's what I have to believe because it's all I can believe. But what you said…" She paused, drew in a deep breath, and braced herself. "This isn't about Michael, is it?" This was the rest of the story, something to do with Cade and Jack, something to do with why Cade was here. And it was a painful story. She could feel that even though Cade had yet to speak. "Please, tell me about it now," she encouraged.

"There's nothing to tell because everything's about Michael! My son is lying in there, in the medical intensive-care unit, fighting for his life."

"But the book you read the back of wasn't Michael's, or even mine." She drew in a shuddering breath. "Whose was it, Cade? Don't shut me out this time, because I have to know."

"Nothing I can tell you will make things better for Michael," he said, stepping out from under the trellis but not leaving. His back was to her now, he was staring off into a patch of tall pampas grass, looking at nothing, seeing nothing but his own misery. "I'd give my life for him, Belle. You've got to believe that. If Michael needed a healthy, beating heart, I'd rip mine out and hand it to them to put in him."

"I know you would," she said, walking up behind him, wrapping her arms around him and laying her head against his back. "But, Cade, you've still got to tell me. Maybe it won't help Michael, but it will help me help you, and he needs you right now—all of you, all of your strength. And you're torn. So for Michael…" At the mention of their son's name, she felt Cade's shoulders slump. Heard him draw in the ragged, tearful breath that finally, when it left him, would leave with the words he needed to say, the words she needed to hear. "Whose book, Cade?" she repeated.

"Robbie," he said. "My younger brother—by blood. Four years younger. Jack's younger brother, by blood, too."

There might have been a time when Cade revealing yet another secret would have made her angry, but not now. The rest of the words didn't matter, because she knew. "Your mother had a child by your stepfather."

He nodded. "Her way of trying to hold on to him, I suppose. And since she was such a good mother to the one she'd already had, as well as the one she'd adopted, why not? Except Robbie—he wasn't like Jack or me. He was…" His voice faded away off as he turned to face her. Then he drew in a bracing breath. "Robbie was autistic, Belle."

This was something she hadn't expected, and she bit down hard on her lip to keep from gasping. "Was it Asperger's syndrome?" she finally managed to ask.

Cade shook his head. "Kanner's syndrome. Robbie didn't connect to people. Certainly not to my mother, not even to his father. He was very much in his own little world, wanted everything to be the same all of the time. Wore the same clothes every day, ate the same food. Robbie was such a sweet little boy, Belle. Yet overall he wasn't very high functioning, and my mother hated that because Robbie made her look…bad. Made her look like a failure in her social circle. She hated it so much that she'd lock him in his room all day when he was home, so she didn't have to deal with him. And she was always sending him away to some sort of institution or program…"

Belle gasped. "Amanda's program. That's why you'd never talk to me about it. You did remember, though, didn't you? And you came here to prevent me from sending Michael because of the way your mother always sent Robbie. But why couldn't you tell me, Cade? Didn't you think I'd listen, or be sympathetic enough?"

"Robbie liked his world simple, and orderly, and that's all he wanted," Cade went on, seeming not to hear Belle. "Except…" He swallowed hard. "Attention from his older brothers. He craved Jack's and my attention."

Cade stepped away from her and returned to the bench underneath the trellis, where he finally sat down. "He loved Jack and Jack was so good with him. Took time, never turned him away. But me…it was never simple, and that's why I couldn't tell you. Because I did things I couldn't even admit to myself, let alone speak out loud."

"To Robbie?" She didn't know what to think yet, except she trusted Cade. No matter what he said, or thought, she trusted him and she was going to hold on to that.

He nodded. "To Robbie. See, the thing was, I didn't want to go visit my mother. Never wanted to visit her when it was her weekend to have me. Or her holiday. I fought to get out of it, but my dad always insisted I had to do the right thing. I mean, I knew the only reason dear old Mom even let me inside her house was for appearances, and the more I was forced to be around her, the angrier I got. The angrier I got, the more I resisted. And poor Robbie—he simply got caught in the crossfire. I think because I wasn't there most of the time, when I was, he wanted so much from me. Just time and attention, really. But I couldn't give it the way he wanted and I always looked for ways to avoid him, avoid the whole damned situation involving my mother."

The end to this story was something she wasn't going to want to hear. She was sure of it, and her heart was already starting to break, even though she didn't know why. But she'd started this, and there was nothing she could do to stop it, so she returned to the trellis and sat down beside Jack, taking care to keep her distance. His body language was rigid now, which meant he was rejecting sympathy, physical or otherwise. "Go on," she encouraged, glancing over at the hospital, wondering how Michael was. Surely Jack would come get her if Michael's condition changed? Still, she was nervous being away from him this long. Yet she couldn't get up and walk away from Cade now, and leave him here like this. "Tell me what happened."

"What happened was that Robbie never changed. He was always this sweet, innocent little kid who couldn't wait to see me. Year after year, that's just the way it was. But my mother hated him, the way she hated everything but her so-called status. And the older Robbie got, the bigger he got. It wasn't so easy to keep him in his room any more, and most of the places she sent him sent him right back to her because Robbie wandered off, and they didn't want to assume any responsibility for that.

"So, one Christmas. I was seventeen, Robbie was thirteen. And living in an institution, by the way, where he was getting picked on every single day of his life. The attendants there were rough on him, other kids beat him up. But it was the place that would keep him because they simply didn't care about their kids...or inmates, as they should have been called. Anyway, it was my holiday to spend with her, and I went grudgingly. Told my dad it was the last Christmas I'd spend in her house because I'd be eighteen shortly, and when I turned eighteen it was my intention never to see that woman again. So I went to her house. Of course, I was in my usual bad mood. Maybe even worse than usual, I don't know, because all I remember about what happened when I got there was that I locked myself in my room, and wondered why Robbie hated being locked in the way he did because it kept him away from her.

"So I was away in my own little world of anger and self-pity when my mother asked me to go and bring Robbie home for the holiday. I, of course, refused. And it didn't have anything to do with Robbie so much as it did me refusing to do what my mother asked. Besides, I knew Jack would go and get him. He was always the hero, the one who came through for Robbie no matter who else let him down."

"But Jack's circumstances were different, Cade."

"Were they? He was being raised by my mother. In fact, he lived under her brutality much longer than I ever had to."

"Without expectations of her. She wasn't his mother, and he knew that. Sure, it might have been rough on him, having to claim her as his mother, but maybe that was something he was able to blot out. I mean, Jack *seems a pretty unyielding kind of a guy, Cade. His sen*sibilities probably weren't like yours, and—"

"You don't have to defend me, Belle. I was who I was, justified or not. I loved Robbie, but I'm not sure Robbie ever knew that because I was too caught up in my own problems to ever reach out to him the way I should have." Feelings he was carrying over to Michael. Now she understood. She was sending Michael away, the way Cade's mother had sent Robbie away. Only the fine distinctions didn't matter, as Michael would have come home in three weeks. Cade's guilt didn't let him sort through the distinctions. All he saw was that his son was getting sent away, and she doubted Cade even knew that's why he'd come to Texas—to stop her. "So, what happened?"

"Jack got home late that night and said he'd go get Robbie the next day. Except no one ever told Robbie that was the plan. He expected to come home the day before, and when no one—when I didn't go to get him, he ran away. Afterwards, the authorities speculated he was trying to get home." He swiped angrily at a tear running down his cheek. "But I didn't have to speculate. I knew. Damn it, Belle, I knew!"

She was the one who drew in a ragged breath, trying to keep her balance, because all she could picture in her head was Michael out there lost and alone, somewhere, trying to get home. The same picture she knew was in Cade's head. Of Robbie. Even of Michael. "And?"

"December nights in Texas can get cold. That night it dipped down into the thirties, and Robbie wasn't dressed for it. Didn't even have on a pair of..." His voice cracked. "Shoes. The authorities found him two days later, but he was..." He shook his head. "The official cause of his death was exposure, but the death certificate might as well have said it was my anger that did him in, because if I'd gone to get him when he'd expected me, instead of hating my mother so much that I wouldn't do anything she asked..."

She scooted closer and took his hand. "I'm so sorry, Cade."

"Yeah, me, too," he said. "Fat lot of good that does Robbie, or even Michael."

But it did her good, because now she knew everything. And understood things in a way she'd never understood them before. Understood Cade in a way she'd never understood him before either. He'd spent a lifetime running away from himself, from his guilt. Spent all those years with his humanitarian causes, trying to make up for something he couldn't make right, not in himself, not in his world. It wasn't her he'd run from. Or marriage. Or Michael. All this time she'd thought it was, but it wasn't. "I, um…I don't know what it was like for you, having a mother like you described. I think it was terrible. Probably still is, because of the kinds of memories you still have. But you were a boy, Cade, and you deserved better. Even when Robbie died, you were still a boy—one who was left to carry guilt he didn't deserve."

"I never had enough time for him, Belle," he said, his voice barely above a whisper. "Robbie didn't know what was going on with me. He was so innocent about the world, the way I see Michael sometimes, I doubt Robbie even knew that my mother despised him the way she did. All he knew was that he had two brothers, and one of them pushed him away." He turned to face her. "And look what I've done to Michael. I pushed you away, which pushed him away."

"You can't compare the two situations, Cade. You love Michael, and you're a good father."

"When, exactly, am I a good father?" he asked bitterly. "Tell me, because I sure as hell don't know."

"When you fly down here every other weekend to see him, even when you know that Michael hasn't yet become responsive to you, which has to hurt you more than anything I can imagine. And when we were back in Chicago and you were there, getting the same kind of response from him, yet you always came back when I'm sure it might have been easier to find reasons not to be so involved."

"And when I get here on my weekends, I'm jet-lagged, and he'd rather play video games. That's your definition of being a good father? Because to me it's just time. I'm spending time with Michael, but that's all."

"You're here now, and now is what counts."

"And he's lying unconscious in an intensive-care bed, and I'm not even able to—"

"To save your son?" she asked, giving in to the tears that had been trying to spill for a while now. "You're not even able to save our son?"

He twisted to face her, his tears as bitter as hers. "I don't know how to be enough for him, Belle. Or for you. I never did. All those years when I was growing up, I got good at shutting people out or running away when they got too close. Had lots of practice. Then you got in. But when it was just the two of us—you were strong. You got along fine in the world and I didn't feel as inadequate because of that. Then when Michael came along…"

"You were afraid to love us because you were afraid of failing us? Of failing Michael?" He'd run because he believed he'd failed Robbie and he was scared to death of failing Michael, too. "Did you know, Cade? Even before Michael was diagnosed with Asperger's syndrome, did you know what his diagnosis was going to be? Did you see something in him that made you think…? Did he remind you of Robbie?"

Slowly, very, very slowly, Cade withdrew his wallet then opened it. Inside was an old photo, one he kept behind his credit cards, library card and driver's license. One that didn't have its proper place in the plastic photo section where he carried photos of Michael. He withdrew that photo, and didn't look at it as he handed it over to Belle. "That's Robbie, close to the same age as Michael is now."

She held the photo for a moment before she looked

down at it. And when she finally did… "They're identical," she whispered, as another round of tears splashed down her face. "Your brother and your son…" It was more than she could bear, more than Cade could bear as well, and as Belle clung to that photo, Cade pulled her into his arms, and the two of them sat underneath the Carolina jasmine with its yellow blooms, and Confederate jasmine with its white blooms, holding on to one another for dear life.

She loved this man. Had never stopped. But had never, truly known him the way she did now. More than loving him, she needed him and maybe this was the first time she'd ever realized she did. Maybe that's why it had been so easy for him to run in all the directions he had when they'd been married. She hadn't needed him enough to hold on to him when his need had been to run. Because she hadn't known him at all.

"I, um…" Jack said, stepping up to the trellis. "I wanted to be the one to tell you…" He cleared his throat. "Michael's…"

Cade and Belle split apart instantly, and she felt the knot form in her throat. The one that threatened to choke her even before Jack's words were out.

"I'm sorry, Belle, Cade. He's taken a turn for the worse. They've just put him on a ventilator."

CHAPTER EIGHT

"I MISS your voice, Michael." Belle wandered from the bed to the window, the way she'd done a thousand times before in the two days Michael had been on the ventilator, and like before she stared out, without really seeing anything. "When you wake up you're going to have to talk to me for a week straight without stopping so I can hear you again." He was stable, basically. The doctors kept telling her Jack's miracle drug was working. But all she could see, since an incident with respiratory distress two days earlier, was that he'd stayed the same. In limbo. A healing process, Amanda had said, and Jack had echoed that. Maybe so, but she was impatient, scared, frustrated. With all her skill, with all Cade's skill, they couldn't do anything for their son except be there. Talk. Reassure Michael. Reassure each other. And pray. "And we need to go get pizza. Do you know how long it's been since we've done that?" She was past the point of tears, at least for now. She was numb, though. Running on the fumes of empty energy. Going through the motions like she was a machine wound up to do what it was supposed to. Move from point A to point B, talk. Move from point B back to point A, talk.

She wanted her life back. All of it. She wanted Michael well and happy again, her medical practice

thriving, and she wanted Cade. When she shut her eyes
and pretended to see her life tomorrow, next week, next
month, Cade was in it. But even that came with complications she didn't want to face as Cade would be going
back to Chicago and she wouldn't. Or maybe she would
go back with him. Right now, she didn't know. Couldn't
plan.

And three more people were sick with *E. coli* in Big
Badger. Jack had called in state investigators the previous day and, so far, they knew nothing more than she
did. Later today the announcement would be made. The
town would panic and blame her, and call her a deserter.
Maybe destroy the cattle from the nearby ranches in
reaction, maybe not. The rest of it was too horrible to
think about.

"Last time we were in the hospital like this, I was
getting ready to wrap you up and bring you home for the
first time. I had this blue blanket for you—I'd bought a
pink one and a blue one, so I'd be prepared either way.
You were such a beautiful baby, Michael. You looked
exactly like your daddy." And Robbie. Her heart ached
for that tragedy as well. And it ached for the Cade she'd
never known when they'd been married—the one who
had loved too much, and too deeply, and carried guilt
that wasn't his to carry. "And he was so nervous carrying you. He's a great surgeon, Michael. I don't know
if you're even interested in medicine, but you could be
great like your dad is, too. In anything you do." With all
her heart, she believed that. And unlike Cade's mother,
who had pushed her boys away and proved her hatred
over and over, she would pull Michael close and help
him achieve whatever his dream would be. Even bugs,
if that's how it turned out.

"Anyway, here was this surgeon who saved lives

every day, and his hands were shaking when he picked you up." A smile of reminiscence touched her lips. Shaking was an understatement. Cade had been a nervous wreck, reduced to a mass of quivering gelatin. His love for his son had been so clear. A love he had been afraid he would betray. "Eventually he managed to get you all the way out to the car, then he had to deal with getting you in the car seat, and…"

She'd been reciting story after story for two days now. They were her lifeline to Michael, and it was like if she stopped she'd lose that connection. "And he just stood there, not even sure where to begin. So I—"

The ventilator alarm suddenly sounded, and the rhythmic, mechanical breathing in and out seemed to strangle and fight against the very machine itself. Belle's heart clutched as she spun round, ready to run to the bed to save her son. But rather than springing into action, which was her automatic response as a doctor, as a mother she didn't move. Not one step. There was no need now, for, across the room, dwarfed in that mass of tubes and wires, Michael was watching her, wide-eyed. Bright, wide eyes. Except he really wasn't watching her so much as he was studying all the machines to which he was hooked up. Analyzing them, trying to figure out the way they worked, the way only Michael would do.

"Welcome back," Belle said, fighting for calm as she grabbed hold of the window ledge for support. Then she pulled her phone from her pocket and texted Cade, who was on his way back from Big Badger with fresh clothes. Her text was simple. Two words. *He's awake.* The two most beautiful words she'd ever texted in her life. "So now, Michael, let me explain to you what all these machines are for." That might have been an odd statement from most mothers, and most mothers might have been crying and throwing themselves all over their sons, but this mother knew her son and her son would want to know every last aspect of every last machine. So Belle kissed him on the head, then began her explanation of the EKG machine, and what the tracing going across its screen meant.

Cade's breath caught in his throat when the jingle indicating he had a text message sounded. It was the jingle he'd set specifically for Belle—Mozart's "Eine Kleine Nachtmusik." A simple piece of music he knew she hated, while she thought he thought she loved it. This time, though, it frightened him as they'd promised to call or text only if it was an emergency. Otherwise they would keep the line open just in case. Since that moment in the garden when he'd told her everything, they'd barely spoken. There really wasn't much to say right now anyway, and he was hoping the lack of words had no significance, while fearing that the lack was more significant than he wanted to know.

For now, he didn't know, though. Didn't want to think about it, dwell on it, wonder about it either. But the jingle of his text message… Rather than looking at it, he pulled off to the side of the road and held his phone between his shaking hands for a full minute, only staring at the icon indicating he had a message, thinking of all the ways his life could be after he read it. Finally, the curdled dread of not knowing forced him to tap that icon, then the message appeared. *He's awake.*

Cade slumped back in his seat, closed his eyes, and let the tears flow. His son was awake. Life just got good again.

* * *

"What comes next?" Cade asked, standing in the hospital hallway, looking through the window at Michael. He had been extubated now, meaning no breathing tube, no ventilator. In fact, most of the monitors had been discontinued, and Michael had protested when they'd been rolled out of the room because he liked them, liked the way they functioned. So typical. Probably in a day knew as much about their functioning as the hospital biomedical equipment tech did.

Belle stepped up behind him, stood so close she could smell a hint of lime in his aftershave. "They're moving him into the pediatric ward tomorrow, and if all goes well, we can take him home in a couple of days." She wanted to lean her head on his shoulder or slip her hand into his, feel his strength, feel anything from Cade, but he was so shut off again. "After that, a normal recovery, I'm hoping. He said he wants to go camping, though. He's already told me that he wants to go every weekend for the rest of the summer."

Just the three of them. "Me, you, and Dad," he'd told her, then added, "Uncle Jack should come, too." A simple, beautiful wish she wanted to make happen, but didn't know if she could.

"Too bad life isn't that uncomplicated," Cade said, on a sigh. He turned to face her. "Look, I've been giving this a lot of thought. I think it's time for me to go back to Chicago. Not now, specifically, but after he's up and about. And I've also been thinking that maybe I should reduce my time with him since my coming and going disrupts his routine. I don't want to do that to him. Also, because of his health right now, Michael's not going to be able to go with me to Chicago later on this summer like we'd planned, and since I don't want to break up his life any more than it's already been bro-

ken up, I'm thinking that I should cancel seeing him
during those weeks altogether, and let him get back to
the life he counts on. But I'm not running away, Belle.
I want you to know that. I'm just trying to let Michael
have what he needs most."

"And what he needs most isn't you?" Cade was leaving? Michael was out of danger and no matter what
he called it, or whatever he believed was his reason,
Cade was running away? This couldn't be happening,
not when she'd started letting herself think that—well,
maybe they had a future. But no. Cade was going to do
what Cade wanted to do. Like always. "You don't want
to disrupt his life?" she added, trying to keep her emotions level when everything inside her was about to boil
over. "So now, when he's going to need you more than
he ever has in his life, you're going to just leave him?
I don't get it, Cade. Why would you do something like
that?"

"Because he needs you, Belle. You're his stability.
Not me. I'm the one who wanders in every now and
then and changes his life for a little while. But Michael
needs the consistency of his real life back, and I'm not
part of that."

"Because you don't want to be part of it! When they
extubated him, do you know the first thing he said to
me?" She didn't wait for his response before she answered, "He asked where you were. He wanted you,
Cade. You! And you're going to walk away from that?"
She shook her head violently. "This isn't about Robbie,
isn't about the guilt you feel over his tragedy. I'm so
sorry about that, and I don't know what it's going to take
to convince you it wasn't your fault. But that's not what
this is about, Cade. It's about your son. You love him,
and you told me you'd come here because you wanted

to establish your relationship with him. Yet when that's starting to happen, you're talking about turning your back on him."

"Not turning my back on him, Belle. Just letting him get his life back the way it should be. That's all."

"You know what, Cade? If you can't be here the way Michael expects you to be, the way I expect you to be, I'm not sure I want you here at all. So maybe you should go back to Chicago now, today. Right this very minute." They were harsh words she knew she would regret later on, but they spilled out anyway. "Because you do disrupt his life. It takes him a full day to get used to you being here, then another day after you've left to get over the sadness he feels when you go. What are you going to do about that? And what are you going to do about the way I feel? Because I'm involved in this, too, and I go through that same sadness. Sometimes when you go back to Chicago, I ache so much I can barely breathe, barely function. And I look forward to your next visit, even though most of the time we barely speak. Even so, I've lived for those moments, Cade. Never dated anyone, never wanted to, because every other week I got to see you for a minute or two. And no one else ever came close to being…you." Bad, good, in between, Cade had always been the only one. "But I can't keep doing that, can't let you do it to me. Or to Michael. So leave. Get out of here. Leave us alone, and we'll adjust just fine without you!"

"But you've never let me in, Belle. Not into your life with Michael. This is where I've always been." He pointed to the spot in which he was standing. "Right here in the hall, gazing through the window at what I didn't have, couldn't have."

"Because that's where you wanted to be." She looked

in at Michael, who was watching them. The expression on his face was unreadable, something caught between sadness and bewilderment, and one that broke her heart for reasons she didn't understand. "I understand now why you did what you did but, Cade, it wasn't me. You're the one who never let me in. So telling me I never let you in…maybe that's the convenient excuse, the one that's easier for you to deal with, but I always wanted you to be part of the family. Wanted you to spend more time with Michael. And more than anything else, I wanted more time with you, but there never seemed to be enough of it, and you were always someplace else. You were doing good things, setting up clinics in areas without medical help, volunteering as a surgeon with your visiting doctors' group. Even though I didn't understand why you were doing it, how could I say something, or even ask you not to go, when you were involved in such great causes?

"Because if I had, I'd have looked…selfish, or petty. Yet I couldn't compete with all those things you did, Cade. Sometimes, though, I was so…lonely. I'd wake up in the morning and ache to have you there next to me, but you weren't. And it was like I had this hole in my heart. One that always reminded me that I wasn't enough to keep you home. So maybe I did overcompensate by smothering Michael more than I should, and maybe it looked to you like I was shutting you out, but you were the one closing the doors, and I didn't know what to do about it because you never told me why. Maybe, if you'd let me in, or told me why you were keeping me out, we could have figured out what to do to help you. I'm not holding it against you, Cade, because I don't know what I'd have done if I'd been carrying the kind of guilt you've been carrying all these years. But you should have trusted me. If you loved me enough to marry me, you should have trusted me."

She looked in at Michael again, who was studying them now through the lens of his camera. "He loves that thing, you know. The second thing he said after they yanked the breathing tube was that he wanted his camera, and I have an idea that everything in his room has been photographed from every angle a dozen times."

"Robbie did, too. I gave him a camera for his eighth birthday…not even a digital one, but one that used film. And he took pictures…" A smile crept to Cade's face. "Mostly of bugs. His world was a lot simpler than Michael's but he loved his bugs. Anyway, he had scrapbooks full of pictures, and he could spend hours looking at them. Didn't know their names the way Michael does, didn't even care. He just liked looking at them. The hell of it was, he couldn't find his way home if he wandered out of the front yard, but if he encountered a bug while he was lost, he could describe it in such amazing ways." He shut his eyes, sighed heavily. "I never meant to hurt you, Belle. But the whole responsibility thing…you did it better than I did. My strong suit was running away. Keeping my distance. And I knew it was wrong, but I didn't know how to stop it."

"Does it bother you that Michael looks so much like your brother?"

"What bothers me is that because of my circumstances I couldn't be the brother Robbie needed me to be. I was so caught up in myself, in my own pain—"

"You were a child, Cade. You can apply adult sensibilities to your situation now, but back then you were simply a child."

"So was Robbie. So is Michael. And I can't be the father he needs me to be."

"Because you couldn't be the brother Robbie needed you to be? Is that why you're still running?" she asked gently. "Because you're afraid you'll let Michael down the way you think you let your brother down?"

"Well, that seems to be my history, doesn't it? One way or another, I've let down everybody I've ever cared for. All my good intentions are outweighed by my deeds."

"Which is why you want to start running again, isn't it, Cade? Why you want to quit seeing Michael as often, for his own good? Or is it for your own good, because you're scared to death that something you do will bring on another tragedy like what happened to your brother?"

"What he doesn't need is disruption, and that's all I am to him. You've said it. I've seen it. I'm nothing more than a great big disruption, and I love Michael too much to do that to him."

She laid a gentle hand on his arm. "So why is he taking your picture right now, if that's all you are to him? Because he's been clicking away, nonstop, for the past several minutes."

Cade turned to look in the window. Smiled, then waved at Michael. "What am I supposed to do, Belle?" he asked. "Tell me. Make a suggestion. Give me a solution. Anything."

"Be his father. Love him the way you do and simply be his father." She slipped her arm around his waist. "He's not Robbie, Cade. He's Michael, and he needs you. I'm not promising it's going to be easy. Not even promising that he'll be very responsive. But he needs you to be his dad, and you need to be his dad."

He spun to face her. "That's all you want from me? Or expect from me? Because here's the thing. Probably the most honest thing you've ever heard from me. If I were to do what I wanted, nobody's feelings or needs considered other than my own, I would move here, live in Big Badger if that's what I had to do to be Michael's father. The problem in that, though, is you live there, and I can't spend the rest of my life seeing you every day, knowing what I lost, knowing I can't get it back. Because I want it back, Belle. All of it. You, Michael, our life—the one I took away from us. I want everything that was good, and that's the real reason I came to Texas in the first place. To see if there was any hope left for us." He shrugged. "But all I see are the ways I've failed you everywhere I look. Even now, that expression on your face—"

"That expression?" she said, her voice barely above a whisper. "Do you know what that expression is, Cade? It's me, telling you I've never not wanted to be a family—the three of us, maybe even four or five of us. Not only Michael and me, but Michael and me and…you."

From his hospital bed, Michael aimed and shot, once, twice, a dozen times. Then he tucked his camera under the covers, smiled, and dozed off.

"I've got a lead on about five different things it could be," Jack said. He handed Cade's laptop computer over to Michael, who was out of Intensive Care now, and was turning his hospital room into his own private home away from home. "I've done every test possible, read the results so many times I've memorized them, cultured things no one would ever culture for *E. coli*, and the good news is nothing is pointing to contaminants in the groundwater. In other words, as far as I can tell, it's not related to the cattle. But the people in Big Badger are pushing for an answer. So far they haven't done

anything more than ask questions, which is probably
the most encouraging news I can give you right now.
Unfortunately, since you and Cade have been busy here,
we've had another four cases diagnosed."

Belle slumped back in her chair. "It feels like I've
been away from there a million years." She glanced at
Cade, who was propped up in bed alongside Michael,
getting ready to help him download his photos into the
laptop. "I think I need to get back. So since Michael
may be released day after tomorrow…" She looked at
Cade. "Do you think you could handle it here, if I went
home for the day?"

Both Michael and Cade waved her off. "We'll be
fine," Cade said, then winked.

"Fine," Michael mimicked, without the wink.

She turned her attention to Jack. "I get the feeling
they don't need me."

"I'm the one who needs you. Between trying to manage your medical practice, and that includes going out
to the ranches as well as doing my investigations…" He
shook his head. "All I have to say about it is, hop into
my car, Dr. Carter, and I'll be more than happy to take
you home and turn your medical practice back over to
you."

"Are you coming back?" Michael asked.

"Tomorrow some time. Not sure when, exactly, but
I'll be back. Why? Do you want me to bring you something?" Any number of his gadgets and books came to
mind.

"Can you bring me my strawberry jam?"

Belle frowned for a moment. "We don't have any
strawberry jam, but I can stop at the grocery and buy
some, if you want it." It was an odd request, as she didn't
recall having had strawberry jam in her pantry in a long,

long time. Probably not since they'd lived in Chicago. But she was so relieved that Michael was on the mend and getting his appetite back as well, she'd have promised him almost anything. "Do you want peanut butter to go with it?"

He shook his head. "Bread and jam. That's all."

Again, another odd request. "Then I'll buy you some jam."

"Not at the store. Mrs. Ellison makes it and everybody buys it from her."

Jack immediately became alert. "Well, I'll be damned," he said, pulling his cellphone from his pocket. "Home-made strawberry jam!"

"Do you think that could be the cause?" Belle asked, totally stunned. She'd set herself up to expect big things, and this was so small. Something she'd have never suspected in a million years, yet Jack knew, or at least suspected, and if the jam turned out to be the cause, she owed him for this one, and she only hoped he would stay around for a while so she could find a way to repay him. Maybe help him find a way back to his brother? Or spend time with Michael? "How could that be?"

"Contaminated strawberries, most likely." He looked at Michael. "What kind of jam is it?" he asked. "The kind she gets out of a cupboard or the kind she gets out of the freezer?"

"The freezer," Michael replied, looking annoyed at being interrupted.

"Uncooked strawberries…contaminated uncooked strawberries. I read about it happening up in Oregon once."

"Which is why the outbreak was limited," Cade said. "Remember, you'd mentioned it to me, wondered why only certain people were getting sick? So now we have the answer—they were Virginia's customers."

Jack clicked a number into his cellphone, then a few seconds later said to the health authority on the other end, "It's probably the freezer jam being sold by a local woman by the name of Virginia Ellison. We need to put out the alert, recall all the jam, check the strawberry supply source…"

"I think you solved it, Michael," Cade said, smiling at Belle.

Michael didn't respond, though. He was too busy putting together a slideshow of his photos. Soon, very soon, he had plans for it. Right now those plans were clicking away in his speedy little brain and nothing else mattered.

"Four days, no new cases," Belle said. She was stretched out on her exam table, head on the pillow, legs over the end, staring up at the ceiling. Life was getting back to normal, and today she'd seen three Big Badger men. Maybe, just maybe, she was making headway in that. "Maudie's on the mend, Jack's enjoying taking care of Michael while we're working. I'd say all is well here. And when Michael's up to it, I promised him another camping trip out on the creek at the Ruda del Monte. Maybe Jack will stay around for a while and go with us—I'm assuming you're going, too."

"I expect I'll have to since I own it. Not the whole ranch. Just those few acres."

"What?" she said, bolting straight up. "You bought it?"

Tossing his white coat over one of the chairs, he walked over to the table and stood at the end of it, taking his place between her knees, looking Belle straight in the eyes. "When you said you wanted to be a family of three, or four, or five, I took that literally. And since that can't happen if I'm in Chicago, I decided to see if that little patch of land came with a price tag. It did, and I'll be talking with an architect in a couple of weeks. Something about a sprawling ranch house up on the knoll overlooking the creek."

"Cade, I—I don't know what to say. The other day, when we were talking, it was all the emotion of the moment. People say things, do things they wouldn't normally do, when they're under stress."

"Like arguing me out of walking away?"

"That was real. I don't want you leaving Michael. He needs you, and he's finally warming up to you."

"What about you, Belle?" he asked, leaning over and rubbing his hands up her legs, from her ankles to her knees. "Tell me what's best for Belle, not Michael, since we both already know what's best for Michael."

She chilled to his touch, and it was such a simple touch. But she always had. "It would be easy to say we should get back together for Michael, but that's not what I want, Cade. Michael has both of us, no matter how we work this out."

"So, what wouldn't be so easy to say?"

"That I want to do this for—for me. The purely selfish me who likes it when you touch me, or wink at me, or smile at me. And I want it for us, too. But it scares me like nothing's ever scared me in my life, because I know what it's like to lose you, and I can't do that again. It hurt too much the first time."

"I never thought I could be good enough for him. I couldn't for Robbie, then after Michael was diagnosed, it was easy to step back because you swooped in and smothered him. Maybe I should have fought harder to stay closer, but when I looked at our beautiful little boy, then thought about what I'd done, or hadn't done for another beautiful little boy, I always knew Michael would be fine with you. You're strong. And fierce."

"But so are you. And Michael needs that strength and fierceness from both of us. It's going to be a difficult world out there for him. Sometimes it scares me, thinking of all the things he's going to have to face. I mean, our child has Asperger's syndrome, Cade. For me, it's simply the way he is. It's normal, he's normal. But that's naive, because I know how people react, and some of them are going to make it tough on our little boy. They won't see Michael first, they'll see his diagnosis. So I've overcompensated because..."

"Because you're *a good mother. It took me a while* to get where I needed to be, Belle, but I've grown up, and I want to be as good a father as you are a mother. More than that, I want to be a good husband."

"But can you make it here in Texas? I know you bought that land because that's what I want. If you practice medicine in Big Badger, though, it's going to be general medicine. Can you do that?"

"Because it's for my family, for a while."

"You can only stay for a while?" she asked, feeling her gut clench into a knot. "Then what?"

"Then I'll be a surgeon again. Maybe not on a large scale like I am now, but even a small-town hospital needs a surgeon on call."

"A hospital? What hospital?"

"Actually, I'm thinking it will be more like a clinic with extended services for now. Something that will grow in the future, though. Michael's already agreed to do the computers for us, by the way. He told me he's getting better at networking, and that he has some ideas to maximize our efficiency."

"You asked your son before you asked me?" she said,

scooting toward the end of the exam table. "He's seven, Cade. Don't you think we should wait until he's at least eight before we turn our hospital's computers over to him?"

Cade chuckled. "If we can keep him contained that long. He's already doing some preliminary designs, and they involve games in the children's ward. They also involve Jack."

"How?"

Cade shrugged. "Not sure, really. But Jack's looking for a place to rent. Said he's got to make up for lost time with his nephew. He really loves Michael, you know. The way he loved Robbie."

"How will you do, having him around?"

"We're OK. Not great, but good enough. Tolerant. We've got a way to go, but he's going to be here for a while, so who knows what's going to happen?"

"Will he be working as a doctor?"

"He didn't say. I suppose that's something he'll have to work out on his own, in time."

Belle scooted all the way to the end of the exam table, locking her knees around Cade's waist and wrapping her arms around his neck. "Well, I've got something I want to work out right now. And this time I'm holding on," she said. "Never letting go."

"This time I'm holding you to that promise." He gave her a quick kiss on the lips, then stepped back, a delicious twinkle coming to his eyes. "We don't have any more patients scheduled in this afternoon, do we?"

In answer, Belle undid the top button of her blouse. "Actually, Doctor, you do have one more patient to see. She has an incurable condition, I'm afraid. One she needs you to check out." Another two buttons came undone. "And I think you should probably lock the door before you begin your exam, then come and listen to her heart because I think you'll like what you're going to hear."

"What am I going to hear?" he asked, putting his stethoscope in his ears, and placing the bell to Belle's heart. He listened for a moment, then smiled. "I love you, too, Belle. With all my heart."

"All my heart," she whispered back

"It's done," Michael said, hitting a few buttons on the laptop and pulling up a banner, "Michael's Slideshow."

OK, maybe it wasn't the most imaginative title, but Belle was bursting with pride. These last weeks had been rough in some spots, good in others. Overall, though, it took both the bad and good to get them to this place, and this was where she wanted to stay, forever. "Bet it's got lots of bugs in it," she said, settling down on the couch next to Michael, pulling her feet up under her, while Cade sat on the other side of him, kicking off his shoes and making himself family-style comfortable.

"No bugs," Michael said, quite seriously. Then quickly changed his mind. "Well, maybe a few."

"Bugs are good," Cade responded, giving his son the thumbs up. "So…" He faked a drumroll on the table in front of the couch. "Let's see it."

Michael hit the play button, and sure enough, bugs. But not the bugs they'd expected. The first several shots were of Belle's dubious reaction to various bugs when they'd gone camping at the Ruda del Monte, including a couple of notorious screams, a few well-placed gasps, and one particularly funny shot of her running away from a moth. Then there were pictures of Cade watching Belle respond to the bugs. Lots of those, actually. And shots of the two of them together, at times arguing, at times frowning, at times smiling. Through Michael's eyes they saw stress, pain, fear…they saw happiness, joy, distance, and separation. It was a mural of a family's struggles, their feelings, their triumphs and defeats, and Belle was stunned. "It's beautiful, Michael," she whispered. So real and so…honest. It's what Michael saw when he looked at them.

"It's you and Dad," he said, more interested in the various ways he could adjust his slideshow. Faster, slower, at times on its side, it all said the same thing. This was how they were, through Michael's eyes. What he saw was the struggle, and the progress. Most of all, he saw the love. And the last photos, of their embrace in the hall outside his intensive-care window, that's the one that said it all. The one that said they were a family again. Well, until a succession of beetles, caterpillars, and grasshoppers crossed the screen. And, at the very end, a moth. Michael looked at his dad, and asked, "Think she'll scream?"

Cade smiled at Belle as Michael hopped up off the couch, finished with all the family togetherness, and scampered to the front porch to wait for his uncle, who'd promised to take him on the bug hunt of his life.

"Will you scream?" Cade asked.

"Could we cuddle instead?" Which was what they did.

Minutes later, looking inside from the porch, Michael aimed his camera and shot a photo of his parents. Then reviewed it and smiled. Tomorrow he'd take out the moth and put this one in instead. "The end," he said resolutely, as Jack came up the steps to get him.

"The beginning," Jack responded, looking in the window at Cade and Belle. "I think, Michael, that this is only the beginning."

* * * * *

A sneaky peek at next month...

Medical Romance™

CAPTIVATING MEDICAL DRAMA—WITH HEART

My wish list for next month's titles...

In stores from 1st June 2012:

☐ *Sydney Harbour Hospital: Bella's Wishlist – Emily Forbes*

& *Doctor's Mile-High Fling – Tina Beckett*

☐ *Hers For One Night Only? – Carol Marinelli*

& *Unlocking the Surgeon's Heart – Jessica Matthews*

☐ *Marriage Miracle in Swallowbrook – Abigail Gordon*

& *Celebrity in Braxton Falls – Judy Campbell*

Available at WHSmith, Tesco, Asda, Eason, Amazon and Apple

Just can't wait?

Visit us Online

You can buy our books online a month before they hit the shops! **www.millsandboon.co.uk**

0512/03

MILLS & BOON® Book Club

2 Free Books!

Get your free books now at
www.millsandboon.co.uk/freebookoffer

Or fill in the form below and post it back to us

THE MILLS & BOON® BOOK CLUB™—HERE'S HOW IT WORKS: Accepting your free books places you under no obligation to buy anything. You may keep the books and return the despatch note marked 'Cancel'. If we do not hear from you, about a month later we'll send you 5 brand-new stories from the Medical™ series, including two 2-in-1 books priced at £5.49 each and a single book priced at £3.49*. There is no extra charge for post and packaging. You may cancel at any time, otherwise we will send you 5 stories a month which you may purchase or return to us—the choice is yours. *Terms and prices subject to change without notice. Offer valid in UK only. Applicants must be 18 or over. Offer expires 31st July 2012. **For full terms and conditions, please go to www.millsandboon.co.uk/freebookoffer**

Mrs/Miss/Ms/Mr (please circle) _____

First Name _____

Surname _____

Address _____

_____

_____ Postcode _____

E-mail _____

Send this completed page to: Mills & Boon Book Club, Free Book Offer, FREEPOST NAT 10298, Richmond, Surrey, TW9 1BR

Find out more at
www.millsandboon.co.uk/freebookoffer

Visit us Online

0112/M2XEA/REV

MP

Special Offers

Every month we put together collections and longer reads written by your favourite authors.

Here are some of next month's highlights— and don't miss our fabulous discount online!

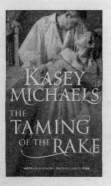

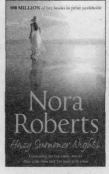

On sale 18th May

On sale 1st June

On sale 1st June